Savage Ecstasy

G·K
Hall
&Cº.

*Also by Janelle Taylor
in Large Print:*

Anything For Love
Destiny Mine
By Candlelight
Defiant Hearts
Love with a Stranger
Promise Me Forever
Wild Winds

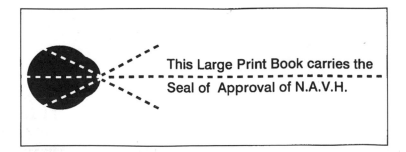

This Large Print Book carries the
Seal of Approval of N.A.V.H.

JANELLE TAYLOR

Savage Ecstasy

G.K. Hall & Co. • Thorndike, Maine

Copyright © 1981 by Janelle Taylor

Published in 2000 by arrangement with Zebra Books, an imprint of Kensington Publishing Corporation.

G.K. Hall Large Print Romance Series.

The text of this Large Print edition is unabridged.
Other aspects of the book may vary from the original edition.

Set in 16 pt. Plantin by PerfecType.

Printed in the United States on permanent paper.

Library of Congress Cataloging-in-Publication Data

Taylor, Janelle.
  Savage ecstasy / Janelle Taylor.
     p.   cm.
  ISBN 0-7838-9306-X (lg. print : hc : alk. paper)
  1. Oglala Indians — Fiction. 2. Women pioneers — Fiction.
3. Large type books. I. Title.
PS3570.A934 S28 2000
813'.54—dc21   00-046552

Dedicated to:
Michael, who made it all possible,
and
Angela and Alisha

This book is a work of fiction. Any historical names, places or events that occur have been used in a fictional context and reflect the author's interpretation of the facts for the sake of her work.

Acknowledgment to:
Hiram C. Owen of Sisseton, South Dakota for all his help and understanding with the Sioux language and facts about the great and inspiring Sioux Nation.

Thank you.

LOVE'S CRUEL ARROW

She came to a wilderness, vast and wide,
Adorned with great beauty and innocent pride.
Searching for freedom and a wondrous new life;
But instead found hatred and bitter strife.
To feel her dreams shatter and fade;
To watch the wanton destruction of plans made.
To first know love and its cruel game;
To endure its counterpart and know great shame.
To meet a man with courage and fame;
To suffer the torment that he is to blame.
To live in darkness and not be spared;
Rejection from the very one whose love she shared.
A forbidden love looked down on with scorn;
Sweet like the rose, but painful its thorn.
Forced to endure prejudice from minds so narrow;
To be pierced in her heart by love's cruel arrow.

Janelle Taylor

Chapter One

Alisha opened the door to their small, one-room cabin and stepped outside to absorb the warmth of the sunlight. The fragrant scents of verdant nature and late spring flowers floated in the balmy air. The bright sun beamed down on the fortress yard, which was cluttered by many one-room cabins, each an exact replica of the ones surrounding it. Only the varying colors of curtains fluttering in and out of open windows or a rugged work bench attached to the side wall of certain cabins marked minute differences to the naked eye. She recalled how quickly and efficiently the cabins had been constructed. The men had insisted on speed, size and style to provide the needed protection against weather and the precious privacy denied on the trail.

She inhaled the fresh breeze from the surrounding forest that gently blew over the tall, spiked fence and through the slightly open gate, cooling its occupants as they labored and played.

She was thinking of how very different it was

here from what she had imagined or had been told. She laughed lightly to herself as she recalled visualizing vast wastelands and tangled forests, filled with clutching vines and thick underbrush. She remembered the tales she had heard about huge, strange beasts and heathen red savages who ran around half-naked, performing terrible rituals and deeds against the whites and other tribes.

Instead, she had found dense green forests; lazy, rolling hills; majestic rock formations; winding rivers and lucid, sparkling streams. She pictured the prairies and vast grasslands that stretched far as the eye could see, acres dotted with small, flowering bushes and mangled trees. She had discovered rugged landscapes which were covered with various sizes and types of cacti and white yuccas.

She wondered how long it would remain this way with groups such as theirs and others ever pressing westward, how long it would be before those great plains she saw would be filled with sheep and cattle. How long before the forests were cut down for lumber needed for homes and new towns or cleared for farms and fields? How long before this wilderness succumbed to progress and change and this very spot was another Liverpool or Harrisburg? It saddened her to think that someday this beauty and splendor would no longer exist. She thought this land should inspire the peace and freedom they all hungered and searched for — but would it?

She hugged the stoop post, swaying back and forth, thinking how wonderful her new life would be. Her mind flitted from one thought to another as a bee from flower to flower collecting nectar. Her thoughts briefly settled on the huge, hairy creature the scout had called a buffalo. She had seen a herd spread out for miles and miles against the blue horizon on the open plains, covering the vast grasslands like a giant, black carpet. She recalled how a sudden stampede had sounded like roaring thunder, shook the ground and was heard and felt for miles. The scout had told her how the Indians hunted them, using their skins for clothing, shelter and shoes; and their bones, hooves, horns and entrails for sewing, tools, utensils and numerous other purposes. He had commented that many tribes depended almost solely on them for everything they needed to sustain life as they knew and lived it.

Lazily Alisha looked around the enclosure at the women as they went about their daily chores and tasks while the small children played. She quickly turned her face away from the place where two men were gutting and skinning a beautiful, white-tailed deer. She wondered why that task could not have been done outside the fortress walls. She watched the strong muscles in the backs of several men flex and strain as they chopped firewood. Many others were going about their chores oblivious to the others around, caught up in their own little worlds of thoughts and work.

She glanced through the half-open gate into the forest and sighed lightly. With June almost over, spring still lingered on the land. She remembered how glorious fall had been and how terribly harsh and cold the winter. This climate was so different from the one back home in Liverpool. She recalled how her mother had hated the fog and cold, damp mist and would constantly ask to go to the South of France during those worst seasons. How she would have loved this warm sunshine, the fresh air and skies the color of periwinkle satin and heather. A note of sadness touched her heart and spirit at these thoughts and memories.

Oh, Mama, her heart cried out, why did you and Papa have to die so young and leave me alone? Why couldn't life go on as before? It wasn't fair . . . such a terrible waste . . . tears glistened in her eyes for a few moments before she could bring her emotions under control.

Alisha wondered what happiness and surprises this new land and year of 1776 held in store for her and the others. Little did she suspect that in just a short time an event would shatter and change her life and thoughts for all time, that all she knew and loved would be cruelly torn from her. Her innocence about life and human nature would leave her unprepared to face the brutality and the drastic changes that she would be forced to witness and endure.

She stood leaning against the post in a dream-like trance, reminiscing about old times and planning new ones. Suddenly she became aware of the loud yells and commotion outside the fortress walls that steadily increased in nearness and pitch. The gate was shoved wide open and she saw a sight that she would long remember.

She stared at the scene in disbelief and astonishment. Some of the men from the fortress were bringing an Indian brave into the center of the yard. He was being pulled forward like an animal by a rope around his neck and with his hands bound tightly behind his back. The raucous group brought many others running forward to see what was going on. They pointed at the brave as they talked excitedly amongst themselves. Some of the men taunted him and shouted insults at him. Others struck blows and pulled at his braids. He was shoved from side to side roughly as in some game of tug-of-war. She couldn't believe what she witnessed with her own eyes and ears.

Ben Frazer, a burly blacksmith from Virginia, yanked on the rope, yelling, "Come on, you savage! Stop that dawdling or I'll break yore neck."

At Ben's movement, the brave stumbled and nearly fell. As he straightened up, he jerked his head backwards with powerful neck muscles, causing Ben to drop the other end of the rope. Ben cursed him as he leaned over to retrieve it. Like a flash of lightning, the brave brought his knee up with a smashing blow under Ben's chin. Ben yelled out in pain as he spit blood onto the brave's chest and drew back his fist and delivered

13

a heavy blow into his stomach. Much to Ben's surprise and anger, the only two noticeable effects of the blow were an exhalation of air and a slight backwards movement.

Ben shook his fingers painfully and shouted jokingly to those nearby, "Damn! He's got a gut of iron. 'Most near broke me hand." Then he slowly added, "We'll just see if'n his back is made of iron."

Jed McDoogan, who Alisha thought looked and acted like a weasel, pranced around him, taunting and shouting, "Blarney! If he ain't a puck! Just look at that face, boys. Why it's enough to scare the hair clear off'n me head."

Horace Swint, the fortress's self-appointed Don Juan, grabbed his braids and forced him to face him. He studied him for a minute, then agreed. "Yore right, Jed. I kin feel me hair jumping up and down in fear. Just look at that face! He must think he can scare us to death with just a look. Well, he won't be so brave or silent when we've finished with him," he threatened boldly.

Ben joined the laughter and shouted above the noise, "I bet we have him begging for mercy within an hour. Just you wait and see if'n it ain't so."

"Shucks," Horace yelled. "I bet it only takes a few minutes. I'll wager you my best gun if it takes more'n half an hour to break him."

Jed whispered, "You think maybe we could do some of them Injun tortures on him? Give 'im a taste of his own medicine? I know of a few things

I'd like to try on him. Couldn't do 'em here in front of the women folk, though." They all exchanged knowing looks and laughed heartily. "Why don't you see just how tough he is, Ben? Put a little squeeze on 'im."

Ben began to tighten the rope around the brave's neck until his face began to discolor and his chest began to show signs of struggling for air. No one tried to stop the malicious actions of the men. Hatred thick as smoke permeated the air. Alisha wondered what had come over these people. They acted as if they had captured a rabid animal. Why?

Many of the people were running about wildly, yelling and shouting. Bedlam had broken loose in the fortress and confusion ruled. They swarmed around him like the sharks had done the rancid meat dumped overboard from the ship on the way over here. What was possessing these people to behave this way? They showed him no mercy or humanity with any of their words or actions to him. As with any mob, sanity and reason had fled and there would be no stopping them. Still, she knew that she must try to do something, anything and alone. . . .

She ran to Ben. "Stop it!" she screamed at him. "He can't breathe! You're choking him, Ben! No!" She slapped at his hands and tried to grab the rope. She shouted at him again, "Ben, you can't do this! Let him go! Stop it now before it's too late! Please . . ."

Seeing her look of anger and disbelief, Ben

15

loosened the rope and spoke to her in childlike innocence, "Aw, Miss Alisha, we was only having fun. We ain't gonna kill him yet."

She looked at the brave to be sure that he was all right. He breathed heavily but his color had returned to normal quickly. She turned to Ben and said, "Strangling a man isn't my idea of fun, as you call it. You could have killed him! Why? I don't understand what this is all about. What did he do?"

Horace piped up acidly, "This ain't no man! This here's a real, live, heathen, bloodthirsty savage. Women should keep their pretty noses outa men's business. This ain't none of yore concern. Go back to your cabin and stay out of it."

Alisha glared at his face so full of hate and contempt for the brave and asked, "Just what did he do to you, Horace?"

He snarled angrily, "He's alive and an Injun, that's enough for me!"

She studied his hate-distorted features in amazement, then inquired, "You mean that you hate him and would kill him simply because he's an Indian?"

Horace gave her a quick, concise, "Yep!"

Alisha retorted, "That's barbaric! And you call *him* the savage? That's really pathetic, Horace. But then again, so like you . . ."

Horace flashed her a look of warning and said, "Don't press me, Alisha."

She quipped back instantly, "Don't call me Alisha! Only my friends can do that." The jab hit

16

home and he flamed at the insult.

Ben intervened at that point. "Miss Alisha, maybe you best go inside if it bothers you to witness punishment."

"Punishment!" she shrieked. "For what?"

"For being an Injun," Horace shouted back at her. "Now stop your interfering or I'll personally see to it that you do."

She glared at him and whispered, "If you ever touch me again, I'll . . ."

Ben warned, "I told you once before, Horace, leave her be." The two men exchanged looks and Horace backed down once more.

The brave remained motionless and silent while they argued over what was to be done with him. Alisha argued, threatened and pleaded against all their suggestions, but was ignored and slowly pushed backwards by the circle of spectators that tightened around the scene. She prayed for her uncle and the others to return soon. She knew the men were not thinking clearly and the group would soon be out of control.

The men decided that first they would flog him with thirty lashes.

Thirty, she thought, horrified. Men have died from less than twenty. I must do something! But what? I'm no match against all these strong men.

The men began to pull him toward the post used to butcher game. Ben was tugging on the rope, trying to drag him to it. The brave held back and resisted with all his might every step of the way. Jed and Horace shoved and pushed him from behind at each delay and hesitation.

Aggravated and angry, Horace suddenly laughed sardonically and tripped him. With quick nimbleness and alertness, the brave flipped in mid-air and landed on his side rather than face down in the dirt. As he was going down, the rope tightened around his neck and he choked and coughed. Swiftly he bounded back to his feet before Horace could deliver a vicious kick into his side. He crouched like a puma about to spring and faced his antagonist with eyes that blazed in unconcealed fury and hate. Horace drew back slightly as he watched the brave's jaw grow taut and the muscles in it quiver. His eyes narrowed and flamed dangerously at the men, who overlooked this warning and would live to regret this day and its events.

Squeals of delight and laughter filled the air. Taunts and jests flew from all directions at his apparent helplessness. "Been drinking too much firewater, Injun?" "They just don't grow Injuns like they used to." "I bet he ain't bathed in a year or more. What'cha say we give 'im a bath, boys?" "Ben, you oughta teach yore Injun some manners." "Hey! how about doing us a little war dance, redskin?" "Heck! I'd like to hear some chanting and praying." "Who's yore tailor, boy? That's really some nifty garb. I bet we could win us a prize with that outfit over in Paris, France." "Somebody get us some paint and we'll fix his face up right for a change." "Yeh! And paint a yellow strip down the coward's back." The ribbing went on and on until Horace became the center attraction with his antics.

He yelled out, "Watch this!" At that, he stiffened his body, held his head high and tried to mock the brave's dignified stance and tried to calm his grinning face to mock his stoical mask. He could do neither.

New bursts of laughter rippled the air and others joined in the gestures and tried amidst howling laughter and encouragement to imitate his walk, stance and facial expression. Catcalls, hoots and hisses filled the air like sirocco winds from the desert during a sand storm.

The brave alertly observed each man and his moves as he stood erect and proud before his enemies. His contempt of them and of the danger he was in was clearly written on his face, and this inflamed the men. His confidence and prowess stung their pride and they tried harder to provoke some emotion, reaction or outburst from him. He rewarded their attempts with silence and stillness.

They pranced around taunting him, but he only stared back in haughty arrogance. The men became more and more piqued by his lack of response to their words and actions. They wanted him to resist or show fear. Their egos demanded that he be broken or humbled before they killed him. Gray Eagle rebuffed all their intimidations and tricks. They refused to recognize the leashed violence and strength of mind and body that he held in such tight control. If they had looked beyond the surface, they would have cringed in fear and respect at what they would have seen.

Horace snarled, "Let's get on with this. We've wasted enough time. He ain't gonna beg yet. Let's just see if'n he bleeds the same color as us. Hell! maybe his blood is as black as that damned heart of his."

Jed shouted, "Tie the bastard face forward! I want to see his expression when he feels the bite of the whip. I want him to have to look us in the face when he pleads for mercy and screams with pain."

Ben remarked, "Maybe I can wipe that smug look off'n his purty face with a few well-aimed snaps of my bull whip."

Alisha pushed and shoved until she managed to get through the crowd. She lunged for Ben's hand and missed. She persisted until she was able to grab the arm of the giant man holding the rope securely in his powerful grip.

"You mustn't do this, Ben! Uncle Thad wouldn't permit such inhumane treatment. No one deserves this kind of cruel abuse, not even him. Please, don't do this terrible thing," she pleaded with him and the others close by.

But no matter what she said or how, the group continued its relentless onslaught of words and actions. Sneers and taunts became bolder and louder, "Dirty Injun!" "You're nothing but a filthy, murdering redskin!" "I say we kills him!" "No! Hang 'im!" "Cut out his tongue like they did ole Timkins . . ." "Hanging's too good for the devil." "Get the whip and give 'im the licking of his life . . ." "Tie him to the hitchin' post and beat him to death." "Let me at 'im. I'll fix him up good."

Talk was running wild and loose and no amount of reasoning or begging seemed to penetrate the vengeance-crazed minds of the men. All the anger, fear and hatred they knew and felt seemed to be centered upon this one man and this moment in time.

Alisha wondered what had sent them to the brink of madness with his capture. They were acting and talking like he was the Genghis Khan of the West. Was this how it had been with Anne Boleyn, Sir Thomas Beckett, or Joan of Arc? Was this how their mobs had screamed for their blood and heads? Were they not as guiltless as he appeared to be? Had there been others like her, forced to watch helplessly?

She had been told about the hatred and differences between the white man and Indian, but she had never before confronted it. They were ready to tear him limb from limb. She had never witnessed such uncalled-for behavior and violence to another. This whole situation went against her beliefs and teachings. How could his being an Indian provoke such hatred and anger from these people?

She watched as the men dragged him over to the post and tied him tightly face forward. Jed fetched the whip, demanding to be the first to inflict some lashes on him. Others grabbed at the whip handle begging for the same honor.

Ben, being the largest and most powerful man present, took the whip and stated, "I'm first! They'll be enough skin on his red arse for all of us to peel some off and leave some for the buzzards."

Alisha made one last desperate plea for mercy and common sense. "How can you people ever hope to have peace and friendship with them when you treat them like this? Can't you see this will only cause more trouble and hatred? Wait for Uncle Thad to come back, Ben. He'll know what is best to do. Please . . ."

Horace snapped, "Who wants peace and friendship with those redskins? Best thing we could do is to wipe them all out and our problems solved for good. Besides, no one asked for your opinion anyway."

Alisha stared at him incredulously and said, "Horace, you can't mean that! You don't know what you're saying. That would be cold-blooded murder!" But she could read in his face that he did understand and mean what he said.

Jed shouted, "Horace, keep her out of the way! Hold her or something. She ain't got no part in this business. Let's get on with this, me lads."

Alisha was seized and held in Horace's strong grip. The whip rose and fell with a loud snap and pop. Alisha flinched at the gruesome sight and cried, "Let me go, Horace! I can't watch. I'll be sick . . ." she stammered.

He was tempted to force her to stay and watch

but decided against it. If she did get sick, it might stop the action and he surely didn't want that. Reluctantly he released her and watched her flee to her cabin. It had been very nice to hold her so close for even such a short time, to feel the heat of her body next to his and to have her under his control. Too bad they hadn't been alone . . . he would not have been so curt and tough with her. Why wouldn't she allow him to be gentle and nice to her? Why did she provoke him into behaving that way to her every time? One day she will come around, he thought. I'll have her yet if it's the last thing I do. In time, Alisha, in time . . .

Again the whip sang out and cut a fresh, bloody gash across the brave's chest. Unexpectedly, Alisha appeared between Ben and the brave with a loaded, primed gun in her hands. Horace was infuriated by her daring interruption and her open concern for the Indian. He halted instantly and paled as she turned the gun on him as he began to advance toward her. How dare she! he fumed to himself.

"No more," she stated firmly, "or I'll shoot the first man who tries. Uncle Thad will deal with this when he returns. Put the whip down, Ben."

Horace moved again and she lowered the weapon to aim directly into his stomach. She warned, "Don't try it, Horace. You're the very man I'd have no qualms about shooting. I won't stand by and watch you beat him to death."

His face flamed in embarrassment and rage, but he didn't dare call her bluff. She held that gun like she knew how to use it and would. How dare she defend that scum and humiliate him like this before the others! He would set her straight later about a few things.

Jed suggested, "If we all rush her at one time, we could easily take her. She can't get off but one shot and that probably couldn't hit the side of a barn."

Alisha glared at him and retorted, "I assure you, Mr. McDoogan, that one of you would be shot in the attempt. Do any of you dare chance who it will be? Will you take that risk?" she openly challenged him. While she had their full attention, she said, "All of you know that this is wrong. We're supposed to be the civilized people, but look how we're acting — like wild animals with a scent of blood and out for the kill. All I ask is that you wait for Uncle Thad and the others."

No one moved or argued with her. She stepped a little to the side. Holding the gun securely, she took a sideways glance at the Indian. Two red slashes crossed his chest. Welts were just beginning to rise. The brave had never winced or moved, nor had his facial expression changed from its arrogant, cold stare at Ben and the other men.

He had said nothing since being forced to walk into the fortress. He glared at his captors with inky black eyes filled with contempt and fury. He surely was a handsome man, and so very brave . . .

Abruptly, she was seized by two rough hands and the gun fired harmlessly into the sky. Horace whispered in her ear, "If you had not been so enchanted with the brave, Alisha, you coulda had your revenge. Too bad . . ."

Her eyes blazed spite at him. She struggled vainly in his tight grip. "Let me go!" she screamed at him. "You'll be sorry for this. Just wait and see. One day you'll push someone too far and they'll kill you. I despise you, you scoundrel!"

He laughed in her face and dragged her back to the edge of the crowd. "Sick!" he mocked her. "This time you'll watch, sick or not You'll watch him die!" he threatened boldly.

As the whip rose for the third strike, a deep voice bellowed out, "What's amiss here? We heard a shot." Observing the scene that confronted him, Thad inquired, "Who's responsible for this? I don't agree to horsewhipping a man and especially not on his chest. Whose idea was this?"

The whip stopped in mid-air and was slowly lowered to the ground. "We's dealing out a little justice to this here Injun," Ben quickly informed him.

Ben always seemed a little edgy when confronted with men in command like Thad, who represented leadership and the law. If it had been anyone else, he wouldn't have even bothered to defend himself or his actions. He would have simply clobbered any man who dared to interfere in his affairs. It galled him to yield to any man, but he did when he had to.

25

"We caught us an Injun sneaking around in the woods," Jed stated at Ben's hesitance.

"Probably planning an attack. I bet he was checking out our defenses and strength," Thomas added.

Many of the others began to shout answers and comments at the same time. Thad raised his hand for silence and said, "One at a time. You start, Ben, since you seem to be at the crux of it all."

Hesitantly, Ben began, "Like they said, Thad, we was out hunting and come upon this here Injun. He had hisself caught in one of Jed's rope snares and was trying to cut hisself free. We captured him, tied him up and brung him here." Ben shifted on his left foot as he watched the effect of his explanation on their appointed leader. Then, he continued defensively, "Hell, Thad, he's just a dirty redskin. Let's kill 'im now and it'll be one less savage to worry about attacking us later."

Thad thought for a minute and asked, "Have you tried to talk with him? Any of you guess which tribe he's from? Didn't anybody try to find out who he is or what he was doing out there?"

"What difference does that make, Thad? An Indian's an Indian! 'Sides, he can't talk or won't. He knows our fortress and how many people are here. We can't let him go now," Ben argued.

"I keep telling all of you that not all Indians are our enemies." Thad was disgusted and exasperated. "Many of them are our friends and have helped us. We can't just capture one of them and

26

kill him for no good reason. First, we should make sure that he's a threat to us. Besides, he wouldn't know our defenses if you men hadn't brought him in here. He might be a valuable hostage," Thad finished quietly.

"Come on, Thad. You know them Injuns don't trade for hostages. They prefer to die if fool enough to get caught. Something about their pride and face," Ben retorted hotly.

"That's pure poppycock, Ben! No man wants to die needlessly." Such prejudice and bull-headedness! Thad thought. "Untie him and lock him in the smokehouse until we can discuss this more calmly and reasonably. Then we'll decide what to do with him and this messy situation."

So amidst the disappointed grumbles and bickering, Ben, Jed and Thomas cut him free from the post and pulled him by the neck rope to the smokehouse. They not only locked him in, but staked him out spread-eagled upon the hard ground, tying his hands to the stakes so tightly that his circulation was nearly cut off. Ben was cursing under his breath as he worked.

Gray Eagle made no moves to stop the men, knowing he could not attempt an escape yet. But he had been in tougher spots before and gotten away. He would be free of this one soon and re-turn to punish them all. He silently accepted their rough handling and insults for now and of-fered them no resistance.

Thomas shivered involuntarily and com-mented, "I'd sure like to know what he's thinking. He has the eyes of the Devil himself. Gives me the creeps just to touch him. You think there's any more of them out there?"

"I wish you'd a killed him before Thad returned," Jed said coldly. "We could have, too, if it had'na been for that consarned niece of his. Damn her good intentions! I'd like to give her a whack or two for good measure."

Thomas piped up quickly, "That ain't what you say when she takes up for you or helps you, Jed. You know why she did what she did. She just don't know these Injuns like we do. Just give her a little time, she'll come around and hate 'em same as we do. You wait and see," he vowed confidently.

"Hell, we shoulda done what we did the last time. Too bad he was travelling alone, right, Ben?" Jed spoke mysteriously to Ben, who understood his meaning and laughed.

Gray Eagle's eyes did not reveal the intense anger that boiled inside. He realized if he had not been so excited by the thoughts of overtaking his father's enemy, he would not have been caught in the wasichu snare by his carelessness. He knew it was dangerous to let his anger and hate blind his eyes and ears in the forest. Now, that sunka ska would escape and not feel the point of his blade in his evil heart. The wasichus will pay for this interference with my tracking and killing of the man who shot my a'ta, he threatened them mentally. I will kill them all, sunka skas! They will no longer kill my people or destroy our lands. This I promise you, Wakantanka . . .

Thomas asked, "Wonder what Thad'll do with him? Sometimes he's a mite too gentle and easily tricked by that kind nature."

Ben reasoned, "Hell, what can he do 'sides kill him now? Can't afford to let him go and have his whole tribe come down on us."

Having secured his bonds, the three men left. Gray Eagle spat after them. He quickly tested the strength of the bonds and found them too strong and tight to loosen or break. He would have to bide his time until his opening came.

When Thad had noticed Horace's grip on Alisha, he had demanded an explanation. Alisha jerked free as Horace loosened his grasp on her arms and delivered a stunning slap to his face. He glared at her for a moment, nearly returning the gesture, but turned and stalked off.

Alisha gave an account of the events before his arrival. "Uncle Thad, it was awful. I believe they would have beaten him to death if you had not arrived in time to stop it. Why are they so filled with hate and violence toward him and other Indians?"

"Now, child, don't judge the people so harshly. You haven't seen the havoc and cruelties these Indians have been accused of inflicting on the whites." Thad raised his hand for silence as she was about to interrupt. "Listen a moment more. Some of these people have lost friends, family members, and homes during raids. I have heard of terrible tortures committed against whites. Women have been attacked, people killed or taken prisoner and homes and farms burned and looted. We've only been here a short time, and you're still unaware of what these people are really like. We tried to make peace with them, but they repay us with death and violence. They seem to understand only strength."

"An offer of peace would carry little weight when written in Indian blood, Uncle Thad. If we treat all the Indians the way we did him today, I can understand why they hate us and don't want us here. We acted more savage than he did. We are the intruders here in their lands and forests. If there is no way to have peace between us, then why do we stay?" Alisha was confused at the il-logic of the situation. "If both sides hate and re-ject the other, but neither will give in or offer peace, the only outcome can be more death and destruction," she said sadly. "Like today . . ."

Thad answered calmly, "When we've been here a little longer, you will love and want this land and life as much as I do. We came here for a new beginning, Lese. We wanted to escape the war and tyranny in England and back on the Colony Coast. Couldn't you feel the noose tight-ening on the Colonists' necks? Life was becom-ing stifling and confining. They've been fighting small skirmishes with the British for a long time now and soon a real war will begin. There will be killing, hunger and ravished lands and homes. You're aware that England is imposing harsh and unfair tariffs and laws on this new land. They will rebel soon, Lese. You mark my words. Men take these things for so long and then they are forced to fight and protect the things they have worked for and built. They have come too far to back down to the Mother Country now. Neither the British nor the Americans are going to give in. War will soon be inevitable. They'll not only have to fight the Mother Country, but some of the Indians as well. Many sided with the British before and will again when it comes to war. Out here, we will be safe from all of that."

"I'm not so sure that is all true. Most of what you have said, Uncle Thad, applies out here between the Indians and the whites. This is their Mother Country and they are fighting to protect it from us. War will be inevitable here someday! Aren't we being unfair to the Indian? Aren't we asking for too much and in the wrong way? I know there is much that I do not know or understand, but what I do see and hear is wrong and unjust."

Thad sighed heavily and knew that it would be futile in the light of the day's events to reason with her. He tried a new approach. "You saw the company books, Lese. We were losing a great deal of money and trade due to the Port Bill and other tariffs. Our end was near back there. I felt our ruin coming. I could not endure to lose everything again, my child. You know that we couldn't have fled south, not with slavery so widespread there. Besides, the war will touch there before it ends. Don't you see and understand? We had no choice but to come here. This is a land of problems also, but in time, we'll solve them and live in peace. It won't be much longer before we start that new trading post and be very busy. By next year, we'll be buying sheep and be into the wool and mutton business again. There won't be any taxes and mortgages to ruin us this time. Perhaps we'll even do some farming . . ."

His mind was filled with dreams and hopes and she did not have the heart to shatter or dim them. He continued, "We'll be happy and prosperous here. We will live in peace and freedom."

"You call this peace and freedom. Uncle Thad?"

He patiently replied, "Soon this will all be over and forgotten and then we'll have a truce. Just give it and me a little time. You'll see. Come, let us speak no further of unhappy things and times. It's getting late and I have some rabbits waiting to be cleaned for dinner."

Relenting and smiling up into the jovial face of her uncle, Alisha realized that she had come to love the old man dearly. There would be plenty of time for talk and understanding later, she thought. She slipped her arm through his and they strolled arm-in-arm to their cabin. Alisha went inside to prepare the vegetables for the stew and Thad went to the side stand to clean his rabbits. As he skinned and gutted the rabbits, he secretly wished for a gigot of lamb and tankard of ale instead of stew and tea.

Horace had been leaning against his cabin stoop observing the talk between Thad and Alisha when Kathy walked over to him. "So, you still persist in chasing Alisha's skirts. Can't you see she doesn't give a fig for you, Horace? She won't even give you a second glance. I could make you forget her if you'd only give me a chance," she promised brazenly.

He glared at the drab, plain girl standing there and said cruelly, "What man would trade one night with her for a lifetime with you? That's like trading gold for rocks!" He laughed and walked inside his cabin.

Kathy stared after him and vowed silently, "She'll never have you, Horace, nor you, her. It will be me or no one. I'll fix you and her. She'll be sorry she ever turned your head."

As Alisha peeled and cut the vegetables, she was absorbed in her thoughts. She reflected on the other Indians she had met since coming here from England a year and a half ago, but none of them had been like Gray Eagle. . . .

A year and a half ago, she was on a ship sailing from her childhood home in Liverpool to the "new frontier" with her parents. She was leaving behind the only home and friends she had ever known. She recalled the great excitement they had felt about coming here, but she also recalled the sadness and heartaches.

The trip to the Colonies had been uneventful,

but tedious. It had been cold, uncomfortable and long. They had left Liverpool in late winter, 1773, and had arrived on the Colony Coast in the spring of 1774. The adventure had been thrilling and frightening to a seventeen-year-old girl.

Alisha was slowly learning what a sheltered life she had led and painfully becoming aware of how naive she was. She knew this was because of her strict, protected upbringing. There was so much her mother had not taught or told her. Each day, she became aware of how much there was to know about life, people and love. Things were not as she had thought and believed. People and times were difficult and life could be cold and hard. Why couldn't people be open and honest as she was taught to be? Why did kindness and friendship not matter to others as they did to her? Why were these men so brash and crude? Where had gallantry and chivalry gone? Alisha did not comprehend that these men weren't so very different from her countrymen. It was just that her father had protected her from the ploys of hot-blooded, eager young men. He had shielded her from the problems in their country. She knew only situations where people were at their very best and never learned what people could be like in hardship. Of her protected life, a gentle, loving spirit was born. Her father would never know what a disadvantage this would give her when she would be called on to step out into the real world with real life problems and people.

She had lived in a world of shadowed illusions and beautiful dreams.

Her naive innocence made facing raw human nature very difficult and harsh for her. How could she hope to deal with emotions, actions and feelings in others that she knew nothing about and could not understand? What made her see and feel things so differently? Was she the only one who did not accept life here? Did she want to learn to think and feel any other way? No! her mind shouted. That kind of hatred would be destructive to herself and others.

She trembled when she recalled how she had tried to stand up against them all. She had done it without thinking, just as she would have gone to the aid of anyone in distress or danger. Let them be angry, she thought defensively. They were wrong and they'd soon realize it and be glad that I stopped them from doing a terrible thing.

She would never know that the financial and political problems her father had shielded her from were the very reasons that they finally left England to come here. Her father, John Williams, had been a merchant and shipper in Liverpool. He was the type of man who radiated charisma and many men went out of their way to do business with him and his firm. They knew they could trust him to deal fairly with them. His reputation became well-known and above reproach during those days. How happy those days and times had been for her.

She began to recall those last days in England

and her trip to the Colonies. So many things had happened in such a short span of time. How she longed to be safe and secure with her parents in their home there. In those happy, carefree days of long ago, she had not known fear, hatred and violence.

Painfully, she recalled the closeness she had shared with her father, a closeness of friendship and companionship now gone forever. They had spent many, many hours just talking, going on outings, discussing books and events that they had both read or heard.

It had been a blessing that her mother had never resented their closeness and special love as some women did. Instead, she rejoiced in their comradeship. Alisha's relationship with him made up for all the missing children and the son that she could not give her husband. She was deeply grateful to her only daughter for this.

On sunny, clear days, she and her father would ride horseback for hours in the nearby countryside, stopping later at some inn or respectable tavern for luncheon. There, they would plan future outings or discuss the morning's activities. They were both great lovers of the outdoors and spent many hours in the forests and dales, collecting treasures and memories never to be forgotten.

As John would watch the sparkle of vitality and innocence shimmer in her eyes or touch her face, he would wonder at his decision to let her see only the happy, carefree side of life, without its usual problems and hatred which tormented many hearts and spirits. But he believed that she would have a lifetime to see and learn to deal with the hate, bitterness and cruelty in life and people. For the time being, he felt that she should have only love, security and happiness. She was still very young and there was plenty of time.

Glancing around the small, homely cabin, Alisha laughed at how vastly different it was from the grand halls and homes she had lived in and visited back in England. What would Lady Margaret say if she could see me now? she jokingly wondered. Out here, there was no worry about what the ladies of society think or say. From the looks of things, Miss Alisha Williams wouldn't even have a coming out ball.

Alisha dreamed about her parents and the grand parties and dinners of the past. She could still see the twirling dancers in their fancy gowns and jewels and hear the lively, soft music as it drifted up the staircase.

She smiled as she recalled that during each party her father would come up to the hallway and dance a waltz with her before she went to bed. They would swirl and twirl to the haunting melody as they made mocking bows and gay, flirty banter. They would laugh and joke in light repartee until the dance was over. Then he would return to his guests and she to her room.

She could still visualize her mother flitting around the room like a beautiful, delicate butterfly, seeing to her guests. Her soft, musical laughter would float up the stairway frequently to Alisha's alert ears, causing her heart to soar in pride and joy. Her mother had been known as one of the most gracious and delightful hostesses in town. It was an honor and a sheer stroke of luck to be among her guests for a party or dinner.

As Alisha grew older, she came to realize that her parents had one of the few arranged marriages that had led to a life of love and happiness for both of them. Thinking about her mother, she knew that her relationship with her had not been as close as the one she had shared with her father. It had been warm and loving, but something had been missing. It was as though her mother always held a small part of her love and feelings back, as if she could not totally give herself to Alisha.

Alisha quickly learned this and turned more to her father. She accepted her mother's feelings, but wondered if she had also held back in her feelings toward her father. Why had Mama been unable to give of herself completely? Did she fear a total commitment? Alisha realized how very different she was from her mother in this respect. When she loved, she loved with her whole being, holding nothing back.

Alisha's smile came quickly and easily and settled in her eyes as well as on her mouth. Her openness and honesty were always evident in her large, lucid eyes, making secrets and deceit impossible. Her mother often told her, "You must learn to veil those eyes, Alisha. Lower your lashes. You tell everything with a glance. And that smile, it will drive a man to distraction and boldness. Watch me once more. Look how I smile demurely. See the lowered lashes? You must go to your room and practice before your mirror." But when she would reach her room, she would stand before her mirror making silly faces instead. She did not like the haughty, reserved looks her mother had told her to practice. She liked the way her eyes sparkled when she smiled and the pretty way her mouth turned up at the corners when she laughed. I will be myself, she thought rebelliously, not an old fishface or prude.

But there were other times which she recalled with great happiness. On every free afternoon, they would have tea and long chats or lessons. She filled Alisha's head, or tried to, with all the facts and knowledge each young lady of good breeding should know. She daily drilled her in manners and etiquette. She taught her how to dress, how to behave in a ladylike manner in private and in public, how to enter and leave a room gracefully, how to sit, stand and walk and how to converse in light banter.

There were hours of tutoring in intricate needlepoint, music, art, reading, writing and anything that her mother thought would give her an advantage over other girls, along with her beauty and charm. She did not want Alisha taken for granted or treated as chattel. Any man looking at Alisha should know that here was a treasure worth winning and keeping. Her mother was confident that she would marry very well indeed for she would personally see to it. Her innocence and artlessness only enhanced her beauty and charm. But at times her mother would sigh and say, "If only you possessed a little guile and mystique, you could enslave the heart of any man you chose."

Often, their chat had dissolved into laughter when her mother would imitate the faux pas of some elegant lady at a recent tea or party. She would try to suppress her giggles as her mother would demonstrate how not to walk or talk. The only topic they did not discuss was what happens between a man and a woman after they marry. Her mother thought there would be plenty of time for this talk later. Her feeling was that a girl could not use unwisely what she did not know. She wanted Alisha to retain that innocent air that was such an intricate part of her charm and never failed to show in her eyes and gentle face.

Also, her mother did not know how to broach and discuss this aspect of life with a young girl. Lese, not knowing what to ask, did not bring up this topic that made her mother so uncomfortable. She assumed she had heard enough until the time came to learn and know more.

But Alisha managed to gain some knowledge by concealing herself behind the drapes in the drawing room when her mother gave intimate teas for a few friends. The women would giggle and reveal certain facts about their new affairs and conquests. Some of the remarks had made her face flame and she had wished she could escape the room. Other times, the talks had sounded a little spicy and risqué. Her mother would have been furious if she had found her eavesdropping on such talk. The women had spoken of passion, pain, love, disgust, and duty with the actual sex act. Some of the things they had described sounded wicked, but others sounded exciting. In time, she would know of these things and feelings for herself. How could a woman do such things? Could I ever be or think like that? she had asked herself many times. She would quickly say no, that for her love must be very special, and to be shared with only one man.

She had completed her schooling, but her mother had insisted that she continue her studies and practices at home everyday with her. Often, these daily lessons had taken place in the large, walled garden to the rear of their townhouse. This had been one of her favorite places. It had always been fragrant and filled with flowers and shrubs of that season. That was the place where she spent many private hours daydreaming and planning. Her mind and heart had lived many a romantic adventure and secret life in that haven. Often, she had read for hours on her favorite subject, Greek and Roman mythology, or practiced her French and her sketching.

Her Uncle Thad had been the first one to come to the colonies, in 1770. Hard times had befallen him back in England. Due to drought and high taxes, he had lost his estates in Sheffield. He had heard and spoken of the rich, fertile colonies in the new world. As his creditors clamored for their loans and mortgage payments, he talked more and more of leaving England. At the final severing of his credit, he sold his remaining possessions and properties and left with his wife and son for America. She sadly recalled his letter two years ago telling her family of Katherine's and Timmy's deaths from a strange fever.

Since his arrival in America he had managed to build up a small but very successful shop in Harrisburg, Pennsylvania. He had written to her parents many times begging them to come and join him in business. He told them of the new life and freedom he had found. Her father had been hesitant to leave England, but was tired of the many conflicts and wars among England and her neighbors.

As the rivalry for trade increased with other countries and wars cut off many of the shipping routes, his business began to show signs of stress and great financial loss. Conflicts were becoming more frequent in the new colonies also. Thad wrote to them telling of how some of the colonists had dressed up as wild Indians, boarded English merchant ships and dumped their tea cargo into the sea as a protest against the tariffs. Tea had washed ashore for many days after the incident. The financial losses were astronomical and England raged at the offense. The culprits were never discovered.

Conflicts increased in spite and frequency after that. Thad wrote to them regularly, giving all the details of newer and more daring escapades. The colonies no longer depended on the Mother Country and wanted independence.

As the threat of a final break became more and more evident to John and his business went from bad to worse, he was convinced to join Thad. He sold all his belongings and properties and the family left for America. It quickly proved to be a wise decision when Great Britain passed the Port Bill. They could have been financially ruined. Luckily, they prospered after they arrived.

Alisha remembered how she had tried to absorb every detail. There had been so much to see, hear and learn. This new land teemed with wildlife, resources and opportunities. Communities had cropped up along the coast and moved inland. She had heard of the huge cotton, rice, tobacco and indigo plantations down South. How she longed to travel there one day and see it all for herself! She had visited the ports and shipyards with her father and they had found them busy beyond belief. His talent and character were quickly accepted by the men already established there. Soon, he was as busy and prosperous as they were.

Time seemed to have wings until that day in autumn. The countryside had been aglow with color and life. The elms, poplars and maples set the landscape ablaze with reds, oranges, golds and yellows. The evergreens and spruces still gave the look of summer with their greens and blues. Splashes of color from late-blooming flowers, redbuds and mountain laurels gave the finishing touches to nature's work of art. Everything seemed fresh, alive and exciting.

Her family had been in the new land only five months when fate dealt her swift, cruel blow. Alisha relived the incident as if it had been yesterday. She saw the young man coming to Uncle Thad's house to tell them of the carriage accident, of how the horses had bolted and gone careening over the steep embankment, killing both her parents instantly.

The following days would have been unbearable except for her uncle. He understood and shared her loss and grief. Some days she felt the pain would never leave her heart, that she would never feel joy and happiness again. But with time, the pain and emptiness began to slowly recede and were replaced with the heartaches and memories of the past.

The winter came and with it more arguing with England over taxes, tariffs and unjust laws. Thad had known that trouble was brewing. Rumors that war would be inevitable in the near future were widespread. A sense of foreboding and impending danger was heavy in the air.

Alisha thought of that first winter. She had never experienced such cold, harsh weather as this land was capable of unleashing. Many days had to be spent indoors because of the extreme cold, ice and snow. How unlike England's foggy, damp winters. How she had longed for spring and warmth for her body and spirit.

The climate and weather-imposed incarceration did nothing for her dismal spirits. To pull her out of her depression, Thad gave food and supplies to several families in return for tutoring from their wives in cooking, sewing and housekeeping for Alisha, who knew very little about these tasks. Her sewing had run more to needlepoint than to making or repairing clothing; her cooking more to sweets than meats, and her housekeeping to minor domestic chores than to singlehandedly running an entire household. She had not been taught these chores for it had been thought unnecessary for a girl of her position and breeding to do such menial chores.

She threw herself wholly into learning these new tasks. By evening, she would be so exhausted that she slept deeply, blocking out all dreams of home and the past. She had not known there was so much to running a household without servants. During the months of tutoring, she became a competent cook, seamstress and housekeeper. She and Thad were both overjoyed with her accomplishments and the housewives were amazed at her intelligence, quickness and willingness to learn.

During those long, cold months, they had rarely ventured out except to attend church services or visit a nearby neighbor. Since there had not been many young women her age in town, she had spent most of her time in their home or helping Thad in his store. They grew very close during those short days and long, freezing nights. A new and rich understanding and acceptance bloomed between them and grew with each new day. He slowly filled the void and emptiness in her life and she in his.

Some nights, they had sat and talked for hours or sang as she had played the pianoforte her uncle had brought from England. Other nights, they had read from Chaucer, Dante, Shakespeare or other writers. They would often discuss the conditions between the colonies and the Mother Country, or the West, which was rapidly becoming of great interest to him.

One night as they dined and talked, he told her he had heard that the Transylvania Company had bought land from the Cherokee Indians near the Virginia Colony and of other tracts of land being bought by other people. They read of Father Kino's Spanish missions out in the far West. News of the exploration of the Northwest Territory and the Dakotas reached his ears. They learned of the exploits of Pierre de Varennes and La Verendrye back in 1731 and their sons in '43. Thad learned there were many settlements, forts and trading posts in those areas. With each new bit and piece of information, his excitement grew. They talked and schemed and planned many days and far into many nights. Soon, they decided they would flee the approaching war and move westward. After that day, the constant questions were when, where and how to make their move.

She remembered how overjoyed they had been when they heard of a group of settlers who would be leaving Fort Henry on the Ohio River in the spring of 1775. From that day on, they had been kept very busy preparing for the trip and taking care of regular chores. There had been so many things to do before spring. The store, house and most of the furniture had to be sold; only absolute necessities could be taken. Many of these items were sold in sadness because of their sentimental value. They selected the supplies and goods needed for the long, hard and possibly dangerous trek. They had purchased a very sturdy wagon and six healthy oxen. At last, all preparations had been made and all the goodbyes had been said.

Now, over a year later, Alisha stood in their small cabin preparing dinner as if they had never lived anywhere else. It had not been a hardship to live in such small, sparse quarters. In fact, it made her work easier. She was glad her uncle had insisted on putting down floorboards. It made the cabin look nicer and kept the dust and mud to a minimum. Later, when the crops were in and the surrounding area cleared, they would all begin new and larger homes. These cabins would be used to store winter food and other supplies or be used by newcomers until they could build their own homes.

Alisha took great pride in their little cabin and kept it very clean and homey. She had made curtains to cover the three small windows and had placed the few statues, vases and pictures that had been too special to sell around the cabin. She beamed with pride as she looked over the furniture made by her uncle.

She studied the home she and her uncle had built and furnished almost entirely alone. Seeing it complete and real still amazed her. The cabin was about fifteen feet long and twelve feet wide. It was built with heavy logs fitted together at the four corners and the cracks were filled with a mud and straw mixture. The fireplace at the left end was large with a small built-in oven for baking bread. It had taken her a while to learn to cook on an open flame in a fireplace, but now she managed quite well.

Near the fireplace was the eating area. There were two handmade, ladder-back chairs and a small, square table used for eating and working. In the front left corner was a sideboard used for preparing food and washing dishes. Underneath the sideboard were shelves for supplies and food. On the left back wall stood a tall, narrow cabinet for dishes and cooking pots. On one shelf was one box containing the utensils and another which held a few precious herbs, spices and tea.

At the other end of the cabin were two built-in bunks and two chests for their clothes. Near Alisha's bunk, there was a small washstand and mirror with a curtain for privacy. There was a window over the sideboard, eating table and between their bunks for ventilation and light. Thad had attached bars across the openings for security and shutters which could be closed for privacy and protection from bad weather.

There were two racks for weapons in their cabin. One was over his bunk and the other built next to the door. The one near his bunk held his extra gun and ammunition and the one by the door held his favorite gun which was always loaded and primed. There were three lanterns hanging from pegs to light the cabin at night. There were also candle holders on the table and washstand in case the lantern oil was low and needed to be conserved.

Without a doubt, the cabin was very sturdy and well-built. It would make a nice home for a long time to come. She and her uncle had made a good working team and their progress proved it. Each was always doing something special for the other, like the shelves he had built one day over her bed as a surprise.

Tomorrow, the twenty-eighth of June, would be her twentieth birthday. She went to the oval mirror to remove a speck from her eye and lingered a moment to study her features. She lifted a long auburn curl and watched it wind itself around her finger in its natural way. She lightly stroked the creamy, smooth, ivory skin on her cheek. She traced the pattern of her heart-shaped lips and pert nose. She ran her fingers up her delicate cheekbones, then down across her small chin. She carefully studied the dark green eyes with the yellow flecks and fluttered thick, long black lashes. Pleased with what she saw in her mirror, she smiled playfully to reveal even, pearl-white teeth.

Placing her hands on her slender waist, she twisted and turned as she looked at her figure in the mirror. She guessed she was what most people would call medium tall and slender. "Not bad," she whispered to herself softly, "but not great either. Maybe in a few years . . ." Her mother had commented many times on her fluid, graceful walk and carriage. She recalled the times she had been told that she was beautiful, but she also recalled her doubts at the speaker's credibility. She could visualize his leering look that accompanied his compliment. "Twenty . . ." she sighed wistfully.

At that moment, Uncle Thad was thinking about Alisha, her gentleness and her innocence. Those were the very reasons he had kept the truth of the Indian situation and their danger from her this long. He had often viewed on scouting trips the brutality credited to the Indians. He had been tempted more than once to turn back when he had seen these incidents. He knew it was too late for that. He had made the mistake of assuming there would be safety in numbers. He had hoped the fort and nearby settlements would offer protection and unification against the red man.

He had been grateful she had been spared the

knowledge of their danger and the sights of many atrocities along the way. He had tried to subtly warn her today, but had failed. He knew that he must soon confess all to her. Would she hate him for bringing her here? Would she want to return east or to England? He prayed not, for she was all the family he had now and he loved her dearly. If the Indians could be subdued or if they could make peace, he wouldn't have to tell her anything.

He couldn't see that he was only dreaming. They were intruders and the Indian was resisting their coming and taking his lands and forests. The pot of gold at the end of his rainbow had tarnished with the sights and sounds of violence and blood. They had failed to understand the Indian's customs, religion and character and many did not even want to try. Thad asked himself, why do we always believe we are right and superior to all other men? Why do we think they should all believe, act and think like we do? Can we not live in peace even if we are different? I hope so . . . I surely hope so for all our sakes and happinesses.

The crowd of spectators had slowly dispersed and returned to their chores after the event of the afternoon. Ben, Jed and Horace talked in Horace's cabin for a long time. They would call a meeting later that night and demand something be done about the Indian quickly. Ben said a guard should be posted at the gate until they were sure he had been alone in the forest. They couldn't afford to leave any witnesses around to report today's events to his tribe. Ben suggested a few men go into the forest and scout around for others in the woods. Carefully he added, "If you do find any more Injuns, kill 'em and bury the bodies. We don't want to give Thad any more problems to worry about." They all laughed and agreed with him. Jed was about to select a few hand-picked men to go with him and Horace was to be placed on guard until the meeting.

Chapter Two

Alisha and Thad ate their dinner in silence, each caught up in private thoughts and worlds. Alisha could not seem to get the haunting face of Gray Eagle out of her mind. She was intrigued by his manner and his virile bronze body. She recalled how he had stood tall and fearless before his captors and taunters that morning. He had exuded confidence and dignity. She recalled the fierce hatred which filled those piercing jet eyes. She visualized his features which lingered in her mind so vividly: the straight, broad nose that flared in anger; the wide, thin, sensual mouth curved in an arrogant sneer and the strong jaw line set in determination and fury. He was dressed in fringed leggings, breechcloth and moccasins. His entire body had bespoken his strength and agility. Muscles rippled and bulged in his broad chest, arms and back with every movement. He was a magnificent specimen of a man. She could still see him standing proud and noble like some knight before battle, issuing an unspoken challenge to any man who dared to accept it. Once again, that intangible, warm, fluttering sensation swept through her body.

His handsome face disappeared and was replaced by the sight of a bloody chest as the beating flashed before her mind's eye in grisly detail. She blurted out abruptly, coming out of her own trance and startling Thad from his, "Uncle Thad! We'll have to go and check on the Indian. He'll need food, water and doctoring."

"I suppose it's up to us to tend to him and feed him as long as he's here. I doubt if any of the others will want to have anything to do with him. You prepare some stew for me and I'll take it out to him and check on his condition." Even if the others believed the man to be a savage, Thad considered himself a civilized man with a gentle nature. He could not bring himself to let a man, any man, suffer unjustly or starve.

"Let me go with you to help him, Uncle Thad," she pleaded innocently. "Let me see what he's like. If I'm to live among them, I should get to know what they're like. I know more about doctoring than you do. I can take care of those chest wounds. If the others won't allow him to be untied, he'll need help eating and drinking."

Thad argued, "I don't think it would be a wise idea for you to have contact with this man, Lese. He's not like most Indians I've seen. There's something about him . . . something that makes me uneasy."

Alisha jested with her uncle, "Uncle Thad, you

sound just like the others now. He's only a man and a prisoner. There's no way he could hurt me or anyone else, now is there? He's just confused and angry about our treatment of him." Truly believing she only wanted to study the Indian more closely, she teased her uncle lightly, "But Uncle Thad, surely his being a man and an unwilling prisoner would encourage him to accept help from a woman easier and quicker. How could he refuse help from a girl who hasn't done him any harm?" She puckered up her mouth in a pretty, mocking pout and Thad laughed in spite of his grave reservations. But Alisha was soon to learn in startling reality that the Indians' hatred and mistrust also extended itself to white women.

Against his better judgment, he reluctantly agreed. He hoped to teach Alisha firsthand that he spoke truthfully and without bias. She quickly prepared the stew, gathered the soothing balm, a wash cloth and a pan of warm saltwater.

She and Thad went to the smokehouse almost unnoticed because most of the other people were eating dinner or preparing for bed. Horace was on guard duty that night and saw the objects they carried. He immediately knew where they were headed and why. Hostility was clearly stamped upon his face as he stopped them at the doorway.

"Let the savage bleed and starve! He's gonna die anyway." He spit the words out harshly, adding sarcastically, "Surely you're not gonna let Alisha near that filthy Injun, Mr. Greeley?"

Angry at his callous attitude and interference,

Alisha retorted quickly, "If you were their captive, Horace, wouldn't you appreciate food and care? If you treat a man like a friend, then he might become one. On the other hand, treat him like an enemy and he'll react like an enemy. Stop being so blind and stubborn!"

"If I was their captive, 'Miss Alisha,' they'd not give a damn about feeding or caring for me or any white man. They'd be too busy torturing me. You're the one who's blind and stubborn."

"Surely they can't be that blackhearted, Horace. It's probably because of the way men like yourself treat and view them. I didn't see a single one of you try to help or befriend him this afternoon. As far as I could see you were too busy torturing him. You don't even know who he is or why he was out there today. Just suppose he was on a peace mission. If he was, surely you changed his mind!"

Horace gaped at her with hardened eyes. He warned her before stalking off, "I only hope you never git the chance to see for yourself. If you do, it will be too late to know you was wrong."

Alisha trembled as a cold, undefinable shiver ran down her arms and spine, nearly causing her to spill the stew. She told herself that Horace was only exaggerating. No one could be that bad or cruel. His words would come back to haunt her many times in the near future.

Thad unlocked the smokehouse door and lit the lantern hanging by the doorway. Its light filled the room with a soft, dim glow and she could make out Gray Eagle's form staked to the ground. She turned a shocked face to her uncle. "He's tied up like an animal! How could they do this? It's inhuman."

Comprehending her uncle's shamed expression and lowered gaze, she accused, "You knew about this? That's why you didn't have to bring a gun. How could you possibly be a party to something like this? Why, Uncle Thad?"

He interrupted her tirade to explain, "Lese, please . . . the others felt it necessary for their safety and peace of mind."

"For their peace of mind!" she shrieked at him. "What about yours and his? Don't his feelings and suffering matter to any of you? I would never have believed you to be party to something so vile and disgusting. Does everyone here despise and fear him except . . ."

Before she could finish her sentence, Ben came to the door. "Thad, I gotta see you right now! There's important things we gotta talk about."

Thad explained to Ben that they were about to take care of the brave's injuries and feed him. Ben shouted angrily, "He don't need or deserve no help or food, the dirty, murdering savage."

Alisha spoke softly to her uncle, "You go speak with Ben, Uncle Thad. I can take care of everything here. How could he possibly hurt me tied up like that?"

Thad looked around in uncertainty. Ben began to argue anew about her intentions, but she told him matter-of-factly that she was going to help him no matter who objected or why. She tried to shame him for his part in this intolerable situation. After all, he did have the lead role in the afternoon's drama.

Ben muttered, "One day you'll be sorry you ever laid eyes on that or any Injun, Miss Alisha. You'll look back and curse the day you helped him. Don't say I didn't warn ya."

To alleviate the mounting tension in the smokehouse, Thad took Ben by the arm and ushered him outside to talk. Ben continued to fume and fuss, but left with Thad. Gray Eagle had alertly observed the scene of the three people both times. He gazed at Alisha's back as she stood staring at the closed door for a few moments in deep thought.

She finally turned and walked over to him, feeling slight qualms for the first time about her decision to help him. Warily, she knelt beside him and looked at him. She was acutely aware of the frigid glare from his eyes as black as the onyx her father had shown her. She avoided looking into them as she spoke softly, trying to stay the quavering in her voice, "I've come to help you . . . to tend to your injuries . . . I've brought some food and water . . ." Her voice trailed off to a near whisper.

There was no answer or indication that he even heard her. Only the icy stare answered her concern. "I'm not sure how to communicate with you or make you understand I'm only trying to help you." She waited and watched for any reaction from him, but there wasn't any.

"I'm truly sorry about what they did to you this afternoon. I can't explain why they acted that way because I don't understand it myself. How can you hate someone you don't even know or have never seen before? Is there something going on out here that I don't see or know about? Can you answer me at all? Do you know any of my words or meanings?" No response. "Do you not understand or just refuse to answer me?" Still, no response. Her heart reached out to him in empathy. "I'm sorry," she murmured softly.

She turned and took the cloth from the warm saltwater. Her mother had instructed her that warm saltwater aided healing and lessened pain. She gently rubbed the wet cloth across his chest. He made no moves. She was startled by a deep, cold voice which rent the silence, "Hiya!"

She jumped at the ominous tone of the command. She instantly met his gaze, but there was no change in his facial expression. She was sure she had felt vibrations in his chest, but it was as if he hadn't moved or spoken at all. She looked confused for a few moments, then decided her tension was playing tricks on her ears. He certainly didn't appear to want to speak with her again, if he had done so before. "Oh, well . . ."

She put the cloth back into the water and picked up the salve. She began slowly to smear it onto the red, raw welts. Again, the deep, icy command seemed to fill the room, "Hiya!"

She stared at him in bewilderment. Was he

telling her to stop or what? She asked, "Did I hurt you? Did you want to tell me something? I do not understand your words."

She held up the balm and said, "Medicine . . . it will make the welts heal and ease the pain. How can I explain medicine in sign language? Can you understand anything I say?" She answered her own question, "I guess not. Even if you could, you would probably be suspicious of people who beat you and then try to help you. You must hate and mistrust all of us. How could they have been so cruel to you? It was wrong for them to do this . . . wrong . . ."

Realizing the futility of trying to explain further, she picked up the stew. Placing her other hand under his head to raise it up a little, she started to feed him. Halfway to his mouth, he violently jerked his head and body away. So sudden and unexpected were his actions, Alisha spilled the stew in the spoon onto his chest and the stew in the bowl to the ground. Startled, she froze and stared at him. Slowly, comprehension came to her and she nodded understanding.

She picked up the bowl and spooned the spilled meat and vegetables into it. She took the cloth and wiped the stew from his chest, noticing old scars from some past injury as she worked. He made no move this time as she spread more balm on his wounds. He refused to show pain or weakness before this woman.

Alisha sat for a short time studying him. "I realize the anger and humiliation you must be feeling under these circumstances, but there is nothing more I can do for you. I am only one against many. They won't listen to me. My uncle will not let them kill you. He can't . . ."

She moved everything away, knowing he could not refuse food indefinitely. He would come to know she meant only to help him and would relent. Before leaving, she knelt beside him with a canteen of water and inquired, "Water?"

He lifted his gaze to meet hers and glared at her. The look in his eyes which bored into hers made her heart pound wildly. She halted the canteen in mid-air as chills ran up and down her body. It felt as if he reached into her very soul with icy fingers of hate and gripped her heart in its spell. She shivered at the intensity of it, but could not pull her gaze from his.

She whispered, "I've never seen such anger and hatred in a person's eyes or face before. How can you possibly feel these things so deeply? Who taught you to hate with such intensity?" Her face and voice softened as she added, "And yet, you're still the handsomest man I've ever seen. Never have I seen a man anywhere to compare with you . . ."

As her eyes searched his features, that heady, intoxicating feeling stirred and played on her senses once more. She longed to reach out her hand and touch him, to comfort him and his hurts. She was confused by this magnetic attraction to a total stranger. Her mind was troubled and her heart saddened by the way he had been treated. Her hand begged to touch and smooth that knitted brow and caress the tautness from his jaw. Her eyes kept straying to his lips. She found herself wanting to bend over and place a kiss upon them.

Gray Eagle watched her with the feeling he was a prize of war being examined. As she raised her gaze to meet his curious one, her look betrayed her reasons for her intense scrutiny. Her color heightened as she tore her gaze away in embarrassment. She did not understand the emotions and feelings he was awakening in her. She missed the knowing smile that passed his eyes and mouth.

A thunderous voice broke into her jumbled thoughts, "You finished in there yet? Ya been in there long enough!"

At the sound of Ben's grating voice, she instantly turned to the doorway. When her attention returned to the brave, he was staring blankly at the ceiling with vacant, empty eyes.

She arose from her kneeling position and gathered the items she had brought with her. Ben was scowling at her and fussing to himself, calling the Indian names and trying to shame her for her interest and concern in him. He grabbed her elbow so roughly that she dropped everything.

"You ain't listening, Miss Alisha! I said I wants you to keep your hands off his heathen body! If given half a chance, he'd attack you and scalp you. These people out here are coldblooded savages. We haveta get them before they get us. You ain't seen the things them red bas . . . them Injuns do to white folks. Best you stay as far away from them as possible. They're devils, that's all they are. People like that don't deserve to live and multiply!"

She had been momentarily stunned by his verbal assault on her and the Indians. She jerked her arm free, crying out more harshly than she intended, "It's attitudes and treatments like those, Ben, that feed hate and mistrust and keep them growing and festering. Why must you hate so ruthlessly? Why can't you try to get to know them and make peace? Surely they want peace and friendship as much as we do. He's only a man like yourself and the others. This was their land before we came. Can't you see that we are just as different and savage to them as they are to us? Have you ever considered they do the terrible things you spoke of because of the way they are treated by us, like he was today? How can you expect a man to trust or like someone who beats him or looks down on his way of life? I bet you they believe we are stealing their lands. Surely they wouldn't resent our being here if we made truce with them."

Ben shook his head in disagreement. "You can't make bargains with the Devil, Miss Alisha. You can't make truce with savages who don't know the meaning of the words truce and honor. They ain't men! They're like animals and that's how we got to treat 'em. They live like wild animals, running around half naked, killing and scalping people, praying to rocks and trees and making slaves outa decent, honest folk. They're good-for-nothing, lazy devils. I hear they make the women do all the work while they lay around smoking or hunting whites to kill and scalp. What kind of life and people live like that? Can't tell me they's civilized people."

"Ben, what am I going to do with you? Don't you know all civilizations and people are different from each other? Look at him, Ben, and tell me that he has the body and muscles of a lazy man who lays around smoking all day. I'm sorry if it angers you and the others but I can't hate someone simply because you all tell me I must. This argument is ridiculous anyway. Neither of us is going to change our minds. Besides, I didn't help him. He wouldn't let me."

Grinning broadly, Ben replied, "Fool! He's too stupid to know you was trying to help him. I told you they didn't want to be friends with us. I didn't refuse help and food from you when me wife was ailing. I still remember those many days and nights you brought my family food and did extra chores. You knows I'll never forget whatcha did for us. Yore like an angel, Miss Alisha. If'n you ever needs help, I'll be there," he vowed chivalrously.

She laughed and questioned in exasperation, "Why can't you be just as understanding about other things, Ben? You know I didn't help you for any thanks. I did it because you needed help and I was there to give it. I didn't help the brave because his pride and mistrust wouldn't allow him to accept it from his enemy. Still, kind sir, thank you for your bold flattery and gesture." She smiled at him and knelt to gather the dropped items. She and Ben joked and laughed as they left the smokehouse together.

Neither of them noticed the watchful, keen eyes of the brave who had taken in the entire exchange. Gray Eagle remained motionless until they were gone. For the seemingly hundredth time, he strained against the bonds. He knew by now the bonds were too tight to stretch or break. He would have to think of some other plan of escape. He cursed his carelessness which caused his capture.

Nettled by his subjugation, he admonished himself angrily. He thought, Wanmdi Hota, son of Chief Suntokca Ki-in-yangki-yapi of the great Oglala tribe and their next leader, a kaskapi of these wasichus, these sunka skas. It is unforgivable and shameful that I, of all warriors, should have been taken prisoner. I am yuonihansni . . . I was not alert and on guard as I passed so close to their camp.

Soon I will be free and they will pay for their treatment of me and for allowing the wahmunkesa to escape. I will have vengeance for myself and my father, if he still lives. When my foot became entangled in the snare, there was not enough time to cut myself free before the wasichu reached me. It would have been foolish to fight so many armed with the mazawakan. The time for escape and vengeance will come as surely as hunwi appears in the night sky.

I have heard how the wasichu have killed and taken the lands of other tribes to the East where Wi awakens and begins his day. They change and destroy the face of Makakin. They bring mniwakan to steal our minds and weaken our bodies and courage. They are lower than our worst enemies, the Ojibwa.

What do they know of our ways? They do not accept or understand what they fear and hate. They look on us in shame. They put up wooden guards to keep land for themselves. They steal what is ours and call it theirs. They kill the game Wakantanka provides for his children. They kill in sport and waste. They bring death and evil to our land and people.

Already some venture to our sacred lands in the Paha Sapa where the Thunderbirds live and the medicines grow. They search for the shiny, yellow rock which they lust and kill for. We hear and see them coming . . . more and more . . . closer and closer . . . they must be stopped . . .

The wasichu do not love and honor the land as we do. It was not given to them, but to us, by the Great Spirit. When the harmony between the land and man is broken or destroyed, the man cannot survive. They do not see that all creatures, men and things have a purpose in life and must be allowed to fulfill this purpose. They know nothing of the great circle of life. Wi and the Thunderbirds feed Makakin; Makakin feeds the game; the buffalo and land feeds the Oglala. All must honor and respect this and allow no man to break this circle. How can they look at the animals and lands and not see the work of the Great Spirit? How dare they destroy and take what He had given to us!

They speak evil of our women and warriors. My people know and accept their tasks and place in our tribe. They are happier than the ista skas who fight and steal amongst themselves. Their thoughts and ways are strange to us. They treat their families and friends cold and deal harshly with those who are different. They call us the savages! They are fools . . .

With thoughts of families and women, came thoughts of the strange ska wincinyanna. He scoffed, she must be touched in the head, crazy, as the wasichu say, to try to help me. And yet, there was no dull, childlike stare in her eyes or her face. She spoke very strangely . . . fool! Does she not know we can kill her and all her kind? Why did she stand up against her own people for me? Is this some kind of wasichu trick? I will see and know more before I decide her fate. Even though her people like her, they did not like her trying to help me. She made them very angry with her, especially the sunka ska called Horace. He would have the girl for himself, but I can see she does not wish it so. Why should she care what happens to me? Why did she look at me that way? She is indeed strange and unlike the others. Still, she is one of them . . .

The harder he tried to convince himself she was mad, the more her soft innocence and beauty haunted him, telling him he was wrong. When he closed his eyes, he saw her face, soft and white with cheeks that went pink when he glared at her. He visualized her long hair as dark as his own which came to fiery light when the sunlight touched it. When she had stood before him this afternoon, she had only been chest high to his tall, lean body. He had been aware that the full bloom of womanhood had not long since touched her. Her eyes and body tell me she has known no man, he thought. He could still hear the musical tone of her voice or the trembling in it when she was afraid or unsure of herself.

He recalled her large, expressive eyes the color of green grass in spring with yellow flecks, much like the treecat's. He could still picture how her feelings and emotions shone openly in them. He was confused at how she looked at him as a man, not as an Indian or enemy. Could it be that she was still unlearned in the ways of men and life? Could it be she did not seek to trick the Indian with her gentleness? If so, she would be hurt far greater than all the others when the red men returned to slay them.

If I truly see the winyan that lives beneath the white skin, Gray Eagle thought, then I will take her for my own and keep her as my kaskapi. He grinned confidently at this last thought and decision. Surely, she will prove to be a most valuable wayakayuha . . .

Once again, he was glad he had forced the white schoolmarm he had captured years ago to teach him the wasichu tongue. She had foolishly believed he would use it to speak with her people for peace and friendship. He laughed sardonically as he recalled the many times he had used it against them for spying and questioning captives. This was his weapon against their lies and deceit. He scoffed at how these wasichu had spoken so openly and freely around what they called "that stupid Injun." We will see who is the stupid one and who is the sly fox.

He knew there was no one who could give his guarded secret away to the wasichu. All who learned of it were killed instantly. This weapon was valuable only as long as it was unknown to his enemies. He would allow no man to use it against him or his people. He smiled a knowing, cynical smile as he vowed, they will pay and pay greatly for their evil. He drifted off to a deep sleep, dreaming of the day he would be free.

The dim glow of dawn's light slowly pushed away the shadows of night as birds chirped loudly to herald her coming. Gray Eagle stretched as much as the bonds would allow, vainly trying to free himself from them again. All morning, plans of escape were reasoned out and then dismissed. He concluded he must bide his time until the best opportunity came along. When it did, he would strike swiftly and deadly and be gone.

It was as the day wore on into evening he realized he was very thirsty and hungry. Stubbornly, he admitted he must bring himself to accept food and water from the enemy to maintain his strength for escape. It would be easier to accept this help from the girl rather than from one of the men. They would humiliate the brave for accepting the food. Pride and anger flared in him and he knew he would accept help only from the girl. Never would he lower his honor to take help from those white dogs, even at the cost of his life or his freedom.

Time passed on and sunset approached. The heat and air were barely tolerable in the smoke-house. Still, no one came. He was restless to be free, to return to the cool forest and his tribe. By this time, they missed him and would no doubt at this very minute be tracking him. Even though he had hidden his trail from the whites, his life-long friend and companion White Arrow would find it and follow him. He realized he might not have to humble himself to take food and water from his enemy, for it appeared they were ignoring him.

He listened to the sounds of the night creatures and to the rustling of the leaves in the gentle breeze. He heard the hooting of the owl, the howling of the coyote and the wolf, the singing of the cicadas and the calling of the frogs and nightingales to their mates. His ears were sensitive to the sounds of the forest and nature. He could hear and sense things the common man did not.

Fragrant odors from the settlers' dinners floated in the air and touched his nostrils, causing him to recall his hunger. He listened to the muffled sounds from the nearby cabins as the people prepared to settle in for the night. Voices and laughter reached his alert ears and he cursed their freedom and happiness while he lay there hungry, thirsty and a kaskapi. Resentment and fury bubbled up in him like a spring of hot water.

Silence began to fill the night air. Did they forget his being there? Were they torturing him this way or did they simply not care to think about him at all? Would they just leave him here to die like some trapped animal? Even the Indian fed and gave water to his captives . . . nearly all were allowed to die like men, not like. . . . His sensitive ears detected footsteps nearby.

Who came in secret with the night? An enemy to slay him? A friend to free him? His nose quickly told him it was not a koda. He waited to see who the foe was . . .

The door silently and slowly opened. He watched as Alisha hastily looked behind her and stepped inside the smokehouse. She lit the lantern but was careful to keep the flame low. She closed the door quietly and looked hesitantly over at him. Her gaze flickered from him to the closed door several times in apprehension. He had the feeling she was defying orders to come there again. She carried some meat pressed between two hunks of bread and a canteen of water.

Slowly, she walked toward him and knelt at his side. Her expression was one of confusion, guilt and fear. Her eyes bespoke inner turmoil. Knowing the time of the night and watching her tension, Gray Eagle was positive no one had permitted her to come to him this time. He studied her curiously.

She spoke slightly above a whisper as she held the food out to him with trembling hands. "Food?" she asked.

She was more than surprised when he lifted his head and bit into the meat and bread. He lay his head back down as he chewed, watching her as she sat there holding the remainder of the food. He noted the pleased look in her eyes. She was encouraged by this small response to her offer of help.

Sensing her fear and tension, Gray Eagle relaxed the hard, cold expression on his face and in his eyes. He must not frighten her too much or she would not come to him again. The secrecy of her help made it more acceptable and tolerable to him. He would accept her help as long as necessary and let the others wonder at his great stamina. A light smile played across his lips at the thought of their amazement at his prowess.

She noted the change in his mood and the half smile. She misunderstood the reasons for them and involuntarily relaxed her own guard. He could not help but notice the smile that lit her green eyes and tugged at the corners of her mouth. As his eyes scanned her features with a strange look, she realized she was staring at him. She flushed a deep red and looked away. She struggled to bring these unfamiliar emotions under control.

Gray Eagle slowly ate the meat and bread, delaying as long as possible to observe her more closely. When he was finished, she held the canteen to his lips for him to drink. As he did so, his gaze captured hers and held it prisoner for a time. She tensed and averted her gaze to the canteen until he had had his fill. He tilted the canteen up with his chin to indicate he was finished. She replaced the top on the canteen and laid it down beside her.

She reached into her apron pocket and produced the jar of balm. She held it up for his approval with the unspoken question in her eyes. He looked from her eyes to the jar of balm, then back to her eyes. Knowing it truly to be medicine, as it had eased the pain and redness of his wounds, he nodded his head for her to apply it once more to his chest.

Alisha removed the top and spread the salve across the red welts as gently as possible. She wondered at the two, perpendicular scars on the muscles on his chest and lightly traced them with her fingertips. His ease and cooperation were taking her off guard and she relaxed as she worked on the injuries.

She admired the hard tone and beauty of his body. She had never before thought of a man's body as appealing and beautiful. She felt giddy and lightheaded touching and caressing the rippling, smooth firmness. His skin was silky and warm to her cold fingers. He observed the effect he was having on her and was secretly pleased. He found himself thinking, if I were not bound, I would take her now.

Just as she was finishing, they heard voices nearby. She stiffened and terror travelled her face. Her head quickly turned toward the door as she waited, quiet and still to see if she were discovered. He read the panic and fear in her expression and wondered what they would do to her if they caught her aiding the enemy. Surely she must be aware of the danger of being caught with him. Still, she had to come. He wondered how much his safety meant to her. Did she now fear for herself or for him?

She was unaware her hand had moved very close to Gray Eagle's face . . . much too close. . . . As the voice moved away, she sighed relief and relaxed weakly.

Like the strike of the snake, Gray Eagle's head came up and his teeth clamped tightly onto the side of Alisha's left hand. Shocked by the surprise and pain of his attack, Alisha tried immediately to jerk her hand free. That only served to increase the pain and his hold. She stared at him with terrified eyes as tears began to roll down her cheeks. Why had he suddenly turned on her like this?

"Please . . ." she whispered in a quavering voice, but he only glared icily at her. Her other hand went to his face and pressed on his jaw, trying to free her hand from his teeth. He bit harder, tasting blood, feeling skin break and touching bone. Horror and pain were evident in her emerald eyes.

She pleaded with him as she pulled gently on her hand. Gray Eagle watched the disbelief in her expression. He thought, I will see just how far her protection for me will go. As her silence continued, he was amazed that she did not cry out for help even though the pain was great and she was only a winyan. He thought, she fears for my life and yet I am Indian and she is wasichu. This I do not understand.

She lowered her head as she wept silently. In an anguished voice she asked, "How long will you inflict this terrible pain on me? How long do you think I can endure this without crying out? If I do, they will surely kill you for this. Don't make me be the cause of your death. Please . . . make your hate and anger go away. Release me . . . I can't scream . . . I can't . . ."

She gazed deep into his antagonistic eyes, pleading for mercy and release. Pains shot through her wrist and up her arm. "Why do you hate me? I have offered you friendship and help. I would only be punished for this, but you would die! Can't you understand this? How can I make you see you must let me go? They will kill you! Please . . ."

Determined to free her hand regardless of the pain or damage, she took a deep breath and flexed her arm. She clenched her teeth together tightly to avoid screaming. Alertly sensing her new intention, he abruptly released his hold on her hand.

She pulled it to her breast and held it there tightly with her other hand. She rocked back and forth on her knees, crying. He could not see her face which was obscured by her long hair falling over her forehead. He waited to see her reaction. It seemed a long time before she finally raised her head and looked at him. Her tear-streaked face betrayed more than physical pain.

She studied him for a few minutes, trying to find the answers in his face and eyes for his cruel behavior. Finding none, she looked at her injured hand for the first time. She saw the jagged, torn skin, bleeding freely, and the swollen, bruised flesh. She tore a strip from the bottom of her apron. She opened the salve jar and rubbed some ointment on the torn skin. She painfully moved her little finger to be sure it was not broken. Immediately, tears returned to her eyes and she winced.

Taking the strip from her apron, she wrapped it around her hand many times and tied the two, frayed ends with her teeth around her thumb. She picked up the salve and placed it back in her pocket. She picked up the canteen and arose.

She glared at him and said hoarsely, "I will never come here again. I won't try to help you again. If you prefer hatred and cruelty, so be it. Maybe I was wrong about you. Horace said you were savage and coldblooded, but I didn't believe him. Maybe for once he spoke the truth." She thought she was speaking to herself for she didn't know he heard and understood her words.

She left as secretly as she had come, never looking back. He watched her go and knew for certain he must have this girl with the courage of the mountain lion and the gentleness of the doe. Alisha didn't realize the fierce determination she had instilled in Gray Eagle to capture and possess her, for she had only seen and felt his hatred and brutality.

Back in her cabin, she asked herself why he had wished for and tempted punishment and death. He must have assumed I would call for help and the others would be furious and kill him, she thought. He seems so sure of himself, so daring and fearless. Why did he attack me so savagely like that? Couldn't he sense I only wanted to help him, that I meant him no harm or contempt? Did he somehow know I wouldn't cry out for help and was testing me? Why?

For the first time, she had seen and felt the cruelty he was capable of inflicting. Soon, this incident would dim in contrast to what she would see and feel at his hands and mercy . . .

His hostility was like an aura surrounding him and stifling the air she breathed. Her body had felt cold and numb at its intensity and depth. When had he learned to feel these fierce emotions toward the white man? Had he been treated like this or worse before at the hands of other whites? Was that why he fought her touch and help? She knew she could not risk going near him again, so she would never know why he did this to her.

She trembled at the thought of her uncle and the others finding out about her nocturnal visit to the smokehouse. What if he had not released me when he did? she wondered. What if he had increased the pain? She shuddered at those thoughts and whispered, "I'll not go near him again. I can't trust him . . . or myself . . ."

Returning from the late meeting in Ben's cabin, Thad joked lightly, "Talking to oneself, Lese, is believed to lead to madness."

She jumped at the sound of his voice behind her. She turned and smiled up at him and quipped, "Maybe I'm already mad."

His eyes went to the bandaged hand and he asked, "What have we here?"

She looked away guiltily as she told him the lie. "Just a slight burn while baking bread, Uncle. No need to worry. I put salve on it and it feels better already."

"Be more careful, my child. I'd hate to lose the best cook around," he spoke lovingly. With a merry twinkle in his eyes, he joked, "Bet you've forgotten what day it is in all the excitement. But I remembered and I've a little gift for you. Been saving it for a long time."

He went to his clothes chest, opened it and produced a bolt of emerald green material. He grinned mischievously and said, "Happy Birthday, Lese."

She squealed in delight as she unfolded a length and threw it over her shoulder. She went to the little oval mirror and turned and twisted several times as she admired its softness and color. "It's beautiful, Uncle Thad!"

She ran to him and hugged and kissed him. "Thank you for remembering. Can't you picture the lovely dress it will make?"

Thad laughed at the way she danced around the room with the cloth. He slyly suggested, "When you get that fancy new dress finished, we'll have to find a suitable young man to come a-calling."

She joined his joking and quipped back, "Uncle Thad, you're impossible! I think I'll remain a spinster and live here with you forever. Besides, I don't recall meeting any 'suitable' young men around here. I don't care to court any of those I've met here."

"Now, now, my girl," he chided her gently. "It's about time for you to start thinking about a family of your own, though I'll put up a fight to lose you. Most young ladies are settled and have their own homes and families by the time they're seventeen or eighteen, especially the ones as pretty as you. You turned twenty today. You don't want folks calling you a *femme seule,* do you? I'm afraid they will if you continue to refuse all gentlemen callers."

She stuck her pert nose in the air and pouted prettily. "Well, I don't care what they call me or say. Give me the name of one man here worth my time and attention and I'll pursue him post-haste. Besides, I haven't noticed any gentlemen callers."

"There is Fort Pierre," he added slyly. "I hear there are quite a few handsome, available officers over there. I could arrange a visit on business to show you off in that new green dress," he teased. "Might find a good catch over there . . ."

"Don't worry, Uncle Thad. I'm sure the right man will come along soon and when he does, I'll know. I promise you'll be second to know. Give me just a little more time to get accustomed to this land and its people. I have a lot to learn about life before I marry."

"As you say, my child. You have a lot of your mother in you. She was stubborn and headstrong until she married your father. I don't think I ever knew any couple happier than those two. You're still young and there's plenty of time for you to find a good man to marry and settle down. I only hope I live to see that happy occasion."

They laughed and talked for a long time. Thad missed the seriousness in Alisha's voice and face when she had said she would not marry any of the men she had met here. All young girls felt that way until they met a very promising young man and fell in love.

Alisha knew she was serious, for none of them had made her heart flutter and her senses reel as he. . . . Forget him, Lese, she scolded herself. He is the last man you could or should ever love. Sadly she added, if only I had known what he was like before I had those feelings about him. Once begun, how do I stop them or control them? Oh why did I have to see and want him of all men?

After the meeting, Thad had sent some men to cut the brave free to move around the smoke-house. Without her knowledge, he had told the men to place a heavier bar on the door to secure it. Gray Eagle was free to move about in the con-fines of the smokehouse.

They had not decided what to do with the brave at the meeting held in Ben's cabin. They had reasoned and argued, but could not agree on the best way to handle this delicate and danger-ous problem. Their final decision could have a major effect on all their lives and futures.

Simon had informed them of his belief the brave was the son of a chief. He based his rea-soning on the amulet the brave wore around his neck. A trapper had shown him a similar one taken from the body of a slain Cheyenne chief's son. The trapper had told him this kind of neck-lace was believed to hold great magic and could be worn only by chiefs and their sons. If this were true, he would be a most valuable hostage in the event of an attack by his tribe. They wouldn't dare attack as long as he was their captive.

Most of the men felt it was impossible to re-lease him after what they had done to him this afternoon. Surely, he would return with his war-riors for revenge. Thad refused to consider killing him and secretly burying him, as some suggested. Thad decided it would be best to wait and see what happened in the next few days. They needed more time and cooler heads to come up with a solution. After a lot of heated arguing, they agreed to go along with him and wait, but for only three days.

Ben, Jed and Horace talked after the meeting, their voices floating to the nearby smokehouse and Gray Eagle's ears. Jed said, "I don't give a damn what Thad says. I say if there's no trouble by tomorrow we kill him."

The other two men nodded in agreement. Ben suggested, "What we kin do is sneak him out one night, take him to the forest and take care of him ourselves. Thad ain't the only one around here with a vote and stake in this. He ain't nothing but an ole fuddy-duddy."

He laughed maliciously and continued, "We could have us a bit of fun with him first and then kill 'im. Hell, we could hide the body where no one would find it. Thad wouldn't be the wiser. 'Sides, what could he do then?"

Jed grinned devilishly and agreed, "Yeh . . . I got me a few ideas I'd like to try on him. What we need around here is a new leader. Thad ain't got the guts for dealing with these redskins. He made a helluva leader on the way out here. He had the smarts and silver tongue to keep the people in line. But out here, he's no good to any of us. I say we git the people to elect you, Ben. We don't need his talking and smarts anymore. What we do need is a man, a real man, to lead us now. I say we force him out."

Horace chimed in, "And I'll take care of that niece of his. She needs a few lessons from a real man and I'm just the one to give them to her. She's turned me down for the last time."

Ben jumped in at those words. "I can't let you harm Miss Alisha, Horace. She's a real lady and an angel. Our quarrel is with Thad, not her. I can't let you harm a friend of mine."

"I didn't mean I was gonna harm her. What I aim to do is marry her. She's the most beautiful woman I've ever seen and I've seen plenty. She makes my blood boil every time I'm near her."

"Now what makes you think you can git her to marry you?" taunted Jed. "From the looks of things, I'd say she hates the ground you walk on. She's paid that Injun more attention than she's paid you."

"Is that so, Jed? I got the advantage over him cause I'm white and he ain't. Besides, I'm available and he ain't," he reasoned further. Thinking of the way she had looked at the handsome warrior, he flared, "I'd like to set a flame to that manhood he's so proud of and shows off with that tight loincloth. Heck, I bet he ain't got enough to satisfy a baby heifer. If we could've finished with that lesson this afternoon, she would have seen him crying and begging for mercy. She wouldn't have been so impressed with him then. Before I'm finished with him, he'll be sorry he ever turned her head his way."

They talked on for a while longer, planning Gray Eagle's tortures and death. Later, they walked off in separate directions to go to their own cabins.

Gray Eagle paced around the smokehouse loosening stiff muscles, ready to spring on the first person to enter the door. He thought on the words of the three men and sneered cynically. If the girl dared to come again, he would capture her and threaten her life in exchange for his freedom. Then, she would know what it was to feel the flame and the knife . . .

The next morning Gray Eagle awoke refreshed and eager to be gone. Morning was crawling by like a snail when his attention was claimed by the voices of two men in conversation near the side of the smokehouse. He eased to the wall nearest them and put his ear close to a crack. He recognized the voices of the two men known as Ben and Thad. He listened . . .

The old man was telling the giant man he could not go hunting with him today. He told of a secret dugout in his cabin to be used by the grass-eyed girl in case of an attack by his people. He said it had not been completed yet and he wanted it finished today. He told how he had concealed it under the boards of the floor under the table. Gray Eagle noted the worry and concern in the voice of the old man. He fears greatly for the life of the girl, he thought.

Gray Eagle heard Thad say, "I'd never forgive

myself for bringing her here if anything happened to her. She's like my own daughter. Ben . . ." he continued hesitantly, "If anything ever happens to me, look out for her, will you?"

Ben nodded and replied, "You don't ever have to ask that, Thad. I'll not let anyone hurt Miss Alisha, not as long as I have life and breath. I'll take care of the hunting today and you work on that trench. We been having good luck lately. Shouldn't be no trouble to get some deer and elk today." Ben was very confident about his hunting and trapping skills; he was one of their best hunters.

Thad returned to his cabin to finish the work on the dugout. Ben called the hunting party together to plan the directions for each small group of men. They all took his suggestions and prepared to leave.

Even though Gray Eagle received no food or water that day, he was glad to be free to move around and to have overheard this new piece of information. It is good she will be safe during the raid, but hers will be the only life spared if she does as I command. He flamed at the thought of having her at his mercy. *"E-cana . . ."* he vowed heatedly, *"E-cana . . ."*

He became alert as a certain voice touched his ears. He peered out a crack and saw the grass-eyed girl washing clothes and hanging them out to dry beside her cabin. He strained to hear her soft voice singing low as she worked. His eyes strayed to where the man called Horace was standing, watching her with great desire.

Gray Eagle's eyes narrowed and hardened. He watched the man stroll over to where she worked and lean against the cabin wall. The girl tried hard to ignore him as he talked to her. Gray Eagle concentrated his eyes and ears on the scene before him.

As if drawn by some mystical force, Alisha turned and gazed wistfully at the smokehouse. Horace followed her line of vision and clenched his teeth in anger. Slowly, she turned back to her work unaware of Horace's cold fury. He sneered, "You been in to see your Injun this morning?"

She glared at him and retorted, "He isn't my Indian. No, I haven't been back to see him." Without meaning to, she added, "Nor do I plan to go again. It appears he doesn't want my help. I can thank the way all of you treated him for it. I doubt if he trusts any white person, male or female, and I can't blame him."

Feigning shock, he commented innocently, "Don't tell me you've wised up to him already! Whatsa matter, Alisha? That beautiful face and body had no effect on a savage? He must be blind, or maybe not innerested in ladies. He's probably the only man who's seen you who hasn't wanted to . . ."

"Horace!" she screamed at him as a red flush lit her face. "That's enough! You're despicable. Why should I care if I have any effect, as you call it, on him? Not all men are filthy-minded like you. He's more of a man than you can ever hope to be." She flashed him a look of cold contempt.

"I have work to do and I assume you do, too. Didn't I see the other men leaving for a hunt?" She dismissed him with the turn of her back and silence.

Believing her words were only spoken to anger him and because he had embarrassed her, he merely chuckled and walked away to join the other men outside the fortress. One day, he thought, that uncle of yours will be dead and you'll be looking for someone to take care of you. I'll see to it that I'm the only one to choose from. If you take too long in coming to me, I might have to arrange that little deed sooner than fate, he threatened mentally.

He glared at the smokehouse as he passed it, and vowed, pretty soon you won't be around for her to compare me with, you red son-of-a-bitch. I'll show her which of us is the better man . . .

Gray Eagle watched until Horace was out of sight and returned his gaze to Alisha. Although I will not feel her touch again, I am glad it will not be the girl who feels my revenge when I flee. That white dog wishes to have her also, but he will not. Maybe, I will let him watch as I take her. Instantly, he knew he would not. For some unknown reason, her dislike and rejection of Horace pleased him. But he was far more satisfied by her words about him. He decided he would think on these things later. This was not the time or place to ponder her meanings and thoughts.

As the hot afternoon moved up into late evening, Gray Eagle excitedly got up to his feet when he heard the horned owl signal from his friend. The hoot sounded three times, twice, then three times again. He was overjoyed and relieved. White Arrow had come and was close by. He waited tense and alert until the night was nearly gone and the moon low in the western sky.

White Arrow's entrance was so stealthful, Gray Eagle almost did not hear him. He smiled as the tall, lean form of his friend was outlined in the doorway by the waning moonlight.

"I am here, Wanhinkpe Ska. Yekiya wo," he ordered and went to join his companion.

As quiet and unnoticeable as shadows in the night, they crept across the yard to the fortress's rear wall. Like agile antelope, they were over the fence easily and quickly with the aid of White Arrow's rawhide rope. He led Gray Eagle through the trees to where he had hidden two horses. They mounted and were riding homeward before the first streaks of dawn were seen.

With unsuppressed bitterness and anger, Gray Eagle related the story of his capture and treatment to his friend. White Arrow listened patiently, but could not conceal his growing anger as the story unfolded.

When Gray Eagle had finished his account of the past few days, White Arrow said, "When Chula returned without you, I knew you were in danger. I followed your trail to that wasichu camp. I have watched all day to learn where they held you captive. There were many wasichu in the forest today. They hide many traps for the animals and Oglalas. When I found the place they had snared you, I was careful not to be tricked in the same way. I do not trust men who use traps for their enemies."

Gray Eagle went into greater detail about the strengths and weaknesses of the fortress. He spoke heatedly about the evil the men had done to him. He explained all his thoughts and observations to White Arrow. When they had finished their talk about the men and the fortress, he told White Arrow about Alisha.

White Arrow smiled and watched his friend curiously as he spoke of the grass-eyed white girl who had made such an impact on Gray Eagle. He carefully listened to the words and tones of his friend's speech. He was amused and surprised by the details of his friend's study of the ska wincinyanna. Gray Eagle left no action, word or contact concerning her untold.

White Arrow listened in amazement and disbelief as he heard all about Alisha's help to Gray Eagle and his treatment of her. He could not believe anyone could be so bold or innocent. The more he heard and learned about this unusual girl, the more intrigued he became about her. If such a creature existed, he would see and know more of her. The look on Gray Eagle's face told him more about her beauty and gentleness than his words did. Truly, she must be a rare flower to so impress the fierce warrior Wanmdi Hota.

Lucky the brave who took her in the coming raid, for surely there would be revenge for this evil act against the son of their chief. He was not surprised when Gray Eagle related his plans for the taking of the fortress and the men responsible for his treatment. However, he was more than surprised when Gray Eagle said the girl would be his. No other brave was to harm or touch her, only Wanmdi Hota.

"Do my ears hear right, Wanmdi Hota? You wish to keep the grass-eyed girl for yourself? Surely, you do not wish to hurt and torture her again? Did you not tell me just now how she went against her people to prevent your death and torture and later she came in secret to care for you and feed you? It cannot be in the heart of my friend to be so cruel and unwise. It is not like you to harm one who has helped you. Will you not show mercy and kindness to this girl?"

"Your words and thoughts are true and wise, my friend. I have never killed one who gave help to Wanmdi Hota, even an enemy. But this time, I must walk lightly and carefully, for this girl stirs things in me that I do not understand. I must remember we are enemies. I fear the thoughts and feelings which come into my mind at the sight and thought of her. It is not good for a warrior to feel fear and hunger for his enemy. Especially one who is so different from the Indian. I do not like the weakness I feel at her touch and presence. I desire her greatly as a winyan. She will greatly warm my mat in the winters."

A black scowl touched his features and he continued, "Also, I cannot allow another to take and use her. She is like the flower of the plains, delicate, white and fragile. She would wither and die as they do when touched many times or handled roughly. . . ."

White Arrow considered the words and feelings of his best friend. "It is unlike you, my koda, to so desire a woman. I feel she will not only warm your mat, but also your heart."

Gray Eagle cast a troubled, cynical look at White Arrow and averred, "I will allow no woman to rule the heart and life of Wanmdi Hota, especially a white slave! Do not misjudge her value and place, my koda."

White Arrow suppressed a secret smile, knowing his friend was the one trying to underestimate the value he placed on the girl and his desire for her. Could it be the great warrior has met his match? he mused. Will it be a white slave who will win the heart of his koda? In time, we will see . . . We will see . . .

"The wasichu must pay for their dishonor to you. They must suffer and bleed as you did at their hands. All the Oglala warriors will want to come and help you punish them. It will be as you say."

"We will give them time to learn fear or become lazy with their guard. In time, their pride will be their downfall. We will strike swiftly and secretly. We will take our enemies in nine hunwi. I have spoken."

White Arrow nodded agreement and asserted, "It will be so. You will take the enemy and the white girl with the grass eyes."

They picked up speed and rode hard and fast to return to the village as soon as possible. Many plans would have to be made and the warriors selected for this task. He smiled a crooked half-smile as he realized Alisha would be his in nine days. He did not know White Arrow was observing him very closely and guessed the reason for the look and smile. She would soon be a surprise to both men.

They stopped at midmorning to water and rest the horses and themselves. As the animals drank and nibbled at the grass by the stream, White Arrow told Gray Eagle the news from his camp. Gray Eagle listened carefully as he informed him of the news sent from the councils of the other six tribes of the Sioux nation during his absence. The increase in white settlers, trappers and traders was also being felt and resented in nearby areas. "You must go speak with the other leaders when we return. They have much to tell you. You must speak for our people against the wasichu coming."

Gray Eagle frowned as he imagined what the other warriors of the area would say and think when they learned the fierce Wanmdi Hota has taken a white slave to his tent. He must prepare himself for the teasing and taunting he was sure to receive when the news was told. No doubt the words would travel swiftly when someone of his importance and power was involved. I must be very careful to keep the girl in her place as a slave, he resolved. I will not allow her to bring shame and dishonor on the name of Wanmdi Hota. She is but a woman . . . she will do as I say . . . she will fear me too much to defy my commands. I will see to it from the start . . .

He recalled how they had tried to scare the trappers and traders out, but they had failed. The value of the furs, skins and shiny rocks outweighed their fear of his people or death. Either they must kill them or accept their unwanted presence, for they refused to be driven back to their lands. Such foolish thoughts and greed to cost a man his life and blood, he muttered softly.

Many of the other tribes were just as angry at the wanton slaughter of the animals and destruction of the forest as was his. He recalled the many wildfires which had burned away many trees and killed many animals. He thought on how careless many of the whites were with their campfires. He had seen entire grasslands black and dead. He was aware of the numerous warriors who had been ambushed, robbed and scalped. The killer would take the warrior's jewelry, life, possessions and scalp. Each time Gray Eagle found the evidence of such a deed, he became enraged and tracked down the culprit when possible and avenged the dead warrior.

He would have laughed at the whites who pretended to own the land and sell it to others, if the situation were not so serious and deadly to both sides. He mused over the white man's obsession with the thing he called money and the shiny rocks from the streams and mountains nearby.

White Arrow was speaking of the ones who came from the East telling the Indians of a strange God who sees, hears and knows all. "They say He made the lands, animals and people. They say we are created by Him and not the Great Spirit. They speak with two tongues and the truth is not in their hearts. They speak of love and friendship with the Oglala and his brothers, but they do not live this love and peace. They live death and hate to us. They call us heathen and savage. They say we must worship this God of theirs or He will punish us. They lie! It is the wasichu who will feel the wrath of Wakantanka.

"Do they expect us to give truce to them when they bring the firesticks of death to kill us and the buffalo on the plains? Many were injured in the last stampede the firesticks caused."

Hate swirled in him like a maelstrom when he recalled the white dogs he had captured while stealing the sacred possessions of fallen warriors from their death scaffolds. The wasichu would stop at nothing! he thought heatedly.

White Arrow told Gray Eagle of the murder of Chenuhula and the raping and killing of Okiliea by the wasichu in the area. "The warriors cried out for vengeance. They await your return to lead them. It is good we did not attack the fortress where the killers hid, for you could have been harmed in the attack."

They remounted and rode on at a steady gallop. They hoped to reach their village by late afternoon. They were both silent for the remainder of their ride, each lost in deep thoughts and plans.

Near dusk, they arrived at the Oglala camp. His tribe was overjoyed to see him safely returned. He shook many hands and slapped many backs in fond affection. He laughed and joked with a few of his warriors. He told them he would meet with the tribal council after he had rested and eaten. White Arrow stood quietly as he watched his friend duck and enter his teepee. His friend needed to have this time alone to come to terms with the meaning of his capture and the meeting of the white girl. It is a grave thing to order the deaths of many people, even one's enemies. It was even harder for his friend to accept the fact he desired one of them as he had never desired one of his own kind. He was happy Wanmdi Hota had the power and strength of mind and body to be a great leader of the Oglala. It was easy for him to see why his people loved and respected his friend above all others. But greatness has its costs, he thought sadly. You will have a bitter, harsh lesson to learn, my koda. The path you chose will be treacherous and painful for you and the white girl if my eyes and ears do not trick me. . . .

The fortress was a cauldron of mixed emotions the next day when Gray Eagle's escape was discovered. Panic and terror ruled the scene for a time. The escape had been brought to light when several of the men and Thad went to the smokehouse to give him food and water. Ben and Jed stationed themselves by the door as Thad unlocked it to enter.

At Thad's hesitation and ashen expression, Ben and Jed peeped over his shoulder. They all stared at the empty smokehouse as reality set in.

Jed was the first to react. He shouted, "He's gone! That bloody bastard's escaped!"

Horace shoved past several onlookers and gaped at the room. He asked suspiciously, "Nobody heard or saw nothing? How'd he git out without help?" He whirled around and glared at Alisha's door.

Jed fumed, "I told you we ought to kill him. I betcha he's out there now planning to attack us. Why wasn't there a guard on the smokehouse?"

Thad muttered something about not thinking it necessary because of the bar on the outside of the door. Everyone quickly realized the brave had been given help by someone, but whom? Who would have dared to release a bloodthirsty killer like that? Hell, they all knew what the revenge from him could be like. All except . . .

Janie began to cry and scream. Her fear and agitation were so great that she fainted. Martha was raving how they would all be tortured and scalped. "We're done for! They'll kill us all!"

People were frantic and confused. Alisha came out of her cabin and stood by the stoop, trying to discover what all the loud commotion was about. Were the people trying to form another mob and take the life of the brave in their hands again? Why was her uncle just standing there silently? Wasn't he going to stop them this time, too? Something was gravely wrong. . . .

She listened carefully to the screams and comments from the group by the smokehouse. Her eyes widened in shock and disbelief when the truth became evident to her. He had escaped! She watched the frenzy of the people in confusion. Did they really fear one warrior this much? She thought rebelliously, they should have thought of this before they tortured and tried to kill him. If they feared him and his people this much, then why didn't they try to make friends with him?

Her own reality of his departure touched her. He's gone . . . I'll never see him again. . . . When she became aware of her sad thoughts, she asked herself why his leaving brought such feelings and thoughts to her. She scolded herself, be glad he's gone and they can't hurt or kill him now. Even if he had still been their prisoner, what good would it have done her? They were worlds apart.

Her attention returned to the scene before her. She wondered what good regrets or questions did now. He was gone without a trace. Ben was yelling for the people to be quiet and listen.

"There's nothing we kin do about him now. Like Jed said, we shoulda killed him when we had the chance. Best we git things ready. Sure as

97

that sky's blue, he'll be back."

The men agreed with his words and angrily appointed him their new leader. With sadness in his face, Thad lowered his head in embarrassment for letting his people down. He was to blame for the Indian's escape and if he came back with his warriors for a raid, he would be to blame for what happened then. If he had it all to do again, would he still stop the torture and death of the brave? Sadly he shook his head, for he could not honestly answer his query.

Now, only Ben had the power to make the men obey his orders and do what was necessary to defend the fortress. There could be no doubt he was better experienced in fighting and killing than Thad. Thad bowed to Ben's place as the new leader and waited with the other men for his orders. He was relieved their destiny was no longer in his hands.

Guards were posted around the inside walls of the fortress at all times, night and day. Weapons were cleaned and primed. Ammunition was placed at strategic points along the walls. Ben ordered the women to check on the food, water and wood supply. He told them this siege could last for many days and the supplies were to be used sparingly and wisely. They dared not leave the fortress to stock up on these things. Who even knew, they could be out there right this minute waiting for them to do just that? They couldn't leave the fortress unguarded or put themselves in a trap or ambush. Time would tell what the brave's plans for them were. When everything and everyone was prepared, the waiting began. . . .

Day after day passed with no sign or hint of a raid. Tension and pressure built daily in the close confines of the fortress. The stress and strain of the situation were telling on nearly everyone. How much longer could they live like this? They were beginning to act like savages themselves. The men rebelled at having to crouch in fear in their own homes. Pride was taking a beating and it was hard to take. To be forced to see oneself as a weakling or coward was unnerving to men like Ben and Thad. Horace was too busy being aware of who was the cause of it all and what Alisha had thought of him.

Time travelled on. Many of the women became edgy and tearful. Men fidgeted nervously and paced the fortress grounds. Even the children weren't immune to the turmoil. They fussed and fought amongst themselves constantly. There appeared to be very few left untouched by the consuming fear that gripped the little fortress. Arguments started breaking out at a single word or action. Tempers flared. Gray Eagle had surmised the effect of his escape accurately. They would help win his battle for him.

As the meat supply ran low and the men feared to risk a hunt, still no raid came. What were the Indians waiting for? t hey all asked. Why didn't they attack and get it over with?

Ben cursed and ranted, "Damn! We're prisoners in our own homes. They're probably out there right now just waiting for us to show ourselves. Hell, they'd pick us off with those arrows like flies. I can hear him laughing at us now. If I ever git my hands on him again. I'll strangle him bare-handed."

"We can't wait here forever like cowards," Jed blurted out. "Our water supply is nearly gone, too. Maybe the bastard has done learned his lesson and don't want to tangle with us again. I bet he ain't as brave and powerful as most of you think he is."

"I wouldn't count on that, Jed. He didn't seem like the type to forget or forgive easily. He'll be back. Just you mark my words."

The people were forced to eat cold food when the firewood gave out. Ben ordered the people to do no washing or bathing until this trouble ended. Women began to taunt the men for not having the courage to take care of "one little Injun." As things became harder for everyone, cruel accusations and foolish actions took place daily.

Martha chided some of the men, "You're gonna let that one Injun keep us from eating and drinking? How long are you gonna stay cooped up here like chickens before you men act like men and bring us some food, wood and water? Maybe the women should go fetch the food and water if you men are too scared. What difference does it matter if we die from an arrow or from starvation and thirst?" No one could argue with her last point, but still the men resisted immediate action.

Black moods and impatience passed from one to the other as the days went by. Kathy Brown cornered Alisha one day and told her flatly it was all her fault the Indian got away and they were in this predicament. "If you had'na been so holy and pure, if you had'na tried to save him, Horace and the others would have taken care of him proper. We wouldn't be in the trouble if you had'na interfered. Ask the others. They'll tell you the same thing."

Alisha knew it wouldn't do any good to argue with Kathy, so she just turned and walked away from her, wondering how many of the others really did blame her for this turn of events. She observed how the Indian's capture and escape had changed things and people at the fortress. It was as if she were seeing these people for the very first time, without their masks of civilization. She felt she didn't know them at all anymore, not even her uncle and her friend Ben. Most of all, she feared and hated the change she witnessed in them. But she was unaware of the effect the situation was having on her personally.

Another day passed as things went from bad to worse. She kept to her cabin as much as possible to avoid the cold stares from several of the people. Most of the others just milled about. The lack of work and abundance of time took the major toll, just as Gray Eagle planned . . .

On the eighth day, Ben, Simon and a few

others decided it was time to risk a hunt and try for fresh water. Ben called the men together and stated, "We've got to have meat, Indians or no Indians! Horace, I want you to watch the gate. Be ready to open it at the first yell or sign of danger. We won't go far. Jed, you and a few others try to cut some firewood for cooking. You other men come with me. If we stay here like this much longer, we'll either starve or cut each other's throats!" The others all laughed, but knew the truth in his words.

The men prepared for their assigned duties. The gate was slowly and cautiously opened. They all went their way and the gate was secured once more. Everyone was beside himself with anxiety until the groups returned unharmed and laden with meat, water and firewood. Simon carried some wild fruit he had found for the children. The people lifted loud voices in cheers and praise for the men and their courage.

Thomas said, "Those Injuns must not be strong enough to attack us or they woulda been here by now. If he was from a long way off, maybe he didn't even make it back to his village."

Matt agreed, "Yeh. He might not be coming or able to come at all. He didn't have a weapon or horse. I bet he could be just laying out there somewhere dead or injured."

Ben spoke up, "Coulda been killed by some animal." He laughed and added, "Or by some other Injun. I hear they kill and scalp each other and that one didn't have no weapons for protection. We didn't see any sign of anything unusual in the woods. I bet he ain't coming back either. I knew all along he weren't nothing but all show. Even if he did make it back to his camp, he's too scared to attack us. I say he don't want no more of what we gave him."

"We gotta show 'em we ain't afraid of 'em," Jed quipped. "If they do come, we'll give 'em a lesson they won't never forgit. I say we kill any of 'em we capture from now on. We should hang their hands on the gates as warning to others. Let 'em know we won't tolerate none of their foolishness."

Two more days went by uneventfully and others began to agree with them. Their opinion gained popularity. Soon, it was accepted by all as fact. The strain and mood of the little fortress relaxed and began to return to normal for everyone but Alisha. Things would never be the same in her mind and heart. She was more confused than ever about her own people and the brave.

The men were so confident and puffed up with pride by the tenth day, they left the gate open while they worked in the nearby forest. No one noticed as the bushes began to close in or the slight movement of the leaves as bodies passed between them quietly and quickly.

It was Janie McDoogan who glanced up, looking for a sign of her husband returning from the forest, to see an Indian near the edge of the forest. He was painted in fiendish detail for war. Once seen, he pointed a finger at her in warning, declaring she was to die this day. She froze in terror as she stared at his outstretched arm and the finger of death. She screamed, "Injuns outside! Injuns outside!" She fled in fear to her cabin, crying and screaming.

Horace was on guard duty while some of the men were cutting wood in the forest. At the cry of alarm, he began to shove the gates closed in a panic with little thought of the men outside. The only time they used a guard was when the men outside carried no weapons. There had been no shouts of warnings from them. Well, he wasn't about to keep the gate open to find out! They would have to fend for themselves now! He had himself and the others to think about, didn't he?

Almost immediately, war whoops and yells were heard, "Hiieee-yaaah!" "Eeee-iiiay!" "Yekiya wo!" The bloodcurdling cries instilled horror and fear in the bravest of hearts. Many of the people cringed in fear, children cried at their mother's knees and shaking hands grabbed for guns and powder. What they had stopped fearing was now becoming a grim reality. The brave had returned with his band of warriors for revenge. This would be a fight to the death of one side or the other. There would be no peace or truce now, only defeat and death. Ben shouted hasty orders to the men, telling them where to go and what to do first. He turned and shouted orders to the women nearby to take the children inside. He called out to others to prepare to help with the gun loading and to tend the wounded.

Alisha had run outside her cabin to see what was going on now. She stood motionless, listening to the words of the people nearby. Did they really say he was back? She heard the whoops of the warriors outside and saw the frenzy of the people inside. In all her life, she had never heard any sound so eerie or frightening. It was like a nightmare. Was he actually going to attack and try to kill all of them? Could the warnings coming from those around her be real? Would they do such terrible things to them? Was this why they had feared to release him? If they had not harmed him, would he have still come back to raid the fortress? The others seemed to believe this.

Couldn't they bargain for truce? Couldn't they beg for peace? They most certainly could apologize for the way they treated him. Surely that would stop this farce! Were they all just going to fight and kill without any attempts to settle this without bloodshed? I do not understand this at all, she thought. There must be something we could say or do to stop him and the fight.

The men had fetched their guns and powder hurriedly and readied them for the coming battle. The men took their places like actors on a stage. But this drama was real and deadly. She heard curses and prayers coming from all directions. Another scream tore through the still air and the blood bath began. . . .

Shooting came from all directions around her. Anguished screams of the wounded were heard instantly. Arrows flew here and there with deadly accuracy. Some set cabins ablaze and some hit live targets which writhed in agony. Frantically, the men fought against overwhelming odds and conditions. Women with ashen faces and trembling hands primed and loaded guns for the men. The worst wounded were dragged to cover near the cabins, while the less seriously injured had to flee for cover unaided. The dead lay where they had fallen. No one could help them now.

Without much effort, the Indians were coming over the fence with ropes. They charged with tomahawk, knife and war club, slaying any and all in their path. Men who were unable to reload fast enough used the butts of their guns for defense or their bare hands. No one of either sex or age was immune to death. Both sides were aware of who the victor would be this day.

At the first warning shout, Thad had forced Alisha into the cabin and down into the trench he had dug under the table. She had begged to help with the gun loading and wounded, but her uncle would not hear of either. "Please, Uncle Thad, someone might need my help! Surely, there is something I can do?"

"No, Lese," he shouted breathlessly at her. "They are far too strong for us to resist for very long. We won't stand a chance against them. You must stay hidden until you are sure they are gone, then flee to Fort Pierre. The soldiers there will help and protect you. You must do this for me! I cannot fight with you in danger. Promise me you'll remain quiet and hidden. Do as I have told you before. The map is in the trench. Promise!"

Tears glistened in her emerald eyes for she knew they were saying good-by for the last time. She thought her heart would surely break. How could she live here all alone without any family? She whispered, "I love you, Uncle Thad. Please be careful and don't give up hope yet. He could only mean to frighten and punish us. Maybe he won't kill us."

He shook his head in despair and answered, "You have given an old man much happiness and joy. I love you as though you were my own child. Be strong and brave. I shall be careful for both our sakes." He forced a brave, last smile for her to remember.

He placed her into the small trench and covered the opening with the floorboards. She heard the rasping on the floor as he slid the table back into place. Faintly, she heard him say before leaving, "May God watch over each of us this day . . ."

For a time, all she could hear was her soft sobbing. "I will never see you again," she cried. "God forgive us all for bringing this day to pass. Good-by, Uncle Thad. May it be done quickly . . ."

Chapter Three

Taking his gun and powder, Thad opened the door and went outside. A noise drew him to the side of the cabin. No one was there; then he felt an excruciating pain in his back. It was as if his body were on fire; pain racked his head, then sweet, black oblivion. He collapsed to the ground, a tomahawk buried deep in his back between his shoulder blades. His dying words had been, "I'm sorry Lese . . . I can . . . no . . . longer . . . help you . . ."

The gates were thrown open and numerous Indians swarmed in and ran in all directions. Their bodies glistened with war paint and sweat. Hands were raised high brandishing tomahawks and war clubs. Arms were stretched out taut with bows. It seemed as if all were yelling and shouting a sound that made the blood run cold and the spirit quake.

Some of the Indians carried highly decorated buffalo shields for protection and wore breast-plates made of the bones of small animals. Faces were painted with lines, dots, circles and slashes in red, yellow, black and white paints. Each man appeared to have his own colors and design for none looked like the other.

They captured guns, horses, supplies and a few people. They took only a few scalps from people who had red or blond hair, as black and brown were common and easily attained. They used these hairs to decorate lances, war vests, jewelry, armbands and shields.

As the battle continued, they slew and maimed with deadly accuracy and speed. The pioneers were vastly outnumbered and even worse, they were outskilled in warfare, for the Indians fought with a gruesome vengeance and hatred.

The shooting and fighting slowly diminished and finally stopped. The only sounds heard now were women crying and screaming and the anguished moans from the still surviving wounded. The Indians shouted victorious, unknown words and danced about happily. Fires burned here and there, destroying months of hard, back-breaking work. Bodies littered the ground and doorways like tattered, broken dolls. Then, the pillage began . . .

They took any and all of what they wanted and could carry, setting fire to the rest. They herded the captives in a group like cattle and tied them together with ropes going hands-to-hands. All others had been killed, some slowly and others quickly, depending upon the warrior at hand.

Jed had been captured while gathering wood in

the forest and tied to a tree near the gate. Horace had been taken as soon as the gates were forced open while attempting to flee for cover.

Gray Eagle had, as soon as possible, taken his place at the Greeley door. He had previously pointed out the four prisoners he wanted taken, alive if possible. Greeley lay face down near the side of his cabin with a tomahawk wound in his back. Gray Eagle patiently watched until everything was under Indian control and things were being made ready to return to their village. Then, he entered the Greeley cabin. He looked around near the table until he spotted the floorboards which did not fit just right. He smiled sardonically to himself and walked over to stand beside the table.

Alisha had never felt such soul-shaking, heart-rending terror. What could be happening? The shooting had ceased and all she could hear were Indian yells, cries of pain, screams, and speech of an unknown tongue. This can't be happening, she thought again and again. It's all a nightmare and I'll wake up soon. But she knew that it was not and that all were either dead or prisoners. What had happened to Uncle Thad? She knew that she must remain quiet and still to avoid discovery.

Thoughts of her uncle had brought tears to her eyes. She trembled in fear and uncertainty. What can I do now? she fretted. What if they burn the cabin? I smell smoke already! The trench was only a little more than body size and allowed for almost no movement. What if they find me? What would he do to me? She heard a crash as the table and stools were flung across the floor. Someone was in the cabin! Her heart pounded so loud and hard that she feared they would hear it.

Suddenly, her eyes went wild in panic and she could not suppress the scream in her throat as boards were picked up and thrown aside. Before she could gather her wits as to what was happening, she was roughly yanked up and shoved out the door. She turned to fight her attacker, scratching, biting and kicking. She was immediately held in a vise-like grip. The smell of fire, sweat and blood filled her nostrils. Terror ruled her senses. She was white-faced and quaking in fear. She stared in disbelieving shock when her captor crushed her to his bare chest and spoke coldly, "Hiya! Ihakam ya, Pi-zi Ista!"

"You!" she murmured, recognizing the brave, and fainted. Gray Eagle laughed to himself as he picked her up and carried her to his horse. White Arrow held her as he mounted and then handed her up to him. "She will have many more surprises before this day is over," Gray Eagle vowed.

The group of prisoners and victorious Indians began their long trek through the forest toward the Sioux encampment. Most of the prisoners were dirty, bloody and weary even before the treacherous walk began. Their clothes were tattered and soiled with sweat, blood and dirt. They trudged along in grief and pain.

The attack had been a complete success. They had been taken unprepared and by surprise as Gray Eagle had planned and predicted. All four and a few other prisoners Gray Eagle wanted had been taken. Many of the warriors led stolen horses heavily laden with booty.

The captives staggered along, tied together in chain-gang fashion, near the end of the advancing column. They coughed on the dust kicked up by the horses and occasionally tripped over protruding roots and rocks. Wearily, they were pressed on and on, some in a daze. Cries and pleas for mercy and pity were heard many times from the women, but only curses and threats from the three men. All went unheeded by the braves.

Alisha slowly became aware of movement, of being held in someone's arms, close to a man's chest. The noises and smells brought comprehension and reality to her fuzzy brain and senses. Her eyes opened and she tried to sit up. Her eyes made instant contact with the brave's. The look in his flinty eyes was enough to instill terror and momentarily subdue her. She sank back into his arms. The cramping and pain in her wrists and arms told her that she was bound securely with her hands behind her back. His right arm ran between hers, then under her right side and held the reins. His left hand lay familiarly across her abdomen. He was now gazing straight ahead. She studied the expressive lines of his face, now relaxed in freedom and confidence. The tightness in his jaw was gone and the coldness in his eyes was missing. She tried to comprehend the brutality this ruggedly handsome man was capable of inflicting. How could anyone do what he just did and look so unconcerned and uncaring? Did it not bother him at all that he had just killed so many people and destroyed their homes? Anger filled her mind at his smug coldness.

A reckless mood came over her and she squirmed and wiggled in his grip. She preferred to be thrown to the ground and forced to walk like the others than to remain so near to him. Instantly, his left hand was on her throat, squeezing off the air. He shook her violently and spoke swiftly and ominously in his own language. She struggled and gasped for air as blackness filled her vision. Shocked by his reaction, she saw how greatly her resistance had angered him. She ceased to struggle and he loosened his hold on her neck. She labored to breathe as she stared wild-eyed at him. She watched the tightness in his jaw dissolve into a smug look. She read the sneer in his eyes as his hand slowly moved away from her neck, across her bosom and rested once more on her stomach.

He could feel the pounding of her heart and the trembling in her body. She will think again before she tries something like that, he thought. His eyes left hers and returned to scan the horizon.

She knew now that she must remain calm and clearheaded until she had a chance to escape.

Recalling his actions at the fortress, she thought, I will do just as he did. I'll not cower or show fear. I will be as brave as he was. She stiffened in determination.

But her brave front and determination began to crumble instantly as she realized that all the things she had heard and been told about these Indians must be true. Unaware that she spoke aloud, she whispered, "It's true! All the things Ben, Horace and the others said? They really are savages and barbarians? What a fool I was not to listen and believe. Maybe he would be dead and the others still alive if I had not interfered. Never in my wildest imagination would I have believed such people existed. What will they do with us prisoners? All those people butchered. . . ." Her stomach churned and she was grateful for the fainting spell which had prevented her from viewing most of it. "So much blood and pain . . . why . . . how could anyone be so cruel?"

She stopped murmuring and thought to herself, he looks like any other man physically, even better than most I've seen. But what matters is his conscience. How could he do what he did? Why did I not see what he was really like? Am I that naive about men and life? The others were right. How could I have been so stupid, so righteous, so stubborn? I'm partly responsible for their deaths and suffering . . . oh God, why didn't I know any better? Why didn't I listen to them and Uncle Thad? Surely, we'll all be dead tomorrow . . .

Tears began to flow down her cheeks and she whispered in anguish, "Uncle Thad, I pray you died quickly."

They rode slowly because of the walking captives. Gray Eagle could feel the dejected, heartbroken emotions of the girl. She has much to learn of life and the Indian, he thought. Hers is a different kind of fear and grief from the other wasichu. They had known what to expect and were not surprised by our actions. But she is confused, hurt and frightened. She does not believe or accept what she sees and feels. Can anyone be this innocent? he wondered. Watching her eyes and face, he knew that his answer was "sha," yes.

The riding and walking seemed to go on endlessly. Exhausted physically and emotionally, Alisha fell asleep in his arms. Gray Eagle felt her body relax and knew that either she slept or had fainted again.

He shifted his arm to look into her face. Her hair was in wild disarray, her cheeks were streaked with tears and dirt and her face was very pale. Even so, her gentleness and beauty came through. Gray Eagle thought of the cruel lessons she must learn before she became his willing slave. He would push her to the edge of fear and despair only to bring her back, grateful and obedient to him and his commands. Yes, her lessons must be swift and harsh to avoid a build-up of pride and rebellion. The sooner she learns and accepts her place, the easier for both of us, he thought.

He lifted his eyes and silently thanked the Great Spirit. Wakantanka and the Oglalas had been avenged. Today and for all days, the wasichu paid for the ravage of the red man's lands, forests and people; for to kill the land and animals, is to kill the Oglalas. You have given us victory over our enemy, he prayed. We give you thanks.

Dusk settled; the night approached as Alisha stirred in his arms. Soon, they halted near a narrow stream. Some of the warriors watered the horses and tied them to a rope tied to two trees. Others built campfires and seemed to be preparing to stay the night. The captives, except for Alisha, were deposited in a heap and tied together back to back for the night. They were given neither food nor water.

Alisha sat beside a campfire with Gray Eagle and the other brave who always seemed to be close to him. The two men ate and talked while she stared heartbroken at the others. She could not make out who was in the group in the twilight. But two faces nearest the light of the fire met her gaze. One was Kathy's terrified face as she struggled to get nearer to the man beside her. That man was Horace. He glared at the two braves, wishing that he had a knife to slit their throats.

Horace's emotions at Alisha's predicament ran from anger to distorted pleasure at her downfall. I'd like to see her refuse him as she's done me so often, he thought with spite. I should have had the courage to take her myself. Now that filthy savage will have her first. Damn! She'll wish later that she had let me teach her a thing or two. But knowing the treatment white female captives received, Horace's desire for her love finally outweighed his desire to see her hurt.

Alisha saw the look of sympathy and anger in his eyes and was grateful that he did not wish to see her harmed. He knew that she was unaware of her situation. He mused, I wonder if that redskin intends to keep her for himself or share her with his friends. She'll never be able to endure what he's got in mind for her. Damn the filthy bastard! Sweet, beautiful Alisha . . .

Alisha thought about Horace and their relationship. Should I have handled the situation with him differently? Was part of the trouble my fault? I was wrong about so many things. Could I have been wrong about him, too?

She recalled what had taken place between them. Horace had travelled here with the McDoogans. He was a young man in his early twenties, tall, lanky with a slender build. He had light brown hair and cow-brown eyes. He had worked as a carpenter's apprentice near the St. Louis settlement. His employer had died when they arrived there. The McDoogans had taken a liking to him and took him under their wing. He was hired to help Jed, who was also a carpenter.

Horace was considered nice looking and a fine catch, but he was crude and brash on many occasions and this disturbed Alisha. She recalled many unpleasant situations with him. He had been sure that he could convince Alisha to marry him . . . it was no matter now.

But at that particular time in her life, marriage and love were the last things on her mind, and especially to Horace. She recalled one day in particular when most of the men were out hunting. Horace, too, was thinking of the same incident, as he gazed at her hungrily.

He had been watching her for a long time that morning long ago, the gentle swaying of her hips, the soft sound of her voice, the sparkle of life in her eyes and the alluring expression on her face. His whole being had flamed with lust for her. He had wanted to stroke that shiny hair, kiss those honey lips, feel her naked body touching his, hear her call to him in heated response and know the full depths of her womanhood and innocence. He had wanted to pull her into the wagon and take her that very minute. He would have forcefully done so many times if she hadn't been so closely guarded by that uncle of hers. He could hardly speak to her or get near her without Thad appearing out of nowhere.

But that day, he had made sure Thad was out hunting before he approached her. Their wagon had been at the edge of the camp at that stop and Alisha had been working on the side away from the circle. He had slowly and quietly sneaked up behind her and whirled her around into his embrace and kissed her hungrily. His kiss had burned with desire as he thrust his tongue into her mouth. He had backed her into the wagon where she had no leverage by which to resist him. She wiggled and kicked at him until he pinned her legs between his. She had felt the hardness between his legs even through her clothes and petticoats. She had screamed at him through a covered mouth and tried to turn her head away, to no avail.

Suddenly, he had been wrenched away and thrown backwards, but not by her uncle. Ben had noticed the scene beside the wagon from where he was chopping wood. He had lashed out at Horace, "That ain't no way to be treating no lady and especially Miss Alisha! You keep yore hands off'n her or I'll forgit that we've become friends!"

Her chest had heaved in anger at Horace's behavior and in frustration at her lack of self-defense. Her eyes flashed insults at him. "If you ever touch me again, I'll . . . I'll . . . Just don't you ever come near me again, Horace Swint! Never!" She was so upset, proper words failed to come. She had wished to heap coals of fury on him, but was so unaccustomed to being accosted by a young man, she could not think of the best way to verbally flog him.

Horace had stalked away, after retorting, "If you weren't so damn beautiful and tempting, I wouldn't give you a second look!" He acted and spoke as though she should be grateful for his attentions.

Kathy had also witnessed the scene between

Horace and Alisha that day. She fumed at the way he begged the slightest crumb of response from her, when she would have given him anything he wanted, simply for the asking. She had watched many such incidents, green with envy. She wanted Horace for herself and he wouldn't give her a simple look or word as long as Alisha was around. She had flirted with him brazenly. In the way of unrequited, distorted love, envy turned to jealousy and jealousy to hate. Kathy felt the first two emotions for Alisha already and the third was quickly following. One day, he'll tire of chasing after her skirts and turn to me, she had thought. I'll have him yet, even if I have to trap him! He's a man and men are always hungry for a woman. Afterwards the men will force him to marry me. She thinks she's too good for him! Why can't he see that I'm the one for him, not her?

But Horace had stubbornly refused to fall into Kathy's clutches. He conceitedly reasoned that Alisha could not hold him off forever. After all, he was the best catch available. She'll come around, he would tell himself.

Alisha's eyes moved to Kathy and tried to focus on the look of hatred written there. Why does she hate me so, she wondered? I tried to be friends many times, but she wouldn't let me. Doesn't she see that I have no hold on Horace? That I dislike him and scorn him? But even now, Horace's eyes were only for Alisha. Kathy could have been a rock for all he cared or noticed.

Kathy's father Thomas had been a dirt farmer back in Tennessee. But just like his daughter and wife Mary, he had the attitude and appearance of bitterness and failure. Alisha once heard that Thomas had pretended to work on the large farm of a relative. She heard that this relative had paid for their trip West just to get them away from his own family and plantation.

Thomas's mealy-mouth whining and leeching had been a problem and nuisance to many on the way out West. Many could hardly believe that he had made it all the way. Maybe he had more spunk than any of them had realized. Maybe there were other reasons for his personality, like his wife and daughter. Alisha always believed that there were reasons for the way all people thought and acted that were not solely their own fault. Life had too many outside, uncontrollable influences. Maybe that was why she tried to give everyone the benefit of the doubt and friendship. She persisted with her offer of friendship and help to all until she was sure that they did not want it or deserve it, just like Horace and Kathy. . . .

Kathy was much like her mother in personality and looks. Both were sullen, drab, unfriendly women, especially to other women. She had what her uncle had called a mousy look. He had told her once, "Stay away from that kind of woman, Lese. They spread their bitterness to those around them. They don't want friendship or kindness. They're like the leeches the doctor uses.

They suck the joy and happiness from the people around them and leave the scars to prove it."

Maybe he had been right in his assessment, for Kathy had rebuffed all her attempts at friendship and kindness. How unhappy and miserable such a life and existence must be! It is too late now to learn of joy and happiness for you, Kathy, Alisha pondered. At least, I have happy memories to remember until . . .

An elbow nudged her ribs and she turned to face Gray Eagle. He held food to her lips, because her hands were still bound behind her. She looked at the food he offered and turned away in refusal. Gray Eagle grinned at White Arrow, who watched with keen interest. He pulled her head into his lap by her hair and tried to shove the food into her mouth. Angrily, she clenched her teeth together tightly, defying him. If the others couldn't eat, than neither would she. He was only doing this to further torture the others who were hungry and thirsty. Well, she would not be part of it!

He clamped his hand over her mouth and nose, cutting off her air. White Arrow carefully observed this clash of wills. She struggled to break his hold on her face. Her eyes were wide with fear and alarm. Her chest began to hurt from the lack of air and her face reddened. Still, he held on and still she gritted her teeth and struggled. Her ears buzzed and lights danced before her eyes. Her vision began to blacken. She blinked her eyes several times and shook her head slightly, trying to clear it.

She ceased her struggles and nearly went limp in his lap. He felt her jaw slacken and her body relax. Surrendering defeat to him, he released his hold. Her lungs fought for fresh air and her chest heaved in relief. Her vision cleared and the ringing in her ears went away.

Just as she regained normal breathing, he stuffed the food into her mouth and held it closed with his hand. She glared at him, but knew that either she had to chew the food or choke. Accepting her defeat, she began to chew the food. She was forced to eat and drink while the others watched in hunger, thirst and envy. Thankfully, he made her eat only a small amount, just enough to prove his power and torment the others.

Ben shouted insults at her treatment and was silenced by a sharp blow to the side of his head. She lurched forward to go to him, but was held back. Poor Ben, she thought, he always seems to be there when I need help.

She thought about the kindly giant of a man, a rogue of sorts. Early during their trip West, they had become good friends during Mrs. Frazer's illness. She thought of the many days she had carried food to the Frazers and helped with the chores. Many nights she had been so tired after doing both families' laundry, cooking and dishes that she would fall into her bed-roll exhausted. Ben would chop the wood for her and bring fresh meat and fowl for her to cook for them all. As soon as Mrs. Frazer was strong enough, she took over her own chores with not so much as a simple "thank you." Ben's gratitude and help ever since then made up for her rudeness and coldness.

Ben had been a blacksmith in the settlement of Virginia back in the colonies. He was a huge, burly man with powerful arms and shoulders, accustomed to heavy, hard work. He had been one of the best and busiest workers and successful hunters on the trail. But Ben was a man of conflicting natures. If a man were his friend, he would do anything for him. But if he did not like someone, if someone did him an injustice, he could be a harsh, cold enemy. Ben was usually an easygoing, well-liked, happy fellow. He was always laughing and joking with the other men and oftentimes the women. He inspired hard work and cooperation among the men, many times taking the lead.

She had no doubts he had saved her from being attacked by Horace that day. He had become like a big brother to her since then and never let anything like that occur again. They had talked and joked at the end of many long, hard days. He had told her all about the smithy business and Virginia. He had said that he had been forced to flee after a fight and the death of the son of the area's wealthiest and most powerful plantation owner. Now, his new smithy shop would never be built. All of their hopes and dreams had been dashed that morning.

For some reason, her thoughts strayed to Jed McDoogan. He was one of the few men who made her feel uneasy and embarrassed. He had a way of looking at a woman with those little, black, beady eyes that made her feel she were naked. Alisha flushed even now, thinking about it. She had been told that the short, red-haired man was an Irishman, but he didn't have the brogue of one to her. Although he was a very good carpenter and had a growing trade, he didn't know how to hold onto money and was usually broke and begging for a loan. In fact, he had been fleeing bad debts and possibly a jail sentence when he joined their wagon train.

His wife Janie was the opposite of him. She was a short, plump woman in her forties. She was a jovial, garrulous sort who made everyone feel gay and relaxed. Alisha could still hear that bubbly laughter that death had stilled forever. She could visualize her fat cheeks and neck jiggling in laughter and the large tummy shaking like a dish of custard. She was forever offering everyone suggestions on how to do anything better or faster. Even though she had been a magpie and slight snoop, she was well-liked by all for her openness and honesty. Many hard, weary, bitter days, she had lightened everyone's spirits with her jokes and antics. She had a way of making even the worst time or event go more easily. Too bad, this love for people hadn't rubbed off on Jed. They were all gone, but why? Why?

Gone were Simon Tinsley, the candle and soap

maker and his wife Elizabeth. They had been almost too weak and slow to make this trip, but with the help of another, younger couple, the Chinners, they had done it. The Tinsleys had provided transportation and some supplies to the Chinners in exchange for driving the team and for doing most of the heavy chores along the way. This relationship had proven to be helpful for both families. The Chinners, a recently married couple and nearly penniless, had been able to make it out West to begin a new life, and the Tinsleys had had the help they had needed along the way. Mr. Tinsley had kept all the people in soap and candles along the way in exchange for the goods and chores needed, other than what the Chinners could provide. In fact, Alisha now recalled that hardly any money had been exchanged along the way. Instead, the people had exchanged goods and services for what they had forgotten or used up on the trail. Now they, too, were dead and gone. Slaughtered like so many others . . .

Joe Kenny, who had been their scout, had already left for his old trapping grounds to prepare for the coming winter. He would no doubt be the sole survivor of this disastrous quest for freedom.

There had been Bill and Alice Cooper, Matt and Cora Dooley, George and Katie Tanner, Dr. Frank and Virginia Blackstone and many others. Even though she had travelled and lived with most of these people for a year, she now realized that she had never really gotten to know them. All these people and many others were all lying dead in the burned ruins of their fortress.

Gray Eagle drove two long stakes into the ground about seven feet apart with a large rock. To one, he secured Alisha's feet and to the other her hands. He knelt on one knee beside her and began to unbutton the neck of her dress. She struggled furiously, but only managed to burn her wrists and ankles with the rawhide thongs. She screamed at him, ducking her neck to prevent his actions. He firmly took her chin in his other hand and held it still while he undid a few buttons to aid her comfort and breathing, then threw a buffalo skin over her.

She stared breathlessly at his profile as he lay on a skin beside her, confused by his actions. Why did her comfort matter to him? It seemed obvious that he meant her no further harm or attention tonight. Anger and fear ran rampant through her mind and body as she thought of all the dead people left behind.

She turned her face toward the sky and tried to still her quaking body and spirits. One good thing about this land was its cool, fresh air and beautiful night skies. The clear heavens were filled with twinkling stars and a full, silvery-yellow moon, which looked close enough to touch. The stars glowed like hundreds of tiny candles on a mirror lake. The night birds and crickets sang praises to the night and to each other. A light breeze played across her flushed, slightly sunburned face and cooled her. She began to relax and her lids began to droop in fatigue. Soon, she slid into the silent, black world of slumber. Her face rolled to lie upon her outstretched, bound arm, and even in sleep, a tear rolled down her cheek and she mumbled softly for forgiveness. But from whom? He did not know.

He propped himself up on one elbow and studied her features. The last time he had been this close to her he had bitten her savagely. His eyes riveted to her hand. The reddish-blue marks, tinged with yellow and purple, were still vivid and unhealed. He wondered how she had explained the injury to her uncle, or if she had told him anything at all. From the looks of it now, he had dealt her a very painful blow. By now, Gray Eagle reflected, she must realize that we are enemies and that I now hold her life in my hands, just as her people did mine.

White Arrow, who was lying next to him and watching her also, said in a hushed voice, "She is as beautiful as you said, my koda. I see this difference in her from the others that you spoke of to me. It is this that makes her stand above the others to you. It is not your skin, but your cruelty that she hates and fears. There is a strange look in her eyes when she looks at you. She is very brave. She wishes to suffer with her people and not be treated differently. Her spirit would be hard to bend if not for the strange looks she gives you. Her feelings will be more of a hurt than your punishments. You are lucky to have found her first."

"You are very wise and alert, Wanhinkpe Ska. You see with more than the eye. You also see with the mind heart and senses. She hates me for what I have done, not that I am Oglala . . . those the wasichu calls a Sioux." They lay down on their skins and were both soon asleep.

That morning, camp broke in a hurry in the pre-dawn light. The others mounted up and pulled out. Gray Eagle untied Alisha from the stakes and put the buffalo skins on his horse. She sat up and rubbed her wrists and ankles. She quickly realized that the others were moving ahead and turned troubled eyes to the brave.

Why were they delaying? What did this mean? Was he going to kill her here or . . . ? Did he have other plans for her alone this morning? She trembled at this last thought. She gazed up into the azure sky and heard the singing of the many birds at daybreak. It all seemed so serene, so out of place after yesterday's bloodbath.

She sat curled in a ball, arms hugging her knees, watching him through eyes wide with fear and dread. He was gathering his weapons and sleeping skins. He came and took her arm and pulled her to her feet. He led her to a group of small trees and walked back to his horse. She looked back at him in confusion, thinking that he was abandoning her here until comprehension set in and she flamed in mortification. She finished her business and returned, not daring to meet his amused gaze.

He bound her hands before her this time and mounted. He leaned over and lifted her up. He pulled her arms over his head and placed them around his waist. As he began to ride away, she had no choice but to lean against his shoulder. They rode all day in the hot sun. She thought sadly, this was what we worked and dreamed and sacrificed everything for? This was the life that was going to bring them peace and freedom?

By mid-day, Alisha was drenched in perspiration. Her hair clung damply to her face and neck. Beads of water formed on her forehead and upper lip and trickled down her face and between her breasts. Her arms and back ached and she drooped in fatigue, thirst and heat.

The other captives had been tied to the backs of the stolen horses to speed up the trip to the Indian camp. On and on the journey continued. Hotter and hotter the sun blazed. Wearier, wetter and thirstier Alisha became. Still, they pressed on. When would they reach his village? When would all of this be over? What was he going to do to them?

The constant glare of the sun hurt her eyes and head. Finally, she lay her throbbing forehead on his chest to shade them. What did it matter what he thought? She was too tired, hot, thirsty and sad to care. The contact with his hard, muscular arms and chest did nothing to prevent the heat in her mind. Slowly she sank into a stuporous sleep from the heat and fatigue. In her sleep, she snuggled closer to him and murmured words which brought a heat to his body. He slid his arm around her slender waist and held her securely while she slept. "Niye mitawa, Cinstinna," he said softly.

She stirred from the embrace of his arm and awoke just as they neared the village. She wondered how she could have slept so long under such conditions, then recalled that she had slept very little since the brave's escape ten days ago. She had been unable to erase his face from her mind's eye or remove thoughts of him from her brain. But these were far from the dreams and thoughts that she had had about him! How could she have so misjudged him? When he had accepted the food and care, she had thought it meant truce between them. How wrong she had been! If only he didn't have that strange, confusing effect on her. If only she didn't think there was more to him than met the eye. From now on, she must let her mind, not her heart rule her thoughts and feelings. His whole being screamed "danger" to her, but she had heeded the warning too late, or was it? Could she somehow find a way to escape this fate? Maybe they would be rescued! Fort Pierre wasn't very far away. But she knew that she was clutching at mist. They would be dead before the cavalry knew they had even been attacked. Sometime soon in this remote village in the new world, the life, hopes and dreams of Alisha Williams would cease to exist. If only there were some sense to it all, she might accept what was happening. But there was none. She had been caught in a war that was not of her own doing. But still, she would be called on to pay its dues with her life. It wasn't fair! She had nothing to do with the situation! Both sides were wrong in one way or another. Didn't it matter to him that she was an innocent bystander? Hadn't there been enough death and suffering? How many lives did his revenge demand? Would anything change with their deaths? She wanted to scream at him, "Why? What's it all for? I offered you truce and friendship and you repay me with hate and death!"

She looked around the village as they entered. Dogs barked noisily at the excitement and the smell of strangers. Women, children, elders and other warriors came forward to greet the returning braves. Gray Eagle moved aside to let the others go first with their prisoners and booty. She watched the expectant faces come alive with the glow of victory and vengeance repaid. The white man's defeat was a happy occasion for the Indians.

She watched as they laughed and talked excitedly with each other. Ironically, it brought to mind the time when Gray Eagle had been captured and brought to their fortress. Were the two groups of people so different then?

Alisha sat mesmerized by the vindictiveness of the people to the three men, who didn't appear to notice or harm the others. They pinched flesh, pulled hair, and delivered blows to unprotected areas of the men. Why them? The three men seemed to have a special place of hate in their hearts. Was it because of what they did to the brave, or was there more to it? She was perplexed by this, but could make no rhyme or reason about it.

The male captives were led to huge posts in the center of camp and bound securely by their hands and feet, but the women were taken in a different direction. Then, the people turned to look over the newfound horses and plunder. Dividing and trading the bounty began immedi ately with great zeal.

Alisha was abruptly returned to the reality of her own predicament by a sharp pinch on her leg. She jumped and cried out in pain and surprise. A female voice, dripping with venom, spoke to Gray Eagle. The Indian girl was very beautiful and shapely. She had long, shining black braids; copper-colored skin and large black eyes which shot daggers at Alisha. She was smiling seductively at him and her voice was sultry. Clearly, the girl had her hooks out for him, if he weren't already hers. Was this his wife or sweetheart, she wondered? The girl ran her hand slowly and possessively along his sinewy leg. To anyone who watched, her behavior and looks needed no interpretation. Her feelings and thoughts were openly flaunted before him and everyone.

A spark of anger, closely akin to jealousy, engulfed Alisha and she stiffened in his arms, watching the girl closely. From the corner of his eyes, Gray Eagle saw her reaction and let the game go on for a time.

Chela asked coldly, "Why is the ska winyan not with the other kaskapis and why do you carry her yourself?" She pulled a knife from her sheath and asked permission to frighten the white girl with "a few cuts." Alisha instinctively knew the girl threatened her in some way.

Alisha pressed closer to Gray Eagle, tightening her grip around his waist, and trembled. "Please," she whispered against his chest.

Gray Eagle gripped the Indian girl's wrist and brutally twisted until she was forced to drop the knife. He spoke through gritted teeth to her, "She is my prisoner and I will allow no one to touch her! You are never to harm her in any way! Do you understand?"

Chela's eyes widened in shock and disbelief, then rage, as she realized the implication of his words and tone. He wanted her for himself! "Am I not enough for you? You want the ska winyan for yourself?" Her jealousy and anger flared even more as she jerked her hand free and stormed away.

Alisha had watched the scene in confusion. It was evident that he had made her very angry with his words and actions. Why had he refused to let the girl harm her? Why had he treated her like that? What was the fight about? Who was she and what was she to him? For some reason, she felt compelled to thank him, even though he suddenly ignored her.

He rode over to where the other three captives were bound and dropped her to the dusty ground. He slid off the horse's back and a young boy led it away. She crumbled to the ground on her numb legs. She made no attempt to rise as the pinlike sensations tingled in her legs.

He stood towering over her like a giant bird of prey as she raised her head to face him, her eyes wide and searching. He stood tall and straight with the look of a fierce Viking god of war. Power and daring flowed from him and hovered all around him.

He reached down and unceremoniously jerked her to her feet and shoved her over to an empty post and bound her there. He took the gold sash that the other brave handed him and tied it around her chest, indicating that she was his personal prisoner and was not to be touched by anyone. Without another word or look, he walked toward a very large teepee, ducked, and entered. She looked at the closed flap and then at the gold sash around her chest. What did it mean? Why was she not with the other women? He looked at her and treated her as if she were some animal that he had captured. She raged inwardly, how dare he do this to me! He has the power to dare anything he wishes! But what were his wishes concerning her? What was the purpose of the gold sash? Thankfully, for the moment the Indians were ignoring all the captives.

Alisha had her first real look around the camp. There were so many of them. There seemed to be at least three hundred teepees, which were arranged in circles, each circle growing wider and fuller. The teepees closest to the center were the largest and most elaborately decorated. Many had stripes at the top and bottom, mostly in red and black, some in yellow. The white, middle area had pictures and designs in red, black and yellow. Many of the scenes nearby were of warriors in battle or on buffalo hunts. The detail and talent displayed amazed her. How could these people be capable of such unusual and artistic talent as this? She studied the style and symmetry in fascination.

The Indians seemed to be enjoying themselves greatly, laughing, talking and smoking pipes. They did not appear to be the cold, forbidding, sullen people that had been described to her. How could a people who seemed so happy and relaxed now have been so vastly different yesterday? Was it this strange, new land? Did it extend its wildness and contrasts to its people also?

Alisha roughly counted five or six hundred warriors and at least two thousand people. Her own settlement had been unaware of so many Indians so close at hand. Only a small band of about one hundred had raided their fortress. Gray Eagle was indeed from a powerful tribe. What would have happened if they had been friendly to him and released him? Would he still have returned to attack them? How would she ever know what he was really like, or could have been like? Why did people facing death always think in ifs and whys? By then, it was always too late to matter.

She wondered if the brave they had captured was their leader. He assuredly was in command and highly respected. If so, the whites would pay greatly for their abuse of him. Would he be lenient with her because of her attempts to help? No! He proved what he thought of her and her aid in the smokehouse that night.

She studied the many breeds of horses tied outside the teepees. She recalled seeing a large corral near the middle of the camp filled with horses. Those staked near the teepees must be the warriors' personal horses. The boy who had taken the brave's horse had placed it outside the teepee he had entered earlier. She looked at the great beast which was an unknown breed to her. He was at least sixteen hands tall and had lean, powerful forelegs and flanks. He was larger than the other horses around and the only one she saw of that breed. A horse fit for a leader, fit for a king, for that matter. He was an off-white color with splotches of gray and brown. He was a magnificent creature. She recalled how easily he had carried both of them and how well-trained he appeared. The horse was indeed as unusual as his master.

She had tried to keep her thoughts away from herself and the others, but now she turned to look at the men beside her. Ben, Jed and Horace were all sagging with fatigue and minor injuries against the posts. They looked dirty and exhausted. Alisha was wondering if there had been a way that all of this could have been avoided.

A frantic, piercing cry rent the air as Alice Cooper ran from one of the teepees which was set out of line with the others near the second circle. It had a red circle at the top and base, with red, geometric designs in the white center and long, red strips of rawhide hanging from the entrance. She was immediately pursued and dragged back, screaming and pleading, into the teepee by a young brave wearing only a breechcloth. The brave had laughed as she struggled with him. Her clothes were torn and dirty, her face streaked with tears and dirt, her hair a tangled mess and a petrified look in her wild eyes and ashen face.

Ben strained against his bonds trying to free himself, shouting curses and taunts to the brave. He finally ceased the useless struggles and lowered his head. In an angry voice, he explained the purpose of the redfringed teepee. The scout had told him once that it was called a wokasketipi. Joe had said that all female prisoners were held there until sold or traded, to be used by the braves as often as they wished or by the women as a slave. When they tired of her, she would be sold or traded to others for the same purpose or kept on as a slave. That was the purpose of the red teepee.

Jed asked if anyone other than Alice Cooper, Kathy Brown and Elizabeth Tinsley had been taken into the teepee. The others all shook their heads no as Alisha stared at the teepee in panic and fear.

Horace could not resist a cruel stab at Alisha, "Where is our food, water and aid, Miss Injun Helper? You remember what I said, but you didn't believe me. I told you they wasn't nothing but bloodthirsty savages. He don't look so good now, does he?"

Her stricken look tore at his conscience as she answered, "Yes, I remember everything you said. I do regret the day I ever saw him and helped him! You were right! You were all right and I was wrong! Is that what you want to hear? Do you also want me to take the blame for us being here and the others being dead? All right! I'll accept that, too! Who's to say or know what difference his life or death would have made now?" She turned her face away and tears rolled freely and silently down her cheeks to drop unchecked onto her dress and the gold sash. She had never felt so wretched and miserable, so frightened and intimidated. Her tears were for the dead souls lying unburied at the fortress, for the women in the teepee whose fates were worse than death, for the men beside her whose blood and lives were yet to be taken and for herself and the death of all her illusions of life and love.

What cruel lessons life teaches in this God-forsaken land, she thought helplessly. Why? What will it accomplish? There is no help or rescue for us. We are all alone now . . .

The cries and pleas went on in the teepee for a

time and Alisha cringed in pity and terror with each one. Jed was the first to make the observation. "That Injun must have something special in mind for you, Alisha or you'd be in there, too! Could be he plans to thank you personally for your help! We coulda taken care of him before if you hadna . . ."

Her eyes had widened in alarm and her face had gone colorless. For a minute, he thought she had swooned. Her heart thudded heavily in her chest.

Surely, he wouldn't . . . not . . . the gravity of her position hit her hard and deep. What did he have in mind for them, for her? How would she be able to live if he . . . if they . . . no, her mind screamed, let me die first!

The three men had watched her closely for the last few minutes, recalling their resentment at her interference and attention to the brave. Of them all, Ben had known her the longest and was the closest to her. He had very special feelings for this slip of a girl who had befriended and helped him many times. Jed had been much too aware of her as a woman and disliked the cool, lofty way she treated him. Then, he would smile and recall that he had a way of making ladies nervous and quiet. To Horace, she represented desire, beauty and hopes of many nights of . . . but, of course, that could never be now. All three men had to admire her hard work and courage, even when her loyalties were misplaced. Each recalled how she was always watching, learning, listening and questioning everyone about everything.

She had a mind that quested for knowledge of life and people. She radiated a happiness and charisma to those near her, at least those who did not fear or envy her beauty and naturalness. To most men she met, she either represented the image of a perfect wife, desirable lover or dutiful daughter.

Their hate and fear of the Indians had caused them to lose sight of reason and her good qualities and blame her for their predicament. If she hadn't stopped them that day, he would be dead and none of this would have happened. But they realized his people would have avenged his death and their situation would be the same.

Each man, in his own way, was trying to show bravery and courage in front of the others and her. We may all die, Ben thought, but I'll be damned if I beg for mercy! They respect courage more, and death will be quicker. What he and the other two did not know, was that the Indians knew who they were and what they had done. Their deaths were for justice and vengeance, not for hate of the wasichu.

All the men had heard tales and rumors of gruesome tortures and inwardly cringed. They did not know that many, in fact, most of those stories were untrue or misrepresented. "Hell, we didn't even stand a chance against them. Damn guns! They can shoot twenty arrows before we kin load powder, ball and prime! Civilized man with modern weapons defeated by savages with archaic arms!"

Alisha leaned her head back against the post and gazed up into the starry sky, wondering if they were destined to die a gory death here tonight while all of heaven watched. God help us, she prayed. She felt as though her mouth was filled with cotton. Her lips were dry and parched and her head ached. She was so very weary and uncomfortable. She felt as nasty and ill-kept as the street urchins back in Liverpool. If only she could sit down and wash her face and arms with some cool water. Her arms were nearly numb and her legs wobbly and weak.

As the Indians appeared to be preparing for something, her thoughts of thirst and discomfort quickly disappeared. A sense of expectation filled the night air. Death and pain loomed on their horizon like shadowy specters. The drums began to sound as the men built a large, bright campfire before them.

She noticed that the children had all been taken inside their teepees while the women stayed in the background to watch whatever was about to take place. The men ruled the scene. They sat cross-legged before the large fire or stood behind it, talking and smoking.

Gray Eagle and White Arrow came out of the teepee that they had entered earlier. He looked truculent and forbidding. His eyes darkened as he took in the captives, but gleamed in anticipation when they came to rest on her. She could not tear her gaze from him. It was as though his eyes were dark pools of water and she was submerged in them, engulfed by their power and pulled ever deeper into their depths. She had no will to protect her from the feelings flaming within her. He studied her for a moment, then dismissed her with a smug sneer.

The two came forward and sat down on a buffalo skin in the center of the group. There were nine men sitting together like leaders of a council. She noted the different colors, designs and positions of the feathers in their hair. It appeared that age or ferocity determined status, as most of the leaders were elderly or fierce-looking braves. She had heard that the chief wore a full, flowing bonnet of feathers, but no one was present wearing one, not even the young brave who captured them.

Would their chief have the power and kindness to stop all this as her Uncle Thad had done for the brave? Where was this leader and chief? If only she could speak with him . . . beg for the lives of the others . . . would his heart also be turned against the whites?

She studied the men sitting there. Most of them were tall, lean and muscular, not the bodies of lazy, spoiled men. Most had well-defined noses, full lips and strong jawlines. As with all the Indians she had seen, these too had hairless faces and chests, making their muscles more predominant. The stoical, expressionless faces now revealed relaxation and joviality. They sat conversing and smoking a long, elaborate pipe in a prayer-like manner, passing it one to the other as in some ceremony or ritual or perhaps just a custom of friendship.

Alisha's eyes moved to the women and studied them. Here, there was a wide variety of looks and shapes that ranged from tall and slender to short and plump. The black hair and dark eyes seemed to be a racial characteristic, for all had them. The skin colors varied from red to reddish-brown to dark brown, with the young woman and the handsome brave a coppery, bronze color.

Her eyes fell on the girl called Chela who stared malevolently at her. The others, except for a few curious stares from young maidens, ignored her for the time being. She seemed to hold no interest for the men in the group.

An Indian came forward dressed in a cape and skirt-like covering of long black and white feathers that must have been taken from a bird with a wide wingspread. On his head, he wore an unusually shaped headdress of matching feathers and leather streamers. He wore wristlets and armlets of smaller, matching feathers attached to leather bands.

He danced and chanted as he shook a gourd-like rattler in front of the three captives. He moved around in small circles, stepping lightly from foot to foot, raising and lowering his head, legs and arms in time to the beat. Then, he moved up close to the three men, dancing before each one as he shook the gourd over their hearts and heads, keeping exact timing to the beat of the drum, never faltering or hesitating. What was the ceremony and chant about?

Wakantanka, see us your children:
We give lives and hearts of the ista skas.
We offer their blood in payment of the blood
  of our kodas.
Wakantanka, see us your children:
We send the spirits of the ista skas; judge
  them for their harm.
Wakantanka, hear us your children:
These ista skas are killers of our people, your
  children.
These ista skas are killers of Makakin and
  your creatures.
Wakantanka, hear us your children:
Hear the cries of Okiliea and Chenuhula.
Hear the cries of the ista skas.
Hear the cries of death and vengeance.
Wakantanka, hear and see us, your children.

They did not know the dance and chant spoke of the coming death and sacrifice. Had they known, it still would not have mattered.

The ceremonial chief stopped and so did the kettle drum. He walked over to a buffalo skin and sat down with great dignity and bearing. The drums almost immediately began to beat again with a different cadence. Some of the warriors from the raiding party rose and danced the Victory Dance, chanting the victory chant and their waditaka. The chant and dance expressed gratitude for safety during the raid and for victory over their enemies. They chanted:

The sun looks on our victory.
The wind hears our victory.
The rain touches our victory.
The Mother Earth drinks from our victory.
We are safe.
We are avenged.
We have victory.
We have victory for warriors.
We have victory for Wakantanka, who guides
    and protects us.

The chant was spoken four times, then the specific coups were chanted. The drumming, chanting and waiting began to wear thin on the three prisoners. Patience was a trait of the Indian not shared by the white men. Alisha, however, watched it all, completely engrossed and fascinated by their movements, the music and the garb. It was as if she witnessed primeval man performing rituals before pagan gods in ancient days. It was an exciting, breathtaking scene and, for a time, she forgot reality.

White Arrow had many new waditakas; the highest of all was the rescue of his koda, Gray Eagle. He had also captured many weapons and horses, which were important deeds of bravery and honor. After all the coups were chanted, the ceremonial smoking finished, and the Victory

Dance completed, they turned their attention to the captives.

Ben spoke softly, "Here they come. I guess it's time. Damn 'em! If I could only get just one hand free, I'd show 'em a thing or two about real fighting! At least I'd die like a man."

Two braves picked up sticks with sharp points and came forward. They slowly circled Jed, jabbing at his body until the many wounds ran blood down his chest and arms onto his pants. Jed, with loathing showing in his face, tried vainly not to cry out and to curse them.

Those braves returned to be seated and others came forward. They held small items in their hands which Alisha could not make out. One of them stepped forward holding a war club. The other one held out small slivers of wood. They began to pound the slivers of wood between Jed's ribs, careful to stay clear of his heart. Alisha's stomach churned and she swallowed hard several times to overcome her feelings of nausea.

Jed, no longer able to suppress it, screamed in agony and begged for mercy and death from them. No one listened or cared. Alisha winced with each scream. Another brave came forward holding hot coals from the fire. She stared in horror as they forced his mouth open, placed the coals inside and tied it shut with a gag. The coals spit and sizzled and smoke came out of his nostrils. He writhed in pain, eyes rolling wildly, until he slowly choked to death before her eyes.

Alisha could not believe what she witnessed.

Could this really be happening? Could no one stop or prevent it? She felt as if she could hardly breathe, as if there was a heavy weight on her chest. Her dry lips stuck together and salty tears stung her pinkened face. How could they?

Horace and Ben looked on in pity and dread, knowing they, in turn, would be next. Ben was more determined than ever to show no fear, only contempt and hatred, when he saw their sneers and laughter at Jed's pleas. He taunted them, trying to show his greater bravery and superiority, hoping they would tire of his taunts and kill him quickly. They refused his ploy.

Horace silently prayed for his death to be quick and merciful. Alisha also prayed for some type of courage in the face of death. Her heart pounded wildly in her chest as fear knotted her stomach. She sagged against the post weakly. She glared at the brave whose eyes never left the scene. He looked on as though he were completely unmoved by it all. How? Why? The sights and sounds of this night were enough to bring insanity!

She looked away from the grisly details of Horace's torture. His courage was short-lived and he cried out in pain. He begged for death and pity as Jed had done. How futile all their deaths were. What hold did this land have over men to demand and receive their blood and lives in payment? She tried to close her eyes and ears to the sights and cries before her. At last, no more pleas came, just silence. He can suffer no more, she thought. She would never have believed that she could have been relieved or glad for a man's death. What has happened to me? she cried to herself. I despise these thoughts and feelings and I hate the reasons for them. Never had she thought of death as a blessing longed for above life. I'm not ready to die, she thought. There is too much that I have not seen or done or learned. I have not known love from a man. I have not had children. I have not walked in the sunlight enough, picked wildflowers in summer, tasted rain upon my lips, seen the beauty and happiness that life and love bring. There is too much unfinished, undone, to die now . . .

Alisha became aware of someone calling her name and turned to find Ben speaking to her. He saw the tears sliding down her cheeks and knew her vulnerability. He bit his lip in anger to think of her impending danger. What will he do with her? he asked himself. She'll never endure what he's got in mind, unless . . .

"Miss Alisha, you gotta try to get that Injun's attention. You gotta try to get him to keep you as his squaw!" Alisha stared at him, horrified that he would suggest such a vile thing and shook her head violently.

"No! Never! I'll die first!" she shrieked at him.

"Dying's the easy part, Miss Alisha. It's what comes before that you'll not be able to endure," he warned her. "I been thinking that maybe he hasn't decided what to do with you yet. He knows that you tried to help him and he ain't put you in that red teepee. You better try to reach him before your turn at this. You got no idea what them Injuns can do to a girl."

Confusion flickered in Alisha's face and eyes. "If he wasn't going to torture and kill me also, then why am I here with you? No, Ben, I'm sure that he means to punish and kill me also. Nothing I could do or say would matter to him now." She spoke, remembering the scene in the smokehouse in vivid detail. Begging had meant nothing then and would mean nothing tonight. No, it would be useless to plead.

Still, Ben persisted, "I always believed a woman should die before giving in to one of these savages, but I'll be damned if I hadn't rather see you as his squaw than see you go through these tortures or worse!"

"I can't, Ben. I just can't!"

Ben tried a new angle. "Alisha, you'll only have to endure his attentions if he takes you. That'd be better than the whole tribe's taking you, and God knows what they'd do to you," he warned.

These thoughts and words raced through her mind. Ben said, "You haveta smile and be friendly to him. You don't need to say nothing. He'll understand your meaning clear 'nuff."

"No, Ben! He'd only laugh and think me a strumpet, or whatever their word for a low woman is. I can't! No matter what he does, I couldn't beg from him again!" Ben did not notice the word "again."

As she searched her conscience for the right

answers, her eyes came to rest on Gray Eagle sitting by the fire. Her eyes met his and were held there by the sheer force of his will. There was a confident, assured look there. She could feel the power he possessed and commanded even at this distance. Slowly, he turned back to the brave sitting beside him to talk. Her eyes lingered a moment longer on his features. Again, she felt that warm, tingling sensation that she did not understand run through her body.

She retreated into her thoughts, oblivious of her surroundings and suffering, only to be pulled back to reality by a moan from Horace. She turned to see him move slightly. He had only been unconscious! His body was covered in blood and sweat. He had numerous cuts, bruises and marks all over his upper torso.

As if this had been the reason for the lull, an Indian came forward to throw water into his face. He quickly came fully awake to his agony and surroundings. "God, how much more can I take? Death come and take me," he prayed in a dry, ragged voice.

Two more braves came forward, one carrying a flaming torch. The other one took his knife from its sheath and reached for Horace's belt. With one slash, the belt fell loose. Another, and his pants fell apart. With a few, swift slashes of the knife, Horace looked on, eyes wide in terror, as his manhood was exposed. He had completely forgotten his threat to the brave.

Alisha, shocked and embarrassed, turned a

deep red. Never had she seen a naked man before, nor did she know very much about men. She knew only the bits and pieces from the teas and silly schoolgirl gossip. Sex was still a mystery to her innocent mind and body. How could she do what Ben suggested? She knew naught of love, men and sex, and the thoughts of lying with a man frightened her immensely, especially with a cruel, wild savage. How could a girl seduce a man with such a lack of knowledge on the matter? She surely couldn't ask Ben to tell her the intimate details of lovemaking and seduction. I wouldn't even know what to do first, she thought. Those are the things a husband should show and teach his wife.

An agonizing scream tore her vision to Horace and she fainted as she saw the torch held to his manhood. White Arrow said, "For you, Okiliea," and the others cheered.

The whole evening Gray Eagle had openly or secretly observed Alisha. He had overheard the conversation with Ben, but knew she feared him too much to follow Ben's advice. With two wasichu dead and the decision to keep the other one until tomorrow, Gray Eagle arose and walked to Alisha.

He lifted her sagging head to peer into the pale face still wet with trails of tears. Enough for today, he thought, as he cut her bonds and lifted her into his arms. He took one look at Ben and sneered.

Ben could read his intentions openly in his

face. He watched Gray Eagle carry the girl into a nearby teepee. She will be safe for a little while, he thought. At least, until he tires of her, if he ever does. For a brief moment, he was grateful for her short reprieve. This is one time I cannot help you, Alisha, he sighed painfully. Would to God that I could drive a knife into your heart and spare you all of this. Damn the red bastard! Don't he know how you tried to help him? Why would any man want to kill a beautiful creature like you? The very time she needs me the most and I'm trussed up like a turkey!

The bodies of the other two men were cut down and hauled away from the village to be left for wild animals to dispose of during the night. Ben flinched at the thoughts of wolves, coyotes and other vultures tearing his body to pieces. My God, not even a decent burial . . .

Gray Eagle gently laid her down on a bed of buffalo skins and covered her with one. He lay down beside her and pulled her into his arms. He had long awaited and anticipated this very moment, but would let her rest for now. Mercifully, her mind had rendered her unconscious to all things for a time. He held her tenderly and slept.

White Arrow had watched with envious eyes and feelings as his friend took the white girl to his teepee. He had thought much about the girl Gray Eagle had told him about. She was everything he had expected. But then, he should have known already. Gray Eagle was not a warrior who took female captives, nor would he set his eyes on any woman with thoughts other than bodily needs.

White Arrow was known to be gifted with mystical insight at times. He knew at this moment that something good and evil would happen to both his friend and the girl. He had unexplainable feelings that she would live here with him and that this was the will of Wakantanka. He thought, I will not tell Gray Eagle of my thoughts and feelings yet. My koda must find and learn this truth for himself. But, I will try to guide him in times of error. I will watch over and know this girl who stirs wilhanmna and iwaktaya in me . . .

Chapter Four

Gray Eagle was later awakened by Alisha's wild thrashing and mumbling as tears rolled from her sleeping eyes. He sat up and watched her for a few moments. A strong one, he realized in relief. He was glad she was not ill and feverish as he had first thought. He gently shook her shoulder calling, "Ku-wa, Cinstinna!" Her eyes fluttered and slowly opened in confusion.

She stared up into the face towering above hers and tried to move away from him. Instantly, she discovered to her dismay that she was trapped under his body. She met his steady gaze with a look of total helplessness, waiting to see what he would do next. His eyes burned with a look she did not understand, or want to . . .

He moved his hand from her shoulder and pushed strands of damp hair from her terror-filled face. He nonchalantly ran his finger up her left cheek, across her damp forehead, down her right cheek and softly over her dry lips. She trembled at his touch and her heart pounded madly as she read the intent in his eyes.

Knowing she was completely at his mercy and the futility of screaming, she forced herself to lie still and quiet beneath him and his touch. He shocked her when he leaned forward and kissed her on the mouth. She fought to turn her face from his kiss, but his hand held her chin firm and secure. He forcefully parted her lips with his insistent tongue and kissed her deeply and hungrily.

She had been caught off guard and did not know how to resist him. He did not stop with just that one kiss, but continued with even more passionate ones. For a time, she was lost in the reality of dreams-come-true. Many times she had conjured up this scene in her mind with him and now it was really happening. His kiss and touch were more than she had hoped or dreamed they would be.

His kiss stirred and brought to life a feeling of not wanting to resist him, of wanting this enjoyable feeling to go on and on. All thoughts and feelings disappeared from her heart and mind, except thoughts and feelings for him and what he was doing to her.

His lips left hers to spread hot, searing kisses over her eyes, face and throat. Never had she been kissed like this or ever felt like this in a man's arms before. Due to her lack of experience, she was unprepared for the fires he sparked to life in her innocent body.

Had she not been consumed with desire or lost

to the throes of passion, she still would have been unable to fight his strength of body and purpose. She had no choice but to accept what he intended to do with her.

As her hunger and passion coalesced into one fiery blaze, she thought, if only we weren't enemies . . . enemies! Reality of her situation and feelings came crashing in on her like a tidal wave. She fought to regain control of herself, but was distressed to find she could not and, even worse, did not want to. Her heart and body cried out for him to continue the onslaught of kisses and caresses. She was absorbed by that tingling, floating, elusive sensation which spread throughout her entire body. Her breathing came in short, shallow gasps and unknowingly she pressed closer to him. Her mouth accepted every kiss he gave and begged for more.

He felt her resistance give way and he pressed his advantage. He caressed her passion-swollen breasts, gently teasing the taut, protruding nipples. A low moan escaped her lips as he buried himself in her hair and spoke softly in his tongue to her. The warmth of his breath in her ear and the husky, deep tone of his voice dashed any remaining self-control from her mind. Her arms encircled his back and she clung to him, offering her mouth to his mouth and her body to his body.

This was the moment he had dreamed of and waited for many days since he had first seen her, and he now knew that she would be his soon. He was surprised at his intense longing for her. He had never wanted a woman as he wanted this small, white girl beneath him. He had to struggle with his own fiery emotions to keep from taking her quickly. He found himself not wanting to hurt, or frighten her too much. He wanted to introduce her to love gently and tenderly on this, her first time. He was far more surprised to learn the full extent of his hold over her feelings. He had no doubts he was the first man she had responded to this way. Her fiery response and desire for him brought him a strange sense of power over her, believing that when the time came she would accept him and her place in his teepee.

Deeply enmeshed in his kisses and caresses, Alisha was unaware Gray Eagle was unbuttoning the bodice of her frayed, dusty dress. But when his lips left the hollow of her throat and marked a path to the hollow between her breasts, the contact of his lips on her bare flesh was like a bolt of lightning. She was instantly aware of his touch and her wanton response. Shamed and shocked at herself and her behavior, she jerked away from his arms and lips and tried to cover her exposed bosom.

His eyes met hers and challenged her to refuse or resist him. For a moment, his glare halted any reaction from her. Well, if it has to be by force, he mused sorrowfully, then so be it. He laughed into her defiant eyes as he pinned her struggling body under his. He held her arms over her head and captured both her wrists with one of his large, strong hands. He pulled his knife from its sheath and carefully cut away her clothing with his other hand. Her feeble struggles and pleading had no effect on him at all. He wanted her this minute and damn well meant to have her.

Soft shimmers of moonlight filtered through the opening at the top of the teepee and illuminated her creamy white skin. It bathed her soft curves in opalescent glow. His breath caught in his throat at the sight of the radiant beauty beneath him. "Ni-ye mitawa, Cinstinna . . ." he said in a deep, hoarse voice.

She stared into the darkness which hid his features from her and pleaded once more for mercy. He watched the moonlight dance in the tear-filled eyes as lust consumed him again. You beg for what I cannot grant or give, Cinstinna, his heart answered her pleas. You cannot leave my arms or my teepee.

He replaced his knife and slightly relaxed his steel-like grip on her wrists. Leisurely, he inspected the naked ivory body with his eyes and hands. His eyes and hands were like branding irons, burning and marking every inch of her body as his forever.

Her face was turned away from him, but he could still make out the glowing, darkened patches on her pale cheeks. As his hand moved up her stomach, the muscles tightened and her skin was covered with chill bumps, in spite of the heat of the night.

Her breathing quickened. She flinched and

cried out in alarm as he cupped one of her breasts. She knew by now there was nothing she could do or say to stop or change what was about to take place. Her mind told her, at least you did nothing to encourage this, as Ben suggested.

He confidently caressed her rigid body, fondling here and kissing there. As his insistent hands brought new hunger to her body, a new battle began to rage inside her. She struggled against him and the unfamiliar emotions threatened to engulf her again. She could not comprehend the intensity of them or find a way to curb or control them. Innocence was her greatest enemy tonight.

With a few swift movements, he lay naked beside her in the waning moonlight. As he moved on top of her, she panicked and was about to scream, but he silenced her outcry with another kiss. She tried to claw and slap him, but he seized her hands in his and pinned them above her head. His mouth claimed hers possessively, as his hands did her body. She mumbled pleas between his kisses as he forced her thighs apart with his knee.

She was petrified as she felt his hard, probing manhood touch her there. No . . . no . . . not like this, her mind cried out. She felt a shard, burning pain as he thrust forward and entered her. He lay motionless within her for a time, allowing the pain to lessen and the shock of his forced entry to settle in. Then, he began slow, easy thrusts as he tenderly caressed her and kissed her unresponsive lips. He realized he did not want to brutally rape her, as was usually done with captives.

She lay immobile beneath him as tears silently slid from her eyes. She wished she could detach herself from this nightmare of pain and degrading humiliation. He had shattered all her dreams and illusions of love and of him. He had forced her to see and feel a cold, cruel side of life she had not known existed until the past few weeks. He had taken everything from her with his actions tonight and the preceding days. Now, she had no one and nothing, not even her self and her heart. He had taken those, too . . .

He claimed her full attention as his thrusts became faster and deeper. He was breathing heavily and hard. She could feel the pounding of his heart and wished she had the courage to seize his knife and drive it into his evil, black heart.

Suddenly, she felt jerking movements within and he relaxed atop her. His body glistened with the sweat of his evil deed. She could feel perspiration from him sliding down her sides and pooling on her abdomen and chest. The heat and odor of lovemaking filled the air. All her senses informed her of what had just occurred between them.

When his breathing returned to normal, he raised himself and spoke to her in his tongue. His voice and tone were firm and clear, but she could not understand his words or meaning.

"Ni-ye Mitawa! Wicasta wanzi tohni icu kte sni!"

She glared at him in anger, hurt and shame and said, "I hate you! One day, I'll kill you for this! If it weren't for me, you would be dead and all the others would still be alive. May God forgive me for saving your life. It was not a fair exchange for the lives of so many of my people. Maybe I deserve this as punishment for helping you and causing their deaths and suffering." She should have known his people would have killed them anyway for revenge of his death, but it didn't occur to her then.

He returned her glare for a few minutes, then rolled over and replaced his breechcloth. He stood up and reached to pull her up with him. She shrank back as she thought, he's finished with me for now and he's going to take me back out there like this, naked and soiled for all to see and laugh. She recoiled in fear and shrieked almost hysterically, "You can't take me out there like this! I won't go! Kill me now, but not that!"

He leaned forward and pulled her to her feet despite her protests. He picked up a blanket and wrapped it around her slender body. She frantically grabbed the edges before it could slip to the ground. He took her elbow and led her out of his teepee, through the circles of teepees and into the edge of the forest. She mutely followed him in a light daze. They had walked a short distance from the camp when he halted beside a large stream.

He motioned to the water, saying, "Yuzaza!"

Bewildered, she only stared back at him. He

snatched the blanket from her grip before she knew what he was doing. Before she could retrieve it, he picked her up and dropped her into the three-foot deep pool of cool water. She came up coughing and sputtering. He quickly stripped and came in, ignoring her as he took water and rubbed his hands over his face and body.

A bath! He means for me to take a bath! she raged. What good will it do now? I'll never be clean again. She turned her back to him and began to wash his sweat and lovemaking from her body, but not from her soul and mind. She would never be able to erase what he had indelibly printed there for all time.

The cool water felt deliriously refreshing after all she had endured for the past two days. Removing all traces of dirt, perspiration, blood and love from her skin enlivened her. She cupped her hands and drank to soothe her dry, parched throat and lips. She shuddered with a sudden chill from the night breeze. Gray Eagle called for her to come, "Ku-wa!"

She gritted her teeth in loathing, knowing she had no choice but to obey his commands. She clenched her teeth to still their chattering. Hesitantly, she came over to the bank as the water lapped at her narrow waist. She held her hands before her to shield her bosom and sex from his keen stare. As she rose from the water with a flaming face, she fought the anger she felt at having to stand nude before him.

As he held the blanket out to her, she knew she

must move her hands to reach for it. She glared at him suspiciously and put out a trembling hand for it. Instantly, she found herself trapped in his strong embrace. With eyes and head lowered in humiliation, she focused on his muscular chest and pleaded, "Please don't hurt me again. Haven't you tormented me enough for one day? What do you want from me?" she asked in a voice filled with anguish.

"Ni, Cinstinna . . ." came the answer in a deep, husky tone.

He wrapped the blanket around her slender body and held the edges together until she took them. Sensing he meant her no further harm, she raised inquiring eyes to his in relief and grasped the edges of the blanket from his grip.

He turned and motioned for her to follow him. She stared at his retreating back and remained rooted to the spot. He halted and without looking back at her called softly, "Ku-wa . . ."

She came up behind him and he walked on. She trailed him like a lost puppy back through the forest and through the camp to his teepee. Only Ben noted their going and coming. He studied her dishevelled state and the dejected slump of her bare shoulders. He saw how tightly she gripped the blanket around her. He shook with violent wrath. He assumed the brave, if not others, had brutally taken and used her. He wished he could kill him bare-handed.

The Indian stepped aside and let her enter his teepee. He turned and sneered at Ben with a mocking half-smile. "You filthy red bastard!" Ben muttered, cursing him over and over.

Gray Eagle went to his pallet of buffalo skins and lay down. He called for her to come to him. Fearfully, she did so. Taking her quivering hand, he pulled her down beside him. She stiffened at his touch. He reached for another skin and threw it over her. She watched him apprehensively as she snuggled under the skin. He lay still and quiet. His slow, even breathing soon told her he was asleep. Still, she continued to watch him warily.

Her gaze moved to his knife in its sheath hanging on a pole nearby. She stared at it, but was too frightened to try to get it. Her eyes went from him to the knife and back to him many times as she lay there unable to sleep. She fretted, how can I sleep nude like this? I should kill you for what you've done and escape.

Hours passed as she lay there recalling and reliving the events of the past few days. Her thoughts were in a maelstrom and her nerves were taut, preventing the peace of slumber. As slivers of grayish light marked the approaching dawn and filtered in the teepee, fatigue and despair brought sleep and blackness to her weary mind and body.

On first awakening, Gray Eagle knew she had slept very little by the dark smudges beneath her eyes. He studied the small, oval face sleeping beside him, recalling how she had unknowingly and unwillingly reached out to him, not to another man or her captor, but to him. . . . Knowing her need for rest and sleep to endure the trials of today and the coming days, he stifled his urge to possess her right that moment.

He smiled sardonically as he told himself, she is yours from this day on, Wanmdi Hota. In time, Cinstinna, you will come to me willingly. This I saw in your eyes and felt in your touch when I took you last night and the day you came to me in the wasichu camp. He was careful not to rouse her when he moved from her side and stood up. He donned his leggings and moccasins and departed with his weapons, pleased that she had not gone for his knife last night as he knew she had been tempted to do several times. He smiled to himself at her show of intelligence — and fear, too.

Soon, the camp was a beehive of activity on this sunny day. Women were moving about preparing the food for the day and tending to their small children. Later, they would go to the stream to wash clothes, bathe and fetch water. When that was done, they would go into the forest to gather wood, berries, nuts and wild vegetables.

Most of the braves were either busy with their weapons, preparing for the coming hunt or supervising the older boys with their warrior skills practice. The younger boys were under the care and command of their mothers, as were the girls.

The noises of the activities reached Alisha's

ears and roused her from her sleep. She sat up, stretching and yawning, and looked around to find herself alone in the teepee. She sat there waiting and watching for what this new day would bring. She wondered if Ben still lived and what they would do to him.

Her stomach rumbled, reminding her she had not eaten since her arrival. She looked down at her nudity and knew she couldn't leave his teepee. She doubted if anyone would give her any food or water if she did ask. She pulled the blanket around her and secured the edges once more.

Very soon, a slump-shouldered old woman entered the teepee carrying food and water. Her skin was darkened and leathery from the sun and lined with age. Her braided hair was nearly all white. She advanced to the center of the teepee where the campfire was located and set the items she carried on the flat rocks there.

There appeared to be a bowl filled with a stew and a platter holding small pones of bread. She hung a skin filled with water on the pole. Alisha could smell the aroma of the meat and bread and her mouth watered with anticipation. Her stomach quickly agreed with a few growls. She watched the old woman working and wished she would hurry and leave so she could eat alone.

A clear, cool voice behind her told her the brave had returned. She turned her attention to him as he entered the teepee. He walked over to the old woman and spoke with her. She listened, nodded several times, and left.

He ignored Alisha's presence and sat down by the food. He began to eat with great enjoyment. For him . . . she realized in anger and sadness. It's for him. Imbecile! she scolded herself hotly. She turned away, knowing the food was for him, not her. Ben and Horace's words came back to taunt her. Had she really expected him to be kind and considerate after yesterday? Yes, she had, if only a little . . .

Humiliated and bitter, she determined she would starve before she would grovel and beg food and water from him or his people. His stern voice broke into her thoughts, "Ku-wa!"

In her black mood and with intense thoughts of hate and anger, she had not noticed the old woman's return. She was carrying more food and a chamois-colored skin over her arm.

Again, he motioned and called for her to come to him, "Ku-wa!" He patted the earth beside him, saying, "Yanka!"

She came forward and sat down near him. The brave had already finished eating and sat watching her closely as the old woman handed her the roasted meat and pones of bread. She fidgeted nervously, all too aware of his keen observation of her.

She had to force herself to eat slowly and lady-like for she was ravenous and the food tempting. It was hot, juicy and delicious and all thoughts of rebellious starving fled instantly.

The old woman had laid the skin, which appeared to be a garment of some type, beside the brave. She slowly and quietly left the teepee, secretly studying the winyan kaskapi. Once more, they were alone. The silence and tension in the air were pressing in on Alisha as she eyed the brave suspiciously. She expected him to seize the bowl from her grip at any moment, but he did not.

She was surprised that he sat immobile, making no attempts to taunt or torture her in any way. He was totally unpredictable and a mystery to her. She ate as he watched her, relieved he did not have to use force on her this time. She is aware of who has the power here, he mused. She will think twice before she defies me. She will come to learn I stay my hand of punishment when she obeys my commands. She finished eating and set the dishes down beside his and turned to him.

He picked up a strange-looking garment and stood up. It was of an oblong shape, a few inches wide with two long strips on either end. He pulled Alisha to her feet and reached to remove the blanket from around her slender frame. Comprehending his intent, she clutched it tightly until her knuckles turned white. She began to back away from him, shaking her head in refusal.

He looked at her with those icy, black eyes and commanded coldly, "Hiya!" as he shook his head from side to side.

Still, she held on in defiance of yet another humiliation. He gripped the edge of the blanket and tore it from her grasp, leaving her standing naked before him. Her cheeks flamed and her eyes quickly lowered in embarrassment. She stood motionless before his gaze. How could she fight against his strength? She was no match, nor even any competition, for him.

His hand touched her leg and forced her thighs apart. Her face reddened even more and spread down her neck and lightly onto her chest. He pulled the cloth between her legs and tied it on either side on her hips by the two long strips. He pointed to the breechcloth and said, "Cehnake . . . cehnake . . ."

She eyed the strange contraption and grasped its purpose and his meaning. She touched it with her fingertips and repeated his word, ". . . cehnake . . ."

He nodded and replied, "Sha."

He leaned over and picked up the other garment. He lifted her arms over her head and this time she did not resist him as he slid the garment over her head and pulled it down into place. It was of a fawn color and very soft to the touch. There were small white teeth from some animal sewn onto the yoke in a pattern.

He touched the dress and said, "Winyan heyake . . ." He lifted her chin and laced the neck ties. She watched him in confusion.

His gentleness as he dressed her had a dangerously disarming effect on her. She asked herself if this could be the same man who just yesterday . . . just last night . . . killed . . . raped . . . and terrified her.

His gaze rose to meet her curious, bewildered stare. She could read nothing in those dark, unfathomable eyes of his. She lowered her eyes to the dress and touching it lightly said, "Winyan heyake?"

He replied, "Sha." He lifted her chin and pointed to the buffalo skins and said, "Yanka!"

Quickly, she went to obey, taking advantage of his good mood and kind treatment. She did not think it wise to anger him unduly at a time when he was like this.

He lifted the flap and went outside. Hours passed as she sat there not knowing what else she could do. She wondered what had happened to Ben and the others. Where had the brave gone just now? What was he planning for her? She was totally mystified by his actions this morning. She realized that he was capable of showing a little mercy and kindness. But why now and after what he had done to her yesterday?

Nervously, she jumped up and began to pace around the inside of the teepee. She was scared, confused, angry and edgy. She tried to decipher some of the noises and sounds that reached her ears. She could make out children's laughter, women's voices talking and singing, men's voices, dogs barking, horses neighing and many other varied sounds that she did not know or recognize.

She doodled in the sand, hummed songs from childhood and paced some more . . . Agitated, she went to the flap and lifted it, hoping for some fresh air and release from her tension and boredom. As she furtively opened it and peeped out, she stared directly into the scowling face of Gray Eagle as he stood talking to that other brave. She blanched and quickly dropped the flap back into place.

She walked over to the buffalo skins and sat down, nervously waiting for him to enter. Would he punish her for her inquisitiveness? From the look on his face, she guessed he would.

When he did finally enter, he seemed oblivious to her presence. He picked up his weapons and placed his bow and quiver of arrows over his shoulder. He turned to her and said, "Ku-wa! Ihakam ya!"

She rose and followed him outside into the warm sunshine, squinting at its brightness. She followed close behind him as he made his way through the village. She was aware of the many curious stares she received and was happily surprised at the lack of open hostility from anyone. Until they met Chela . . .

The two women locked gazes for a short time. The Indian girl's hatred could be felt in the air and noted in her voice when she spoke with Gray Eagle. To Alisha, she appeared to be pleading with him about something important. As the girl talked, she gazed hungrily into his face, laying her hands on his bare chest. Her pleading and begging turned to anger as he seemed to refuse her words and wishes. Alisha watched the many emotions of love, hate, anger, desire and jealousy come and go on the girl's face and in her ebony eyes. He was a man to stir and evoke all of those feelings in a woman. Had she herself not felt all of those for him at different times? She could easily understand the girl's turmoil of emotions.

Jealousy! The thought struck her like lightning. Could that be her source of anger and hate? She is furious because I am his captive and . . . sensing Alisha's stare, Chela turned and glared contemptuously at her. Chela returned her full attention to Gray Eagle. She caressed his face lightly with her fingertips as her other hand seductively fondled his smooth chest and broad shoulders.

Chela's tone, mood and intention became clear and embarrassing to Alisha and she shifted restlessly at the heated scene before her. Alisha looked away as Chela tried to put her arms around Gray Eagle's neck and kiss him.

He roughly pushed her away from him and pulled back. He grabbed Alisha by the hand and walked off. Chela's stare bore into Alisha's back until they were out of sight. Alisha knew if their places had been reversed, she would feel the same way Chela did now.

She was alarmed to find herself thinking, if he were mine and he brought another to take my place, I would fight for him and hate her. What is that girl to him? I wonder. Surely not his wife for she does not live with him. Perhaps his fiancée or sweetheart? If so, then why does he treat her like that? It is cruel and mean. Maybe their relationship is one-sided. Maybe, this love and desire she feels for him is not returned. That thought brought a smile to her lips and a leap of joy to her heart . . .

Just maybe, he does not love or want her. The way she touched him and behaved toward him . . . a spark of anger and jealousy flickered uncontrollably in her own heart and mind. Defensively, she asked, why should I care what is between them? He can have whom he pleases! Perhaps she could take his attentions from me. Fearfully she realized, if she did, then what would he do with me? Would he give me to one of his friends? Maybe Ben was right. If I do what he says, perhaps he will keep me for himself. That way, I would be under his protection . . .

But why did he choose to keep me? Surely my help meant nothing to him or he wouldn't have been so cruel to me last night. She frantically asked herself, if he only desires me or wants to hurt me, what will happen to me when his lust and revenge are sated? While I remain here in his demesne, she resolved, I shall endure until the time for freedom comes.

They strolled toward the forest and entered the trees. It was exhilarating to be outside in the fresh air and sunlight, to smell the greenery, flowers and nature's aromas and to move about with a small measure of freedom. It was delightful to walk barefooted in the cool grass and inhale the heady, woodsy air. It was almost as if they had suddenly stepped into another world

174

and time. All around Alisha could hear the sounds of the forest creatures and the rustle of the leaves in the light breeze. Sunlight filtered through shady trees, sending shimmering rays to the ground or playing on the leaves and flowers. The bushes and trees were covered with heavy green foliage. Wildflowers sprang up here and there, offering their color, fragrance and beauty for them to see and enjoy. A gentle wind whipped through her hair and dress and played across her skin.

The singing of many birds filled her ears. A quiet calm settled in her mind as she walked along the forest path behind Gray Eagle. She was reminded of the many long walks she had taken with her father at Thad's estates back in Sheffield or in the park near their townhouse in Liverpool, especially in the early spring or fall.

She stopped and gazed up at two squirrels chattering noisily and shaking their tails in warning to each other. It appeared as if they were arguing over who would be the owner of a cluster of spruce cones. She laughed softly as she stood observing the animated scene. Forgetting where she was and why, she called out quietly to Gray Eagle, "Look! Aren't they cute?" She pointed to the scene above her as she suppressed her laughter with her hand.

She did not know he had halted when she had and had been watching her the entire time. He had noted the sparkle of life and gaiety which lit her eyes like stars. He saw how the bright eyes and dazzling smile intensified and heightened her beauty. As he listened to the musical laughter, he almost joined her merriment.

Displeased with himself for his lax, unguarded reaction to her, he spoke roughly, "Ku-wa!"

Startled at the unwarranted iciness in his voice, she jumped and stared at him. The smile and laughter faded instantly. As he turned and walked on ahead of her, she impishly stuck her tongue out at him, then proceeded to follow along behind him again. He knew he had extinguished her newfound lightheartedness and regretted his harsh tone. Hadn't this walk done exactly what he had hoped for, by slightly relaxing her fear and mistrust? That was until she had caused him to relax just a little too much too soon . . .

Later, they came to a wide, rock-filled brook and he sat down. He patted the ground beside him and said, "Yanka, Cinstinna."

She glared at him, then sat down a little way off with her back to him. He grinned in amusement at her open display of hurt feelings and her attempt to punish him for his harshness. He would allow her to lick her wounds for the time being.

He watched her as she unconsciously plucked wildflowers and one by one picked the petals off them in anger. He thought teasingly, she pretends it is my body she tears apart with her bare hands.

Alisha listened to the drone of the bees collecting nectar. She heard the singing of the katy-dids and cicadas. She watched the flowers and leaves dance in the sunlight and breeze. She listened to her heart beg for truce and understanding between them. Its pleas tugged at her. Hadn't there been enough hatred and cruelty between them? How could she bear to live this way forever? Would he . . . could he . . . accept truce between them? She was lost in her illusions when White Arrow came up and joined them.

White Arrow sat down and began to talk with Gray Eagle as he threw small pebbles into the water. The stones hit with a "plip" and rings rippled in ever widening circles until they disappeared. Alisha watched the ripples, wishing she knew their tongue. If she did, then she could hear and know their secrets.

She was thinking this place was a glen for lovers, not a place to speak of death raids and vengeance, as she was sure they were doing. Lovers could lie among the flowers in the cool grass and . . . Her face pinkened as she realized what she was thinking and visualizing with Gray Eagle as her lover. Alisha! she scolded herself. What are you thinking? Have you gone completely daft?

Gray Eagle caught her elbow and pulled lightly on it. She turned to see what he wanted. He said, "Wayaketo!" pointing into the forest across the brook.

Her gaze followed his direction to where a female red fox was coming to drink with her young

177

pups. No matter how hard she tried to appear disinterested, her eyes kept straying back to the scene on the other bank. The mother had a reddish-orange coat of silky fur which was thick and fluffy. Her ears, throat, paws and tail were tinged and tipped with milky white. The pups could hardly be more than a few weeks old.

The vixen sniffed the air and walked along cautiously as her pups ran and tumbled in the tall grass behind her. One pranced and chased a grasshopper before starting to tumble with one of his companions in the grass. She could hear their immature growls and laughed in spite of herself.

The pups discontinued their play and began to nip at their mother's tail as it swished from side to side. She would nudge them lightly and send them rolling in the flowers. She came to the water's edge not far from them to drink. She watched the three people very carefully as her pups came to drink, ready to give the warning cry to flee if necessary. Sensing no danger from the humans, the mother turned and led her pups back into the forest and out of sight.

Alisha had been totally captivated by the little drama and had not realized she was the center of attention of both the men. They had both been watching her as beauty and wonder lit her face and jade eyes with fascination and tenderness. Never had they seen such warmth, depth and in-nocence radiate from a female before. Her eyes had a way of coming to life with a sparkle and vitality all their own. Without knowing it, she had created stirrings of desire in both men.

Gray Eagle cleared his throat as he gave White Arrow a warning glare at the heated gaze in his eyes which rivalled his own in depth. White Arrow groaned, smiled and nodded understanding. He said, "Pi-Zi Ista has much inner beauty also, my koda. It is rare to find both beauty and gentleness in a woman, and almost impossible among the wasichu. I see why you wished to have her for yourself. It is a shame that she is so much afraid of you, my koda."

Gray Eagle's eyes left Alisha's features to meet White Arrow's gaze. He answered, "Sha, she is much afraid of me for she has cause to do so. But there is more to her feelings for me than fear. She tries to hide her hunger for me from both of us. When I am gentle with her, she forgets and accepts my touch. She forgives my being her enemy. I have done much to cause this mistrust and fear you see in her."

White Arrow laughed heartily and jested, "Then you must only be gentle and loving to Pi-Zi Ista. I would think her touch and acceptance would be much more enjoyable than her fear and anger."

Gray Eagle quickly retorted, "And have my warriors think me weak and wayakayuha to a winyan's touch? Never! She will be the one to show weakness and be my wayakayuha. She will learn to obey my commands. You know our people would view any kindness to her from me in jest and anger. She must earn the right to be treated well."

"She is unlike most winyans. She has already earned the right to be shown mercy because of her help to you at her fortress, my koda. I would be careful not to punish her too greatly as you teach her obedience. Perhaps, you might instill too much hate and fear for her to overcome and accept you," White Arrow chided and warned his friend. "I see her as one who responds to love and gentleness more than strength and hate. She will give more in love than by force."

His tone carried a solemn sound as he continued, "I have spoken to Chela. She is like the mountain lion ready to pounce, teeth bared, claws out and filled with the urge to defend what she calls her own. She does not like the place you have given the ska winyan in your teepee. It would be wise to watch her closely."

Gray Eagle's face showed a look of concern and worry for a moment or two. He replied, "Sha . . . I have seen this also and it angers me greatly, Wanhinkpe Ska. I belong to no winyan and never will! Chela challenges me when she pushes me this way and this far. She cannot stand in the shadow of Cinstinna in many ways. She forgets that she is Oglala and behaves as the ska winyans. She will soon learn that I will not be forced or told what to do. Her kiss and touch stir nothing in me since I have found and taken Pi-Zi Ista. If she is not careful to guard her tongue and ways, I will refuse to join with her when the time comes!"

White Arrow stared at him with astonishment and disbelief in his eyes and on his face. "You cannot refuse the ways of our people! You must take Chela to join! Does the white girl so inflame your blood that you turn against your laws and customs? It will not be accepted, Wanmdi Hota. This will bring much hate and anger to her and you. They would accept her place in any teepee for life, but not in the life and heart of their leader and greatest warrior, my koda. Think on my words before the act is done and cannot be changed."

Gray Eagle answered, "I do not turn my heart from my laws or my people, Wanhinkpe Ska. But I will not allow Chela to show her anger and jealousy at my yuonihansni! No woman will take my honor and face before my people. The white girl is mine and I will let no man tell me what I must do with her, nor any woman! If I choose, I will keep her! I did not mean the white girl would take the place of my chosen one. But if Chela dares me long and hard enough, the chosen one will not be her."

As they continued to talk, Alisha stood up and walked to the edge of the brook and knelt to drink. She lifted water to her lips with cupped hands, then patted some onto her warm face. She knew she needed privacy but did not know how to ask for it. She pondered her predicament. She rose and went to kneel before him, her face glowing with embarrassment and discomfort. When he looked at her and asked,

"Sha?" she pointed to herself and spoke hesitantly, "Lese . . ." and pointed to the grove of small trees across the water.

He followed her gaze to the trees, then looked at her rosy face. "Lese wonahbe . . ." He pointed to her, to the trees and then repeated, "Wonahbe . . ."

Hoping he understood her request, she got up and walked across the rock-covered stream to the clump of trees on the other side. She turned to see him sitting and calmly talking to the other man. She went behind the trees and excused herself.

When her business was complete, she returned to sit by the water, splashing in it with her bare feet. After White Arrow left them, Gray Eagle touched her shoulder and called, "Ku-wa, Cinstinna." She stood up and followed him back to the camp in a mildly relaxed mood and spirit. She forced all her yesterdays far back into the recesses of her mind — at least, for today . . .

Not too far away at that same moment, Ben was also thinking of cool water and a big, tall, green shade tree. He had been bound spread-eagled on the hard, stony ground in the blazing sun since dawn.

The sun continued to beat down unmercifully as his upper torso burned and cooked. His eyes hurt from the constant strain of squeezing them tightly shut against the harsh brightness. His mouth felt as if it were filled with cotton and his throat dry and parched. His lips were swollen to the point of cracking and bleeding. He knew from the past experience of finding a man lost for two days in the desert that the sun could be a relentless tormentor and killer. It slowly and painfully sapped a man's life from his body.

Sweat poured from his burly body. Salt stung his eyes and lingered on his lips and tongue. A man his size and strength would be very slow dying this way. Of course, they knew and wanted just that very thing for him.

His thoughts wandered back to the smithy shop he had built in Virginia. He recalled how the scouts and returning traders had recruited volunteers for wagon trains West to where land, game and opportunity were abundant and for the taking. They had painted a rosy picture to all the innocent, gullible people who were tired of poverty, injustice or who were just trying to flee pressing problems.

"Land for the taking! That's a joke! Freedom! That's a joke, too! All we found out here is blood-thirsty savages ever'where, hoarding the land and game like it all belongs to them alone. Stingy Injuns! Bloody red bastards! There's enuff land and game for ever'body. Damn selfish bastards! Nobody told us they'd be like this, killing, raping, scalping and God knows what else they've done to others. Hell, they said we wouldn't have no problems controlling them or pushing them out. We's stupid to think we could fight 'em and win. There's too many of 'em and they're too powerful. They took that fortress like it was made of straw and we was using toy guns! Damn them lousy, lying scouts! Damn 'em!"

Ben shuddered as he recalled the height of the attack, realizing there would be no escape for them. He had killed his wife and retarded son to prevent their capture. That was how he had been taken alive. He hadn't seen the Indian come up behind him before he could turn the gun on himself. The Indian hit him on the head with a war-club, rendering him senseless. Upon regaining consciousness, he had found himself a prisoner.

At first, he had assumed he was being tortured for killing two potential slaves. But when he saw Gray Eagle walk up to him and laugh in his face, he guessed vengeance was the real reason for his still being alive and a captive. He wants blood payment for that beating, Ben thought.

"This heat's murder," he groaned. At least, his family did not have to witness his torture and death, or worse, to be tortured and killed themselves. Suddenly, the thought came to Ben, only the men who were directly connected with the brave's capture and beating were taken prisoner. Sure, they had taken a few females captives, but no other men. Did that mean he wanted personal revenge on them? But why had he placed Alisha with them instead of with the female captives? Did he intend to torture and kill her, too? That is, when he finished with his other ideas first?

She hadn't done anything bad to him. In fact, she tried to help the devil. He wondered if the brave was keeping her as his slave because she did try to help him. Could it be he likes her? Or could it be he plans to let her be an example for all the other white women? Ben trembled in anger and fear at thoughts of her position. He wondered where she was now and what was happening to her.

Maybe I was wrong to suggest she be nice to him and do whatever he says, he thought with regret. Could only make him madder. Hell! How kin you ever tell what they's thinking or what they'll do? I guess she's learned by now, the hard way, we told her the truth about them savages. I bet she wishes now that she had let us kill the devil.

His emotions and thoughts ran one way and then another. The sun climbed higher into the azure sky and grew hotter. He felt as if his very brain would cook and his head split open. Blisters began to appear on his torso and face. "I'd give anything for a sip of water and a little shade," he sighed in misery and pain. He drifted in and out of semi-consciousness. He experienced crazy hallucinations, realistic mirages and weird dreams. Still, the heat and torment continued. He knew the heat could drive a man mad if no succor came. And none would, he realized, not this time.

Once, he dreamed the brave stood over him, taunting and mocking him. "So, the wasichu is now a red man, too. Your arms can no longer hold a whip, ista ska, nor your tongue cry insults and curses to me and my people. You will suffer and die as all other ista skas who steal our lands, kill our game on the great plains and forests, as those who desecrate our sacred burial grounds and rape our women and girls. We would have shared our game and land with kodas, but your greed made you hunger and take more and more. You leave behind only death and destruction. You kill the hehoka, mato, capa, suntokoa and our brothers the buffalo. We must stop you before there are no lands, forests and game left for the Oglala and his brothers. Your name and face are known to us as a killer of our people. The winyan Alisha will also taste of my vengeance for her deceit," he taunted to further torment Ben.

With a few swift kicks in Ben's ribs, he spit on him and said, "I curse you and spit on you, sunka ska! You will pay with your life and blood for the lives of Chenhula and Okiliea as the other two did. If Wi does not take your life, Hehoka Sapa will with his knife. Okiliea was to be his winyan."

As the sun finally began to sink in the far horizon, Ben was only vaguely aware of being untied and taken back to camp. He was retied to the same post once more. To his surprise, he was given water, but only enough to keep him alive for a little longer, not enough to quench his great thirst. Water was then thrown into his face and onto his bare chest.

Reviving him only made him more aware of the intense, fiery pains on his face, mouth, chest, arms and his left side. Pains shot through his mid-section with each breath. Ben questioned, my left side? Why should it hurt like hell? Memory flooded his foggy brain and he knew he had not imagined the Indian's visit this afternoon. He knows our tongue! he realized. He knew ever'thing we said to him and about him at our fortress! No wonder he's so damn mean. That explains what he did to Horace. Ben tried to recall all they had said to him and about him, looking for some clue to his fate.

If he hears and knows all we said, he reflected, then he knows what Miss Alisha did. Damn him to treat her like that knowing all along she saved him! That sorry son of a bitch! He knows she helped and he don't give a damn! She ain't got no idea what a fix she's in. He'll know ever word she says to him. He'll go to punishing her right and left and she'll never know the why of it all, poor girl. I gotta find a way to warn her afore he uses that evil agin her. But how? I kin hardly move or swallow, much less yell loud enough for her to hear me. "Gawd, help me this one time," he prayed. "Give me the way and voice to warn that innocent girl. She don't deserve none of this hell and punishment."

His opportunity would present itself very soon. Alisha had been left in the care of the old woman while Gray Eagle had gone hunting. She was to teach the new kaskapi part of her new duties, such as how to cook the Indian way, where to fetch water and where to gather wood. The old woman showed her how to prepare the meat for roasting and the aguyapi for cooking on the hot, flat rocks in the edge of the fire. They had gone to the stream to fill the skins with mni and to the forest to gather can in a sort of back sling made of leather.

The water and wood were placed in Gray Eagle's teepee and the cooking lessons were being given in the old woman's teepee. Alisha suspected that she might be watched, so she did as she was told and made no attempts to escape or disobey. She had made a few attempts to converse with the old woman, but was rudely and coldly ignored and silenced. That is, except for the old woman telling her how to say the words for wood, water, bread, food, no and be silent. There were a few other words and signs she could not say or understand, like "witkowin." It was a word the old woman used frequently when she did something wrong or too slow.

Alisha thought how lonely life would be in a world of icy commands and silence. When the lessons were finally over, the old woman took her by the wrist and said coldly, "Ku-wa, witkowin!" and led her toward Gray Eagle's teepee. Alisha mutely followed.

As they were passing the center of camp, a scratchy voice called low, "A . . . li . . . sha . . ."

She jerked her head up to see who called her name for she had not recognized the hoarse voice as Ben's. Her eyes widened as she took in his condition and appearance. What had they done to him? He looked terrible and was obviously in great pain. He looked like he had been burned.

His skin was blood red and covered with numerous tiny blisters. His eyes were swollen nearly shut and his mouth was cracked and bleeding.

"Ben!" she screamed his name in alarm and pity.

She tried to pull her wrist from the old woman's grip and run to him. The old woman yanked her back. "Hiya! Ku-wa, witkowin!" she ordered.

Alisha could not pull free from the woman's grasp. She was amazed at the old woman's strength and the tightness of her grip.

"I must go to him! Sha!" she pleaded, using her other hand to try to free the imprisoned one. "What have you done to him? Ben . . ."

Seeing Alisha could not get free to come to him and knowing his only chance could be lost soon, he waited no longer. He began to stammer low, "A . . . li . . . sha . . . the . . . brave . . . he can . . . he can . . ."

Without warning, a yellow-tipped arrow was imbedded deeply into his throat. All she heard was a swift "swish," a heavy thud and a bubbly, gurgling noise as blood and air gushed out. Alisha screamed in horror and fought to pull free and go to him. She gaped at the callous murder as she watched Ben's blood flow down his neck and spread over his bare chest. She watched the torment fill his eyes, but he never cried out.

She whirled to trace the flight of the deadly arrow. She should have known who she would see standing there before she turned. Glaring at her with eyes narrowed in fury was Gray Eagle. She felt suspended in time, between reality and illusion, of knowing what she had just witnessed and not wanting to believe it.

Her lips were parted in an unspoken curse. Before her stood the very person responsible for all the torment, pain and mental anguish she had been forced to see and endure. There stood the man who had killed her people, friends and uncle, the man who had destroyed her hopes, dreams and life, the man who had reduced her to a mere slave and chattel, and now this . . .

She watched as he walked toward her, his eyes never releasing their hold on her. Those unfathomable jet eyes blazed with fury and that stern, stoical face was taut with rage. She trembled visibly as fear raced throughout her body and mind.

He grabbed her by the arm and began to forcefully drag her toward his teepee. "Hiya! Ku-wa! Ya teepee." His tone was cold and ominous.

She stumbled along beside him until they reached the entrance to his teepee. Suddenly, it was all too much for her. She dissolved into near hysterics. She jerked back on her arm and screamed at him in a shrill voice. "You murdered him! You're just as coldblooded and savage as they said you were! I hate you! I hate you! If you ever touch me again, I'll kill you. Murder . . ."

She raised her hands to slap and claw at his face as she continued to scream at him. Instantly, he had both her hands caught behind her back and imprisoned there with one of his. With his free hand, he slapped her several times as he demanded, "Iyasni! Hiya!" But she refused to stop or be silent.

"I hate you . . . I hate you . . ." she cried out over and over.

Her head rollicked from side to side from the force of the blows. Livid red prints appeared on her ashen cheeks and blood began to flow from the corner of her mouth. He shook her roughly by the shoulders and warned, "Lese! Hiya!"

The use of her name caught her attention and she froze for a moment, staring at him. She ceased her struggle and verbal assault on him. Her frenzied fury spent, she faced her antagonist in quaking terror and dreaded alarm. The comprehension of her wild attack on him petrified her. She immediately realized her grave mistake. Her chin began to quiver with suppressed tears and growing fear.

Her trembling fingers covered her lips. She shook her head in disbelief and cried out in dismay, "My God! What am I doing? What is happening to me? Now you have me acting like a savage, too. I'm sorry . . . Wanmd . . ." She left the sentence unfinished. It was too late for apologies and he wouldn't even understand her anyway.

She was panting in short, labored rasps. She backed away from him and ran inside his teepee. She flung herself down upon the pallet and wept as if her heart were being torn apart. He stared at the quivering flap and listened to her heart-rending sobs for a time, knowing what must be done and somehow dreading it.

Ben lived just long enough to hear and witness her tirade. He died praying her death would be swift and merciful. Surely, the brave would kill her now . . . or worse . . .

Eventually, her weeping subsided and she lay drained of all emotions and tears. She lay in the semidarkness imagining all sorts of gruesome tortures and punishments. What now? she asked herself. Anguish filled her heart and mind, knowing she would be the next and the last to die.

Gray Eagle did not return for a long time. Near exhaustion, she drifted into a troubled, restless sleep. Her dreams tumbled together in a colorful kaleidoscope of images and scenes, each one coalescing with the other.

She watched Gray Eagle smirking at Ben. She saw the yellow arrow embedded in Ben's throat. She watched as he struggled vainly to tell her something urgent. His lips moved, but she could not hear his words. She saw her mother and father riding rapidly in a phaeton into total darkness and oblivion. She cried out for them to stop and wait for her, but her only answer was the tolling of the death bells from the cathedral tower.

She tried to flee from the sight of dead bodies covered in dirt and blood. She was surrounded by them. They were lying all over the ground, floating face down in the river, hanging from trees and piled up like stacks of wood for burning. She saw women stripped and dragged to a teepee drenched in fiery red blood. She covered her ears with the palms of her hands to shut out their screams and pleas.

Her nostrils were filled with the smell of smoke. Her eyes burned and teared from its irritating sting. The smoke obscured her vision and breathing became difficult. The heat of the flames grew hotter and closer. There was no escape. Suddenly, she was imprisoned in a deep, dark pit as cold as death itself. She realized she was trapped alive in a grave.

Her lungs ached and burned in her struggles to breathe. Her heart pounded wildly as she thrashed about on the pallet in a cold sweat. Her terror mounted as she realized someone was holding the grave closed, preventing her escape. Unspeakable fear gripped her. She opened her mouth to scream, but no sounds would come forth. Strong hands held her down as dirt was shoveled into the grave and her face. Soon, it would be too late for succor.

"No!" she cried out, "please don't bury me alive! I can't breathe! No! Father help me . . . help me . . ."

She fought the hands that prevented her escape. She pushed at the imaginary dirt in her face. She gasped for air, and coughed from the omnipresent smoke.

The image of Gray Eagle formed before her. He stood straight and tall before her, emitting power and strength. From somewhere deep inside her mind, she knew he was her only salvation. She held her open arms out to him and pleaded, "Wanmdi Hota, save me . . . help me . . ."

His hands closed on her shoulders in a grip of iron as he shook her and called out to her. The voice from far away reached her. "Lese! Ku-wa! Lese . . ."

The bonds of the nightmare gave way and released her. As she came fully awake, she was looking up into the face of Gray Eagle leaning over her, shaking her and calling her name. "Lese, Ku-wa!"

And come she did! She threw herself into his arms. She placed her arms around his neck and clung to him tightly, crying in relief. For a minute or two, he held her in his embrace and let her draw comfort from his touch and gentleness.

Then he pushed her down onto the skins and took her brutally and forcefully with no tenderness or preliminaries as punishment for her earlier display and outburst.

Shocked back to cold reality, she struggled fiercely against his attack. She whispered words of hatred and defiance to him. When he finished, he rolled off her and lay beside her. She turned her back to him and lay facing the teepee on her side. She vowed softly, "One day, I'll make you pay for your cruelty. I'll escape and you'll never be able to hurt me again. I hate you and all your people . . ."

He listened to her words, knowing he must keep a watchful eye on her for a long time to come. Earlier, he had remained in his father's teepee until his anger had lessened. He was furious with himself most of all. He had allowed his hate and anger to talk to the ista ska today, and he had almost told the girl his closely guarded secret. His actions this day and just now were unlike him. Usually, he held his anger and emotions in rigid control. He was greatly alarmed and concerned at the feelings the girl gave him and for his reactions to her and the situation she created. He was disturbed by the position she had placed him in today. She had forced him to strike out at her to save his face and honor before his people. He was even more alarmed to find it bothered him to do it. Who was she to come into his life and wreak such havoc with his emotions and judgments? Who was she to force him to show his feelings openly and be unable to control them completely? He knew his answer was that she was the first and only woman to cause such stirrings and desires in his heart and body. Why did she have to be white and his enemy? Why did it have to be that girl he wanted above all others? Why had he been unable to forget her? Why did she steal into his mind without warning? She is only a winyan, Wanmdi Hota, and a white one at that! But, never had he known one like her.

She was like the white buffalo, very rare and special. He was lucky to have been the warrior to find and capture her. He was relieved he had returned to camp in time to stop Ben's tongue from revealing his secret to her. He was sorry the death had taken place in front of her, causing her to resist and hate him even more. He listened to her soft weeping and wished he had not been so harsh with his taking of her just now. She is still new to the ways between a man and a woman, he reminded himself. I have hurt her both times I have taken her. Next time, I will show her it does not have to be so. There is no need for pain and fear . . .

He recalled her words of hatred and her threats to him. He recalled her show of defiance and disrespect to him before his people. She had tried to dishonor him. She had dared to yell at him, to fight with him, to strike him! Her! A mere winyan and wayakayuha! He was torn between anger and astonishment that she had dared to hit him, Wanmdi Hota, son of the chief! She has much pride and daring, he thought, amused. It is sad to crush such spirit, but it must be done to also crush her rebellion.

Did she not know he could have easily killed her for her actions and words? Did she not know his people would think he should do just that? Could she not guess what it had cost him to spare her life after her tirade? He had forced her to suffer shame and hurt just now as he had done this afternoon. She should be grateful I did not slay her on the spot where she stood! he thought. Next time, I must punish her more severely and openly or be subjected to ridicule. A man who allows a winyan to rule his ways is looked on in shame for weakness. To allow a wayakayuha to make a man show weakness is unforgivable!

He knew then he must cause her to fear him so deeply that she would not dare to defy him or strike him ever again, at least not before his people. She must learn to obey without hesitation or rebellion. But the memory of her crying out to him in her dreams haunted him. He dismissed it with the thought that she had done so only because she realized that only he had the power to help or hurt her. Suddenly, he recalled that she had used his name. She must have heard others call him Wanmdi Hota and assumed it to be his name, he reasoned.

He also recalled her words of apology, but they had come too late. The damage had been done. Even though he understood her reasons and feelings for her actions, he could not overlook them or withhold his punishment. He was reminded anew of the loneliness and problems which confronted a leader. Many times, he was called upon to think of his people or laws above himself or his wishes.

He looked over at the slow rise and fall of Alisha's chest as she slept beside him. It had taken her a long time to calm down and go to sleep. He longed to reach out and comfort her before she slept, but knew it would be unwise to do so. To do so would only erase the lesson he had just tried to teach her. He was perplexed at how deeply her pain and suffering touched him. At all costs, he must keep her at arm's length. He must not let her get too close to him, even

197

though he wished it could be so. His life was committed to his people and way of life.

Softly, he whispered, "Much as I wish it, Cinstinna, it cannot be. Your place in my teepee must always remain as wayakayuha. Even with all my power, I cannot change the fact we are enemies . . ."

Alisha found herself alone the next morning when she awoke. She lay there for a time thinking about yesterday and last night. Anger filled her and she vowed, "Damn him and his cruelty! He'll pay for what he did. Somehow, some way, I'll make him pay for doing that to me." Haunting thoughts and memories filled her mind from long ago and far away. Once more, she was hiding behind the drapes in their drawing room listening to the idle gossip of her mother's friends. Now I know why they said it was painful and disgusting. Those who said it was different lied. There is no passion and pleasure involved, just lust and taking for him and pain and endurance for me. Liars! All of them . . . liars . . .

Gray Eagle entered the teepee and called for her to come with him. Having no choice and afraid to defy him again so soon, she arose and followed him. They walked through the forest to the same stream he had brought her to before. He seized her arms and, despite her protests and struggles, stripped her and tossed her into the water as if she were a small pebble.

He sat down cross-legged on the grassy bank and watched her intently. She immediately tried to shield herself from his burning gaze, but quickly realized the futility of such actions. Angrily, she wiped the water from her eyes and coughed to clear it from her throat and lungs. She glared at him with hate and anger dancing in those emerald eyes, then turned her back to him to bathe.

Without a sound or warning, he was beside her in the water. She gasped and once more tried to shield her bosom from his view. He grinned in amusement as he ignored her feeble efforts to hide behind her small, delicate hands. He handed her a white cake of some kind of soap. She looked at the strange bar of soap for she had never seen or smelled anything like it before. It was very hard to lather in the cool water and had a gritty texture. She shrugged and thought, at least, I will feel and smell cleaner.

As she finally managed to get the soap to lather, she forgot his presence and watchful eyes and scrubbed her body until it was pink all over. She washed her hair twice, grateful to have the dirt and oil gone and to hear it squeak in answer. As she dipped over and over in the water to rinse her body and hair, Gray Eagle was reminded of the playful antics of the musquash.

He suppressed a secret grin as he listened to the low rumbling of his hungry stomach. He called to her, "Kuwa! Ya!"

She did not look his way as he stepped out of the water to dress. He smiled at her turned back and called to her to come again. Slowly, she turned toward him, hoping he was finished dressing. She came to the edge of the stream and handed him the soap. Seeing the futility of trying to shield herself, she stepped onto the bank as gracefully as possible under the humiliating circumstances.

When he refused to give her back her clothes, she wrapped the blanket she had dried off on around her. He led the way back to the village and to his teepee. She had not realized it was the custom of his people for the men and women to bathe separately.

Gray Eagle did not want the other women taunting or showing unnecessary coldness to Alisha during this adjustment period, so he overlooked the custom and took her with him. Also, he could not trust Chela's hate and anger to be stayed when they were alone. He had to admit to himself that he enjoyed watching her and being with her. So far, he had not received any teasing for this action. Seeing her great beauty, the other warriors guessed his motives and knew they would have done the same thing with her as their captive.

Alisha was completely unaware of the many ways and times he had gone against his ways and customs for her. His mind and heart battled many times with what he wanted to do and what he felt he had to do. He did not like leaving himself open to ridicule by the other warriors, if not from his tribe, then other tribes who saw and learned of his actions. His leniency toward Alisha was pointed out to him many times by the strange looks and whispers from the women in his camp and by the open accusations from Chela. Only his position and respect had silenced the words of his warriors, but not their thoughts. How much longer could he allow this leniency toward her and in himself to continue? She would have to accept his power over her and her existence and cease this rebellion or he would be forced to become harsh and unyielding toward her.

If things came to that, she would never be his other than physically. Somehow, he found himself wanting more from her than a place on his mat at night or her duties as his slave. She must bow to his authority soon and accept a mild truce between them, or accept his power and her hate. If he could not have her willingly, then he would take her forcefully and her hate with it. He resolved, I am a man and a warrior. I will not be brought low by a winyan, even one such as she. I wish she would realize how much easier it would be for both of us if she accepted her new life here. Surely, what I have to offer her is better than the red teepee, or death. I must teach her this now.

She was overjoyed and relieved to find a clean change of clothes on the mat. Without waiting for his approval or suggestion, she quickly put on the cehnake and winyan heyake. She picked up a pair of small moccasins and slid them on her tiny feet. She sat down on the mat and tried to finger comb the tangles from her wet hair.

Gray Eagle dropped the other clothes by the wood sling for her to wash later. The old woman called out to enter with food. He felt Alisha was not quite ready to take over his cooking yet and let the old woman continue this chore for a time. She entered, put the food by the campfire, and left.

He sat down and called for her to come. He patted the earth beside him saying, "Yanka, Lese!" She watched him warily as she sat down and waited for him to finish eating first. He handed her the food that was left. "Wota!" he commanded firmly.

She did not know if the word meant food or eat, but repeated it back to him, knowing it should be learned and remembered. His language would be very difficult to learn and speak if it should ever become necessary or desirable. She couldn't speak with him or anyone else yet, for all she knew were commands and single words.

Would he mind or care if she tried to learn his tongue? Did he want her to know only what was needed for her chores? Since they were so obviously enemies, he surely wouldn't want to carry on a conversation with her. He had made no attempts to teach her any words other than his commands. She would see just what his intentions were.

She looked up at him and softly called his name to get his attention. He turned curious eyes to her, bewildered by her tone, and desire to speak with him. At his look of intense scrutiny, hesitation filled her eyes and she lowered her gaze and became silent.

"Sha?"

Summoning up her courage, she pointed to several objects while saying the Oglala word for them with a questioning note in her voice after each. Each time, he replied "sha" when she said the word correctly.

She made the sign for being bound by the wrists and asked, "Kaskapi?"

He shook his head and replied, "Sha."

She tried all the words she had learned. She came to woman. She pointed to herself and asked, "Lese winyan?"

Again, "Sha."

She stared at him with great confusion in her eyes and asked, "Witkowin? Lese witkowin?" She lifted her shoulders in question.

His eyes darkened and narrowed as he tried to decide if she was asking if he thought this or if she were asking what the word meant. No matter, he grabbed her roughly by the forearms and shook her. Icily, he said, "Hiya! Lese hiya witkowin!"

She was shocked by his tone and reaction to her question. "I do not know what 'witkowin' means," she offered in fear and explanation. "The old woman calls me this and I do not understand."

She watched him as he brought his anger

under control and put his cold, expressionless mask back into place. Firmly, he stated, "Lese hiya witkowin. Lese mitawa."

She stared into those unreadable eyes in bewilderment and reasoned, "I am not what? If the word is bad and makes you angry, then why did the old woman say it to me so many times?" Comprehension settled in. "Of course, she knew I would say it in front of you and you would become furious and probably punish me. What a mean thing to do. She only wanted you to hurt me more. I will be more careful of her and her motives from now on."

She was very quiet and thoughtful for a few minutes. She looked over at him and asked, "What could the word mean to make you so angry? What did she call me?" She puzzled out loud, "Lese is not . . . my woman? No, winyan means woman . . . I think . . . maybe, she called me your sweetheart or love. I'm sure that would infuriate you. So . . ." she daringly teased him, "I am not your woman or love. If you don't watch out, I just might find a way to change your feelings for me. That would really prove to be a shock to you." She could not suppress a laugh as she added boldly, "For their great warrior to fall in love with the enemy he captured, that would really be something to see. If I weren't so well acquainted with your hatred and cruelty, I might be tempted to try it. Your hate is more of a reality to me than the coming night."

Gray Eagle fought to suppress the smile and

laughter he felt at her words and comments. She couldn't be further from the truth if she really believed he hated her and that she was not his woman. Anger raged deep inside him as he recalled her last question. He would deal with the old woman later. How dare she call her a whore!

He moved over to the buffalo skins and sat down to work on his arrows. Alisha put the remains of their meal on the rock beside the fireplace. She studied him from under lowered lashes. He had not seemed to mind her trying to speak his words until she used that particular one. She must remember never to say it again. Still, he had not offered to teach her any other words. He must think I only need to know those kinds of words that concern the work of a slave to his highness.

She went to sit upon the other end of the buffalo skins near him while he worked. She began to pull and work at the tangles in her long hair with her fingers. She moaned and yelped as she pulled at the entwined tresses. Soon, he got up and left the teepee. He returned shortly with what appeared to be a brush made from the tail of a porcupine. He handed it to her and returned to his seat and work. She stared at him dumbfounded.

Clean clothes . . . food . . . a hair brush. . . . What was he up to? Why was he being so nice for a change? She would never understand him, so why try? She began to brush her hair, thankful for any kindness or consideration from him, no matter how small.

When she had managed to free all the tangles, she brushed it until it was shiny and silky. She decided the coolest way to wear her long hair would be in braids as the Indian women did. That should also help to prevent tangles. As she finished one braid, she realized she had nothing to hold the end secure. She thought for a moment, then moved down to where Gray Eagle worked and knelt before him. He ignored her until she lightly touched his arm and called his name.

"Wanmdi Hota?" she said hesitantly, unsure of how he would react to her forwardness and the use of his name, if it was his name.

He raised his eyes to meet hers. "Sha?"

Timidly, she held the end of the long, heavy braid out to him and said, "Thong . . ." touching his hairband with her finger. He knew what she wanted from him and nodded understanding. He picked up a long strip of rawhide he was using to secure his arrows and cut two lengths from it. He handed them to her and said, "Pahin iyakaska . . ."

She stared at him, confused by his new words. He touched the thong ties in her hand and repeated his words. She realized he was telling her the name of the hairbands. She nodded her head in understanding and then slowly repeated the words to him as she held up the two ties.

"Sha."

Automatically, she smiled at him and thanked him. She returned to her former place and continued with her hair. She had not noticed the strange look he gave her when she flashed him that dazzling, bright smile. She lay the brush down on the mat when she was done and sat watching his hands work so quickly and skillfully.

Soon, her eyes began to wander across his proud, handsome features and down his strong, virile frame. She could still feel the pressure of those powerful arms around her. She could recall the feel of his lips on hers and the touch of his hands on her body. His smell and presence filled her senses.

Suddenly, she became aware of her rapid, erratic breathing, the trembling in her body, and her thoughts about the warrior sitting near her. Horrified, she turned her back on him, praying he had not noticed the effect he was having on her. Her prayers were in vain, for he had been all too aware of what she was feeling and thinking. He had not dared to speak or look at her, fearing that to do so would break the spell he was having on her. It would be best to let such feelings and thoughts flourish and grow in her. He wanted her to see she could reach out to him and accept him as a man. He waited . . .

Nervously, she jumped up and began to pace around the teepee aimlessly. This close and private confinement with him nibbled at her nerves and emotions. Her eyes and attention kept straying to him. She would find herself watching him hungrily and intently. He could feel the heat and tension of her eyes without looking up.

She wanted to breathe fresh air, or walk barefoot in the cool grass, or feel the warmth of the sun on her face or just feel relaxed and free. Most of all, she wanted to be away from him and out of his reach and sight. But how? she fretted.

The chores! She picked up the water skins, the dirty clothes and soap. She approached him. As she held the items up for his approval, she asked, "Ya mni?"

He looked up at her and the things she held so tightly in her trembling hands. "Sha."

She left his teepee and followed the trail to the stream. She knelt by the water's edge to wash the clothes. Later, she moved upstream a way to fill the water skins with clear water. She gathered everything together and stood up to head back to the camp.

She was startled to find him sitting not more than ten feet away from her, just watching her nonchalantly as she worked. She expelled the air in her lungs with a sudden rush, not realizing she had been holding her breath. Her pounding heart slowed to normal as she thought, so, he does not really trust me. But why should he? After all, they were enemies and she was his prisoner.

He stood up and leisurely stretched his lean, tall frame. He headed for his camp with her trailing along close behind. When they reached his teepee, she hung the water skins on side pegs and the dress on another peg to dry. She picked up the wood sling and came to him again. "Wanmdi Hota, can?"

He looked up and nodded yes, then returned his attention to his work.

This time, she looked behind her several times as she headed for the forest, but he did not follow her. She scoffed, he knows I am not stupid enough to try to escape. Or does he? He probably thinks I have no brains at all. How could I blame him? Who but a dimwit or dunce would have tried to help him in the first place? I doubt if I'm the only person to give aid to their enemy unknowingly. Maybe that's why I'm still alive. Perhaps they are superstitious about killing lunatics and idiots. When I find a way to escape from here and him, he'll see just how smart I am.

She let her thoughts ramble as she gathered the firewood. She scouted around picking up small branches and pieces of scrub wood and placing them in the wood sling. When it was full, she folded it up and left it where it was for now. She assumed most of the Indians would be inside napping or resting as was their daily custom in the heat of the day. Those who chose not to sleep would work or rest quietly while their family members did.

She believed there was no one around at this time. Carefully, she looked around and seeing no one, she sat down on the plush green grass. She admired the beauty of the landscape; the full, verdant trees and bushes; the tall, willowy grasses; and the small wildflowers of blue, yellow and white scattered all around her. She stretched her face to the sun and absorbed its warmth and life. She inhaled lungs full of fresh, crisp air. She lay down on the soft, fragrant bed of grasses and flowers, not wanting to return to the village just yet and Gray Eagle's watchful gaze.

She lay on her back studying the clouds as they lazily drifted in the sea of blue above her. Impishly, she imagined each cloud was a person or object as she had done so many times as a child with her father. Often, she would laugh out loud at the impression the shape made on her mind. It was as if she were the only person alive in this garden of nature.

Unfortunately, she was not. She sighed deeply and sat up. Reluctantly, she got up, knowing she must have been gone too long. She must hurry back or he would come looking for her. If only she had the means and courage to flee right this minute and not go back to him. But there were many dangers besides him in this wilderness.

She leaned over and picked up the wood sling. She hooked it over her arms, allowing it to rest on her back. She headed back along the forest path. Suddenly she halted and stared straight ahead. She was not alone . . .

Chapter Five

Startled, she exclaimed, "How do you move about so quietly and secretly? You frightened me!"

She sighed in relief. Surely, he had been nearby all the time. He leaned against a large tree, chewing on an aromatic twig which smelled like peppermint. Strangely, she felt relieved by his guard instead of angry at his mistrust. As long as he was nearby, no one and nothing could harm her.

She laughed and commented in jest, "My very own cavalier. Who or what would dare to harm me with the bravest and strongest warrior as my . . ." She flushed a bright pink as she realized what she was saying, but, more so, for what she was thinking. She tried to force a closed expression and guard on her face.

Her thoughts and words pleased him as much as her relaxed mood. He could read her face like the signs on his teepee. In time . . .

He straightened up and headed back toward

the camp. She followed close behind him as usual. Along the path, they met several Indian women headed for the stream with garments, water skins, and wood slings.

He halted and moved aside to allow them to pass with their burdens. They nodded and spoke their thanks, for it was their place to allow his passing first if he so chose. Alisha stood quietly and respectfully at his side as they passed them. The women stared ahead, ignoring her presence completely.

It was at that moment she saw Kathy Brown not far behind them. She was being led by a rope encircling her neck. She was filthy! Her clothes were torn and nasty and her hair was in tangled, matty disarray. Her head was lowered and shoulders slumped in sad dejection, fear and submission. Alisha stared at her in shock and pity. She had the appearance of some terrified wild animal.

As filthy as she was, Alisha could still make out the signs of abuse and ill treatment on her body and face. Her eyes quickly scanned the small group for the others, but they were not there. They must either be with other Indian women or still in the red teepee. She couldn't bear to think of them tortured or killed. She refused to think about what had happened to Kathy or the others in that terrible teepee Ben had told them about. Although she could not pronouce the Oglala word for it, it meant no more than a slave brothel. How could they treat helpless women like that?

Kathy was slowly staggering along behind the woman who held the rope in her hand. As she yanked on it to speed her up, Kathy tripped and fell. She saw Alisha as she was pulling herself upright, amidst pokings and taunts. Her sad, hollow eyes livened for a time, until she took in Alisha's appearance and companion. Her stare went from Alisha to the handsome, virile brave next to her. She instantly recognized him and the meaning of the situation before her. Her eyes took on a look of contempt, envy and hatred which could rival Gray Eagle's for the wasichu.

Her expression and its abrupt change were noted by both Gray Eagle and Alisha. Alisha still made an attempt to go to her aid. Gray Eagle instantly seized her arm and commanded, "Hiya!"

She turned pleading, sympathetic eyes to him and begged, "Please, let me go to her. She's one of my people and she needs help. She needs food, water and care just as you did once. Please, Wanmdi Hota . . . Wota . . . Mni . . . Yuzaza . . . Sha . . ."

His cynical look told her he would show Kathy no mercy or pity, but not why. She turned back toward Kathy. Alisha's eyes widened in disbelief and her face paled as she watched Kathy mouth some of the vilest words and curses she had ever heard. She didn't know the meaning of many of them and was glad. As Kathy cast cruel accusations and words of hatred at the shocked Alisha, the Oglala woman yanked on the rope and led her away down the forest path.

Alisha stared after her in despair and torment. Gray Eagle had watched and listened to the brutal confrontation between the two women. Her suffering did not bring gladness to his heart.

She spoke just above a whisper in a voice filled with anguish, "She hates me far more than I realized. Such vile and cruel words from a woman . . . I am not to blame for your suffering and problems, Kathy. I'm not . . ."

In great need of some understanding and consolation, she lifted tear-filled eyes to Gray Eagle and asked, "Am I truly responsible for all of this because I saved your life? Would your death have changed anything for my people?" She cried out to him, "Tell me I'm not to blame for all their deaths and sufferings! Tell me I only did what I had to! Tell me I am innocent and guiltless, Wanmdi Hota! Tell me!" She covered her face with trembling hands and sobbed.

He watched her, wanting to pull her into his embrace and comfort her. He longed to ease some of her guilt and hurt, but dared not. Someone could come along the path. How could he explain his comforting, or even caring, to anyone? Instead, he said softly, "Hiya ceya . . . Ku-wa. Winyan Brown witkowin!"

At his words and tone, she looked up at him. He touched her tears and repeated, "Hiya ceya . . ."

She gazed into his softened eyes with confusion and questioned, "The Brown girl is what?"

When he did not offer to explain further, she

tried again, "Brown winyan witkowin?" He nodded yes, nothing more. "But what is witkowin?" No answer or response. Exasperated by his refusal to explain, she replied, "It cannot mean what I thought or you would not have said it about Kathy. You said it in contempt like the old woman did. I do not understand."

She realized he would not, or could not, answer her and was forced to let it drop for now. She knew now it was something bad.

She stared down the deserted forest path and asked him, "Is that what will become of me when you tire of me?" She didn't expect any answer. She added bitterly, "I'm sure the girl called Chela would love to have me at her mercy and command." She visibly trembled at that thought.

Impulsively, she grabbed his arm and pleaded, "Please do not give me to her, Wanmdi Hota! Let me stay with you forever! I promise I will be good and give you no more trouble. I only want to belong to you!"

Wanting to be sure she knew and meant what she was saying, he pressed her for an explanation. He would see if she would try to make him understand her pleas. He lifted his shoulders and eyebrows in question. He touched his forehead with his fingertips and said, "Hiya."

She knew he did not understand and was asking her to try to explain her meaning. For the first time, he actually cared what she wanted and was trying to communicate with her. She was dumbstruck at first, but did not want to give up this chance for truce.

She thought for a few moments about how to explain herself to him. She used the first words which came to mind. "Lese . . . Wanmdi Hota's winyan . . . Kaskapi . . . Sha?"

He nodded understanding or agreement and waited for her to continue.

Slowly and hesitantly, she did. "Lese hiya ya Chela . . . Hiya ya . . . teepee . . . Lese ya Wanmdi Hota teepee . . . Sha?"

He searched her features and replied, "Lese de mitawa. Ya Wanmdi Hota teepee. Hiya Chela. Lese Wanmdi Hota kaskapi."

Hoping he meant she belonged to him and he would keep her, she flashed him a warm, radiant smile and sighed with relief.

He turned and headed up the path once more for his camp. She followed close behind with a lightened heart. He took her to his teepee and left her there. He was gone for about two hours. He returned with two fat rabbits, already cleaned and gutted for cooking. She smiled timidly as he handed them to her.

He had purposely brought her the rabbits. He knew she could prepare them for eating, since that was what she had brought to him at the fortress that night. Until she learned more about his ways and foods, he would try to bring back game she was familiar with preparing. He was aware of the differences in their diets and cooking methods. It would take time and patience for her to learn these things and he had a lot of time and patience in that area of their life together. This was a difficult period for her and he was willing to be lenient in some matters.

She started the fire as she had been taught by the old woman. She used the hot puck and small twigs, then slowly added larger pieces of wood. When she had the fire going well, she took two long wooden skewers and placed the hunks of meat on them. She reached inside the pouch the old woman had called a wozuha and sprinkled some of the finely ground herbs onto the meat. She placed the skewers between the two forked posts on either side of the campfire.

She took a round, bowl-like container and poured some of the corn meal, acorn flour mixture into it from another wozuha. She slowly added water from a mni skin and mixed it together until she had the right consistency for the aguyapi. At this moment, she was happy she was needed for something other than bed service. She would show him she was more than a mistress.

The rabbits roasted slowly and the air began to fill with a delicious aroma. She placed little pats of the aguyapi mix on the flat, hot rocks at the edge of the fire. She watched as the little pones of bread began to cook and brown. She lifted them with the utensil made from a buffalo horn and turned them over. Within a few minutes, they were done, crisp and brown. She smiled, pleased with herself and her new talents.

Gray Eagle glanced up and studied her as she

worked. He was sitting on a buffalo skin near the opened flap to catch the breeze as he worked. He was using a flat, smooth rock as a tool to sharpen his knife and tomahawk. He was relaxed and content in the scene surrounding him. He, the warrior and man, was sitting in his teepee working on his weapons after a successful hunt, while she, the woman, prepared their evening meal. He glanced around at the evidence of completed chores, the clean clothes, the full mni skins, the full sling, the nuts and berries, and his woman kneeling by the fireside cooking their wota. She was singing softly to herself as she worked, unaware of his keen interest and observation.

This is what has been missing in my life, he thought. This is how it should be between two people who . . . He laughed at such silly thoughts and feelings. He chided and warned himself, your vision grows old before your body, Wanmdi Hota, and your mind thinks thoughts of foolish old men. Do not see what is not here. The only two people here are the warrior and his kaskapi. She only does as she is commanded and has promised. Do not dream the dreams of fools.

But he secretly wished it could be like this every day. He slipped back into his dream. Perhaps she is learning to accept me and her new life. Will she allow the feelings she showed to me back at her fortress to grow? Perhaps I have allowed my harshness to flame like the fire and destroy them. She might have felt only pity for me as she now does for the Brown winyan. I could have been wrong in what I thought I saw in her eyes and face. This conclusion disturbed him. What if she really did hate him and only obeyed out of fear? What if he had forced her to see him as a savage warrior instead of a man?

When Alisha knew the meat and bread were done, she turned to him and spoke with difficulty and hesitation. "Ku-wa, Wanmdi Hota. Wota, aguyapi . . . yanka."

He looked over at her and surprised her with the expression on his face. There was actually a pleasant look there with a slight half-smile playing across his lips and in his dark eyes. Was she only imagining it, or was it perhaps a smirk instead? It could be for the food, her use of his tongue or maybe just her docile, servile behavior. No matter, for it made him look more handsome and relaxed.

Rarely was there a look such as that upon his face and rarely was that cold glare missing in those obsidian eyes. She stared at him openly. She was very aware of his strength and virility. Recalling his fiery kisses and light caresses, she flushed and looked away.

He came to sit beside her and be served. She was careful not to meet his gaze, nervous and alarmed by his effect on her. She didn't understand why this cold, cruel man had any effect on her in any way other than fear, hate and disgust. When he had finished his meal, she ate in silence as was their custom. After she was finished, she cleared away the remains of the cooking and eating.

She turned an embarrassed face with lowered eyes to him and said, "Won . . . ah . . . be . . ." She did not see his amused smile at her shyness.

He stood up and stretched languidly, then called for her to follow him. They walked along the forest path into the dense trees. He led her to a copse and left her alone. Later, he rejoined her to return to his teepee.

Once back, she sat down on the mat to await his next order. He was moving about in the teepee, collecting some items from his personal belongings. He walked to the flap with long, easy strides. He halted for a moment and turned back to face her. He flatly stated, "Wanmdi Hota ya Oyate Omniciye. Lese hiya ya. Lese yanka."

She stared at him in bewilderment. He called her to him and repeated his words as he made the signs for his intentions. He lifted the flap and pointed to the council lodge as he was speaking.

She nodded that she understood his commands. She watched him cover the short distance between the two teepees and disappear inside. She wondered why he bothered to explain his actions to her. He was such a confusing, unpredictable man! She would never understand him or his ways.

She lowered the flap and returned to her place on the mat. After a long time, she lay down upon the mats, thinking about this turn of events and his new, relaxed behavior toward her. Her emotions and thoughts were in an upheaval, for none of this made sense.

She could visualize his face in cold fury and contempt. She could melt that expression into one of relaxed acceptance or desire for her. She had never met or known anyone like him before. Her heart and brain were raging a heated battle between resistance and acceptance, love and hate, escaping and remaining.

Gray Eagle was like a magnet, strong and forceful, pulling her helplessly to him, making her unable to break or resist his hold. Instantly, he could reverse polarity and repel her in anger and coldness, shoving her away with those very same arms which had so recently held her in a tight, tender embrace. It was as if two men forever at war occupied the same body. He could be passionate and tender one minute; then cold and cruel the next.

She never knew how he would behave or react to any given circumstance at any time. She could not comprehend two such strong, opposing emotions as hate and love in the same man at the same time. Then, again, she corrected herself, she should really say hate and lust, not love. He could easily be a lover as well as a warrior if he so desired, and this knowledge terrified her.

Angrily, she thought, he is cruel and taunting one minute; then kind and thoughtful the next. He rejects me brutally; then accepts me tenderly the next time. She unwillingly recalled his kiss and touch which brought fires to her body. But, the actual act of lovemaking had been painfully unbearable for her.

Could it be his kindness was only a taunt within itself? He withheld his wrath and punishment as long as she was subservient. She remembered how brutally he had taken her after her open defiance of him at Ben's death. She had never seen him so angry. She trembled just recalling it. She knew she had seen the look of death in his eyes that day. She knew he had forced himself to overcome his temptation to do so; but she did not know why.

Poor Ben, what did you have to tell me that was so important it cost you your life? You said, "The brave can . . ." Can what? Can kill me? Can punish me or ravish me? I already know those things. What did you feel was so urgent I learn?

Would it make any difference to him if I could learn to accept this life of thralldom? Would total submission to him change anything? Does he prefer for me to remain his enemy or accept him and his dominance? I think he loves to be a ruthless tyrant, making me cower before him in awe and fear, showing off his power and superiority over me and my people.

If only I had the courage to remain aloof and resistant to him and his threats. But how long could I hold him at bay, mentally or physically? I can't go through with those tortures like the others did, or be sent to that teepee like Kathy . . .

If I pushed him too far or too hard, he would surely do one or the other to me. Would he kill me if I blatantly refused to be his harlot and servant? I can't risk testing him, even though I despise living like this at his beck and call. I dare not defy him. And yet, I dare not leave my heart open to him. He would rip it from my soul and devour it like some demon.

Don't let a little kindness and a brief reprieve erase his deeds, she warned herself. You must keep your guard up and never trust him or his motives. To trust or love a man like that would only bring anguish and then death. The only place he can have in my life is as my mentor and protector, for now. Later, none . . .

In all her anxiety, she never thought to question why he chose that very moment to kill Ben; nor how he knew what Ben was saying to her. Had she thought more on the scene and words, she would have grasped the deadly truth — he heard and knew exactly what Ben was saying and wanted to silence him forever. Far worse, she would have realized the full extent of her predicament — he knew and heard all her words to and about him. She pushed the painful scene far back into her mind and tried to forget it.

She wondered, is Kathy the only other prisoner left? Were the other women dead or sold to other tribes? How could Kathy hate me so much? I can't bear to think of the terrible abuse and suffering they must have endured in that teepee. For her to see me clean and free with the very man responsible for it all must have angered her. Can I really blame her for her feelings, no matter how wrong she is? If only she knew the truth! At least, she doesn't have to live with the guilt that she might be responsible for all the deaths and sufferings.

I guess I should be grateful to him for taking me and keeping me here with him. I couldn't endure being a harlot for his tribe as she is. I'd die if he ever took me there. I'd just die . . .

Tears filled her eyes and began to roll down her cheeks as she recalled the arduous trek to this land of death for men and their dreams. They had begun the trip with great anticipation and high spirits. They had moved slowly and seemingly endlessly at times. Living in a covered wagon for a year had proven to be a hardship for many. To others, it had been exciting, stimulating, educational and strengthening. She recalled all she had learned, seen and done.

At times, the going had been hard, but there was always someone or something there to inspire them to press on. There had been many complaints, heartaches and problems along the way, but they had overcome them all. There had been good and happy times, too.

She reflected on the ones who had given up along the way and returned to the colonies, or settled where they were at that time. Others remained at the nearest settlement to where they had lost the strength to go on. She remembered the many graves left along the trails from sickness, accidents or just loss of the will to live and push on and on.

She thought of all the things they had so carefully carried for such a long way, now lying burned and ruined at the fortress. All of their hard work had gone up in smoke and ashes. All because of one man . . .

The blurred details of their trip slowly returned to her. Most of their days had been spent traveling or doing chores, and their nights in exhausted slumber. There had been little time to socialize with the other settlers, for there had never seemed to be enough time to complete their chores.

They would travel until the last streaks of light were gone and be up again at the first light of dawn to push on once more. Joe told them they were moving too slow and had to hurry to make more progress before winter halted them. Once it hit, they would have to stop where they were during the worst of it and wait it out. He hoped to make this stop near an established settlement or fort.

To get her mind off her present problems and turmoil, she began to reminisce about the trip. She recalled the first stop they had made at a settlement built in 1758 and named Morgantown. They had lingered there only a short time for rest and supplies. They had planned to follow the Ohio River west in order to have their backs protected and to be near water. It was at Morgantown she had her nineteenth birthday. It came and went, unnoticed by all except her and Uncle Thad. Perhaps that was why she thought of Morgantown first.

Later, they had passed the settlement of Clarkesville in the Indiana territory. It was there she realized most of the exploration and settlements were French. Nearly all the forts, towns and trading posts they visited were run by and surrounded by the French. It was immediately made clear to everyone the French and Indians were friends and it behooved the settlers to be friendly to the French. That situation had proven very difficult for many of the men who had fought against the French many times before coming to the colonies. Bigotry and prejudice were slow to die in the hearts of many of the men.

When their group made stops at these forts or posts, they would stock up on depleted supplies, rest, and talk with the trappers and traders about newer and better routes and newly settled places. Alisha thought, if we had all been French, everyone would probably still be alive. But, of course, the brave would not have been our enemy or treated as he was.

These Plains Indians were entirely different from those she had seen and met along the trail. The Miami and others had been pleasant or ignored their passing. There had never been any open hostility from any of the tribes or bands they had contact with. Alisha had not realized the tribes they met had been friendly with the white man for a long time. Other tribes had simply learned the futility of resisting the white man and his weapons. The Miami had thought it wiser not to attack a group of whites who had no intention of settling on their lands.

It had been about that time the men had decided to abandon the river trail and head overland to the settlement of St. Louis. Some of the men had argued bitterly about this decision. Along that trail, they had passed a settlement named Vincennes and moved on to Cahokia in the Illinois territory.

Their longest stop had been where the Mississippi River, referred to as the "Big River," joined with another river called the "Big Muddy." There they built rafts. It had been a slow and dangerous crossing on the light rafts. Some of the wagons and a few lives had been lost in the swift, swirling red waters. She recalled how awesome and terrifying it had been for her. How had she found the courage to keep from crying that day?

Some of the others had been too frightened to cross after witnessing tragedy and failure by others. Those who refused to make the crossing headed for the settlements of Kaskaskia and Ste. Genevieve. The ones who were successful were jubilant and proud.

She had found their stay at St. Louis enlightening. There was a very large trading post built in 1764 situated near the river and surrounded by numerous homesteads and small settlements. She had learned the Spanish had controlled this area at one time and had offered large land grants to anyone who would come and help settle it. Their ploy had been unsuccessful and they soon lost and sold their claims to the French.

The owners and proprietors of the trading posts there were the ones who convinced them to head on for the Dakota Territory. They told many stories about the vast, open ranges for grazing and farming; the forests filled with game for food and skins; the numerous streams and rivers for water supply; the serenity and safety because of the nearby military post, Fort Pierre; and of the gold brought back by some of the traders and trappers.

Alisha asked herself, what good had that fort been to them? Had it helped or protected them in their greatest hour of need? It might have been on the other side of the world for all the difference it had made for her people.

She reflected again on her journey. The traders and trappers in St. Louis did not, in their desire to see this area settled and more populated, tell the settlers of the dangerous living conditions and strife between the whites and Indians, especially the Sioux. They had believed the increasing number of settlers and soldiers would help their businesses to grow. A greater number of whites would increase the chances of their pushing the Indians farther north or west, leaving the trapping grounds and gold-filled streams and hills open for the taking. Either way, they were sitting pretty at the crossroads between the East and West. It would be far safer for them to have whites at the back door than hostile Indians.

Their journey had been much rougher after they left St. Louis. Winter had overtaken them sooner than expected. Joe Kenny, their scout, had told them they were lucky for that was one of the mildest winters he had seen in these parts. If that was what he called a mild winter, Alisha joked to herself, I would hate to be caught in one he considered harsh.

I can recollect days we didn't make any progress and others, only a little. I remember those worst days when Joe would make us form a circle and wait out the storms and deep snows. Then, he would push us on and on as soon as the weather cleared and the trails were passable. Perhaps he was in a big hurry to be out of this area. No, if he had known what we really faced, he would have told us. If he did, they didn't listen or wouldn't turn back.

If our men were smart enough to bring two extra wagons of feed and hay for the animals when grass couldn't be found in the snow, why couldn't they be smart enough to sense our danger or the signs of trouble brewing? We should have been wise enough to turn back on those days filled with overwhelming problems and bickering.

Thank goodness for those books I brought along or I would have been as irritable and edgy as they were on those layovers. But there were good times, too. Alisha smiled as she recalled their Christmas on the trail. It had been wonderful and beautiful. For a change, nearly everyone had been helpful and friendly to each other.

Thankfully, that Christmas brought out the best in their group. Perhaps it had been because of the children. They inspired a happiness and gaiety all their own, and spread it to those around them.

That was the time I gave Uncle Thad that funny little pipe Mr. Parsons carved for me, Alisha thought wistfully. It had taken nearly all my small savings, but it was well worth it. Uncle Thad, I miss you so much. Why did they have to take you from me? Why did you force me into that trench? I would not be in this situation if I had refused.

Oh, God, how I dread another winter here! Those high snowdrifts and ice; I've never been so cold in my life. I hated the way the wind made my nose and cheeks hurt and turn red. My feet and hands would get so numb they didn't move. They felt like dead weights and ached with the cold. There were even times when it hurt to breathe and my teeth would chatter so loud I couldn't sleep all night. I was never so happy as the day when winter was over and spring came.

That Christmas day had not been cold or wet. Perhaps the good weather that day had been a gift to all of them. She suppressed laughter as she pictured the little tree the children had cut and fixed. They scampered around like chipmunks confiscating and collecting anything they could to decorate it with. Mrs. Dooley had conniptions over her missing red ribbons and Mrs. Blackstone over the cotton puffs from her husband's medicine bag. But how lovely the tree had been when they finished! Everyone had been delighted and amazed by the children's pooled efforts.

I can still hear the singing and laughter . . . Ben and his deep voice . . . I bet he had been nipping from that little jug he kept hidden away for "special occasions," as he called them. When he started to dance around the tree, I thought I would die laughing. Mrs. Frazer sure was angry with him for acting that way. You always were a show-off and clown, Ben. Sadness touched Alisha as she realized she would never hear his laughter or see his antics ever again.

The remainder of that night had been spent drinking hot buttered rum and tea and exchanging small sentimental presents. There would be no old-fashioned Christmas with plum puddings and yule log, as they had planned. But she did have beautiful, wonderful memories no one could ever take from her.

Alisha tried to sleep, but it would not come, for her mind was too full of thoughts of those days and times. Time had slipped by swiftly after that night and spring was near. She vividly recalled the first buds on the trees, the early shoots of grass, the unfolding petals on impatient wildflowers, and the first warming of the sun after all the snow and ice were gone. The sky had never seemed clearer or bluer. The air had smelled fresh, crisp and clean. It was like witnessing the rebirth of nature in a virgin land of unexcelled beauty.

Her uncle had commented to her, "This land's a woodsman's delight, Lese." It was abundant in lush green forests filled with elders, pines, spruces, red cedars, elms, ashes, poplars and others which even he could not name.

He had shouted excitedly, "Look, Lese! Wood for every need! Hard woods for furniture, homes and fences, and soft, pliable woods for carving everything we need or want."

Game had once more become abundant. The hunters had had no problems bringing back plenty of meat. During their rest stops, the girls and women could pick wild berries and fruits to be used in delectable pies and desserts. The lengthening days gave more time and light for chores and socializing.

She recalled the loud cheering and joyous celebrating when they finally reached their goal in May. None of them knew the war they had feared and fled had already begun back East.

The first thing they had done was to set about building a strong, high fortress for protection. Then each family built a small, one-room cabin. They had worked hard, long hours to finish before the violent thunderstorms, accompanied by hail, heavy rains, and crashing lightning, hit them. They had been told this was a common thing in June. The few storms Alisha had witnessed had been at a distance.

She greatly feared violent storms.

She had thought the fortress a waste of time and energy, for the Indians she had seen and met had all been friendly. Bitterly, she added, it was a waste . . . it did not protect us or our homes. It might just as well have been made of blades of grass.

I thought the journey had forged me into a stronger, braver person. Where is all that courage and strength now? To think I actually held a gun on my people to prevent the brave's beating and death! How he must have laughed at me! This new land and search for freedom was not worth its cost. To think of all we sacrificed and endured . . . for what? To die! Those who died on the way here were lucky! They will never know that all the sacrificing and suffering were futile. I will never forget the day it all began to shatter — the day I first met Wanmdi Hota!

She rolled over on her side and faced the teepee, listening to the sounds of nightingales calling to their mates. Stillness settled in as the night darkened.

Chapter Six

Gray Eagle lifted the flap and entered his teepee. The fire had died down to glowing embers, casting a soft light inside the darkened teepee. His keen vision could make out Alisha's form on his mat. Opalescent moonlight filtered down on her, creating a soft, romantic setting.

He moved over to a side pole to hang his weapons. He undressed and came to lie beside her. His alert senses had already told him she was not asleep. He remained still for a time, relaxing and thinking. He rolled to his side and propped up on his elbow, gazing down at her. Instantly, he saw her stiffen and alarm race across her face. She wanted to move away, but it was too late to feign slumber. Besides, it would not make any difference to him if he had other things on his mind.

He read her thoughts. She fears I will take her roughly as before. No, Cinstinna. Tonight, I will show you love and desire.

She trembled as he leaned forward and kissed

her. She spoke so softly he almost could not hear her. "Please, Wanmdi Hota, don't hurt me again. Hiya . . ."

He pulled her rigid body to him and began to kiss her. He pressed warm, moist lips to hers. Light kisses began to linger and deepen. He halted to remove her dress and breech cloth. She offered no resistance, for fear he would cut this one off, too. There was no doubt in her mind if he wanted it off, it would come off one way or another. She would rather be naked before him in private, than before his people.

"Please, hiya . . ." she pleaded against his lips as their naked bodies met. "Please, Wanmdi Hota, hiya . . ."

He raised his head and looked down into her terror-filled eyes. He spoke to her in a firm, husky voice, "Sha, Lese. Niye mitawa. Kokipi sni." She did not understand his words, but his tone of voice and gentle mood had a soothing quality. She did not beg again, but tensely waited for him to continue.

His hands roamed over her quivering body with soft caresses. Combined with his fiery kisses, his touch made fires ignite and burn deep within her. This time was unlike the others. Why didn't he just take her and stop this slow torment to her senses? What was he doing to her? What were these strange, tingling sensations inside her and all over her body?

Soon, she found it impossible to resist the emotions he was loosening within her. Nor could she stop them. She felt herself weakening and her resistance giving way to his lips and touch. His kiss and touch brought ecstasy and hunger she did not understand.

Reality flooded her. He is using my own body against me! I must fight these feelings. I must not give in to him willingly! I will act the harlot for no man, especially him! He has taken enough from me! I will not give him my heart and soul as well!

Her mind screamed warnings and rebellion to her traitorous body. Fight him, Lese! Don't show a weakness for him. Resist! Be anything, but his lover! Slave, yes, prisoner, yes, lover, no, no, no . . .

But as he continued his slow, deliberate assault on her, she knew she was losing ground to his greater knowledge and vast experience. He is a savage! her mind screamed. Why does he make me feel this way? He will only use me until he tires of me, and then cast me aside. Why doesn't he hurry and be done? How much longer can I fight this hunger for him? I must concentrate on other things — his cruelty, the dead, their suffering and pain, of anything but what he is doing to me . . .

Her breasts were swollen and firm and her nipples taut with passion and desire. When he teased or kissed them, she felt she would surely go mad if he did not soon possess her completely.

She could not free her lips from his, nor her body from his grip. She could not stop the hands which started an aching deep in the pit of her being. Her pulse and heart raced madly with each other. Finally, she could no longer restrain her desire for him nor could she reason with her conscience. She was as pliable as putty in his hands.

What did it matter anyway? He would take her, willing or not. Why fight him? Why resist him? These feelings which refused to be quelled tore at her reason. His kisses and touches had whetted her love-starved appetite, and it demanded to be fed and sated.

She couldn't understand how he could hold off like this. She could feel his heated ardor. Was he only teasing her? Was he showing her he had complete power and control over her in every way? He was tantalizing her to the brink of begging for fulfillment. She was his prey, and he devoured her with his hunger.

She wanted . . . she needed . . . what? She did not know for sure. At last, he heard what he had been waiting and working for, "Sha . . . sha, Wanmdi Hota. Sha, sha . . ." she moaned the words out in final defeat and desperation.

He moved to top her, parting her unresisting thighs with his knees, and gently entered her. She inhaled deeply as he filled her. His thrusts were slow and deep. Her resistance sank lower, until their lovemaking was the only reality to her. She moaned softly as she was caught up in the heat of passion. She didn't know when her arms had encircled his back and embraced him tightly.

Her lips and body responded feverishly to his kisses and non-verbal instructions. Passion climbed higher and higher. Soon, his thrusts increased in depth and speed. As she molded herself to him, it happened, for the first time. As the shock of release came, her eyes flew open wide and she stared into his. There was no pain this time, only the sweet passion and pleasure they had bespoken.

He smiled down into her astonished face as his lips reclaimed hers. Waves and waves of ecstasy crashed over her. Together, they rode the crest of passion-filled waves until they had subsided. Afterwards, they lay spent, breathing heavily.

Suddenly, full comprehension came to her of her unbridled behavior and what had just taken place between them. She fought to pull away in shame and anger at herself and him, but he held her tightly and securely, refusing to release her.

"Hiya, Lese," he said firmly. She ceased her futile struggles and lay limp in his embrace.

She cried out weakly, "What have I done? Why did I let you make me act like some . . . like some . . . oh-h-h! You're mean and cruel. How could I let you, of all men, make love to me? How did you force me to lose control and respond to you like that? Well, never again! I'll never submit to you again. Never!"

The wild spouting of words ended, but he still held her and would not let her go. She was totally bewildered by her fierce abandonment, but more so by the emotions and pleasures she had just experienced with him.

She struggled again. "Let me go! I can't sleep like this, with you touching and holding me. Leave me be! Hiya, Wanmdi Hota," her last few words spoken with intense pleading in her voice.

Tears of self-betrayal and anger slid down her flushed, rosy cheeks until she finally relaxed in his embrace and went to sleep. She slept peacefully and was still all night in his powerful arms.

He smiled into the darkness, knowing she did not possess the knowledge to resist him, nor the willpower. He gazed down into her sleeping face and tenderly pushed little wisps of hair from her dampened forehead.

"Waste cedake." He suddenly realized he had spoken the very words he had feared to think or feel, that he loved her . . .

For the next few weeks, it was as if there was an unspoken truce between them, during the days. He was not the harsh, cruel master to her, and she behaved as a perfect slave, doing all the things expected of her without defiance and showing great ability and intelligence in her strange new life and surroundings.

But each night she fought his touch, kiss and lovemaking until he overcame her resistance, and then she would cling to him passionately in surrender and hunger. Emotions she had never felt before were alive and in full play. Gray Eagle did not seem to object to her resistance in his mats. In fact, he relished the nightly duel of wills and her final defeat each time. He knew she wanted him as much as he wanted her, but her pride and honor forced her to hide this from him and even from herself.

"In time . . ." he would muse to himself each night.

It was the Indian custom for captives to be turned over to the women to be taught chores or for punishment to be meted out to disobedient slaves. But Gray Eagle chose to keep Alisha to himself, allowing no one else to conquer her spirit. If he could not manage to be with her or nearby, he would have Matu or White Arrow accompany her around the village or to the forest. This unusual situation was quickly noted by many of the women and warriors. Only his great respect and honor, along with her total submission and obvious value and beauty, prevented any open talk or taunts. Without her knowing, his people began to see her lack of contempt and hatred for them. Reluctantly, they came to accept her presence. Only Chela and Matu refused to look past her skin color and position in Gray Eagle's life to see the woman Alisha.

Even though no one spoke to her or acknowledged her, she was not treated cruelly or taunted, and for this she was thankful. It seemed to her that she was invisible to everyone except Gray Eagle, White Arrow, Chela and Matu, but she was wrong. She was noticed by envious women who saw her in Gray Eagle's teepee and at his side, and by the other warriors who agreed with his good luck at finding such a prize. He received many offers for her in trade, but lightly turned them down. His spirit would soar with pride at those times. She was indeed a rare prize, fit for the son of a chief. If only she were not white . . .

When Matu was busy and Gray Eagle was out hunting or gone on a raid, she would be left in White Arrow's care. As the days passed, she found herself spending more and more time with him. She found it easy to respect and like him. He seemed the only person who liked her and viewed her as a friend, not a slave. She felt completely at ease in his presence, and he in hers. He had never known it would be pleasant to be with a winyan, especially one who was an enemy. He was soon very fond of her and enjoyed her company over his own kind. Acceptance and friendship came quickly and easily between them. Within days, he found himself wanting more.

With her small Indian vocabulary and signs, they could almost talk to each other. He would catch himself smiling or laughing with her when she struggled with his tongue. Once she was filling the mni skins and leaned over too far and tumbled into the stream with a big splash. Another time she was caught in the briars while gathering berries. She did not get angry at him for laughing at her. Instead, she usually laughed at herself with good humor and honesty. She was alive and vital, one who enjoyed life with its ups and downs. She found happiness and joy in the smallest of things.

White Arrow recalled the time she made him climb the thorny wanhu tree to return a baby bird to its nest. Or the time she tricked him into releasing the beautiful, colorful pheasant he had snared. She possessed a tender heart and did not like to see anything or anyone suffer. Since this was an intricate part of his religion and beliefs, it pleased him greatly. He came to respect and admire her more and more for these qualities and traits.

Sometimes when all her chores were finished she would run through the meadow chasing the wind, or butterflies, or picking wildflowers. Once, she had made a headband of flowers and placed it on his head. She had merrily danced around him, bowing and laughing, calling him a "wasichu chief." Only his dignity as a warrior had kept him from joining her playful behavior and game.

He enjoyed watching her eyes sparkle with life, and listening to her voice ringing with laughter. He was alert and quick to notice she preferred his company and guard over others, and was the most relaxed and happy around him. When they would return to the village, or others were around, she would adopt an air of respect and reserve. She had never brought embarrassment or taunts to him for her attitude or behavior toward him. His heart would warm with admiration and love for her because of her concern for his honor. He would seek some small way to repay her kindness.

White Arrow did not realize Alisha's demure actions were brought about by her fear of the others' intolerance and misunderstanding of their closeness. True, she did not wish him to be taunted for his acceptance and friendship; but she feared their taunts would halt their friendship and happy times. She knew she must not make herself a burden to him, or he might withdraw his affection, leaving her totally alone in this demesne. She became more and more aware daily of what White Arrow and his friendship meant to her. She did not want to do anything, *anything,* to dampen or destroy it.

Without knowing how or when, White Arrow came to accept her as his koda and Gray Eagle's winyan. He no longer thought of her as a wasichu, but he tried not to think of her in other ways. He found he had to remind himself constantly that she was his best friend's woman. It would bring great shame to him and dishonor to his friend if he allowed himself to forget this for a minute. He would sometimes find himself wishing she were the slave of another, for then he would not feel guilt at taking her or wanting her. If she had been the slave of an enemy, he would dare any danger to go and steal her for himself. The more he was with her, and the more he came to know and understand her, the harder it became to pull back from her emotionally. Still, he knew he must.

What did he care if some of the warriors taunted him about being a man who watches over winyans and kaskapis? He would grin and chide them for their envy. They would all laugh and jokingly challenge him for his coveted position. Soon, it became a joke they played and enjoyed, knowing White Arrow's courage and daring were beyond reproach. Luckily, White Arrow was an easy-going man and did not mind their jesting, serious or not.

One warm, sunny afternoon, he explained his pet name for her. He had never called her Lese or Alisha as she had told him many times. He would call her "Pi-Zi Ista." She did not know what it meant, but came to answer to it. She was sitting by the stream with her bare feet dangling in the water. She turned to him and asked, "Pi-Zi Ista?"

He threw back his head and laughed heartily. He pulled up a handful of grass and pointed to it, saying, "Pi-zi." He then pointed to her eyes and said, "Ista." Pointing to the grass first, then her eyes, he put the two words together, "Pi-Zi Ista."

She looked bewildered for a moment, thinking, grass . . . eyes . . .

She exclaimed in delight, "Grass Eyes!"

Her green eyes had looked like grass to him and he had chosen to call her this. "Sha," she said, smiling her pleasure at his choice. "Pi-Zi Ista . . . Sha."

He stood up and called to her, "Ku-wa, Pi-Zi Ista."

She smiled up at him and rose to follow. "Sha,

Wanhinkpe Ska." They both laughed at her way of saying his name. "I should give you another name, too. Something easier to say, like Daniel or Brandon. How about Sapa Ista?" He grinned, knowing she had made some reference to his black eyes. He walked on with her following close behind.

Many more days passed by, but Matu still refused to change her attitude toward her. She persisted in treating her with coldness and contempt. She disliked having to teach Alisha her chores or watch her doing them. She was openly pleased Alisha preferred White Arrow's company, for he surely did not seem to mind hers. In fact, Matu read more than tolerance in his eyes. She blamed Alisha for this also.

Alisha was unaware of Matu's deep-rooted hatred for white women, especially those with auburn hair and green eyes. Each time she looked at Alisha, she did not really see Alisha, she saw Jenny. She would silently curse her as she recalled past pain-filled days.

Matu would ask herself what Alisha possessed that her kind did not possess better. She would think, she is soft and spoiled. She must be shown and taught everything. She cannot be left alone and must always be guarded. She is weak and beneath my people, the Si-Ha Sapa. She is even beneath the Oglala and all other tribes.

Why do great warriors like Wanmdi Hota and others lower themselves to capture and keep these white women? "Ska witkowins!" she spit out bitterly. They could have their choice of any winyan in their villages, or even winyans from other tribes. Any winyan would be honored and pleased to take a man such as Wanmdi Hota or Wanhinkpe Ska. It was beyond her to understand and accept this.

Matu knew she must do as Wanmdi Hota told her, but she did not have to like it, or the girl. She would not dare to call her a witkowin again. He had been very angry with her. But why? She was his whore, was she not? Still, she must not call her that again, at least, not out loud.

On those days when Alisha was in Matu's care, she was taught which berries, wild vegetables and herbs to gather. She was shown how to properly prepare and cook them. Certain berries were used in the pemmican they called wasna, others in soups, others for eating plain, others for cooking in breads, some for dyes and as medicines. They would gather certain roots to be cooked in several ways; some boiled, baked or smoked.

The hunters had just returned from a very successful hunt, and meat was plentiful. Along with the buffalo meat, the hunters would bring home other game, such as deer, rabbit, squirrels and hehoka, the Oglala name for elk, moose or antelope. Most of the buffalo was used in preparing the wasna for winter rations and the remaining meat for eating now. Alisha quickly learned how to cook buffalo meat in various ways for the different cuts and parts. She had been surprised to find it had a venison flavor which was very tasty and nourishing. Matu was very careful to suppress and hide Alisha's progress as a cook and worker.

Alisha learned which herbs and greens to use to flavor and tenderize the tougher cuts of meats. Her most disliked chore was helping with cleaning and gutting the animals for cooking. Each time she did this chore, she had to fight constantly to overcome her feelings of weakness and nausea. The sight of blood on her hands and the mutilating of the animals' bodies made her nervous and uneasy. At this time, she did not realize the reason for her discomfort and tension.

Nearly every day or two, Gray Eagle and White Arrow would bring home fresh meat of some kind to her, Matu or other women who had no warrior to hunt for them. It appeared to her that generosity and assistance to others in need were great deeds to be honored and praised. She became very much aware of his actions and deeds. She saw the great respect, honor and love his people felt for him and showed to him. But she was unaware of her heart softening and reaching out to him more and more as the days passed.

Days began to slip by more swiftly as she worked under the watchful eyes of Matu. She gathered pokeberries, which they called pakon. The shoots were cooked and eaten, the purple berries used for a dye, and the roots dried and pounded into a medicine. They also gathered chokecherries for food, medicine and dye. They gathered buffalo berries for eating. Other days, they collected wild cabbages, onions, prairie turnips, horsemint, camass bulbs, and roots from the bitterroot plant. All of these she learned to identify and cook, much to Matu's frustration and chagrin. Her polite manner, interest, quickness and gratitude did not sit well with Matu.

Alisha thought the hardest task was gathering the buffalo berries. They grew on trees which were about fifteen feet tall and covered with thorns. The tree had silvery leaves and an egg-shaped fruit which was sweet and delicious. This fruit turned a yellowish-red when it was ready for picking. Matu had tricked her the first time they gathered this fruit. She had made her climb the sticky tree to pluck the fruit and drop it down to her.

After White Arrow had removed all the thorns from her arms, hands and feet, he taught her to use a long branch to dislodge the fruit with a light touch. He was very angry with Matu, but Alisha would not let him punish her.

"Hiya, Wanhinkpe Ska," she begged, holding his arm. She did not wish to tattle or cause more conflict between herself and Matu. It would be unwise to force him to take sides between them. The deed was done and punishing it would only lead to more hatred and resentment. Perhaps her forgiving attitude would ease some of the tension between them.

One of her favorite tasks was the gathering of items for dyes and paints. They would join some of the other women as they gathered and collected earth pigments and plants. They would make yellow from buffalo gallstones; yellow, orange, and red from ochers; blue from wanhu and pokeberries; red from vermillion; black from charcoal; and other colors from grasses, clays and flowers. Sometimes they would mix the extracts and particles with water, and other times, with grease or oil from animals or plant stems. Perhaps one day, Alisha daydreamed, Gray Eagle would allow her to paint some scene on his teepee or designs on his horse. She secretly wished to do even the body painting for ceremonies, but not for war or raids against her people.

Early each morning, she would hear their prayers and chants to their god, Wakantanka, or to the sun, Wi. She was taught in the beginning what things she was not to do or touch. She was taught never to touch his weapons; his pipes, called canduhupa; his candi tobacco; his medicine bundle, called pezuta wopahte; or his ceremonial headdress, which was the top part of a buffalo head.

He had shown her these things and shaken his head and said, "Hiya!" firmly after each one. He had repeated the sequence to be sure she understood his instructions. She nodded her understanding by pointing to each one and stating "hiya" after each.

Even on those nights when she was alone or bored, she did not dare to disobey. She would often look at or study the items, but never touch or handle them. Such an offense was considered bad medicine and evil. For an enemy, or sometimes a woman, to touch such personal things could cause them to lose their power and magic. Such an offense was punishable by death or the loss of a hand.

She had soon comprehended the woman's place in Indian life. Even though she labored hard and long hours, she was highly respected, and treated with dignity. The warriors did no domestic tasks of any kind, or anything which appeared to be female work. The Indian women accepted this way of life as easily as breathing. They did their work with efficiency, reserve and pride.

It was quickly apparent to Alisha that the men were the supreme rulers in this domain also, just as it was back in her homeland. But there was a very noticeable difference in the attitudes and manners of these women. They quietly and willingly accepted their lot in life, whereas many of the white women hated their lots and destinies. She had witnessed many of her friends' anger at their pre-arranged lives and marriages. Alisha knew she would have done the same if she had been forced to marry one of those same men. She wondered if women would ever be free to choose their own mates and ways of life.

She came to understand that his tribe was ruled by a council, of which Gray Eagle and White Arrow were members, and called the "Oyate Omiciye." They would often meet in one of the most elaborately decorated teepees in the inner circle. The most influential leaders and warriors lived in the first three inner circles. She could see they were the ones in charge of the laws, punishments, raids and hunts. Many times she had watched as a group of hunters or warriors would raise Gray Eagle's arm and cheer him as the "tiospaya itancan" for their coming raid or hunt. She had watched him leave their teepee and go to the council lodge when the old man called out, "Oyate Omiciye kte lo."

White Arrow had pointed out the medicine lodge to her one day. He had called it the Pezuta Teepee. He had pointed out where the Yuwipi Wicasta lived, but his teepee was empty at this time. She thought perhaps he had gone to collect some special herbs for medicines, or to perform some secret incantations. With her small, inadequate vocabulary, there was no way for her to ask about the things she did not understand.

She also noticed there was another teepee empty in the inner circle. It was the largest and most beautiful of all. Its skins told tales of many fierce battles and daring hunts. The hero in all scenes wore a flowing, full bonnet of yellow feathers. She knew this must be their chiefs teepee. But where was he? Why was he not here? She had no way of knowing Chief Suntokca Ki-in-yangki-yapi and Pezuta Wapiye Wicasta Itancan Torlac were in the Paha Sapa, their sacred lands of healing.

She still had not learned or guessed Gray Eagle's true status, but knew him to be in high esteem in his people's eyes. Perhaps he was the chief's son as Simon had said. She tried not to show too much personal interest in him and forced herself not to ask him or White Arrow those questions which plagued her mind. For some unknown reason, she felt danger in asking or knowing about their chief. This was a wise decision, for it would only have reminded them he was not here because a white trapper had shot him, nearly killing him.

The women's lives were filled with various chores each day, and there always seemed to be something new for her to learn. On this occasion, she was helping the women gather sumac berries to be used in the treating and tanning of animal skins and hides. She had observed them for a long time in silence, watching and learning. They would stretch the skins taut and secure to a wooden frame, then scrape the fat and bits of meat from the skin with a sharp tool. When the scraping was thoroughly done, the skin was rubbed with animal brains to soften and condition it, then tanned.

Later, she had helped for a short while, until Matu became impatient with her sluggishness and nausea as she worked with the brains. Matu pushed her aside to observe some more. Alisha was only too happy to obey this time.

There were other women sitting close by collecting and treating sinews, which were used for binding skins and clothing together, much like the thread her people used for sewing. She watched as they removed and collected claws, teeth, feathers and quills to be used as decorations on clothing and belongings.

The Sioux favored the use of the porcupine quills for adorning pipe bags, bow quivers, men's vests, moccasins and women's clothing. First, the quills were softened in warm water, then flattened and pressed with a heavy rock. Later, they were braided or sewn onto the skins and hides.

The first time she had attempted this task, she only succeeded in pricking her fingers numerous times with the sharp quills. Unfortunately, the design was incorrect and had to be taken apart, inflicting more painful, bloody pricks. Matu had delighted in her pain and trouble. She had continued to instruct Alisha until Gray Eagle guessed what was really taking place with the lessons. He had called for Alisha to come to do a chore for him. She had immediately answered his beckoning.

She had reddened when he took her two small hands into his large, strong ones to examine them. Embarrassed, she defended her lack of ability. "I guess I wasn't very careful. I'm not very good at it yet, but soon . . ." She halted when she realized what she was saying and doing. Angrily, she continued, "You probably think I'm stupid and careless, just like the old woman does. I'll learn to do it yet, even if my hands are covered with pricks and blood," she vowed, determined not to be bested by him or Matu.

He had made no comment, but had taken her to the Pezuta Teepee. There, he put some oily substance into the palms of her hands, then motioned for her to rub it in. She did so, and was surprised to find it numbed and soothed the stinging pain. The bleeding soon stopped. She looked up into his eyes and smiled her thanks. He ignored her smile. He called for her to follow him back to their teepee to prepare their evening meal. Each such event would gnaw at her diminishing fear and mistrust of him.

At all times, except during lovemaking, he held himself away from her in dignity, arrogance and coldness. He was lofty, forbidding and unreachable. He accepted her presence and services, but offered no outward friendship, attention or concern.

She mused to herself, perhaps he pretends I am Indian in the dark. Or, at least, he can ignore my white skin as he makes love to me. It was apparent to even a naive girl like Alisha that he enjoyed her body, her resistance, her submission and her docile behavior, but not as a person. She would have been greatly shocked if she had but guessed how he truly felt.

He worked hard at suppressing and denying his feelings and thoughts about her to everyone, including himself. He constantly reminded himself she was only his slave and enemy. He would keep her at arm's length at all times, except when he made love to her at night. On those occasions, he would think of it as a game, a show of power, or as punishment. He enjoyed forcing her to betray herself and submit willingly to him, night after night. He did not realize how deep and strong his feelings for her were becoming. He dismissed such ridiculous thoughts.

In her plight of slavery without friends or family, she turned more and more to White Arrow for the affection and happiness missing in her life. In return, White Arrow was drawn to her beauty and vulnerability like a bear to a honey tree, aware of both its dangers and rewards. To see her smile, to hear her soft laughter, to be a part of her happiness, and to watch her grow and bloom into a desirable creature before his eyes, was well worth a few stings. Only the knowledge she belonged to his best friend, who was like a brother to him, held his attentions under control.

As long as she belongs to Wanmdi Hota, White Arrow thought, I will not touch her and dishonor him. When the day comes that he casts her aside, she will be mine. Wanmdi Hota will not dare to keep her much longer. The others will begin to question his feelings for his white slave. The time for trading her will come soon. When she is mine, I will not be forced to give her up, for I am not a chief's son. He must soon take his mate and cannot keep her then. What mate, especially one like Chela, would allow him to keep a slave such as Pi-Zi Ista? He rationalized, when the time comes, she will come to me willingly, for we are friends and she trusts me.

One night later, she sat watching Gray Eagle as he put some feathers in a pouch. She picked one up and admired its strength and beauty. She questioned, "Eagle?" making the sign for a bird.

Instantly, his head jerked up at her word. She was examining the feather and did not see this curious reaction. He sighed in relief, but took advantage of this situation.

He said, "Wanhinkpe Ska." She looked up at him in confusion. He went on. He held up an arrow and said, "Wanhinkpe."

She brightened and replied, "Wanhinkpe, arrow," touching the arrow he was holding.

He nodded and continued with a list of things which had to do with the color white. He said, "Wasichu . . . ska . . . ," touching her skin. He pointed to her eyes and said, "Ista . . . pi-zi, ska . . ." He picked up a feather and, touching the white tip, said, "Ska . . ."

Concentrating on his meaning, she surmised, "White man; eyes, green and white; feather tipped with white . . ." The answer was obvious. She exclaimed with delight, "White Arrow! Wanhinkpe Ska means White Arrow!" She smiled, pleased with herself.

He went back to his task. She studied him curiously for a few minute, then timidly inquired, "Wanmdi Hota?"

He looked up and met her soft, steady gaze. He picked up one of the eagle feathers and said, "Wanmdi," making the sign for a large bird. He spread out his upraised arms like giant wings, indicating the bird was large and powerful.

She studied his motions and words. The bird must be large and the feather was from an eagle.

Quickly, she guessed, "Eagle! Wanmdi is eagle. Hota?"

He took the two containers of paint which he was using on his new buffalo shield. He pointed to the black, saying, "Sapa." He pointed to the white and said, "Ska." Knowing she had guessed that word correctly, she could not suppress a smile. He slowly mixed the two colors together until he had the color he wanted.

He began, pointing to each color in turn, "Sapa, ska, hota . . ."

"Gray Eagle . . . yes. The most powerful and courageous ruler of the heavens. Arrogant, untamed, unafraid, untouchable; but also a beautiful, brutal killer. . . . A name well suited, my love, for you are all of those and more. You fear nothing and no one. You yield and bow to no one. You conquer and take what you desire, and kill anyone or anything in your way. The day will come when you turn those claws on me and kill me, just like you did to all the others. Perhaps you will use those talons to tear my heart from my very soul. Gray Eagle . . . well chosen indeed," she nodded agreement.

He had carefully listened to her words, heedful to keep his face and eyes blank and empty. He reflected on her description of him. He mused, she knows me well, or thinks she does. Her use of the words "my love" is interesting. Is it only a phrase used by the wasichu, or does she mean them in another way? She has said them with softness and a touch of mockery. There is still much to learn about this winyan, he noted ruefully.

Alisha had taken over his task and was separating the feathers and putting them in their appropriate pouches. She was very careful not to bend or muss them, especially those to be used on arrow shafts. The feather controlled the aim and flight of an arrow.

When she had put all the pouches away, she turned to find him staring at her with an intense, nearly imperceptible glint in his eyes. That look never failed to spark flames in her own traitorous body.

"I know what that look means, you insatiable dragon!" she accused teasingly, then added, "Does the noble eagle open his wings and nest, if not his heart and life, to a ska winyan?" She could not suppress giggles at her analogy, but missed the gleam in his blazing ebony eyes at her words.

He nonchalantly retorted, "Ska winyan ku-wa Wanmdi Hota o-winza." He motioned for her to come to him on the pallet.

She playfully taunted, "And what if the ska winyan says hiya? Perhaps she's not in the mood to make love to Wanmdi Hota."

So, he mused, she wishes to play games with me. He was very tempted to call her bluff. His eyes glimmered as he wondered what her reaction to his command in her tongue would be. No, he cautioned himself, it is too soon for such things to be out in the open.

He called to her a little more sternly, "Lese ku-wa o-winza!"

Feigning humility and shyness to tease him further, she came to kneel before him. She looked up into his face with large, innocent eyes. She softened her tone of voice to a low, sexy whisper. Placing her small hands on his hard, bare chest, she cooed, "Yes, master. Your adoring slave comes and yields to you. Oh, great and noble warrior of the skies, take me and let us soar like your namesake, wild and free. Make me burn with hunger for you. Come to me in love, not hate. For once, love Alisha and not your kaskapi. Pretend I am the winyan of your heart for one night. Tonight, let this be the joining of love and hate, of Alisha and Gray Eagle, not slave and master. Is one night so much to ask for?"

Suddenly, it was no longer a joke. She realized she meant every word she had just spoken. She truly wanted him. But she also wanted him to need her in the same way. Why couldn't he accept her for herself and not only as his slave? Why couldn't he want and need her as she did him? Why couldn't he love her as she loved him?

These thoughts and emotions frightened and confused her. A shadow of bittersweet torment passed across her features. She lowered sparkling emerald eyes and dropped her hands to her lap. That was a stupid, foolish thing to do, Lese. Some things are best kept hidden and suppressed, even to yourself.

He scrutinized her closely for a time, allowing her new discovery to sink in and take hold. He placed his hand under her chin and raised it until their eyes met and locked. He lay back on the pallet and called softly to her, "Ku-wa, Lese . . ."

Without a minute's hesitation, she went into his open arms and to his waiting lips. Time ceased to move at this first contact. Never had their nights together been more passionate or tender . . .

To her utter distress and disappointment, he was back to his old self the very next morning. He was once more the cold, forbidding warrior, first and foremost, as if last night had not even taken place between them. It was obvious to her that it had meant nothing but sex to him.

When she halted to speak to him, he cast icy, impatient eyes on her. She had started, "Wanmdi Hota, ku-wa. Lese needs . . ." Her words trailed off and stopped. She felt as if someone had just thrown ice cold water on her, chilling her very soul. His look did far more damage to their relationship than he could imagine. She paled and stared at him.

Tears sparkled in her eyes as she turned and ran back inside his teepee. She had needed him to come and sharpen her knife for cutting up the deer meat. She cried bitterly as she worked on the meat with the dull knife, trying to focus her attention on her chore. She would never forgive this insult.

When he came in later, it was evident from her puffy red eyes she had been crying. He casually tried to find out what she had wanted from him earlier. She appeared to either not understand him or pretended not to. She had remained quiet and withdrawn the rest of the day, and had cried herself to sleep that night after he had finally forced her submission to him.

He realized she had placed a wall around her heart and feelings, much like the wall the blue-coats built around them to protect them from Oglalas. She was trying to protect her heart against his attack on it. He still failed to realize the depth and pain of the wound he had inflicted on her, trying to protect his own heart against her attack.

She made no attempts to communicate with him. She would only answer to his commands, or call him to eat. She would battle with her eyes to keep them away from him. She tried to remain as distant mentally and physically as possible from him. She forced herself to stay busy or out of his sight during the day. At night, she would sleep with her back to him. She would not allow herself to be ensnared by his tricks and traps any more.

Her withdrawal gnawed at him day and night as time passed on. It stung his pride to see and hear her with White Arrow, smiling, laughing and talking. When he walked in upon them, she would instantly become subdued and aloof. Her smile and laughter would fade, to be replaced with silence and a glum look.

White Arrow did not understand what had happened between them to cause this reaction in his koda. Gray Eagle's anger and agitation were obvious to him, and he also noticed Alisha's mistrust and hurt. He wondered what his koda had done to her this time, for surely he had wounded her deeply and cruelly with some deed. White Arrow surmised, I read two fears in her eyes — fear of him and fear of what she feels for him. Perhaps she has learned he must give her up soon and fights to control and stop her love and the pain from it.

Alisha's withdrawal from Gray Eagle was as hard on her as it was on him. It demanded so much from her emotionally and physically. She had to be on guard against him and her reactions to him. The battle was becoming too hard. She was weary of this pretense and loneliness, day and night. She wanted him, needed him.

Gray Eagle was at the end of his patience. He hungered and thirsted for her smile, her laughter and her full warmth and attention. He knew he could not tolerate this situation any longer. She had punished him long enough. It was time for a new truce between them. He needed her completely. How dare she treat me like this! he raged. I am the warrior! She is but a ska kaskapi. I will end it this moon! I will not allow such treatment from her.

That night, Gray Eagle could no longer contain himself. He grabbed her chin in his steel-like grip, forcing her to look at him. He stated in a commanding, deep tone, "Ni-ye mitawa!"

She glared back into those stygian eyes which challenged her to deny what he had just said. She did not know those words or their meaning. But her answer was perfect. She hotly retorted, "You can force me to be your harlot; but you cannot force me to love you or want you. And I will not . . . I will not!"

Immediately, he had angrily thrown her down on his mats and made consuming, fierce love to her, taking her quickly and coldly. He would prove his words were true!

She had struggled against him and his brutal attack. She had cried out words of hatred to him over and over. Afterwards, she had wept for a long time, giving him the time to realize what he had just done, and the error of it.

She sat up and glared down into his face. "I hate you! I wish I knew how to explain those three words to you. Lese hates Wanmdi Hota! Lese hates Wanmdi Hota!" She continued shouting those words to him until he forcefully pulled her rigid body into his arms and kissed her tenderly, again and again.

Powerless to resist him for very long, she clung to his embrace and returned his kisses with desperate longing and hunger. Soon he was making love to her once more, but this time with gentleness and passion. When it was over, she snuggled into his arms and slept peacefully, which she had not done in many nights.

The following morning, he realized her coldness, but not her protective wall, was missing. His actions had shattered the fragile trust he had instilled in her, and it would take time for it to come again.

Chapter Seven

Alisha's idle time was spent in various ways. Tonight as she lay waiting for Gray Eagle to return from a council meeting, she studied the teepee they shared. It was constructed of twenty-five poles and covered with about forty-five buffalo skins, as best she could count. As with all teepees, theirs faced the east to catch the rising sun and to avoid the northwest winds. She knew it was the woman's chore to dismantle and put up the teepees. She fretfully wondered if she would be able to learn and perform this important task when the time came for her to do so. She had been entranced by the scenes and designs painted on the interiors and exteriors of the teepees. She was still amazed at the talent and ability they displayed under these conditions with such crude supplies.

She had immediately learned the meaning of the position of the teepee flap — open meant "enter" and closed meant "absent or privacy." No one entered another's teepee without permission when the flap was down. As was the custom, their flap was always open from morning till dusk.

Many evenings after eating, she would sit for hours watching Gray Eagle as he worked on new arrows, his shield, lances, or other weapons. The care and construction of weapons was a very time-consuming job for the warriors. As with hunting, it took a lot of skill, strength and patience.

Tonight, he was working on his new buffalo shield, which had been made from the neck hide and toughened to withstand arrows or blows from his enemies. The edges were trimmed and decorated with scalp hairs, feathers, and colorful strips of rawhide, but the white center was still blank and unfinished. He would paint the sign given to him by Wakantanka when he chose to reveal it.

Some night or day, the Great Spirit would reveal to him in a wowanyake what akito was to be painted on the shield. This sign given to him in the vision would be his protection and guide in battle. Until the vision was given, the center would remain empty and white.

She watched him as he put the shield away and picked up a pointed stone. He began to hone the tip into an arrowhead. She had watched him do this many tunes, but always observed with fascination. She was secretly happy with his great intelligence and knowledge. He appeared to know so much about everything. She had often studied him in the forest, noting his unending knowledge about the animals and their ways, and nature. He was as one with his surroundings and in nature. He belonged here in this savage wilderness, just as this wilderness belonged to him and his kind, for they were much alike in character. He accepted things the way they were and tried to change nothing. She realized as long as the Indian lived here, this land would remain unchanged and ever self-renewing.

Alisha came to understand the Indians' closeness with the land and nature. She saw how they helped and depended upon each other for survival. She recalled the "Canhdeska Wakan" White Arrow had shown her on the ceremonial lodge skins. The scenes painted there symbolized a sacred life circle. They depicted a baby within a circle, probably a mother's womb; a small child; a grown man; a warrior's body on a death scaffold; a warrior on the Ghost Trail; and the circle closed. Their belief signified man came from the Great Spirit, was born, lived, died, and returned to the Great Spirit for eternal life. Alisha was amazed to see how similar to her own religious beliefs this was. This made it difficult for her to understand why the white man called them pagans and heathens. Was it only because they called the one deity Wakantanka instead of God? Her increasing knowledge of them forced her to see they weren't so very different after all.

She had learned that this concept applied to all men, animals, and objects. Each was to live for the purpose for which it was created. The Oglala appeared to revere all life — except the white man's, whom they viewed as the destroyer of nature. In the Oglala way, animals were killed only for food, shelter, clothing and protection from harm. The Oglala never destroyed or changed any part of the lands or forests. They conformed their lives and needs to the land, rather than conforming the land to their needs. These beliefs were ingrained in the Oglala from the day of birth. Anyone who tried to alter this way of life was viewed as a threat, to be removed or destroyed. This was a proud and courageous nation. They would never allow the white man or other tribes to force them from their home-lands. She prayed her people would see and learn the folly of trying to conquer this land and its people.

Alisha realized that her people had brought guns which killed and maimed with a strange, evil magic. They brought liquor which robbed the senses and powers of the warriors. They brought strange, new diseases and deaths to the people.

The Oglalas watched as we moved their lands and forests, Alisha thought. They watched as we cut away the forests and hunted their game. They watched how we treated them with malice and disrespect. Why shouldn't they hate us and want to kill us? Could we ever have become friends and allies with such totally different concepts of life? Could we ever have accepted each other in peace and honor? But Alisha was afraid to answer her questions.

As each new day came and went, she continued to cook; wash; gather wood, food and water; and became more and more confused with her position among the Indians. The others had been killed soon after their arrival, but she was still alive. Perhaps it was because she had made a good slave and he had decided to keep her.

No one had been permitted to harm her. But no one other than White Arrow, Matu and Gray Eagle associated with her. What does it all mean? she would question. If they aren't going to kill me, then why don't they accept me? If I'm going to live here forever, they could make me their friend, couldn't they? Will I always be a slave and outcast forever? she sadly wondered.

On some days, she felt like a schoolgirl, being tested for what she had learned and for her obedience. One thing was certain: she was definitely Gray Eagle's personal prisoner, under his command and power. She had tried to do all that was demanded of her because he had halted his cruelty and violence to her.

The hardest part of her captivity was accepting his daily lovemaking, and trying to resist the ever-growing hunger for him, a hunger which was not only physical, but emotional. She found herself wanting to be his friend and companion, as well as his lover. She desired the freedom and acceptance to be herself with no restrictions and restraints, to be able to talk with him and the others, to have his friendship and company and that of others. She yearned to be liked, and to find peace and freedom here with them. She wanted to run through the forests and meadows laughing and singing. She wanted to be accepted with honor and respect. She wanted . . . the impossible . . . She wanted to be an Oglala, living in peace and happiness with friends and family . . .

As she feared, the time came when she found herself waiting and watching for his returns from hunts and raids. When he would go to the lodge for a meeting, she would peer out and watch him until he disappeared inside the other teepee. She would catch herself listening for the sound of his voice speaking or chanting. She would tremble with longing when she heard his deep, rumbling voice. She would stand watching the smoke from numerous pipes as it escaped from the teepee vent. She would wonder what they were talking and laughing about in there. She would find herself looking for a glimpse of him at every turn, or hoping for a chance meeting, or observing him intently as he spoke with others. Even at night, she would frequently wake up and lie watching his relaxed features, or just listening to his even, steady breathing. The harder she tried to suppress these growing feelings, the stronger and bolder they became.

Once, she had panicked when he and White Arrow had ridden off and stayed away for two days and nights. She had been terrified something had happened to them. At first, she convinced herself she would be relieved, then realized without his protection she would be at his people's mercy. White Arrow, who was with him, would not be able to save her.

As she lay unable to sleep most of the second night, she knew it was Gray Eagle she actually feared for, and not his protection of her. He might have had an accident, or have been killed, or captured by whites again. She was beside herself with worry and fear. Was it possible she really did love him this much? How could she be sure? She had never been in love before. How did love feel? What was this love between a man and a woman? Perhaps she only reached out to him for protection or in lust. If that were true, any man would suit her needs. But it was his voice she strained to hear, his face she longed to see, and his touch and kiss she hungered to feel.

Those two days and nights seemed endless without him. On the afternoon of the third day, she was walking up the forest path, daydreaming. She happened to glance up and see him dismounting his horse. Her heart and pulse raced with joy and relief. He's back! He's safe! Without stopping to think, she ran toward him, calling his name, "Wanmdi Hota! Wanmdi Hota, you're home!"

She beamed with happiness and tears of excitement sparkled in her emerald eyes. Abruptly, she hushed and stopped as the surprised, gaping stares and silence of those around them alerted her to her actions. She lowered her eyes to the ground, face flaming.

He and White Arrow exchanged grins. White Arrow remarked, "Pi-Zi Ista is happy at your return, my koda." Secretly, he wished that look and smile had been for him. Perhaps one day it will, he thought. I fear she grows to love him and that is not good. I must speak with him soon about her trade to me. The time is near for it.

Gray Eagle walked past her, heading for his teepee. Casually, he called for her to come with him. Mutely, she did so. Thankfully, he made no reference to her outburst or behavior. He put away the pizuta yutas that he was carrying.

He took the cactus buttons with him to the lodge meeting later that night. Alisha was angry and frustrated to have him leave on his first night back home. He had hardly even noticed her or spoken to her since his return, or so she thought.

Just a slave! she cried in hurt and humiliation. I mean nothing more to him than someone to do his chores and relieve his male anxieties! I hate him! He's mean and cruel! Nothing but a chattel, she scoffed bitterly at herself.

She paced the small confines of his teepee in a black, stormy mood. What cut even deeper was the fact he did not return at all that night. When she managed to bring the tempest she was feeling under some kind of control, she lay down and went to sleep. Even if he had ignored her, he'd returned safely. This reality enabled her to relax and sleep after two long, sleepless nights.

The warriors had gathered in the lodge to listen to White Arrow as he told about their trip to the village of their friends and allies, the Cheyenne, to trade for the peyote buttons. These buttons were used during or before certain events and ceremonies. Tonight, they would be eaten during a ritual, a quest for a vision from the Great Spirit. They hoped to find the answers to how to deal with the wasichus and bluecoats in their lands. The final effect of the drug was sedative, which induced relaxation and deep, peaceful sleep. The ritual lasted far into the night and Gray Eagle did not return to Alisha until the next morning.

Last night's rebuff and rejection, as Alisha saw it, brought a renewed caution to her. She placed a watchful guard over her words and actions toward him. Once more, he had shown her what her true position in his life was. He was aware of the withdrawal and change in her, but not the reason behind it. He watched as she and White Arrow drew closer in companionship. Helplessly, he saw her reaching out to his friend and saw his friend accept it. He watched as they communicated with a combination of words and signs she had learned. But most disturbing, he observed the way they both changed in his presence. They became quieter and more subdued with each other. It was as if they sensed he would object to their closeness and behavior, and he did.

Perhaps they were becoming too close and friendly, he surmised. She is behaving with my koda the way she should be acting to me. Why does she fear being open and honest with me? Is there more than friendship between them? Is her withdrawal from me a turning to my koda? Could it be because of the way he treats her? He gives her what she hungers for and needs — friendship and acceptance. He gives what I cannot. Do not turn to him for more, Lese, he warned, for I will not allow it. I will not allow Wanhinkpe Ska to turn your face and heart to him. I cannot allow you to come between him and me, nor will I allow him to come between us. I must keep a watchful eye and alert ear on this thing. It is far easier to dam and halt a small stream, than to wait until it becomes a larger, more powerful river . . .

Alisha and White Arrow had gone into the forest to gather wood and fetch water from the stream. He was keeping an eye on her today while Gray Eagle was off hunting with other braves. Matu had been busy tanning hides from the last hunt and did not wish to stop, which suited Alisha fine. Near the big tree by the stream, White Arrow had met a friend and had stopped to talk.

She quietly gathered her wood in the sling and filled the water skins. She looked back to see the two men still talking. She strolled along the bank in dreamy thought. She occasionally leaned over to pick a wildflower which caught her eye. She stopped and played in the water with her fingertips. She picked leaves from low-hanging branches she passed under. She was completely caught up in a world of her own making. She was unaware of how far she was walking.

She meandered along, her head filled with fantasies and warnings concerning Gray Eagle. White Arrow assumed she was on private business and did not come after her for a long time, almost too late . . .

As she leaned over to pluck some black-eyed Susans, a hand clamped over her mouth and a strong arm encircled her chest like a band of steel. Panic seized her heart and mind. She fought like a wildcat, kicking, scratching, and biting at the hand over her mouth. She fearfully thought she was being captured by some enemy tribe. She went rigid. Her eyes widened in astonishment and disbelief.

A voice behind her blurted out, "Why, you little she-cat! I'll teach you to bite Ole Smitty! You got some lessons to learn in manners, gurl."

English! A white man! her brain screamed. At last, help. Rescue . . . freedom . . . no more slavery . . . no more Wanmdi . . .

Because of her lack of struggling, Smitty was able to turn her around to face him. He was instantly shocked at what he saw. He stared incredulously into her beautiful ivory face with wide, frightened green eyes.

"Well, I'll be damned! Bless my soul and good luck if'n it ain't a white gurl. A good looker at that. How'd you git out here, gurl? Where'd you come frum? What's yore name anyhows?"

He rapidly fired many questions at her numbed brain in his great excitement. She only stared at the trapper blankfaced and dumbfounded. He was filthy and smelled foul. He was wearing fringed buckskins and a beaver hat. From his odor and appearance, he had not bathed in months, perhaps even a year. She noticed his long, shaggy, dull hair; bushy eyebrows; unkempt, wiry beard; and rotting, yellowish-brown teeth.

She nearly fainted from the stench of his breath and body odor. He shook her and asked again, "I asked kin you speak English, gurl?"

Still unable to force any words from her mouth, she nodded her head yes. He questioned, "Can't you talk? You look as'o you never see'd a white man afore. Whatcha doing out here alone? How long you been with them Sioux?"

She finally managed a soft whisper, "A few weeks or months . . . I'm not really sure . . ."

At the softness in her tone and the view of her delicate beauty, Smitty was reminded of the painful urgings of baser needs which had prompted him in the first place to attack what he assumed was an Indian girl.

Atta boy, Smitty. This gurl is some'em else. His dull, slaty eyes filled with increasing lust as he eyed the small, fragile creature before him. He glanced around and inquired as to how and why she was so far from camp alone.

She hastily looked around, realizing she was in unfamiliar surroundings. "I just wandered off. I better get back before he comes looking for me."

Alisha instinctively sensed danger from this man. She was alarmed to find herself alone and defenseless with him. She was becoming more frightened as time passed. She was troubled at the leering way his eyes engulfed her entire being.

A lewd gleam flickered in his eyes and he licked dry lips in anticipation. His eyebrows lifted as he questioned, "He? So, you be an Injun squaw. Don't matter none to Ole Smitty. Should've guessed it from yore looks. Even an Injun wouldn't pass up a gal like you. That'll make it all the easier and better. Won't have to hurt you none. We'll jest git ourselves a little ways off frum here. We don't want them Injuns disturbing us just when things are gittin good. If'n you knows what I mean . . ." He flashed her a licentious grin as he laughed wickedly.

The stark reality of her situation and his intentions was as clear as water. She was petrified. She instantly broke into a run, screaming loudly. He immediately came after her, cursing and yelling for her to shut up. He caught up with her and snatched her backwards by her hair. They struggled for a few minutes before he threw her roughly to the ground. He quickly fell on top of her and began to madly rip at her clothes.

He pulled at her dress, trying to push it up. She fought with all her strength, praying for help. He managed to undo the laces at her neckline. He savagely bit into her soft shoulder. He cruelly squeezed her breast and silenced her pleas and yells with a slobbery, bruising kiss. She nearly retched.

He forcefully tugged at the bottom of her dress, finally succeeding in getting it up to her hips. He painfully parted her slender thighs with bruising, insistent fingers. She fought with renewed urgency and terror. She could feel his hardened manhood rubbing against her inner thigh. His hand touched her there as he yanked on the breechcloth. Her hands pulled desperately at his hair and pushed at his towering face. She bit into his lip as he tried to kiss her again. He jerked his head back in a black rage.

His arm came down across her throat, cutting off her air and voice. She shoved at his arm, twisting her head to one side. He grabbed her hair and pulled her face back to his, covering her mouth with his. Tears of disgust, pain and fear slid from her eyes and ran down into her hair. She vowed she would fight him to the death before she would submit to this.

A concerned voice called out, "Pi-Zi Ista, ku-wa!"

Smitty's head jerked up for a look around. That was all the time Alisha needed to scream out at the top of her lungs. He quickly slapped a hand over her mouth. "You stupid bitch! You wanna git us killed? I kin help you git away from them Injuns. All I wants is a little piece fur me services and trouble. You dun called out to him. Hell, you acts as tho ya prefer him to yore own kind! Guess

I'll have'ta kill him afore I takes care of you."

He pulled his knife and she was certain he was going to take her life right then. He hesitated as he gazed down into her large, innocent eyes and nearly lost his chance for revenge. Abruptly, he had to jump up to meet White Arrow's attack. He had seemed to come from nowhere. He bounded forward like a cougar, screaming, "E-ee-eei-ay!"

They slowly and cautiously circled each other, sizing each other up. Never once did one's eyes leave the other's. Smitty knew he was looking into the face of his death. Those stygian eyes burned with hate and fury. His muscles were taut with apparent strength and nimbleness. He moved with the quickness and agility of a mountain lion. There was no trace of fear or doubt in those black eyes. White Arrow's aura told of his abundant courage and self-confidence. He reeked of vengeance and power.

Smitty realized there was no chance for him in a fair fight. His face paled and he heaved in loud, ragged gulps. He slashed out wildly at White Arrow, who easily maneuvered to stay clear of his knife and attack. White Arrow mockingly circled with him, letting him wear himself down. He lunged at White Arrow and was tripped. He pretended to strike his head on a rock, knocked unconscious. He hoped the brave would turn his attention to his squaw, allowing him to jump him from behind. He would kill that damned Injun and take the girl with him. If his trick failed, then he was finished.

Smitty had hit the ground with a loud thud and moan, then lay motionless. White Arrow disregarded caution in his concern for Alisha. He turned his back to Smitty and came to her. A few long, easy strides, and he was beside her. He gently lifted her body and carried her to the stream. He knew the trapper had not succeeded in his attack. He noted her disheveled state and tear-streaked face. He saw the red finger marks and spots of blood around her mouth, but no cuts.

He quickly scanned her for other injuries. She had bruises and scratches on her arms, legs and neck. His eyes darkened in fury when he found the vicious bite on her shoulder. By now, she was crying uncontrollably and shaking violently.

He examined the redness on her throat where the trapper had tried to choke her into silence and submission. His anger flamed higher and his eyes glinted with the death warning. He glanced up and caught her eyes searching him. He forced a warm smile at her as he took a cloth from his waist and dipped it into the cool water. He washed the tears, dust and blood from her face. He was as gentle with her as a mother to a newborn baby.

He leaned over to scoop up mud to make a pack for the nasty bite. A shadow fell across her lap. She jerked her head up in time to see the trapper coming at White Arrow's back with his knife held high and threatening.

She lunged at the man, screaming a warning to

White Arrow, "No-o-o! Wasicun ku-wa! Wayaketo!"

White Arrow was instantly aware of danger and was on his feet, braced and ready to face and fight his enemy. Thanks to her attack on the man, his knife was quickly in his hand. The trapper had as easily tossed Alisha aside as if she were merely a feather. He met White Arrow's fierce attack head-on. They clutched and fought furiously. With one swift, accurate slash, the trapper lay dead at his feet, his throat slit from one side to the other.

White Arrow rose and stood over the body of the trapper. He lifted his head toward the heavens and gave an eerie howl like a ghostly wolf in victory.

Alisha ran to him in relief and fear. She grabbed his arm and turned him to face her. Boldly and fearfully, her eyes searched his tall, lean frame for any serious injuries. Frantically, she cried, "Are you hurt, Wanhinkpe Ska? He could have killed you! It would have been all my fault." She shuddered in revulsion. "He put his hands on me. He was going to . . ." She lowered her face into her hands and wept.

He pulled her into his embrace and held her quaking body tightly. His fingers gently caressed her rigid back. His thoughts were in turmoil as to how close this call of danger was to her. He had only let her out of his sight for a short time, but it had almost cost her her life. He was furious with himself for allowing such a brutal thing to happen. He hungered to kiss her, to make love to her, and to blot out everything that just happened.

As he comforted her and spoke soothingly to her, he had to fight rising, heated emotions, which threatened to engulf him. He lifted her tenderly into his strong arms and carried her back toward camp. As he walked, he murmured reassuringly, "Sh-h-h, Pi-Zi Ista. Kokipi sni. Hiya ceya. Waste cedake."

She did not grasp the meaning of his words of comfort or love, but his tone was comforting. She was so shaky and weak she did not protest his attention and help. She laid her face against his hard chest as she cried his name over and over.

Gray Eagle was returning to camp just as they left the forest path and headed toward his teepee. He curiously watched the way his friend carried her pressed close to his chest, tenderly and protectively. More alarming was the way her arms tightly encircled his neck and back, and the way her head lay familiarly on his shoulder. His eyes darkened and narrowed in suspicion and alarm. What was the meaning of this bold display?

He handed the reins of his horse to a young Oglala brave. He quickly covered the distance to his teepee. White Arrow had taken her to the pallet and laid her down gently. He was stroking her hair as he spoke to her in his tongue, "Kokipi ikopa, Cante Cinstinna." She held his other hand clasped between her two cold, trembling ones and continued to cry.

Gray Eagle entered without a sound, but White Arrow was instinctively aware of his presence. He pulled his hand free from her grasp, stood up, and came over to him. He met Gray Eagle's gaze slightly uneasily. He related the events in the forest. He told him all about the trapper's attempted attack, the fight, and her warning which saved his life.

Gray Eagle listened in silence, then stressed, "Do not become too protective of 'my' winyan, my koda."

White Arrow met his steady gaze in guilt and understanding. He replied, "She is yours, Wanmdi Hota. This I will not forget. Were she not the winyan of my best koda, I would have finished what the wahmunkesa began. When the time comes that you must give her up, I will trade anything I possess to have her." He turned and left Gray Eagle staring after him.

It was distressing to have his friend confirm his suspicions and fears. He did not like his friend's attraction for Lese.

He walked over to her and stood gazing down at her with those dark, unreadable eyes. Sensing his eyes on her, she raised a distraught face to him. She shifted to a kneeling position, then lowered it again. He dropped to one knee before her and placed his hand under her tremulous chin. He raised her head until her jade eyes met his ebony ones. He slowly turned her head from side to side as he checked her injuries.

His blank expression and cool silence alarmed

her. He pushed the neck of her dress over to view the bite White Arrow had spoken about. As he touched it, she winced in pain and began to cry.

She fought to control the fresh flood of tears. She tried to apologize for the trouble she had caused. "I'm sorry, Wanmdi Hota. It was all my fault. I walked too far away. He tried to . . . to . . ." More tears filled her eyes. "Wanhinkpe Ska might have been killed. I would have been to blame, just like the other time with my people. I seem to cause trouble wherever I am."

Teardrops sparkled in those large, sad eyes and slid down her rosy cheeks. To her surprise, he caressed her cheek with the back of his hand and ran a finger lightly over her bruised lips. He went to get the water skin and came back to wash her face. She sat still and silent under his ministrations. His eyes met and locked with her curious ones. He searched her features for signs of more than White Arrow had told him. But her clear, innocent look verified what he hoped to be true.

He pushed her down to the skins and closed her eyes with his fingertip. "Istinma, Cinstinna." She knew he told her to sleep, but the other word she did not know, even though he had used it many times before. He stood up and left. She began to weep sadly, in need of his comfort and embrace, until sleep finally came.

Things returned to their normal pattern and the incident was presumably forgotten. But Alisha could never forget the leering way the trapper had looked at her, nor the brutal way he had tried to rape her. White men could be as savage as he was . . .

White Arrow could not forget how much he had wanted her, nor how hard it had been to stifle his urge to take her himself. He also recalled the way she had clung to him for help and protection. I must have her, he decided, but only after she is mine . . .

Gray Eagle had been unable to forget Alisha's close call with death and danger. Nor could he dismiss thoughts of the dangerous emotions growing in his friend's heart for his winyan. What if she had been killed, taken prisoner by another, or raped? What would he have done? He could not bring himself to think about her death, but the other two thoughts sent him black with rage. How dare anyone try to take or harm what is mine! he raged. I would have tracked him down and slain him!

But what if it turned out to be his koda who stole her or her heart? He wondered what he would do if she turned to his friend for more than friendship, or his friend took more from her. Would his friend keep his word not to touch her, or would he be overcome with her beauty also? Pride and honor were two of the most important things to a warrior. Surely his friend would not sacrifice either for a mere white slave. But his Lese was far more than a mere white slave, far more . . . He hoped he would never be forced to face either of those two situations. He might kill his best friend for such an insult, and her also if she responded . . . Confidently, he decided he would trust his koda's honor and love, and Lese's fear and love for him, to prevent anything like that ever happening. He would not even consider Wanhinkpe Ska's warnings and hints about his having to give her up one day soon.

The days marched on as this pattern of truce dropped back into place. He had not taken her for three nights after the incident. He had sensed her apprehension and fear, and sought to give her a few days to calm down. The first night he had taken her, she cried out in panic and fought him wildly. He had finally managed to quieten her and incite her into submission to him. When it was over, she had refused to leave his embrace all night. She would cry out and toss restlessly in her sleep. Each time, he would comfort her, and she would sleep peacefully again.

Her days slipped back into their schedule of regular tasks, chores and activities. But she could not seem to relax completely. She always worked in a pensive, tense mood while in or near the forest. A short time ago, Matu had returned to camp with the berries and greens they had gathered while she remained behind to gather the firewood.

She glanced around frequently as she worked, in fear of a similar incident like the other day. She tried to calm her fears by talking to herself as she worked. You must forget what happened the other day. It's over. He can't hurt you ever again.

Wanhinkpe Ska killed him . . . for you. Why doesn't Matu come back? Wanmdi Hota wouldn't like it if he knew I was alone. Just a little more wood, and I won't wait for her! I'll go back alone!

As she worked faster, trying to finish quickly, she had not noticed the wind was rising and the sky growing darker. It was so hot and humid today, and her thoughts were on a cool, relaxing swim in the stream. She was reflecting on the summer days she had spent with her father before she had returned to school in the fall. She had often gone swimming with him on many of those days.

Suddenly, a loud crash rent the still air, jarring her back to reality. She looked around for Matu who still had not returned. She was completely alone. The wind picked up and gusted through the trees and grass. She ran out into the open field to see if she could catch a sight of Matu. Her braids swayed in the breeze. She had dropped the wood sling and covered her face as dazzling bolts of lightning zig-zagged across the gray sky. Thunder boomed and vibrated in the air. Rain began to pour down and she was scared.

The heat was almost stifling and the feeling surrounding her awesome. She had been caught in a few storms, but none as violent as this one. There was power and intensity in this storm. The thunder sounded its warning to all who could hear.

She was shaking in fear. She did not know which way to run as lightning struck a nearby tree and sent it crashing to the ground. The storm seemed to cut her off from the village and surround her. She looked around in confusion about what to do.

Above the howling winds and peals of thunder, she heard her name, "Lese . . . Lese . . ."

Her heart lurched in joy. Wanmdi Hota! Overcome with joy and relief, she called out, "Here! In the field . . . Hurry, Wanmdi Hota. Please hurry."

In a moment, he was at her side. She ran into his arms and hugged him tightly. His arms encircled her and pressed her close to his chest. When Matu had returned to the village alone, he knew she was still in the forest. Matu had told him she had returned to bring the mni skins and wota while Alisha gathered the wood. She was going back to fetch her, but secretly hoped she would try to escape, or some ill would befall her again.

Gray Eagle had scowled at her and said she was never to leave her alone again. He said he would go and bring her back this time.

The storm had broken in fury as they talked. He left to search for her. Alisha trembled and clung to him, burying her face on his chest. He pulled her to the ground as other bolts flashed nearby and the storm's fury heightened. Her terror and fear increased.

He covered her trembling lips with his and kissed her passionately, trying to block out the raging of the storm and her fear. They clung together in the tall, wet grass and wildflowers. She did not know when her dress was pushed up above her waist and the breechcloth removed, but she was well aware of the hunger he filled when he entered her.

The storm now raged inside and outside. Their unleashed passions rivaled its very fury. Soon, they were oblivious to the bright lightning, the roaring thunder, and the rain pouring down on them. They were soaked, but all they felt was their heat and thirst for each other.

She responded to his lovemaking with such fierce, unbridled desire, he would be astounded later when he would reflect on it. They flamed their love and desire higher and higher until a final, explosive ecstasy was reached. The pounding in her ears and chest was far greater than the thunder.

As they lay spent in each other's arms, they returned to reality of the wind and rain. The storm had subsided slightly, but a gentle rain continued to fall. Laughing, they replaced and adjusted soaked clothes and started for the village.

She halted and exclaimed, "The wood!" She ran to retrieve the sling and came back to where he waited for her. He wished he could carry it for her this one time, but dared not.

They entered the village unnoticed. All the others were inside to avoid the storm and rain. He built a fire and they exchanged wet clothes for dry ones. She sat by the fire to dry her hair.

When he looked over at her, she smiled serenely as if were the natural thing to do. Her eyes had a soft, happy glow.

The remainder of the day was spent inside. She napped as he sharpened his weapons. As he worked, he would occasionally stop and study her sleeping features. Had her fear of the storm been responsible for her uncontrolled submission to him? He recalled her passionate yielding. She had offered no resistance, mentally or physically, this time. He was aroused just recalling her wild, carefree behavior. Stubbornly, he refused to take her again so soon. It would not be wise to let her see how much and how often I desire her, he reasoned thoughtfully. He smiled contentedly to himself at her slow, but assured, defeat to him. Life was becoming easy and relaxed with her. This both pleased and worried him greatly . . . far too greatly, he mused.

Chapter Eight

Morning arrived with a clear sky and a bright, warm sun. The peaceful, sleepy village began to stir and come to life almost immediately. Gentle rays of sunlight filtered down into the teepee from above. Birds were singing and chirping in the crisp, freshened surroundings. It was going to be a glorious day.

Gray Eagle and a few of his braves left to go hunting. The soft, damp earth made tracking game very easy and quick. They had been gone for a number of hours when loud whoops and yells pierced the still air.

Alisha had finished most of her daily chores and was about to prepare their evening meal. The excitement drew her attention away from her task. She put the knife and meat down to go outside. She wondered what the hunters were bringing in to cause such a wild clamor. Perhaps something huge, dangerous or rare, she mused.

She stepped outside into the dazzling sunlight, squinting momentarily to focus her eyes. The pounding of horses' hooves pulled her line of vision to the right where the braves were charging into the center of camp in an uproar of dust and noise.

Automatically, she halted and stared. Not only were the braves leading several horses laden with fresh game, but also two white trappers, as revealed by their clothing and appearance. The two prisoners were bound securely with their hands behind their backs. She quickly noted they were being pulled forward by ropes tied around their waists leading to the horses laden with game. The pace of the horses forced the two men to a slow run to keep up. One tripped and fell into the dust. The braves continued, allowing the man to be dragged along in the rocky dirt.

Her eyes frantically scanned the group for a sight of Gray Eagle. Suddenly, he came from the rear of the group and moved forward with ease and confidence. She studied his tall, lean frame to be sure he was unharmed. Gray Eagle mistook the intense scrutiny for a show of accusation.

When her searching eyes returned to his, hers met with a cold, dangerous glint which she had known so well, but had not seen lately. She instantly recognized the message he was sending to her, but knew she could and would not obey it. She remained rooted to the spot where she had halted only moments before. Her eyes and brain begged, not again . . . please, not again . . .

His eyes turned to burning coals, warning her not to interfere, to remain silent, to return to his teepee and not defy his authority. She read and ignored all his commands.

She turned and looked on in pity and anger at the men who were stumbling wearily and weakly into camp and the angry braves who were leading them. Tears threatened as she watched the mob preparing for more torture and death. The hostility of the Indian hunters was evident to her. She watched it spread to the people around as they spoke in angry voices, pointing several times to the two men.

The brave who appeared to be the spokesman for the group of hunters told the people how the two men had attacked and killed three of their party. The two men were in the process of scalping the braves when they were taken prisoner. A cry of vengeance roared through the air and filled her ears. She stared at the scene, bewildered by the talking and shouting by the brave and his people. If only she could understand what they were saying and what was happening! With each new burst of words, the people grew angrier and fiercer. Hatred as thick and heavy as an England fog blanketed the camp.

Her eyes were drawn down the line of horses and men to a sickening, saddening sight. There were the bodies of three braves strapped to horses. Most of their bodies were covered by blankets, but she could see bright red blood running down their arms and dripping onto the stony ground. Even the blankets covering them were saturated with blood in several spots. They must have put up a fierce struggle. Once more her eyes scanned the group to see which of the braves was missing. Mahpiya Luta, Hehoka Sapa and Tatanka Yotanka were missing. Sympathy for Gray Eagle touched her raging heart, for Red Cloud had been one of his best friends and companions. She had come to respect and like the aging warrior.

Five more lives . . . she realized she was just as sad about the deaths of the three Oglalas as she was about the deaths of her own kind. Even if death was such a common, expected event in the lives of these people, she still found it difficult to accept. It was far more difficult when it was cold-blooded and unnecessary, like today.

More blood shed . . . more death . . . more suffering for both sides . . . would the hating and killing never end? All the torment and anguish she had witnessed and endured for the past weeks flooded in on her, blocking out the peace and love of the past few days. Without any doubts, she knew what was about to take place. Grief and distress prevailed over common sense and judgment. It was too much . . .

Gray Eagle had watched her face, reading all her thoughts. He had hoped her expression at the sight of Mahpiya Luta's bloody body would overrule her rebellion. He had hoped she would realize the serious gravity of the situation and not interfere. Noting the look on her face, he knew he had hoped in vain. The lives of the two white men were still more important to her than the deaths of three of her enemies, or so he thought. Unaware of the crime the whites had committed, she could not know the justification and demand for their punishments and deaths. He made a very unwise decision when he refused to explain the truth to her.

He maneuvered his horse in front of her, blocking the scene from her vision. She raised her emerald eyes to his, seeking mercy and understanding which were not there. To his dismay, he caught the spark of rebellion and anger which flared in her somber eyes.

He pointed to their teepee and said tersely, "Hiya, Lese! Ya! Iyasni!" Silently, he prayed she would do as he commanded.

She argued with herself. Helplessly, she knew there was nothing she could do for them. Do not risk his wrath and temper turning on you, she warned.

Trying to understand, she asked, "Why, Wanmdi Hota? Why must more suffer and die? Five more lives sacrificed. For what? Surely you don't expect me to stand here in silence, watching while you torture and murder them like you did my own people. I can't!" she nearly screamed at him. "I beg you, do not kill them. Do this much for yourself and me . . ." her voice was filled with pain and sadness. In anguish, she whispered, "If only I knew how to make you understand what I say. Talking to you is like talking to a rock . . ."

More firmly, he repeated his commands again.

As tears began to flow down her cheeks, she turned and ran inside his teepee. He sighed in relief at his victory and her submission. He called White Arrow over to him and said, "You must watch her carefully, my koda. These are her people, but I cannot allow her to interfere. She must accept and deal with her sadness and anger in private. I will take care of this matter while you watch over her. Do not let her leave my teepee or call out."

White Arrow nodded understanding. "I will watch over her." He knew if she openly defied his friend again, he would punish her severely. He did not want to see her suffer or hurt. Her courage, beauty and gentleness played havoc with his reasoning.

White Arrow handed the reins of his mount to a nearby youth. He crossed the short distance to Gray Eagle's teepee, ducked and entered. He stationed himself just inside the opening. He had lowered the flap when he had entered. He thought it best that no one witnessed his concern and guard.

She lay sobbing on the buffalo pallet. He longed to go to her and comfort her. He knew what a grave and foolish mistake that would be and forced those thoughts aside. She is Gray Eagle's winyan, he reminded himself. I must not reach out to her in any way. When he realizes he must give her up, I will bargain for her with all I possess. I will comfort her when she is mine.

His ears and senses became alert as the death

chant began. He listened to the words as he had done so many times before.

Wakantanka, see your children . . .
We come to give lives and hearts of wahmunkesa.
We offer their blood for the blood of our warriors.
Wakantanka, see your children . . .
We send the spirits of the wahmunkesa to you.
Judge them for their evil.
Wakantanka, hear your children . . .
These wahmunkesa are killers of your children.
These wahmunkesa are killers of your animals, our brothers.
Wakantanka, hear your children . . .
Hear the cries of Mahpiya Luta, Hehoka Sapa, Tatanka Yotanka.
Hear the cries of the wahmunkesa, death and vengeance.
Wakantanka, see and hear your children . . .

White Arrow again turned to Alisha. His eyes watched her so intensely she could feel the power in his stare. She was surprised when she raised her hand and found White Arrow standing there instead of Gray Eagle. Their eyes met and locked with an undefinable emotion.

The spell was abruptly broken by a yell which rent the air, followed by a tormented scream. She blanched as white as the snows on the mountain tops. Her chin trembled visibly. Another, and still another yell and scream tore through the silence. As many more followed, she glanced around the teepee in agitation and helplessness. Her hands twisted and fidgeted nervously in her lap. Her teeth tugged at her lower lip. With each new cry, she flinched as if she felt the pains herself.

Soon, she lowered her head and covered her ears with the palms of her hands. Still, this did not shut out the anguish of death. She began to rock back and forth, humming softly to herself. This new ploy did not shut out the pleas and sufferings. A pain-filled voice reached her ears as it pleaded for death and an end to his torment.

Unable to restrain herself, she bounded forward. Before she could reach the entrance, White Arrow seized her by the arms and held her securely. He warned, "Hiya!"

She lifted tormented eyes to his and wept. He put his arms around her and held her gently, but securely. In need of this comfort, she clung to him tightly, her arms encircling his waist.

All of a sudden, Gray Eagle entered and noted the tender scene. His fierce gaze flashed ominously at his friend. Nagging doubts and fears plagued his mind.

White Arrow immediately guessed what his friend thought. He calmly explained he was only giving her comfort in her pain and fear, and preventing her from going outside. Gray Eagle saw how distraught she was and begrudgingly accepted his friend's words. He watched how Alisha clung to him, like a small child.

He came forward and reached for her. As he pulled her unwilling body from White Arrow's embrace, their eyes met for a brief moment. He was shocked and alarmed by the bitterness he read there. Angrily, he knew the truce was ended between them. He felt sadness at this knowledge, for their truce had been so pleasant, but so short. Still, she was his and he would not allow this mood.

Furiously, she jerked her arm from his light, easy grip and backed away without speaking. She stood not far away, glaring at him. His eyes darkened like the deepest night and his jaw tightened noticeably. He looked like a man devil-possessed by her defiance.

He spoke through clenched teeth, "Ku-wa, Lese!" There was a deadliness in his tone which brought panic to her heart. She remained frozen to the spot, noting his rapidly rising fury. She made a foolish move in White Arrow's direction, but he was instantly between them, blocking her escape. She looked past him to White Arrow for assistance, but he lowered his head in refusal.

For some wild, unexplainable reason, she made a grab for Gray Eagle's knife in the sheath at his waist. He seized her small wrist painfully and pulled her struggling body to him. He pinned her arms behind her back with one of his powerful hands in a grip of steel. He slapped her a couple of times, brutally bringing her back to her senses.

Immediately, livid prints appeared on her ashen cheeks. She quivered like a leaf in a strong March wind. Her panic-stricken face drained of all its remaining color, except for the bright red prints on her cheeks and the bruises already forming on her delicate cheekbones. Her lips were slightly parted and dry. She breathed in erratic, shallow pants. He released her and stepped back a few paces.

He held out his hand to her, repeating his previous command and daring her to refuse again. She stared at the outstretched hand as if it were a snake about to strike. She raised her hands to touch her stinging cheeks. She stared incredulously at the man she had come to love and fear above all others. Too terrified to refuse, she extended a cold, quivering hand to him.

Yielding to his command and power would not be enough this time. The look in her eyes and on her face moments before demanded to be punished and corrected. He captured her hand in a grip of iron and began to bend her fingers backwards. He would wipe out any and all defiance left in her this very night. Never would she look at him that way again, nor treat him with such open disrespect and hostility. She would see and feel what it was like to push him too far.

In his fury, he increased the pressure as his eyes blazed into hers. Knuckles cracked loud in the still silence. Pains shot into her wrist and up her forearm. Furiously, he vowed, you will not fight or resist me this way, Little One. You will do as I command without hesitation.

Once more, she gazed pleadingly at White Arrow in agony and fear. He watched the scene in suppressed hostility and rage, but dared not interfere. She comprehended she could expect no help from him. Her eyes returned to Gray Eagle's face.

She recalled the night in the smokehouse clearly and knew it would not do any good to beg or apologize. He would do as he wished. Tears blinded her vision and she had to blink several times to clear it. She determined he would have to break her hand before she would grovel further to him, like some whimpering, beaten animal. Why did he receive so much pleasure from her suffering?

Incensed, her other hand flew up to slap him. Before the blow landed, he easily captured it in the same viselike hold. Inflamed at her daring action, he increased the pressure again. He could not believe she had dared to strike him. Would he be forced to break her hand before he broke her will? Why could she not learn her lesson and yield to his greater power and position?

Thankfully, only White Arrow had seen this audacious outburst. The penalty for striking a chief or his son meant certain death! Would she never fear or respect him so much that she would cease this futile and foolish struggle?

She bit into her cheek to keep from crying out.

Blood began to flow from the corner of her mouth and eased down her chin. You must yield and beg mercy, he vowed. I will have it no other way!

It took every ounce of her willpower to remain silent. He gritted his teeth and tightened his hold, increasing the tension. He wondered just how much more she could stand before giving up. Her bravery and determination annoyed, yet pleased him. But it also angered him to be forced to continue this display of power.

As he applied more pressure, she began to kneel in hopes of reducing or weakening his grip. By the time she was to the ground on her knees, he had eased to one knee, staying just close enough to retain his hold and the pressure.

"The past few days have all been lies and tricks! You still hate me as much as ever. You will never allow me to penetrate that wall around your heart. That is, if you even have one. I will not beg mercy from you this time, Wanmdi Hota. You'll have to crush both my hands before I yield. I hate you! You're a savage! A bloody savage! I'll never belong to you, ever! I'll die before I let you touch me again." She accused boldly, "Murderer! Killer of women and children! Beast! One day, I'll cut your evil, black heart out with your own knife!" She yelled at him in anger and pain, hoping he could grasp a few of the words, or at least their tone and meaning.

Disregarding the Indian custom, Chela threw the flap aside and entered at that heated moment. She had heard the angry voices coming from inside his teepee and could not resist the chance to see Alisha punished or shamed. She smiled sardonically as she witnessed the duel of wills, knowing who the victor would be. She was surprised and angered he did not kill her immediately for her actions. He is too easy with this white whore, she fumed. He will be sorry for this one day and for the way he has shamed me before the other women. He is mine and no other will have him . . . no one . . .

She looked at the determination and rage on his face, and the suffering and defiance on the white girl's. This was more than she had hoped for. He would see now he must kill or trade her. His pride demanded he break her spirit and will first. She felt heat spring inside her loins and fill her with desire as she watched him hungrily. His hard muscles rippled with each movement. He possessed a spirit no other warrior could compare with. She watched the handsome face with the crooked half-smile and the flashing, angry, black eyes, the color of darkest night. Her ebony eyes caressed his body like a physical touch. I must have you soon, Cante, she thought. These fires which burn within me will surely go wild if they are not fed! How can you desire a white whore over your chosen one? She must be destroyed to end this magic she casts over your eyes.

Chela remained at White Arrow's side watching happily. "What has the ska winyan done to lose favor with him? Is he going to kill her? He must!" She boldly taunted, "How much longer will the greatest Oglala warrior yield to a mere ska witkowin?"

White Arrow whirled to face her in disbelief and anger. He ordered her to silence and respect. His look momentarily did just that. He looked forward again. Chela continued to glare icily at him. Comprehending his true meaning, she hissed, "She has you under her magic also. You will both regret the day you found her and brought her here. She will only bring trouble and an evil curse. If he cannot find the courage to kill her, then he must trade her to the Cheyenne. She must not remain here."

She stared at him contemptuously, then sauntered over to Gray Eagle's side. She encouraged more pain and suffering for the white girl she hated above all others. Sarcastically, she implored, "Let me help you, Cante. I will happily cut her to pieces. I can remove that face which blinds you both. A few cuts and scars and she will no longer be so beautiful and desirable."

At Chela's appearance and the sound of her vindictive, venomous voice, Alisha stiffened in renewed determination. She would not yield before them. Gray Eagle saw the new spark of fire and rebellion in Alisha's face and eyes, and was furious at Chela's appearance.

Soon, the pain became excruciating and she knew she could not hold out much longer. He saw the flickering of doubt and hastily pressed his advantage.

In desperation, she struggled to think of some diversion. Noting the smirk on Chela's face, she thought, I will teach that cruel, selfish girl a lesson of my own. I will tempt him right before her eyes. Recalling how she had seen Chela flirt with him in front of her, she copied her actions.

Softening her gaze and tone, she spoke to him, "I love you, Wanmdi Hota. No matter how much you hurt me or hate me. I have loved you since the first time I saw you." A note of pride tinged her voice and face as she continued with the first thing that came to mind. "You stood there so proud and daring that day, challenging them with your very presence and power. How I wanted you, without even knowing it or why. But in time, I will escape from you, for you will never forgive or forget that I am white and your enemy. Why must it be so, Wanmdi Hota? Why did you act as though you wanted me all these weeks? Why did you allow me to believe I could . . . that we could . . . no matter now . . ." As she pressed her body to his, her eyes searched his for a flicker of hope.

She tried to concentrate on anything other than the pain in her hands and Chela's chattering voice. She wanted to scream at her to shut up and to leave. She whispered to him, so close he could feel the wind from her breath, "I would gladly have been your slave if you did not force me to endure the torture of my people. I could love you with all my heart if you would only allow it . . ." She leaned forward and shocked them all by kissing him passionately and boldly.

Chela went wild with rage and jealousy. She grabbed Alisha's hair and yanked fiercely, pulling her away from him. She screamed at Alisha, "Witkowin! How dare you? He is mine! I will kill you for this insult."

Without a change in his expression or position, Gray Eagle spoke to White Arrow, "Wanhinkpe Ska, get her out before I kill her."

Chela released Alisha's hair and stared dumbfounded at him. The deadly calm of his tone told her he meant what he said, but still she questioned, "Surely you would not punish or kill me because of this ska witkowin? What is she but a kaskapi and witkowin? Do I hear you right?" She glared at him in fury, challenging him to deny her words or defend himself. He did neither.

He did not respond to her accusations in any way as White Arrow dragged her out of the teepee. Boldly, she fought, kicked, and cursed him as she hurled insults and threats at all of them. He would deal with Chela later. Right now, there were more important things at hand. His obsidian eyes bored into Alisha's.

Unable to resist any longer, her resolve crumbled and she wept openly. She wondered why she had not been fully aware of his sadistic nature by now. Hadn't she been shown enough evidence of it?

She moistened her dry lips and swallowed her pride. Solemnly, she spoke, "I am no match against your strength or hatred, Wanmdi Hota. If it matters at all, I yield."

She could not check the flow of tears which followed her submission. As they streamed down her cheeks, she lowered her head in defeat and despair.

His victory concluded, he released his grip. She gently massaged her hands and wrists as the tears dropped onto them. Time passed, but he did not move away or speak. He lifted her chin with his fingers and gazed into it, trying to decide how much to believe of what she had said. Were her words only lies brought out by her pain or as a taunt? Why should it even matter what she thought or felt? But for some reason, it did.

Reading the suffering in her emerald eyes, he knew he should have controlled his anger. He should not have struck out at her so brutally. Were her feelings so wrong or her actions so un-expected? Perhaps she would not have fought him if she had known why the prisoners had to die. But he would and could not be placed in a position of explaining his judgments and actions to her or any winyan. She must accept these things without defiance or questions.

She looked sadly into his eyes and asked, "Why do you hate me so much, Wanmdi Hota? What have I done to you that you want to hurt me this way? Is it only because I am white? If only you could talk to me, or I to you, then you could tell me how to stop this hatred between us. There is so much I do not know or understand. If only I could hate you as you hate me . . ."

Her words and torment cut deeply into his heart. He was tempted to tell her everything, but could not. For a time, he wished he were not Wanmdi Hota, but only a man. But man cannot change who or what he is and what he must do. He pulled her into his embrace and held her tightly for a long time. Can she not feel or know that I do not hate her? he anguished. Can she not see this is how things must be for now and accept it? If only I were freed from my obligations and responsibilities to my people, then I could tell her the truth and reveal my love to her.

Alisha was bewildered by his fierce embrace and brooding silence after what had just taken place between them. He was as changeable as the winds. One minute he was as violent and destructive as the monsoon; the next, as warm and gentle as a prairie breeze.

Her battle-weary spirit offered no resistance. What good did it do to fight him? He was always the victor in their wars. Besides, she needed this small comfort he offered. She willingly and limply melted into his arms and clung to him, maybe for the last time, she grieved.

He is probably deciding my fate right now, she thought, and there is nothing I can do to influence it in any way. Abruptly, he released her and left quickly, without a word or backward look. She sat staring at the trembling flap for a time, pondering what his actions might be. I was a fool, she thought with dismay, to interfere tonight or to have believed everything would work out some day. How could I have forgotten for one minute what I am or what he is truly like? What difference does it make now? It's too late to recall my words or actions. It would be far easier to recall the sands of time in an hourglass. I will die as all the others did before me. But why has he waited so long? Why did he even bother to keep me at all? There is no understanding him or his ways. She sat there still and silent awaiting his verdict.

Gray Eagle had left quickly, not trusting himself to be near her any longer. Something drastic must be done, he decided, and I dread it. I must be alone to plan how to handle this matter.

He walked along in a deep, solemn mood. Quietly, he passed the rows of teepees and corral where the horses grazed contentedly on lush buffalo grass. His scent was so familiar they hardly noted his passing.

He finally halted on a small, sandy knoll and gazed intently out across the vast, empty plains. Barren, and yet, he knew even now in the soft twilight, life was just beginning for the night creatures. When hunwi showed her face at night, she gave them the signal to come to life and carry on with their purpose.

This night was so like, and yet so unlike, many others before it. Many times, he had walked alone in the night or ridden off alone in the cool pre-dawn to ponder his thoughts and troubles. When he would go out alone and sit quietly on a grassy knoll or on a high boulder in the rosy dawn or silver twilight, he was as one with the land and the Great Spirit. He could think, plan, and listen with his mind and heart. He could reason what was best for him and his people. His burden was so great with his father away. He must prove his wisdom, courage and leadership to himself and his people.

Why now, of all times, had he found this white girl who was such an obsession with him? Why was her life so important to him? Was he not a great and fierce warrior of the mighty Oglala? Was he not Wanmdi Hota, son of a chief, and she, a mere white female slave, worthless of all possessions? Why had the wasichus not remained in their own lands to the East? Why did they have to encroach and defile his lands and forests?

I cannot hold out my hand to her in love or acceptance. I must stand true in strength and honor before my people and the Great Spirit. The laughter from the other tribes at my taking her would be heard as coyotes in the wind. They think she is unworthy of my touch and acceptance, or any warrior's. They do not see the winyan I see and know. They did not see her courage at her fortress against her own people for me. They have not seen her suffer at my hands for herself and her people.

He could not comprehend why this should matter to him either. He should be rejoicing in her suffering, or that of any white eyes. He should laugh and be happy when he saw her pain and sadness. But my heart does not beat happy at these things, he grieved. I cannot tell her what she must do or why. I cannot tell her why her people must be punished and die. I cannot praise her work and learning, even though both have been great and good. These are things a slave must accept in silence. Why is this problem so difficult to solve and understand? The sadness and pain in her eyes and voice rip at my heart like the eagle rips at his captured prey.

The time for possessing her heart and spirit was the night of the storm when she came to me so openly and freely. That time has passed and cannot be returned. If I had but given her a word or a sign of love that day . . . no! She is a ska ista and I am Oglala. Our paths are set and guided by the Great Spirit. Each must walk his own. She will forever be a white slave, and I, an Oglala warrior.

I must be strong! I must not let her love and my desire for her reach me, except on my o-winza at night. We met as enemies and so it must remain until Wakantanka wishes to change it. I can only pray and hope he will some day.

The capture of the wahmunkesa tonight forced her to turn once more to Wanhinkpe Ska instead of me. If only for one moon I was not Wanmdi Hota, then I could love and comfort her. In my anger and suspicion, I strike out at her too harshly, causing much more pain and hate. Submission will be easier for her if she did come to fear and hate me, but do I want it so?

His heart cried out, you do not wish her to

hate you. Fear you, sha, but hate, never. His brain replied, but why should it matter to you if she hates you? You could kill her with one slash of your knife, or sell her for only one crippled horse! He smote his breast and shouted aloud, "I am Wanmdi Hota! How dare she do this to me. I could crush her with my bare hands if I wished it so." Pride and power surged through him at these thoughts.

He stood up and stared up at hunwi. "I will yield to no winyan! Does she not see I cannot? Surely she cannot believe a warrior could love a white slave! Winyans are to work for their owners and obey them in all things. She is not even my winyan. She is only my slave. I own the very life she has. She must come to learn this. It is not my way to feel these things for a winyan. She brings out a weakness in me which I cannot allow to show. These thoughts and feelings send warnings to my mind. A warrior cannot hold these feelings in his heart for the life of an enemy."

Tormented, he asked himself the dreaded question, "Why do I not remove this temptation from my life and sight? Why do I not kill her this very night?" But his heart answered for him, if you do, you will be forever parted, for the wasichus do not walk the Mahpiya Ocanku. His mind argued again, why do you not sell her to another? Once more, his heart responded, you cannot allow any man to take what has been yours, or place his seeds of life were you have placed yours. Nor can you allow another to feel and know the love which beats in her heart for . . . Fool! he scolded himself. After tonight, she will hate you forever.

During the past few months, he recalled, life has been happy with her. Each time I have forced her to admit her love and need for me has brought happiness and joy to my heart. Each time I have seen her learn something new, my pride has soared like the eagle. She has learned much since coming here. If she is as different from the others as I truly believe, then why do I treat her as the same? Why do I not accept this one, special wasichu?

Why do my heart and blood pound wildly when she is near? Why does the very scent of her, or sound of her voice, or sight of her bring this longing to my heart and body? Why does her image appear before me in the stream, or in my mind at night? Why do I wish her close to me at all times? He could not face the answer to his questions, for it would be to admit he loved and needed her.

He thought, I knew as soon as I saw her face tonight she would defy me and the death of her people. The others would not have accepted her attack on me again. If she had raged out at me or fought me as before, I would have been forced to kill her to save my honor before them. Why can she not see and know these things?

I have her, and yet, I do not have her. I cannot keep her, and yet, I cannot give her up. "Help me, Wakantanka," he prayed fervently. "What must I do with this girl? Is her death necessary to free me from her power of love? Must I sacrifice her life for my honor and that of my people? Is there not some way I can save face and keep her also? Can I not have both?

"You have given me great strength and courage. I now ask for wisdom and strength for what must be done. How can our lives and hearts touch when we remain enemies? Why did you let me find and take her if only to lose her now? Do you test my courage and obedience once more?

"I am a great warrior in my people's eyes. Give me the girl's life and the freedom to take and keep her. You are all powerful and all knowing, Wakantanka. Give the heart and life of Lese to me and the acceptance of my people. This war within my heart brings out only my cruelty to her."

He sat down cross-legged and stared off into the darkness, waiting for an answer to his prayer. He tried to clear his mind of all thoughts and his heart of all emotions so the Great Spirit could speak to him. Patiently he waited . . .

The night creatures became still and silent for a time. Clouds drifted before the full moon, obscuring its light. The whole land seemed to be hushed and waiting. This quiescence seemed to be Wakantanka's way of saying, I cannot see or speak to you. It is not the time for my answer. Soon, I will show you what you must do. Until then, you must wait and be patient.

Perhaps the Great Spirit was testing both of

them. Perhaps he waited to see if the white girl deserved to live and belong to him. Perhaps he waited to see just how important she was to him and to see what changes she would bring about in his heart and life. Perhaps she must be taught obedience and respect first. Thankfully, the Great Spirit left him with hope by not asking for her death. Did he have some plan for them which he did not see or understand yet? Somehow their destinies were locked together, but he did not know how.

His mind reasoned with him, the eagle soars alone and so must you, Wanmdi Hota. At least, for now. You must be strong and show no weakness. You must take this girl when you desire her, but you must not allow her to touch your heart until Wakantanka says it can be.

Until the Great Spirit tells me what I must do, her defiance must be struck down. If I cannot do this, then she must die. His decision was hard and bitter, but he accepted the truth of it. He arose and began his way back to his teepee with heavy heart.

As he walked along, he pondered, how can I force this obedience? I must prevent her turning to Wanhinkpe Ska. What punishment would she fear the most? What would bring this fear to her heart? Would she fear losing me and my protection enough to yield to me completely? If she feared I was going to give her to another, or others, would she come to me and beg me to keep her? Would she promise to never interfere or disobey again? If I could show her how bitter and harsh her life would be without me, would she come to me once more in submission and love? She must be taught this lesson. She must see and know it is Wanmdi Hota she needs and must obey. She must learn I have the power to keep her or to cast her aside. She will learn that no one, not even Wanhinkpe Ska, can help her if I forbid it. This lesson must be quick, cold and cruel. I must find the one thing which will reach her . . .

He sat down by the stream and tossed small pebbles into the water, watching the ripples spread out into the darkness of the water. He could see her in his mind's eye as she splashed in the water and ran laughing through the tall grass and flowers with his koda. That's it! Wanhinkpe Ska . . . He is the one person she likes and trusts. He will be the one to bring her the most hurt and sadness. She thinks he is her koda. Cruelty from him would serve both purposes. It will force a wedge in their closeness and cause her to turn only to me. It will also force her to see I control her life.

But how could Wanhinkpe Ska punish her without really hurting her? What would cause her to hate him and fear me? It must be a pain to her spirit and not her body. She is very brave and suffers too long in silence. What would bring pain to her heart? He searched his thoughts. The wokasketipi . . . yes, she would meet him there. After that, she would no longer have these mixed feelings for him. She will fear my sending her there again as punishment if she defies me again. I will be the only one she can turn to in her sadness and shame. She will be sure to never provoke me to such anger again. Yes, the wokasketipi is the answer, but it must be done quickly.

But for the first time in his life, his courage and daring seemed to falter.

He returned to the village and went to Wanhinkpe Ska's teepee. He clearly and slowly related his plan to him. He told him exactly what to do and how. He was determined to teach her of her place this very night and have it done with. He said only the Brown girl was in the red teepee.

He stated his plan to White Arrow firmly, "I will bring her there to you in a short time. You will handle her very roughly with great desire. You will kiss her and place your hands on her as if you are about to rape her. You can do what you must to convince her she is about to be attacked by you, but you are not to hurt her. After she is filled with great fear and the truth of her position, you will let her flee the teepee sa. I will be close by. She will run to me, begging for my mercy and help. I will grant both. She will be so scared and grateful to me that she will never defy me again."

White Arrow stared at him in disbelief as he related this brutal plan. He blurted out, "You cannot be serious, my koda! You cannot truly wish to do this thing to her! Is this lesson so important that you would hurt her this way? Did you not already punish her this night? You will cause her much sadness and shame. I do not wish to be a part of this trick. You must ask another to do this for you. She is white, but I cannot find hate or contempt in my heart for her."

Gray Eagle exclaimed tersely, "No! It must be you for the plan to work."

White Arrow paced around nervously and pondered just what it really was his friend was asking him to do. He was fully aware that he would be able to embrace, kiss and caress the woman he loved and desired for the first time and with his friend's consent and knowledge. Many times he had longed to take her into his arms and never let her go. He had hungered to feel her lips pressed next to his, to feel her arms around his neck, and to have her beneath him in love. Surely she would resist my forced attack on her, he assumed. Or would she? Is it possible she will be too frightened to fight me, or be submissive to provoke Wanmdi Hota? Could this night reveal things Wanmdi Hota will be forced to face which he does not expect? Perhaps she will turn to me completely in revenge. She will know he orders this thing. I must not be brutal to her. I must let her feel my love in my kiss and touch. These thoughts brought a raging fire to his loins.

Suddenly, prickling, cold sensations ran down his arms and spine.

"I cannot do this for you, my koda," he stated

317

simply. "You ask too much of me, and perhaps of the girl also."

Gray Eagle demanded, "You must! It will be quickest and cruelest corning from you. If I chose someone else, she would only turn to you instead of me out of anger and hurt. I cannot allow that. It must be you and tonight."

White Arrow was apprehensive at the approaching deception. "But she trusts and accepts me. Is this why you really chose me? You know she will hate me and reject my friendship after this. I feel you will long regret this night if you go through with this."

White Arrow's reasoning was to no avail. Gray Eagle ordered his friend, "Go to the teepee sa and I will bring her to you. May this night bring an end to her resistance and renew our truce." He left White Arrow standing there looking after him with a pain-filled heart.

White Arrow gazed up at the full moon and thought, this will be a night long remembered. It will cause great pain for many. I feel a coldness in the night air like death. He shivered again uncontrollably. He went to his appointed place to wait.

Gray Eagle returned to his teepee and called for Alisha to come with him. She had been sitting on the buffalo skins, silently praying for his mercy and understanding. His voice told her nothing. Dispirited and unsuspecting, she rose and followed him.

It was but minutes before she realized they

were standing before the entrance to the wokas-ketipi. She focused horrified, disbelieving eyes on him. Surely, he doesn't mean . . . His expression quickly told her that her darkest fear was a reality. Anything but this, her mind screamed.

She began to back away in panic. White-faced and shaking, she shook her head and protested, "No! You can't put me in there. Please, Wanmdi Hota. I'll do anything you ask. I'll never defy you again, in anything or any way. Please, hiya."

His granite features never changed. She turned to flee, but he easily overtook her. He captured her arms in a grip of iron and pulled her struggling body into the teepee sa.

Instantly, she was humiliated by what was taking place between Kathy and a young brave. She turned away, face flaming, to come face to face with White Arrow. She begged help from him. The look on his face made her blood run cold and her body stiffen in alarm. There was no sign of compassion or kindness written there. Instead, she read a look of bold, open desire. He licked his lower lip in anticipation as his burning eyes caressed her. He reminded himself he must play his part in this game to the fullest.

She panicked. Had she been brought here as punishment? Or was she here as payment for some deed he had done for Wanmdi Hota? Perhaps she was going to be put here for good to be used by any brave. Was he giving her up? Did he no longer want her?

"No, not you, Wanhinkpe Ska . . ." she whis-

319

pered. "You can't be a party to this new degradation."

Any doubts vanished. She knew he was and there was nothing she could do about it. "He has chosen my persecutor wisely and carefully." She felt crushed and defeated by this new torture and betrayal. She suddenly felt totally alienated from both of them, and even from life itself. It was more than she could endure.

She turned to Gray Eagle and intently searched his face as she had done with White Arrow. She knew immediately she had guessed correctly. All doubts were dismissed. Her pulse raced wildly as she panted through slightly parted, parched lips. That wintry face told her all she dreaded to believe. His icy eyes bored into hers. She swayed slightly at the full comprehension of the meaning of her situation. He would never want her back after tonight. He was far too proud to accept a common, used squaw. The full extent of his hatred and cruelty was like a vicious slap in the face. To find he could do something like this tore savagely at her heart. This was incredible after all they had been to each other. Lies! All of it had only been lies and taunts.

She knew it would be useless to yield defeat this time. It had gone far beyond a battle of wills between them. Yes, he had chosen her attacker wisely, for he had selected the only Indian who was her friend. Tears welled in her eyes and she blinked to clear her vision. She shuddered visibly and struggled to breathe.

She spoke almost inaudibly, "I'll never forgive you if you allow this. I'll hate you and curse you until the day I die. If you feel anything, anything at all, for me, then stop this charade now before it's too late for both of us. I'll die before I let him or anyone else take me this way. This I swear to you, Wanmdi Hota!" She shivered and trembled as if she were standing in snow.

White Arrow pulled her around to face him. He entwined his fingers in her soft, silky hair and pulled her face to his. Her pupils became suddenly very large and a dull glaze settled over them. Her crying had ceased and her face paled. She did not plead again, nor did she resist when White Arrow pulled her into his loving embrace. He lowered his lips to hers and kissed her passionately.

Only moments before, Gray Eagle had heard her mutter softly, "I hate you . . . I hate you both . . ." This was the last thing she would remember of this treacherous night.

White Arrow's lips traveled across her face and throat with hungry, fiery kisses to return to her unresponsive lips. He took her mouth fully with great desire. Still, there was no reaction from her. She stared unseeing beyond him into space. Her skin chilled like ice covering a winter pond. Her body was rigid as the rocks. Her mind had traveled a great distance away. Her spirit had gone to hide in that secret world where one neither sees, hears, feels nor knows any pain or reality.

She did not feel his kisses or caresses. She did

not see him rip her dress to the waist. She did not see the look of lust or love in his eyes for her and her beautiful body. She did not feel his hand gently caress her breast. She did not hear the words he murmured softly to her. For Alisha, time stood still . . .

White Arrow was the first one who was alerted of something wrong. At first, he had thought her reaction as one of shock and fear. But now, he knew better. She neither responded nor resisted him in any way. He leaned back and gazed into her pale, trance-like face. He studied it for a few moments, then looked past her to Gray Eagle with a look of worry and concern on his face.

Gray Eagle had not left yet and knew from White Arrow's expression something was wrong. He had observed her rigid body give neither response nor fight. He came forward and pulled her around to lace him. He, too, noted the vacant stare and a chill passed over him. He passed his hand before her eyes . . . nothing. He shook her by the shoulders and called her name . . . nothing. Alarmed, he slapped her. Still nothing, except for the livid red print upon her ashen face. She had not even blinked. From all appearances, she did not even breathe. He recalled her words of death before submission. He panicked. Could a person wish death upon himself? he wondered in dread. He looked troubled and bewildered, not knowing what to do.

White Arrow spoke up, "I told you this would be too much for her. She has fled to the Great

Spirit for protection. He has accepted her and will not allow her to be hurt anymore. She is important to him in some way for he has watched over her many times. He may not let her return to you for I have felt the chill of death in the wind this night. There is evil in this deed, my koda. I tried to warn you, but you would not listen."

Gray Eagle ignored his admonishment and told him to go for the shaman's helper. "Bring him to my teepee. I will return her spirit to her body this very night. I will not let her go. She is mine, Wanhinkpe Ska! He will send her back to me." But silently and prayerfully he added, He must!

He wrapped a blanket around Alisha. He gently lifted her body into his quivering arms and carried her toward his teepee. White Arrow quickly went to summon the shaman's helper in the medicine lodge.

Kathy would never know just how lucky she was that neither of the two men had seen her vengeful smile or heard her pleased, cruel laughter after they left the teepee. If either had, she would have been killed instantly. She maliciously thought, she has seen what it is like to be a real prisoner for a change. Whatever she did to lose favor with her brave, I bet she does it again. How I would love to see him put her here for good! If she were here, I'd never have to be used again. She would be the one to claim all those red savages' attention. Perhaps I could choose whom I would like to give my attentions to. Maybe even go to one brave as his own. Perhaps the handsome brave who has her now, or his friend. Both are handsome and powerful and neither appears to be very mean if you don't cross them. If I plan it just right, I could wind up in his teepee in her place. She laughed to herself thinking how nice life would become as a slave to such a virile warrior.

The brave above her grunted and thrusted forcefully into her. She surprised him by hungrily taking all he gave and begging for more, mentally pretending it was Gray Eagle who was taking her. She squirmed teasingly and raised her hips to meet each thrust. Her arms went up around his back and she clung to him in animal lust. Her response inflamed him to greater hunger and passion, believing his lovemaking had such power even a white slave couldn't resist him. Arrogance and pride swept through him and he worked on her with greater lust.

His fire and passion soon passed to Kathy. Forgotten were thoughts of pretending he was Gray Eagle or of resistance and deceit. Animal lust and pleasure filled her mind and thoughts. All the nerves in her body were tense and tingling. Liquid fire ran in her veins. She was consumed with the desire for fulfillment of these strange new cravings and feelings. The more she responded and worked with him, the better the feelings and the higher the cravings. When ecstasy was reached, she realized what she had been denying herself all these years with men and all this time here in the teepee. She thrashed about wildly under him and moaned with pleasure. Slowly, the feeling ebbed and passed and relaxation came. At that moment, she decided she would give her all to any brave who came to her from now on. Just look how her meager response had been rewarded — the brave had openly desired and wanted her, and there were the other rewards deep within her own body. How she wished she had known of these things sooner!

Soon, Kathy thought, Alisha's brave or his friend will come to me. I will fill him with such pleasure he will be unable to resist me. And you, my little Alisha, will take my place here. He will learn that I can please him in ways she knows nothing about. She smiled, confident she would soon possess Gray Eagle or White Arrow for her own and leave the tipi sa forever. Pathetically, Kathy did not realize she had just set and sealed the pattern and destiny for the remainder of her life.

Chapter Nine

Gray Eagle rushed straight to his teepee with Alisha and laid her down on his mat to wait for the shaman's helper. Tension mounted inside him as he stared into the blank, unseeing eyes before him. He held her cold, rigid hand in his and spoke softly to her. Nothing . . .

Ckulaketua entered the teepee and examined the inert girl. He asked many questions about what had brought on this state. Gray Eagle painfully related the events in the wokasketipi. Ckulaketua pictured this gentle-spirited girl in his mind and what she must have endured. He fully understood and recognized her condition. He had seen it a few times before. He told them it usually followed an event which was too difficult for a person, most often women or children, to accept. He called it spirit-hiding. He explained how her spirit had gone to hide and heal the hurt and shame the brave had forced on her tonight.

He said this condition could last for hours, days or longer. There was no real danger to her life unless she refused to awaken soon. Her fight to keep her spirit hidden would be determined by how deep and painful the hurt and shame were. Spirit-hiding was used as a protection against madness and reality.

He mixed a fine yellow powder with water in a small crucible. He forced this potion down her throat, holding her nose to force her to swallow. He began to shake a small wagmula as he chanted softly and melodiously. Slowly the potion took effect. Her eyes closed and the color began to return to her face. He ceased his chanting and touched her arm. The chill left her body and she relaxed in a deep sleep.

Ckulaketua smiled and said this was a good sign. It meant her spirit did not hide too deeply or resist being forced to return to them. In his chant, he had called on the spirit helpers to lead her wandering spirit back while she slept, and to protect it on its dangerous journey. He told Gray Eagle she would sleep for a long time, then he departed silently.

Ckulaketua paused outside the teepee to lift his head and give thanks to the Great Spirit for his help. Never had the pain of a white-eyes touched him before. Why this fragile creature brushed his heart and pity, he could not understand. As surely as I am Oglala, he thought, she is protected and used by the Great Spirit. He has used me to heal and restore her spirit for his purpose.

Sleep for a long time was exactly what she did.

She slept all night, the next day and all the following night. Gray Eagle watched over her closely and protectively during the long hours.

When she finally awoke, she still felt drowsy and weak. The facts of the night before, as she recalled them, painfully flooded her mind. But she could not recall anything past the first few, agonizing minutes. What had happened after that? Had Wanhinkpe Ska raped her? She couldn't or wouldn't remember. If so, she hoped and prayed she never would remember that night.

She was filled with anguish as she recalled how close they had become and how good he had been to her. She had trusted him and accepted him as her friend. She had helped to save his life. Her only friend . . . how could he do this horrible thing to her? Had he only feigned his acceptance and friendship? Had he only been waiting for the day when Wanmdi Hota would let him take her? Surely he hadn't believed she would respond out of gratitude to him. Perhaps she had misread his intentions all along. Was it all deceit and lies? Was it all some cruel joke to taunt her and make a fool of her? Were they all laughing at her stupidity?

How could he have done this to me if I am truly his koda? My whole life here has been filled with lies and deceptions. I am all alone now. No one loves or cares for me. I doubt if he ever did. She wondered if the wokasketipi would be a part of her life from now on, perhaps as punishment or reward to friends for deeds.

In torment, she cried out, "I wish I had never awakened. I wish I had been murdered at the fortress with all the others. No torture could be as brutal as last night's. Ben and the others are lucky — they can suffer no more. Will this Hell never end? How much more suffering will I be forced to endure for helping and loving him? Let my debt be paid or forgiven.

Gray Eagle had entered moments before and stood silently listening to her tormented words. She felt his presence and turned. She glared at him as though she could punish him with only a look. There was no visible light or sparkle in those large, sad eyes which glowered at him.

Her thoughts screamed at him. Her eyes chilled and narrowed as she thought vehemently, I will never accept this kind of brutality to my people or myself! Never will I go willingly to the wokasketipi! I will be your slave and harlot, but never the other things! I will force you into killing me first!

He remained still, returning her long, chilly stare until she turned away from his scrutiny. Why did she always feel as if he were reading her deepest, most secret thoughts? It was as though he probed her very heart and soul with those piercing, ebony eyes. He would gaze deeply into her eyes and read her like a map or open book. She mused bitterly, if he really can, then he knows how much I loathe and despise him, and long for the day I am free from him and this place, even if death is the only way out . . .

He touched her shoulder and said, "Woyetu, mni, Lese. Ku-wa." His gentle tone angered her greatly.

She jerked her shoulder back as if he had burned her with his touch. She moved so abruptly she nearly fell over. Struggling to remain upright and show no weakness or pain to him, she shouted, "Don't touch me! Ever! I hate you!"

She lowered her face to her hands, trying to conquer her confusing dizziness. Her head felt light, but her body heavy. Unaware she had been unconscious for two days, she was bewildered by this strange feeling. She wanted to refuse the food and water, but quickly realized she would need her strength to escape if the chance ever arose. Surely a chance would come some day soon.

She reluctantly gave in. She turned to look where he had been standing, but he had silently left, leaving the food and water where he had been only moments before. Angrily she thought, if starving me would only hurt and not kill his slave and harlot, chances are he would do it. To be completely dependent on him for her very life and existence was maddening.

I must be free of him, she resolved. I must! I will surely go mad or die if my chance doesn't come soon.

Don't wait for a chance to slap you in the face, Lese, she scolded herself. Make your own chances . . . She toyed with the idea for a time. I must plan and prepare. I must be ready to flee at a moment's notice. One day, he will be looking the wrong way, or be gone hunting, or stay all night in the medicine lodge, and I will escape him and this savage land. He will never see or hear of me again. I only regret I can't repay his cruelty or make him feel the shame and hurt he has inflicted on me. If he were my prisoner for only one week, I would . . . I would . . . Her train of vindictive thoughts halted, for she knew deep inside she could not do anything any different than she had the first time he had been a prisoner to her people. Damn him! she cried, for I still could not bring myself to hurt or hate him. God help me for I have lost my heart and soul to a brutal savage.

Weak and exhausted, she reclined on the mat and laid her limp arm across her eyes. She vainly tried to drive all thoughts of him and what he had done to her from her battle-weary mind and heart, at least for a little while. She needed to rest and plan.

As she dozed lightly, she did not hear him enter. He stopped at the teepee's entrance and studied her for a minute to see if she were sleeping. Guessing not, he called for her to come to him. At the sound of his voice and command, she lowered her arm and sat up. Her new resolve and determination to rebel against him were quickly forgotten as she faced him. He called for her to come with him once more. This time the command was given more sternly.

Why do I always cower in fear to him? she asked herself in disgust. Why not just refuse and stand up to him and his evil treatment of me? What more can he do to hurt me? Instantly, she knew what he could do. Fear stormed her brain. The wokasketipi . . . Surely he wouldn't take me there again. Is he angry at the way I treated him a while ago? Can't he understand how upset I was? No, he wouldn't understand anything like compassion, mercy or pity.

When will I ever learn to curb my tongue and outbursts? It doesn't do any good to argue or resist. It only makes things worse for me. Wouldn't he have left me there last night if he didn't want me for himself? Maybe he won't tolerate the slightest rebellion from me now. I proved to him last night how powerful and devastating this new weapon is. He'll use it without mercy against me.

Her head and heart were pounding wildly. No . . . not again! She placed her cold, trembling fingertips to her temples and began to massage them with small, circular movements. She closed her eyes. He saw her fear and hesitation, and came over to her. He pulled her to her feet and guided her outside. He released her hand and said for her to follow him. He headed in the direction of the forest, away from the wokasketipi. She watched his retreating back and turned to stare toward the tipi sa.

Realizing she did not follow, he halted and returned to her. He followed her gaze with his eyes and read her thoughts. He pulled her around to face him. Lifting her chin to force her to look at him, he stated firmly, "Hiya wokasketipi. Ku-wa, yuzaza." He caught her arms to steady her as she nearly swooned with relief.

At least for a while, I'm safe, she thought with relief. But I won't go back there. I must do exactly as he says and wants. Soon, I will be free. I won't give him any reasons to take me there again before I can get away.

They went along the forest path to the stream in silence. Gray Eagle glanced back at Alisha. She was looking up and did not catch his look. He saw the warm sunlight play across her face, shine in her eyes and bring her auburn hair to life. How he wished this beautiful girl was not white! He returned his attention to the path, wondering what Wakantanka thought about this white girl he had taken captive. Would he object to one so innocent and so like his own people in her thoughts and ways? She seemed to revere and respect the work of Wakantanka and Makakin. Many times, he had thought she was like an Oglala except for her skin. At times, she totally accepted him and her life here.

He looked back once more, thinking how Wi seemed to caress and touch her in some hidden, special way. She closed her eyes, and let her face and body absorb the sun's warmth as he watched curiously. Why did the Great Spirit watch over and protect her, a white slave and his enemy? Was he not there at her fortress to capture her? Does he not leave her in my keeping now?

She was like the work of Makakin herself — hair of fiery bark, skin of white snow, eyes as green as newborn leaves or grass, and voice like a babbling brook near a waterfall. Hunger for her smile and warmth came to him, and he knew he must have her touch and tenderness again. She must be mine in body and spirit, he resolved. I know and feel this is what she wants, but she is afraid. She cannot resist my touch, but fears and hates the touch of others. When she forgets for a time that we are enemies, her eyes sparkle with love and she smiles with tenderness. Her laughter sounds of a gentle breeze in the leaves at night. The day will come when she accepts her fate here and she will stop this resistance. We will both be happy then.

Her resistance forces me to hurt and punish her over and over. She must come to learn the place of the Indian winyan is not as it is with the wasichus. When she learns this obedience and submission, then I can withhold my hand. She must learn I cannot show weakness to her before myself or my people. She must learn to yield to me before the others and not to defy me openly. Her courage and gentleness are winning many of my people to her. If she would but learn respect and obedience, she could earn their acceptance in time.

When my father returns, he will know of her value. He will agree with the council's decision this day that I be allowed to keep her as my kaskapi. I have earned the right to have her if she will only accept my captivity without defiance. They have shown great wisdom, for they, too, have seen more than a white girl in Lese.

When I marry Chela, I will keep Lese with me. I have not felt such joy in my life since entering manhood or since the day of my sun dance. The Great Spirit has accepted my flesh and blood in gratitude, and given me flesh and blood in return in Lese. I have seen this in my vision last night and this day, she was returned to me. She is a part of my sacred life circle and without her my life will not be complete. She was sent to fill the loneliness and hunger in my heart. She is my reward from the Great Spirit.

They had reached the stream and were bathing as troubled thoughts filled both their minds. It no longer bothered Alisha that he watched her when they came to bathe. If she refused to undress and bathe, either she would be the one to suffer, or he would simply force her to bathe by stripping her and tossing her into the water. She had always loved long baths and swimming. She slowly learned to accept his watchful stare and bathe happily and leisurely with her back to him.

This daily event of bathing in the cool stream was one of her most cherished things. It seemed to have a soothing, relaxing, and reviving effect on her. She would not leave the water until he called for her to come. Only then would she reluctantly leave and dry herself off.

She had to admit Gray Eagle had shown her one great kindness — she did possess three deerskin garments, each beautiful, soft, and trimmed in a different design of beadwork or quills. Three garments provided her with a clean change every day. For this, she was very grateful to him, and to Matu who had made them at his command. She had one to wear, one to wash and one drying from the day before. This hot climate, so unlike the English one, made a daily bath and change of clothes a miracle.

She had become accustomed to the strange undergarment and liked it better than the bloomers she used to wear. It was much more comfortable and definitely cooler.

On the days she washed her hair, she would re-braid it later in their teepee. Other days, she simply left it braided and squeezed the water out after her bath, When all was completed, she would gather her things and follow him back to camp and their teepee.

Such was their routine on most days, but not today. This day was different from the others. Today, her mood was melancholy, and her thoughts and feelings in upheaval. She had undressed, bathed, dried off, dressed, and sat down to wait for him to finish. Today, she did not linger in the water, nor did it soothe and relax her. Today, she was not singing or happy. Today, her mind was on freedom from the cruelty and love of Gray Eagle.

Subconsciously, she sat watching him. He lifted water in his hands and chanted in his deep voice as he shook the water into his face and onto his chest. He performed this same ritual each time they came to bathe. She was completely unaware of the effect his voice and the sight of his nude body was having on her. The melodious baritone of his voice made her skin tingle and the virility of his body inflamed her emotions. His lithe body moved with ease and grace. She would feel the warmth spread throughout her body and ache with longing for him at times like this. She would have to force herself to tear her eyes from him before he caught her admiring him so openly and boldly. She tried to forget the many times he had turned and found her staring at him, those alluring, green eyes pools of darkened desire. He often wondered if she realized how great her desire for him was. The heat from her eyes was enough to burn and inflame him at any distance.

Today as she watched the ritual, she sarcastically thought, even savages pray to their pagan gods. She had given a great deal of thought to their worship of the sun, but without a wider vocabulary, she would never be able to fully comprehend or understand their beliefs and ways.

She could shut her eyes and picture him as he faced the rising sun each morning and chanted a prayer. This was the first thing he did each new day. On rainy days, he would sit cross-legged just inside his teepee, face east and chant softly. At these times, there was a different lilt to his tone. Why, she did not know.

When she would face the sun with closed eyes to absorb its warmth and life, she would find him studying her and looking bewildered. He would look as if he were trying to solve some deep mystery about her and this act. Then, he would simply smile as if she had pleased him in some way.

As he finished his ritual and bath, she looked away as he came out of the water. She shifted uneasily as the sounds of his drying off and dressing reached her alert ears. She was still too timid to openly look at his nude body, but had done so several times secretly. She had watched from lowered lashes, unable to prevent her eyes from straying there. He was as graceful as an antelope — long, sinewy legs; flat, hard belly; brawny, powerful arms and back; hard, smooth, muscular chest; and . . . He was like Apollo in human form. She flushed and fidgeted just recalling these images and thoughts.

He had dressed and was calling for her to follow. She arose to accompany him back to his teepee. Shortly, they were back inside. She sighed with happy relief because they did not meet either Kathy, Chela or Wanhinkpe Ska. She could not deal with contact with any of them. In fact, she wished she could avoid all three forever.

Before Gray Eagle had come inside, he had halted to speak with a brave. When he finally entered the teepee, he took a small parflech and began to pack it with bread and strips of dried meat. He took a full mni skin and extra buffalo skin he used as a mat on hunts and put them down beside the parflech. He gathered his weapons and sat down to check and prepare them.

Comprehending what these preparations meant, her heart leaped in joy. He must be going on a raid or hunt. This is the chance to escape I have wanted and prayed for, she thought eagerly. Freedom, at last! She could hardly keep from shouting and singing. I have been here long enough that I can come and go without much notice from the others. If he does as usual and leaves me unguarded, I will be long gone and far away before he returns. Never again will I see or feel his hate. By tomorrow, I will be free. She smiled.

Gray Eagle glanced up to see her smiling secretly to herself as she watched him gather his things for the raid. But the smile quickly faded and she looked away when he studied her with suspicion. She cautiously tried to behave normally.

He guessed, she will be glad to have me away for a time. But this is good. It will give her the time to be alone and think. There are many things she must come to understand and decide for herself. She will come to know she is mine and always will be. She will come to understand she can be happy if she comes to me of her own free will. There is no choice but to accept me and all my ways.

Just to nettle her, he called her to come and sit down beside him while he prepared to leave. Knowing her freedom was near and not wanting to provoke him, she instantly obeyed. She sat down in elated spirits at his side. She looked on as he rolled some items into a buffalo skin and neatly tied them up.

As he began to fill his empty quiver with new arrows, she retreated to her mind to plan. She unconsciously toyed with the gold locket around her neck. He had believed the shiny yellow circle was an amulet against evil for it resembled the sun in color and shape. He had allowed her to keep it for that reason.

She lovingly touched it with her fingertips, caressing it lightly between them. She did something she had not done since leaving Pennsylvania. She opened the locket and gazed at the small miniature of her father and herself. Her elation at thoughts of freedom made her long to have contact with something from her past as encouragement and to give her strength of purpose.

The miniature had been done shortly before his death. The two of them had been out shopping for a birthday gift for her mother. They had stopped in at an "artiste atelier" to have it made. It had been a wonderful surprise, but her mother had only worn it for a few weeks before she had been killed. It had been given to Alisha, along with other small personal effects. The destruction and fire at the fortress had taken everything but the locket she wore. It was her one and only link to her past. Although she could not guess his reason, she was glad he had allowed her to keep it. She had not had the heart to look at it until today.

She had been so full of life and happiness that

day and it was evident in her sparkling merry eyes and dazzling smile. She studied the girl in the locket. How naive and unworldly she had been! Would she have smiled so brightly and innocently if she had known then what life was truly all about?

She covered her mouth with her hand to suppress a laugh as she noted the expensive clothes and fashionable hairstyle; then looked at how she was dressed now and touched the long braids resting at her breast. Which girl are you, Lese, she pondered. The one in the miniature or the one here now? Two such totally different girls, lives and fates. Why had the Fates chosen this as her destiny? It wasn't fair.

She then looked at the tall, ruggedly handsome man at her side in the locket. Tears came to her eyes, but remained unshed. How young, vital and dashing he had looked that day. She studied the angular jaw which told of a strong character and honesty. She gazed at the sparkling, devil-may-care, steel-blue eyes. His hair was the color of a raven's feathers and his face golden-bronze from his sporting life. He had been a man to cause the heads of women to turn for a second and third look and to look at her mother in envy. She noted the charisma in his expression. He had possessed a natural charm and polite manner which drew people to him in both private and business circles. She had been so very proud of him. She had treasured the love and closeness they had shared for so many years. Even now, his death was unbearable.

Oh, Papa, her tender heart cried out, why did it have to end this way? Why did things have to change so cruelly? I love you and miss you as much as in the beginning. Will this terrible emptiness and pain in my heart never heal?

When Gray Eagle finished what he was doing and looked over at her, she was sitting and staring intently at the little locket with tears glimmering in her eyes. He studied her curiously for a short time, confused by her expression and mood. His eyes followed her line of vision to the gold circle she held in her fingers. It was open. He leaned toward her and stared at the scene inside the locket. It was Lese with a young, handsome, smiling, white man. His eyes instantly riveted back to her dreamy-eyed look.

His thoughts went black with rage and jealousy. He struck out at himself in anger. Fool! She has a white-eyes she loves and longs for. She has lied and deceived me. She has tricked me with her soft words and loving ways. She hopes I will feel love and pity for her. But she will know my anger and feel my wrath!

Eyes blazing hot fury, his hand snaked out and snatched the locket from her grip. He roughly yanked the delicate chain around her neck. It broke, leaving a red scratch along her neck. She was startled by the sudden, aggressive brutality of his action, and gasped in shock. She stared wide-eyed with fear at him.

He held the little locket up and scrutinized the man in the miniature with her. She did not realize how hard he was straining to keep his emotions and fury under rigid control. He tightly clutched the locket in his hand, fighting the overwhelming urge to slay her immediately for her deceit. She will never look upon his face again. She will regret this trick and beg my forgiveness. He walked to the fire pit and dropped the locket into the flames.

Unaware of his coming intentions, she was too late to stop him. She lunged forward and tried to reach for the locket in the swirl of flames. He quickly grabbed her hand back before it touched the fire. He shouted angrily at her, "Hiya!"

He crushed her small hand in his powerful grip. She struggled to free it and rescue the locket. "No!" she cried in anguish. "Please don't destroy it, Wanmdi Hota. My father, no, it's all I have left from him. Please, I beg you, don't!"

He loosened his iron-like grip on her hand, but still retained it in his fist. She stared in torment as flames licked at the images; charring, melting and fusing them into one small multi-colored dot of nothingness. The gold locket turned a glowing red, then, white hot as it melted into the same nothingness. Soon, the only thing left was a very small, glowing ball. The last reminder and connection to her past life was now but a memory.

The intense agony in her eyes and face knifed at his heart. It was too late to save the locket. He released his grip. She slowly sank to the ground before the pit and stared into the fire which flickered in a bright kaleidoscope of colors. She murmured to herself, detached and in shock, completely unaware of him or her surroundings.

"It belonged to mother. It was a birthday surprise. We gave it to her just before she was killed. Father was a handsome man, wasn't he? Mama said he could even make a spinster turn green with envy. They gave it to me after she died. It was the only thing left which truly belonged to me."

She smiled as she recalled the day she and her father had given it to her mother. "It was such a grand surprise. We kept it a secret. I can still see her face and hear her words of joy. 'Now I have my two favorite people closest to my heart all the time.' I haven't looked at it since they died. It brought too much pain and loneliness." Tears rolled down the pinkened cheeks.

"It's all gone. Nothing left, just like everything at the fortress — burned and destroyed. All gone . . . everything and everyone . . . Why, Wanmdi Hota? How could a little locket with my father's image harm you? It was mine. You had no right to destroy it. I hate you!" She shot the stinging words at him like a flaming arrow.

Coming to full consciousness, she turned on him in a sudden fury and pummeled him on his bare chest. She shouted, "I hate you! I hate you! I hate you! You're cold-blooded and heartless! You'll stop at nothing to hurt me! You had no reason to do that! It was mine! Mine!"

She lowered her voice to a deadly, icy tone, "I hope you're captured and killed on this raid! I hope they torture you and beat you until you're dead. You should be made to bleed and suffer for all your evil. I hope you pay dearly for your hatred and cruelty."

Too late, he realized his grave mistake, but knew it could not be changed or undone. He was alarmed by the full extent of his feelings and jealousy. He was shocked by the brutal way he had struck out at her, but was more concerned with the reasons behind his actions. He was a man who prided himself in his control over his emotions. But this girl had a way of wreaking havoc in him. She revealed things in him which he did not understand. When he was confronted with situations like this one with her, all his years of training and practice fled and failed him. He had openly vented his anger on her too many times lately. What magic did she possess to bring out such feelings and reactions in him? How did she make him lose all reason and judgment when she was the center of the problem? I do not like the way I strike out at her, he thought, but somehow I cannot seem to stop or control it.

He reached out and tenderly gripped her shoulders, saying, "Hiya, Lese."

She ignored his order and continued her tirade of hate and hopes for his coming doom. Fearful someone might hear her, he spoke sharply in warning, "Hiya! Iyasni! Ya wokasketipi . . ."

She was immediately frozen into silence and

stillness. Trails of tears were still wet on her flushed cheeks and the wild despair still filled her eyes. Between gasps for air, she vowed, "You'll have to kill me first! You'll never take me there alive again. I will never endure such shame as that again. Never!"

The warning had done its job, so he released his hold on her. She sank to the ground before the fire pit and gazed into it. Staring into the dying flames, she mentally cursed him, damn him and his threat! I will not let him have this new power over me. Either I will escape or I shall kill myself.

Tears filled her emerald eyes and silently rolled down her face. The firelight appeared to dance in those large, sad eyes and sparkle on her teardrops. Such a cruel price to pay for broken dreams and shattered illusions . . .

She whispered in a tone tinged with anguish, "There is nothing you have ever done to me which has brought me more pain. You could hurt me no less if you drove an arrow into my heart. You and those bloody arrows which bring death and suffering. Would they could be more like Cupid's instead — arrows to bring love and desire." She turned on him and accused heatedly, "But you know nothing of love. All you know is hatred and lust. You wish everyone else to be as unhappy and bitter as you are."

Emerald eyes met and fused with jet black ones. Softly and tenderly she asked, "Don't you ever feel longings for love and happiness,

Wanmdi Hota? Have you never loved or wanted any woman so much it actually hurt? Does your hatred flame so deep within you that no one will ever be able to put it out? If I could borrow that mythical bow for only one moment, I pierce your heart with love for me and never release you from my hold. There has been so much anger and hate between us. Will you never allow it to end? Is there no hope for a lasting truce for us?"

She could have answered her own questions. She lowered her face into her open hands and cried, "Oh, Papa, why? Why did I have to be left alone? I can't face these fears alone. Why did we come to this godforsaken land? Why am I at the mercy of a man whose hatred and cruelty knows no limits?

"I wish you would kill me and end this torment. Why did you have to spare me and bring me here?" She dropped her head into her hands once more and wept in total despair and hopelessness.

He watched and listened as she cried to release the pent-up pain, loneliness and suffering. A desire to comfort and love her flooded him. Hunger to heal the hurt he had caused her surged in his heart. He lifted her into his arms and took her to the mat. She did not resist until he pressed her down to the mats with his body. Guessing his intention, she began to fight him like a cornered wildcat.

"You'll never touch me again, not after all you've done to me. If you think you can crush my heart in your hands one minute, then hold me in your arms and make love to me the next, you won't! I hate you!" she hissed at him.

His superior strength of body and purpose enabled him to easily and quickly pin her beneath him, naked, breathless and fighting. She had never fought him so fiercely before. He was afraid he would hurt her in their struggle. He knew he must end her resistance quickly. His eyes narrowed to a dangerous glint and his voice lowered to an ominous tone. In slow deliberation, he said, "Wokasketipi or Wanmdi Hota?"

She was so distressed by the implication of his threat, she did not register the use of the English word "or." She would never know how much that mistake and oversight would cost both of them. Gray Eagle had instantly realized his slip, but knew her lack of reaction meant she did not catch it.

He spoke once more in a more demanding tone, angered by what almost took place just now. "Hiya ku-wa Wanmdi Hota, ya wokasketipi! Hiya ya wokasketipi, ku-wa Wanmdi Hota."

When she did not answer him, but only stared back into his ebony eyes as if hypnotized by them, he gave the choices again. She thought on his words, "no come to him, go to the teepee sa; or no go to the teepee sa, then come to him." Understanding filled her mind — a choice! He was telling her to choose between him and that brothel! He would certainly carry out his threat.

She glared at him as she reasoned the two choices.

"A choice, is it? Go to the teepee sa where any man can take me . . ." she shuddered to even consider this possibility ". . . or come to you and let only you take me. But do I dare trust you? With your love for taunts and cruelty, it's probably just a trick. Even if I chose you, you'd more than likely take me there anyway afterwards. You've never offered me a choice before. Why now? You have the power to force me to do anything. Why the choice?"

She hurriedly tried to figure out his motives before he demanded an answer again. He lowered his face to hers and was about to kiss her when she abruptly turned away. He warned, "Hiya Wanmdi Hota . . . sha teepee sa."

He took her two hands and placed them around his neck. Holding them there, he repeated his choices with a tone of impatience. His complete and true meaning hit home. Her eyes widened with comprehension.

"Now I understand. The real choice is between the teepee sa and willing submission. Oh yes, you could rape me. But that isn't what you want. You want yielding and groveling. You want me to feel shame and guilt. How cunning and wise you are in some things. Is this your new threat to hold me in line? I act as your harlot or as one for your whole tribe."

He remained quiescent, allowing her to work out her decision. "If only you put half this much effort and wisdom in other paths. . . . What difference could this possibly make? You've taken me many times before. To be stripped and raped by others . . . by Wanhinkpe Ska. . . . You chose your weapon well that night, too. To allow my one and only friend to hurt me was cruel, even for you. Only you have hurt me more. Why will you not allow me just one koda? I hope I never recall that night. I have no doubt you forced him to do what he did. Still, we can never be kodas again . . . if we ever were. You use your position and power like a knife, Wanmdi Hota. You cut deeply and painfully into the hearts of those you hate or wish to punish."

She drowned in those pools of black. "Why me, Wanmdi Hota? Why do you make me a special receiver of your hate and revenge? Why did you have to take my one friend and the small happiness we shared? If only you could feel just a little love in your heart for me. No . . . I would settle for just a little less hate."

Killing her friendship with Wanhinkpe Ska was a mistake, he realized. So was the wokasketipi. She has withdrawn further from me. Whether it be by force and fear, or love and submission, Lese, I will have you.

The tautness left his body and he relaxed his tense jaw. She met his gaze to discover the icy glare was missing and in its place was a calm, pleasant, almost tender expression. She shifted uneasily beneath its glow. There was a look of smug anticipation gleaming in his eyes. Arrogant savage! she fumed. He knew all along I would do anything before I'd let him send me back there.

"Hiya teepee sa . . ." she answered with firmness. "Sha, ku-wa Wanmdi Hota . . ."

To her utter confusion, he gave her a broad smile, or perhaps a victorious sneer. It really did not matter which, the effect was shattering to her resistance and hate. His eyes softened to a dark slate color. The taut lines at his eyes and mouth relaxed into gentle lines. He flashed even, white teeth in an almost breathtaking smile. If possible, he looked even more handsome and desirable.

Her heart seemed to skip a beat, flutter wildly, then pound madly. With lips dry and slightly parted, those emerald eyes could not leave his face. He calmly returned her heated, surprised gaze. There was a strange look in his eyes which she could not fathom. Time ceased to exist. She was lost in those black, bottomless depths. The power of his will drew her deeper and deeper, until there was no hope for survival — or any will for it.

The close contact and heat of his body made her tremble. She inhaled and exhaled in quick, short rasps. His warm breath on her face and the heat from his smoldering eyes set her blood afire. He watched as desire replaced hate and anger in her flushed face.

Sensing she had lost the will to resist him, he released his hold on her hands. He remained propped on his elbows staring down into her face. Her hands remained behind his neck. All past feelings and events were irrelevant to what was taking place between and within them. There had been a change, for no longer did a slave and warrior lie amidst the buffalo skins; only a man and a woman . . .

Each was aware of the strangeness which filled their bodies, minds and the very air in the teepee. To each came the thought, "here is the one I love and want." There were no thoughts of past or future, only of here and now.

He was both happy and shocked by the effect of only a smile on her. Why had he not tried this way before? His present actions held far more power over her than any force or threat. He had her totally under his power with only tenderness. It was a sad pity he would soon disregard and reject this new discovery. He had found the knowledge and key to conquer her love and defiance, but he was unable to admit or accept it.

His lips found hers and kissed her long and deep. He soon found her hands held him there for another and another. Her fiery response answered his call. She returned every kiss and offered others. She yielded to the hunger and warmth he offered. He began to whisper soft words in Oglala to her as he caressed her and rained hot kisses over her face and throat. Even though she did not understand his meaning, his tone had the desired effect.

"E-cana, ni-ye mitawa. Kokipa ikopa, Cinstinna. Kte lo Wanmdi Hota. Lese. Waste cedake . . . waste cedake . . ." For the first time, he allowed his emotions to run free. This time, there would be total giving and taking from both sides.

Completely forgotten were her former intentions of giving in to avoid the teepee sa. She clung to him passionately. This was the joining she had long awaited. When he came to her, she met each thrust with a desire unbridled and out of control. She responded to him with instinctive moves. Lost in the heat of love and passion, she obeyed every command his mouth gave her. All reason fled in the face of consuming love.

Her senses were spinning. He was everywhere — his smell filled her nostrils; his voice sounded deep and husky in her ears; his touch burned like fire on her flesh. Her body ached for fulfillment and ecstasy. For these few, precious hours, there was no Indian or White; nor hate and cruelty; nor slave and master. There existed only man and woman; only Alisha and Gray Eagle; only love and desire, joined together in the act of giving all to each other, physically and emotionally.

Caught in the spiral of climbing passion, she wondered how she would ever want to escape him now. How could she bear to live without him after this night? How could she bear never to see him again? She had never known or possessed him this way, nor had he ever come to her with such tenderness before. How could she ever stop wanting or loving him now? She did not understand this change in him, but she hoped it would last forever. She had been wrong, for he was capable of love and tenderness.

As the final thrust was given and accepted, both were lost in the throes of love, consummated to the fullest. He laid his head down beside hers as their breathing slowed to normal and a calm, relaxed serenity came. He was the first to realize how deep he had been lost in her love. He had been caught unprepared for both his or her response. He was alarmed to recall how nothing had mattered for those hours except Alisha and his need for her. He had been completely unaware of everything but her. Perhaps she had been the one with the power over him. I cannot allow her this power or knowledge, he thought. It is too soon . . .

Her passion ebbed and reality returned. She recalled her wanton, fierce surrender to him. Had she only imagined his response to her? She must know the truth now. "Wanmdi Hota . . ."

Forcing his expression under control, he lifted a blank face and fathomless eyes to her. She waited for some sign or word. He offered nothing more than an expressionless glare. He knew what she asked him without words, but he could not bring himself to reply. She realized her love and desire had been so great she had let herself pretend he felt the same way to offset her shame. Humiliated by her discovery, she tried to pull out of his embrace. She was frightened by her emotions and behavior.

What is the matter with me? she raged against

herself. How could I have responded to him like that? I had no will or desire to stop him or myself. I have lost all control over my body and mind. He rules them just like he rules my life.

He raised his head and peered into her face as she struggled to pull free. She reddened in guilt and hurriedly looked away. He knew her fear and uneasiness at this sudden unleashing of hidden emotions, for he, too, felt the same panic and alarm he sensed in her. He also understood her loss of pride. She sees now she is mine of her own choice, he thought, and it confuses and frightens her.

To alleviate the tension in the air, she said defensively, "Ya Wanmdi Hota, sha . . . hiya ya teepee sa . . . hiya teepee sa!"

Nodding understanding, he guessed the purpose of the statement. He would let her believe she was only choosing him over the wokasketipi. She was aware of the full truth about him and herself. He would give her time to accept these new facts about her feelings.

His thoughts were also in turmoil. He would soon be forced to face and deal with these same facts and emotions in himself. Could he ever accept the fact that he loved a white girl who was his slave and enemy? Could she ever become more a part of his life than being just his kaskapi? The Great Spirit would reveal the answers to these questions very soon.

He rolled over and covered them both with blankets, then went to sleep. She lay a long time contemplating her actions. Recalling the passion and ecstasy she had experienced, she trembled with renewed desire and fear.

If he gains this new hold on my heart and body, I will never be free of him, she reflected. It's horrifying enough to be his slave, but to love him would be damning. I can't allow that to ever happen. Tomorrow I must escape and be free of him and his spell forever. She vowed, tonight will be the last time my body will ever betray what my heart feels. He will always believe I acted out of fear of him and the teepee sa. I will not give him the weapon of love to use against me.

After tossing restlessly for hours, she began to dream . . .

Chapter Ten

She saw herself running through a field of flowers. She frolicked in the warm sunlight, tossing her silky hair to and fro in the light breeze. She twirled and danced merrily. A soft love ballad filled her ears. As she moved along, she plucked daisies until her arms were full.

Abruptly the sky darkened. A fierce wind howled around her and in her ears. It whipped her hair into her face and eyes, and tore at her dress. The daisies scattered everywhere. Peals of thunder sounded above and all around. Where had the azure sky, the white, billowy clouds and bright sun gone?

A blood-curdling yell rent the air. She whirled around to see five Indians running toward her. They were painted up in gruesome, fiendish detail. They wore only breech-cloths and deerskin moccasins. Their entire bodies were covered in color and strange, bizarre designs. They wore no feathers or headbands in their sooty, loose-flying hair. The malevolent, demoniacal expressions on their faces instilled terror in her.

She turned and fled in alarm. For some reason, her legs were like two dead weights which moved in very slow motion. Panic gripped her heart and she instinctively knew there was no escape. She tried to scream for help, but not a single sound would come out. The Indians swiftly overtook her. Hands were pulling and grabbing at her from all sides. Her clothing was torn from her body and hot, clammy hands were all over her flesh, pinching, touching and squeezing.

She finally managed to scream and scream and scream, but no help came. She was thrown to the ground and held spread-eagled, each man taking a limb and holding it tightly to the earth. Never had she known or felt such degradation and shame. There were insistent, cruel hands at her breasts and thighs. She struggled with all her might, but realized she could not prevent the assault.

The fifth Indian, who was towering over her, removed his breech-cloth. He leered sadistically down at her as he stood there fondling his enormous, protruding manhood. She turned her head from the horrible, humiliating sight before her. Rough hands immediately forced her head back to face her first attacker. They laughed and sneered at her fear and useless exertions. The others shouted encouragement and teased him in a deep, guttural language she did not know.

The man standing above her dropped heavily on top of her, knocking the wind from her. He savagely entered her with a brutal thrust. She screamed at the tearing, burning, excruciating pain which seemed to rip her apart inside.

Gray Eagle gripped her shoulders painfully and shook her violently, trying to awaken her. He had pieced most of her nightmare together from her cries and pleas. He knew what she was dreaming and believing to be real. This was probably brought on by her visit to the wokasketipi.

His voice reached her inner mind, and he, too, joined in the nightmare. He seemed to come from nowhere, swinging his tomahawk and slashing with his knife. She watched, fearful for his life and safety, as he overpowered and killed them all. Blood was everywhere — on the flowers, the earth, on her and him, and over her attackers. All the braves lay dead and mutilated. Suddenly she was in his arms and he was holding her tenderly, telling her she was safe. She clung desperately to him in the dream, little knowing she did so in reality. Soon, she came fully awake. She stared at him through tear-soaked lashes, comprehending it was only a horrible dream. She clutched at him for comfort. She began to kiss him hungrily. She begged him to make love to her and blot out the nightmare.

He tightened his embrace on her and pulled her willing body beneath his. They made love with an emotion akin to animal mating. Her fiery capitulation and heated response to him kindled him with a fire which could only be quenched with her total possession.

Later, she lay enfolded in the security and warmth of his arms and slept peacefully the remainder of the night. He held her all night, letting her draw comfort and love from him. For the first time, she had come to him to seek the love and comfort she needed and wanted. She had begged him to make her his, and he had.

When morning came, he hesitated to study her sleeping face. She had moved only slightly when he arose. Her hand had gone to the place where he had lain and still held his body heat. She snuggled to the warmth and odor he left there. Softly she whispered his name in her slumber, and a smile formed upon her lips.

Her vision had shown her she is mine and she accepts it, he triumphed. She is truly mine now. The love she has felt will bring the changes in her which must come. It is time. Sleep, Cinstinna. When I return, we will speak of these things. It is time for you to understand my feelings for you and for you to know of your place here with me. The Great Spirit has prepared your heart to learn and accept these things. You will no longer fear me or my love. The time for hate and suffering is past. We will know of love and happiness, but only here in our teepee. When I tell you of these things, you will understand why it must be this way for now.

He smiled, confident of her total commitment to him. He leaned over to gather his bedroll, weapons and supplies, and went to join the others.

Capa Cistinna had brought the news of a wagon train moving into their lands from the East. He had spotted it yesterday when he was out hunting. He had counted about fifteen wagons which were driven by many people dressed in strange black and white garments. Gray Eagle and some other braves would go and scout this area to learn of the white man's intentions. Perhaps they only passed through their land on the way to some other land. If not, the braves would attack and force them to move on or be killed.

Gray Eagle left his teepee and walked to his horse. He spoke gently to the powerful appaloosa as he fed and watered him. He stroked Chula's neck with great affection, smiling to himself in apparent high spirits.

White Arrow walked up with his pinto Aluzza and began to tease his friend. "Your head soars as high as the eagle in the sky, my koda."

Gray Eagle had not felt this relieved or lighthearted in a long time. He laughed and replied, "Yours would also, my koda, if you possessed the woman of your heart. She is truly mine now. She will never resist or defy me again. The council, the Great Spirit and, now, she herself have agreed that she is mine. From this moon on, she will be my kaskapi only in the eyes of others, not just in our teepee."

White Arrow arched his eyebrows in surprise at this sudden change of heart. Astonished, he asked, "How so, Wanmdi Hota?"

Grinning with self-confidence, the reply was, "Last night, she came to me and gave of her heart and body completely and willingly."

Perplexed, White Arrow asked skeptically, "How did this come about so quickly and without warning?"

Gray Eagle explained the events of the previous night in minor detail, including her feelings and words about White Arrow.

"In time, we could become kodas once more. It is good to my heart that she does not hate me for what I did to her."

"She will learn and understand all things when we return. It is time for peace and understanding between us. She will again accept you as her koda. I will tell her of the things she must know. If she accepts and understands these things, then I will tell her of my feelings and needs for her. Then, she will accept her life here with me and our people. We will know happiness for many moons."

"It is good you do this, Wanmdi Hota. She has suffered too much for a long time. It is the time for healing and understanding. She will be greatly shocked and surprised to learn of your feelings for her as a woman. She does not guess you love her and want her as herself."

"It will be new to her, but it is time for the truth between us. Only you, my koda, will know she is more than a kaskapi to me. For a time, it must remain this way."

They went to join the other warriors who were preparing to go on this raid with them. As they went along, White Arrow casually asked who was to be left as a guard and protector for Alisha.

"There is no need for her to be guarded now. She is safe here and the old woman will see to her needs while we are away. There is food in our teepee and the stream is close by."

White Arrow was again astounded by this much trust and assurance in Alisha. He did not tell me all of the things which happened last night, he thought. It takes more than one night of love and submission to earn this honor from a warrior like him. Was it truly love which has brought on this final giving in? Could it be she has grown weary and disheartened from all her resistance and suffering? She does not want to be farther punished or sees the futility of defiance. May the Great Spirit protect you, Cinstinna, if you fail to be worthy of his trust.

A chill touched White Arrow, causing him to tremble with its intensity. He knew what he must do.

He scanned the group for a sight of Gray Eagle. He must warn him to reconsider a guard for Alisha. He saw him speaking with Matu, giving her orders concerning Alisha. The command was to leave her alone unless she appeared to need help or protection. White Arrow hurried to him. As they walked away from Matu's teepee, he asked his friend to reconsider his decision on this matter. He told him of his uneasiness at leaving her alone.

"There is a warning in the air but I do not grasp its meaning. You must leave a warrior to protect and watch over her this time."

Gray Eagle scoffed at his friend's urge for caution and chose to ignore his words. He was too proud and arrogant to think anything could possibly go wrong for them now. Everything had been settled. There was no need for further worry or concern.

Gray Eagle rode away with his warriors without realizing the truth to Wanhinkpe Ska's warning. Excitedly they rode toward the valley where Capa Cistinna had seen the strange wasichus camped. Gray Eagle dismissed all thoughts of Alisha.

The air was crisp and clear on this bright morning. Fluffy, snow-white clouds drifted lazily in the giant sea of blue sky. The braves struck a pace which would tire neither the men nor the horses. As was their custom, they spoke rarely. Each man concentrated on what was to come. One slight hesitation when action was necessary could cost one brave his life or even the life of his friends. They knew their mental readiness was one of their greatest advantages over their enemies. A wasichu would often give a split-second hesitation before slaying his foe. Many times this resulted in his conquer or death. But the Oglalas fought with ruthless fury, courage and undivided attention.

At dusk, they reached the deserted camp. Some of the braves dismounted to search the ground and camp for signs of the wasichus. They scattered out in several directions and found the trail the people had taken. The campfires were cold, indicating they had been out for a long time. Their tracks were filled with loose dirt. It was evident the people had risen early and pulled out for some curious, unknown reason to return in the same way they had come. The wasichus would be forced to travel slowly with their great load.

The Indians saw no need to pursue the departing enemy. It would be a long, tiring journey to catch them. By leaving the Oglala land and forest, the wasichus' lives would be spared. The Oglala did not seek out wasichus to slay for the love of killing.

The braves voted to camp there for the night and get an early start home in the morning. They made camp in the very same spot the wasichus had used only a day ago. They ate their quick, light dinner of dried meat and bread. Later, they sat around small campfires, talking and smoking.

There was no race anywhere who loved storytelling and talking more than the Indians. As with many past nights, they spoke of old glories and battles. Often, the one speaking would act out his tale or speech with great to-do. Gray Eagle's people were a happy, easy-going, intelligent tribe who enjoyed their lives and existences as they were.

When the time for sleep came, Gray Eagle lay on his back on his buffalo skin gazing up into the starry, clear night. He would be happy to get home and to again taste the sweetness of Alisha's surrender. He recalled many things about her as he lay there. I will teach her the ways of the Oglalas and she will become as one someday, he dreamed. A final truce has come between us now. He smiled as he thought of the simplicity of things to come.

White Arrow observed the mood of his friend closely. He saw the smile come and go. He thinks of Pi-Zi Ista and her defeat to him, he deduced. I do not fully believe she yields her all to him yet for her suffering and pain are still too great in her mind and heart. Wanmdi Hota sees as he wishes it to be, not as it truly is. Who will suffer the most when the time for this truth is here? I fear our people may accept her as his kaskapi, but never as his winyan. My greatest fear is she will not be able to accept this life of slavery forever. Only the Great Spirit knows and controls the truth and only he can help either of them now.

Alisha's image formed before his mind's eye. He saw her soft, snowy skin; her proud, graceful walk; the sparkle of life and innocence in those grassy eyes; the fiery shine in her auburn curls; and her courage in the face of danger. She makes any man, Indian or wasichu, desire her for his own, White Arrow sighed.

How does he bring himself to hurt her these many times? he asked himself. If she were mine,

I would be firm, but gentle, with her. I would love and protect her from all shame and hurt. He thought angrily, she clings to me for comfort and understanding, not him. She begged me to go against him to help her. Wanmdi Hota will never know how close I came to doing just that!

Dreaming of how he would like to someday possess Alisha, White Arrow finally dropped off to sleep.

The warriors ate quickly the next morning and were hurriedly on their way before dawn broke. This time they rode swiftly, eager to be home after the long, fruitless journey. There was no need to conserve the strength of the horses or men.

It was mid-afternoon when they reached their village, horses lathered and pawing loose dirt. The younger braves came running forward to take the horses. They would feed, water and rub them down in the cool stream water. The other warriors came out to hear the news of their ride. The group of men talked and laughed for a while.

The younger braves joked and planned for the day when they, too, would be with the warriors on hunts and raids instead of caring for the horses after the excitement was over. They led the animals to the stream and entered a shallow area. It was their daily task to feed, water and exercise the warriors' mounts. In this land, a man's horse could mean his life, and the animal was treated with great care. After he had been cared for, he was exercised to loosen and firm taut muscles.

The warrior's horse was put through a daily regimen of selected drills for speed and agility. The bridle was used only for securing and leading him. He was directed and commanded by knee-pressure and verbal commands from his master. When properly trained, an Indian horse could only be ridden by his owner. Unless verbally ordered by his master, he would not allow anyone else on his back.

This style of knee-pressure riding was necessary for their type of hunting and warfare. A brave needed the use of both hands for his weapons. His horse must be trained in alertness and nimbleness to adjust to sudden changes of direction when pursuing an enemy or game. The young braves knew the importance of their task and did it with great pride and efficiency. After the horses were exercised, they were tethered near the warriors' teepees.

Gray Eagle grew restless with the continued talking. He dismissed himself from the group of men to go to his teepee. He lifted the flap and entered. He looked about — she was not there. He went to find Matu and question her. Matu informed him she had done as he had commanded. She had left her alone. She had not seen Alisha since yesterday morning when she was returning from the stream. Alisha had gone inside his teepee and remained there.

A quiver of apprehension disturbed Gray Eagle's mind. He tried to brush it away. Alisha must have gone to the stream and Matu had not noted her passing. He walked there, but found no Alisha. He strained his ears and eyes for a sight or sound of her. Surely she must be close by. She could be out gathering berries, but why alone? He walked around, calling her name. There was no answer. He scouted the edge of the stream and forest for her. The incident with the trapper haunted his thoughts. Had something happened to her? Could she be hurt or taken prisoner by another? Had she gotten lost in the forest or been attacked by some wild beast? He knew the answers to all his fears, for there would be some sign of danger or warning to his keen eyes. He must have just missed her in the village. There was no other place she would dare go. The camp was a large place . . .

He returned to have another look around, trying not to show his worry. It did not take him long to realize she was not in the village, at the stream or in the nearby forest — the only places a kaskapi could go. That intangible feeling of danger touched him again and he fought to suppress it. He was gazing off into blank space when White Arrow came over to him. Gray Eagle explained his futile search for Alisha. White Arrow saw the black scowl mixed with anxiety on his friend's face. They walked back to his teepee for a clue to Alisha's disappearance.

His eyes scanned the teepee thoroughly. They

darkened in fury as they noted the missing mni skin, wasna pouch, the garments, the blanket — and Alisha. His face went almost white with shock and rage at the implication of the missing items and his Alisha. White Arrow observed a tic in the taut muscle of his friend's jawline. As the full truth settled in on his koda, he watched Gray Eagle's eyes narrow, and his brow tense in rapidly growing anger. He could hear the gritting of his teeth as he clenched them together as he paced the close confines of his teepee. As he planned what to do, he continually pounded one fist into the palm of his other hand.

When he spoke at last, he vowed ominously, "This day, she will regret above all other days she has ever known, my koda! She has dared to dishonor my trust in her and make a fool of me before my people. She has betrayed me and my acceptance of her. To think of what I was going to tell her this very day! I will shame her before the very ones she shamed and dishonored me. They will see and know Wanmdi Hota yields and bows to no winyan or man. She will pay greatly for this betrayal. I will never again make this mistake. I cannot forgive this thing, Wanhinkpe Ska. I cannot . . ."

White Arrow listened to the words which were tinged with anger and anguish. He tried to reason with Gray Eagle and to help him understand Alisha's escape, but Gray Eagle was past hearing any excuses or reasons. White Arrow comprehended the meaning of his premonition — the time had been too short to bring forgiveness, no matter how much love she felt for his koda. I tried to warn him, he thought, but he would not hear my words. She has betrayed not only his honor but his love. They will both suffer for this deed, just as the warning promised.

As he watched Gray Eagle gather his supplies in order to track Alisha, he feared what Gray Eagle would do to her when he caught up with her. I must force him to take me along, he decided. I could prevent his killing her out of anger. He must not kill before his hurt and rage have lessened. Wanmdi Hota is not a man to dishonor as she has unknowingly done. Can he not see how greatly she fears him, and rightly so? Can he not see she hungers for freedom and peace just as he did? It takes more than love to make a winyan stay here willingly.

Gray Eagle refused to allow White Arrow to go with him. "This is between the girl and me! No one can help or protect her from me, not even you, my koda. The Great Spirit will guide my path. He will show me what to do when the time comes."

"Be sure it is the voice of the Great Spirit you hear and obey, my koda, and not the voice of vengeance within your own heart."

White Arrow knew it would not help to argue further with Gray Eagle for he was determined to go alone. White Arrow remained silent.

Gray Eagle allowed White Arrow to help him search the surrounding area for signs of her escape. Now that they knew she was fleeing, they would know what to look for. It did not take long to discover her tracks near the stream. Each man went in an opposite direction to find where she had left the water to enter the forest on the other bank. She possessed a light step and small foot which made her tracks easy to define and follow. Earlier, they had taken no particular notice of her tracks near the stream for it had not seemed unusual for them to be there. As Gray Eagle moved along in the stream searching the bank for her trail, he realized she had purposely tried to hide her tracks.

He scoffed bitterly, knowing her ability to hide her passing from his keen eyes would not hold a twig to his tracking skills. There was no way she could hope to hide from his alert senses. When he spotted the place she had left the water, he whistled a signal to White Arrow to come and join him. They studied the tracks. It was evident she had passed here about mid-day the day before. He told White Arrow to return to camp and wait for him there. He stepped out of the stream and replaced his moccasins, then disappeared into the forest on the other bank.

White Arrow knew it would not take his koda long to overtake Alisha. He is sure to move swiftly, he thought. He will have her within his power and mercy by nightfall. I pray he brings his anger under control before he finds her.

But the opposite thing was happening to Gray Eagle. The faster he walked, the greater his anger built within him. He snarled angrily, her love was a lie, a trick! I have not been a fool of a winyan's deceit before. I have allowed no one to fool me with these games. She is not unlike the winyans everywhere. Fool! It was unwise to trust a winyan and to open my heart to one, especially an ista ska. She will pay for this. She will never have the chance to dishonor or trick me again — if I do not kill her first.

Gray Eagle knew he must come to terms with the rage which gnawed at his insides and the fire which burned a message of revenge across his thoughts. She had dealt him an unforgivable, crushing blow. He knew if he did not bring his emotions under rigid control he would surely kill her with his bare hands. He concentrated on self control, but hardened his heart against Alisha.

Gray Eagle was accustomed to covering many miles swiftly without food or rest when necessary. Even amidst his great anger, he knew he must find her soon before she came upon a wild animal or other warriors. To imagine a wild animal tearing at his Lese's body agitated him immensely. He felt uneasy and tense. He instinctively quickened his pace. Her death was more alarming than her escape.

Far worse were his thoughts of her capture by another tribe. After her reaction to the teepee sa, she would never endure many rapes and abuses. If they mistook her for an Oglala maiden, her beauty would be her downfall. No man could refuse to take her once he saw her; and after once taking her, he would not want to give her up.

His anxiety mounted with each passing minute. He now travelled with new angers and concerns. She had no weapon to protect herself with. She would be powerless to ward off any kind of attack, by man or by animal.

In spite of his attempts to prevent them, happy days and times began to storm his mind. Little things began to sneak in around the edges of his heart and lodged there, unwanted and resisted. Many incidents of his cruelty and her resistance flashed vividly before his mind. For a brief moment, a flicker of understanding glimmered, but he quickly extinguished it.

He asked himself if he were only trying to find excuses for her, trying to pretend she was innocent of blatant defiance and purposely trying to dishonor him, and trying to convince himself she did not love him and her response to him had not been deceitful.

He knew it was beyond his power to protect and save her this time. He tried to force himself to accept the inevitable. His people would expect and demand her punishment for this deed and he could not lose face by refusal. What reason could he give for withholding it? He cried, if only there was some way to save you, Cinstinna, without the cost of my honor. This time my hands are bound by my laws and customs. You have chosen our destinies and we must live them.

He came upon the place where she had spent a restless night. He could imagine her fatigue and fear. She could not be too far ahead of him now — her signs and tracks were still fresh. The gap was closing fast. He must soon decide his course of action when he found her. An action which would affect the course of both their lives.

The sun was slowly sinking on the horizon and blazed like a giant fire in the heavens. Darkness would soon be upon him. Suddenly, he sighted her. He halted instantly to quietly observe her, alerted by a sixth sense of impending danger.

She was standing immobile, staring wide-eyed and white-faced at the ground before her. His gaze followed her line of vision. Coiled and ready to strike, a large rattlesnake blocked her path. She was poised between two high boulders in a narrow gap, which obviously had only one exit — the one now occupied by the viper. Evidently she had intended to hide and sleep in the gorge, but had changed her mind. Perhaps she had felt trapped without another means of escape. It appeared to be a test of patience and courage between Alisha and the rattler as to which one would make the next move.

He stood frozen in his hidden position until he was sure of his next move. He did not take the life of one of Wakantanka's creatures lightly. He carefully studied all angles of the scene from where he was. He could not afford one error. She was surely too scared and tired to remain still and silent much longer. He dared not show himself for she might move or call out, inciting the snake to strike. A snake-bite was a horrible way for one to die. Her death or life was his to decide . . .

Had he been shown a way out for both of them? Had the Great Spirit sent one of his creatures to do what Gray Eagle did not have the heart and courage to do? He carefully calculated the wind, the speed of his arrow, and the distance between them, knowing he would get only one chance to seal their fate. Fervently, he prayed to the Great Spirit to guide his aim and give his arrow true flight and speed, hoping he had made the right decision. He was ready. . . . He gazed intently at the fragile white girl who had brought stirrings to his heart as no other winyan had.

He silently and cautiously released the arrow from his bow, instantly knowing that now, all was in the hands of the Great Spirit.

Alisha stared transfixed into the face of death. It was too late for Gray Eagle to come to her rescue. She had prayed he had already returned to his village and found her missing. Surely he would come to search for her, if only out of pride and anger. She knew it was too soon for him to have returned from his raid and have tracked her down. He had taken his bedroll. That meant he was planning on being gone for a couple of days. By the time he discovered her escape and tracked her here, he would only find her body, distorted in agony and death. What a stupid fool I was, she raged against herself. Perhaps he will be glad to be rid of me. If he misses anything at all, it will be my services in and out of his mats.

She had once seen a man die of a rattler bite. It had been terrible to witness. His leg had swollen to twice its size, turning a flaming red, then a purplish greenish blue. His tongue became so enlarged he could not swallow or breathe. He had burned with a raging fever for days and ranted wildly in delirium. His eyes began to redden, bulge and glaze on the second or third day. After a few days, the leg began to turn a greenish-black and rot right off his body, producing a putrid stench. When the end came, he could no longer scream or even beg the men to kill him to end his torment. They couldn't even force whiskey down his throat anymore to assuage his suffering. The venom had travelled throughout him without mercy, ravaging him completely.

Alisha now knew she should not have attempted to escape. She was no match for this savage land . . . or for Gray Eagle. If only he would come and save her from this horrifying death, she vowed she would never try to escape again.

While standing off the rattler, thoughts rushed through her mind. If I do somehow manage to escape this snake, I could be attacked by other animals or starve or get lost forever on the plains. I could even be captured by another Indian and . . . Horror flooded her senses. The reality of this fate was worse than death by the snake. No man would treat me like he has, she realized. They would treat me like Kathy . . . the teepee sa . . .

many men and nights of . . . She weighed the things he had done to her against the things she knew were done to other female captives. Nothing he had done could compare with the terror, shame and torment of those things.

Please, Wanmdi Hota, she begged inwardly. Please find me . . . if I must endure a life of slavery, then let it be with you. If I survive this ordeal and you do come for me, I'll never try this again. If only I could go back to yesterday, I would be safe in your teepee, waiting for your return.

But the day before, Alisha had thought only of escape.

Gray Eagle had been gone when she awoke. She had immediately peeped out to see if he had left her guarded, but saw no one. She prepared the fire and did her daily chores. After she had cooked maize cakes, she took a pouch and packed it with food and a change of clothes. She clutched it tightly to her bosom and made ready to go to hide it for later. She took the mni skin and blanket, and concealed them in the wood sling. To anyone who noticed her, they would see only a kaskapi fetching water, wood and behaving as a good slave should.

She followed the path to the stream and hid the bundle in some thick, leafy bushes near the water's edge. She hurriedly collected some wood, filled the mni bags, and bathed. She knew this could be her last bath for a long time. She scrubbed away the last traces of their lovemaking from her body, wishing the same could be done for her mind.

She retrieved the wood sling, water bags, and her soiled clothes and returned to their teepee. Matu saw her leave and return. Then, seeing no reason for Alisha to leave Wanmdi Hota's teepee again, she dismissed her from her mind. She had not even thought it unusual to not see her again.

Alisha added more wood to the fire to give the appearance of her presence. She placed more aguyapi on the flat, hot rock by the fire. The smell of the fire and aguyapi cooking would avoid any suspicion toward her until it was too late.

It was mid-afternoon. The women had taken the smaller children inside for their naps. Many of the braves joined their women at this rest time. The other braves went to the meeting lodge to talk and smoke with friends or to plan new hunts and raids. The older boys and girls were at the far side of the village doing chores or playing games. This was her chance. It was to be now or never.

No one saw her as she cautiously slipped from the teepee and headed into the forest. She walked quickly, careful to notice if anyone was following. She retrieved the bundle she had hidden by the stream. She removed her moccasins and stepped into the water. She had recalled her father's lesson on scents and trails being concealed in water. She walked a long way in the stream, observing the trees and bushes for signs of discovery or danger. When she thought she had gone far enough, she left the stream by the other bank and entered the forest.

Every nerve in her body was on edge. She was too frightened to feel the scratches from the briars, or the scrapes from the twigs which slapped against her, or to hear the sounds of the wild forest creatures.

She traveled for what seemed like hours, not daring to stop for rest. She came to the edge of the woods. Before her, she could see only dirt knolls and sand flats which appeared to go on and on forever. The far landscape was etched with high bluffs and ravines, and in the far distance, dark mountains and plateaus. There were many sagebrushes, dried and withered from the harsh sunlight, to nip at her bare legs. From her viewpoint, the terrain looked rocky, dangerous, and very desolate, but for the occasional beauty of the yuccas and flowering cacti. The sparse patches of tall grass seemed barely enough to support any kind of wildlife.

The boulders and canyons she noted in the distance could provide many hiding places for her. The trek would be slow and treacherous, but she had made her decision and resolved to push on quickly. She gazed around once more and stepped out into the open. She hesitated for a time as if she waited for some evil to swoop down and devour her on the spot. Nothing . . . no movement or sound . . . only the blazing sun beating down on her in welcome to this arid, deserted wilderness. She ventured forth slowly.

It was getting late and she knew she must soon find a safe place to stay the night. She searched the sides of the ravine as she moved along. Her eyes lit on a small clump of bushes located on a semi-flat area a short distance up the embankment. She would have a good view of her surroundings from there. The bushes would offer some visual protection from intruders and a slight shield from the cool night breeze.

She gradually worked her way up to the bushes after many slips, falls and scrapes to her hands and knees. She spread out the blanket and sat down on it, breathless and panting. She coughed to clear the dust from her nose and lungs. Perspiration dampened her body. The hard, stony ground instantly made its discomfort known to her posterior. She wished the buffalo skin had not been so large and obvious to carry. She would surely miss its warmth and comfort tonight. She shifted restlessly on the thin blanket and moved closer to the scanty shelter of the bushes.

She rested for a time. She soon became aware of the numerous stinging cuts and scrapes. She picked up her water skin and gingerly bathed the dirt and blood from her face, hands, and legs. The water did little to soothe her minor injuries. A little later, she ate her meager meal. She was so weary, but so uncomfortable she could not fall asleep. Too many fears, doubts, and questions plagued her thoughts.

She watched the effect of the brightening

moonlight on the nearby terrain. It was lit by the ghostly, sinister glow. The sky was clear and the heavens filled with hundreds of milky, iridescent stars. A chilling breeze leisurely swayed the tall grasses back and forth in hushed silence. The rock formations loomed dark and forbidding against the graying skyline. She studied the cacti and trees which were bent and mangled by age and weather. It gave them the appearance of hideous specters to a fatigued mind.

Somewhere out there Wanmdi Hota either sleeps or sits beneath this same moon and stars, she mused. How different our thoughts must be. Our paths have crossed and now veered from each other. Sadly she thought, but we gained nothing from our touching of each other's lives. I have lived as chattel for these past months. I doubt if he will even think of his white captive when he is gone.

She instinctively reached to finger her gold locket, but knew instantly it was missing and how it had gone. Drowsily she stared at the landscape. She slipped into a light stupor and without being aware of when or how, she drifted into a fitful slumber.

Within a few hours, she was abruptly awakened by loud, mournful wails of a nearby animal. In the distance, a coyote was on the prowl. She shuddered and fearfully glanced around, expecting to be pounced upon and ripped to pieces at any minute.

Her exhausted mind played many tricks on her

imagination. She saw and heard all kinds of evil things lurking in the nearby shadows. For the remainder of the night, she sat in wide-eyed fear, clutching her knees to her chest. She shivered from the chill of the night and lack of warmth from the light blanket. How she longed for a fluffy, thick buffalo hide and Gray Eagle's body heat.

By daybreak, she was worn down mentally and physically. She wondered how she could push on, but knew she must. This was no time to look back or falter. She watched the huge, orange sun rise from the bowels of the earth and sluggishly ascend upward into the periwinkle sky. Its hue gradually changed from orange to ocher, to yellow, to a brilliant platinum. It spread its warmth and dazzling light all around her, dispelling all the demons of the night.

She ate very little, knowing her food supply and water would have to last for a long time. Surely there would be places to refill the water skin, but no way to kill or find more food. She had no idea how far or how long she would have to travel before she found other whites or the fort. She wasn't even sure if there were any other white settlers nearby. If she could only make it close to the fort, hopefully someone would find and help her. She remembered Fort Pierre was to the northeast on the map her uncle had shown her. But the map was in the charred ruins of their fortress and the fort was northeast of that fortress, wherever it had been located.

She didn't even know in which direction the Oglala camp was from her fortress. The only thing she could do was head east, toward the rising sun. Somewhere in that direction lay her civilization, Fort Pierre, and hopefully her England.

She gathered her things and began to move on. The going became harder and slower. So much of this terrain was perilous with its sharp, slippery rocks jutting up to trip and cut the feet of a careless traveller. There were so many pitfalls and hidden snares to avoid, she was forced not only to watch the countryside for dangers, but her footing as well. Her progress went even more slowly.

Unaccustomed to long walking and the rocky terrain, her feet and legs ached. Her shoulders, arms and back begged for some relief from the constant strain of pulling, pushing, bending and carrying. Alisha was hot, sweaty, dirty, scratched, bruised and weary before noontime. Never had she been so tired, not even on the journey to this savage country. How much longer could she continue in this heat?

The sun beat down harder and harder. Its heat sapped her strength and its bright light pained her eyes. She did not realize how frequently she drank from her water skin.

It was almost sunset when she was so weary and sore she could go no farther. With shock she discovered she had used all her water. She squeezed and shook the water skin in panic. She glanced around for any slight sign of moisture.

The arid, dusty land told her it had seen no rain for a very long time. There was no chance for escape without water. Escape, she scoffed. There is no life without water, Alisha. How could I have been so wasteful and careless? All this suffering just to die from a death worse than one Wanmdi Hota would mete out.

She racked her brain for any shred of information about dry climates and water. Underground streams . . . springs bubbling up near bases of cliffs . . . an artesian spring . . . vegetation which holds moisture. . . . She scanned the landscape for the highest bluff. To her right, she spotted two high rock formations with a narrow pass between them. Perhaps in there, she thought with eagerness. She dropped her bundle and headed for the opening. The lack of water had panicked her into believing she was thirstier than she had reason to be.

She walked the length of the narrow pass until she came to where it was blocked by fallen rocks. On her way, she had examined the walls and ground for any sign of moisture. She found none. The shadows on the sides of the cliff walls and the receding light reminded her it would soon be getting dark. She hurried back to the entrance. At least I have food, she reassured herself. I can eat, then find a place to sleep for tonight. I'll have to wait until the morning to search for water.

As she reached the entrance to the small gorge, she halted, then froze in that very spot. One of the most terrifying sounds she had ever heard pierced her ears. Like a powerful magnet, her eyes were drawn to the ground before her. A deadly quiver passed through her. She glared as if hypnotized at the six-foot long, diamond-backed rattlesnake that lay directly in her path, blocking the only exit.

She was mesmerized by the snake which was as large around as a huge apple. He had a triangular head with protruding mounds above his slanted eyes and minute pits on either side of his mouth. She noted the brown, black, and white diamond designs on his back. She watched the forked tongue as it darted swiftly in and out, and listened to the ominous rattling of its tail. The tail caught her attention and she vainly tried to count the number of rings on it. It was almost impossible with its rapid movement, but there appeared to be twelve to fifteen. He had been around for a long time.

In a flash, Alisha recalled Ben's warning about this particular snake and its aggression against its enemies. After Luke's death, Ben had told her all he knew about rattlers. He said that with their sense of smell, they could pursue their quarry relentlessly for miles. Most snakes would back off from a larger enemy, but this one would stand his ground and attack.

The rattler had made no move to strike at her so far, but neither did it slither away. It just lay there, waiting and warning her. It was a game of cat and mouse, with her as the mouse and the snake, the cat. It sensed her fear and toyed with it.

Her body ached in every part, but she knew she must not shift her weight in any way or it might instantly strike at her. She would not stand a chance of avoiding those deadly fangs. Her only hope was to remain completely motionless, as lifeless as the rocks around her, until the snake tired of this cruel game and moved on to other prey.

She could not venture a guess as to how much time had elapsed. Thoughts of her precarious position were foremost in her mind. Even if she avoided its first strike and fled into the gorge, it could pursue her. There was no way out of the boxed gorge.

Wanmdi Hota, where are you? Alisha begged silently. Please come! I need you. Let him be in time, please . . .

A faint swish and heavy thud were suddenly heard as a yellow-tipped arrow was embedded deep within the snake's head. Her eyes retraced the flight of the arrow. Relief flooded her features. She screamed his name and nearly swooned in joy.

With Alisha's life in danger, Gray Eagle had made the only decision possible. He was sure the snake had no intention of leaving any time soon. It would have been only a short time before she had done something to incite him to attack. The snake's life had to be taken with great silence and caution. If he had missed, all would have been lost. She would have screamed or moved and the snake would have ended her life. He was sure the Great Spirit understood and agreed with his decision. Her life was now back in his hands.

Alisha leapt past the still thrashing snake and ran straight into the arms of Gray Eagle. She clung to him as she cried hysterically. She babbled almost incoherently, releasing pent-up fear and joy.

"You came . . . so frightened . . . found me . . . almost too late . . . wouldn't leave me here to die . . . sorry . . . never again . . . promise . . . learned lesson . . . prayed you would come . . . so tired . . . don't be angry . . . don't . . . hate . . ." The last couple of sentences, although rushed, were clearer to him. "You do care what happens to me, don't you? You wouldn't have come to save me if you didn't. Hold me, Wanmdi Hota. Just hold me and never let me go, ever again."

Her statement about his caring for her rifled through his mind and he reacted violently. He seized her by the shoulders and shook her. He shouted to be heard over her babbling.

"Hiya! Iyasni! Iyasni! Hiya wohdake! Sica!"

He continued to shout at her, but his tone and expression only gave her more reason to cry, which she did uncontrollably. She comprehended only a few of his commands — to be silent and that she was bad.

He realized he had little choice but to let her get it all out. When she did calm down a little, he bound her hands before her and tied a long rope to them. He left her standing there while he went to the snake. Taking his knife from its sheath, he cut the rings off its tail. The rings were believed to contain great magic. They were usually made into a wanapin and worn to protect the wearer from evil and danger.

He came back to where she waited, still silently sobbing. He glared coldly at her for a minute. He reached for the rope and gave it a tug. She nearly stumbled as she was abruptly yanked forward by both her hands. She mutely followed him to where he had dropped his own belongings. He retrieved his weapons and pack, and began to lead her away. He ignored all her attempts to explain her actions and to plead for forgiveness.

They walked for a very long time. Alisha was so exhausted she soon walked in a near stupor. She stumbled and tripped many times and then fell face forward into the dirt. Her elbows and knees were scraped and bleeding. She couldn't force herself to get up again and move on. Why was he being so mean? She couldn't go on anymore . . .

"Mni . . ." she pleaded hoarsely. But when she wearily raised her head, she faced Gray Eagle's moccasins, firmly planted on either side of her head. She lifted her eyes to him. His expression was one of total indifference concerning her needs.

She dejectedly dropped her head back to the stony ground and wept anew. She was in need of water and rest, but knew he would grant neither. He leaned over and jerked her back to her feet.

He gave the rope a pull and led her forward again. She tried to hang back, but he grabbed her hand and forced her on and on.

It was not long before she faltered and cried out, "I can't go any farther, Wanmdi Hota. Please let me rest for a while. Couldn't I have just one sip of water? I'm so tired! Please . . ."

She staggered on for a short distance until she began to hear a buzz which sounded like hundreds of insects flying around and inside her ears. Minute, brightly-colored lights formed and flashed before her vision like numerous fireflies darting about. The moon must have gone behind some clouds, for it was suddenly very dim and dark. The droning hum grew louder, the night grew darker, and the fireflies increased in number.

She weaved back and forth, shaking her head to clear her senses. She could not think where she was. He mouth was very dry and her knees unsteady. She could hear a faint voice from far, far away calling her name, but she could not seem to answer. She could make out a blurred image before her, but the face swam from view before she could tell who it was. Total blackness engulfed her as she collapsed into Gray Eagle's arms.

Gray Eagle had surmised only moments earlier what was about to happen. He had planned to make camp as soon as they cleared the open plains. He was pushing for the edge of the forest before they stopped for the night. The dense cover of the trees would offer the needed protection from the night and his enemies. He had refused to realize how weak and tired she was. Her face and lips looked bloodless. There were blue smudges beneath her eyes, and her breathing was too shallow and labored. He should have allowed her to rest and drink. He was using her to vent his anger and frustration.

He tenderly lifted her limp body and carried her the remainder of the distance to the edge of the forest. He spread both of their blankets out and laid her on them. He forced water between her lips and made her swallow it by holding her nose. After her parched mouth and throat were wet and soothed, she drank instinctively from his mni skin, but did not regain consciousness. She did not even come to when he bathed her face in the cool water.

He made a small campfire near where she lay. He was too agitated to sleep. He gazed into her colorless face, then into the flames. He ate the dried meat and aguyapi with little appetite, but drank thirstily from the same water skin from which she had begged only a sip. He had been consumed with an overwhelming need to force her to suffer because he had found her missing. He was determined to crush the rebellion which had caused them both such suffering and shame.

But her suffering had not eased his pain or fed his hunger for revenge. In fact, her suffering had only served to increase his own. The hardships of the past two days would not compare with the sufferings she would endure when they returned to his village. I must not push her so hard tomorrow, he decided, or she will be far too weak to survive the icapsinte. Without her knowing, I must find ways to let her rest and drink . . .

He stood up, flexing his muscles to release their tautness. He went to sit beside her. His eyes surveyed her condition, the dirty, pale face which had lit up with such happiness at the sight of him. He could not prevent his hand from reaching out to caress her soft cheek. He was too mindful of a similar night two moons ago as he lay down beside her. How foolish his thoughts and plans had been on that night which now seemed so long ago.

She whispered his name in her sleep and snuggled closer to him for warmth. He pulled her into his embrace and held her tightly. His lips brushed hers in a lingering kiss. Even in her deep sleep, she responded to his kiss.

Why did you flee from me after our last night together, Cinstinna? he pleaded silently. Did you not feel my desire for you? Sleep well, Cante. Tomorrow you will hate me and curse my rescue. My heart will bleed for you, but it must be done. Perhaps you will one day come to forgive and understand why I must do this thing. Until you return your love to me, I will hold you to me as my kaskapi.

At last, his troubled mind and weary body found the peace of slumber.

Chapter Eleven

Early the next morning, Gray Eagle was awakened by the shrill cry of a hawk. He lay for a time listening to the piercing cries of a hawk in warning to another who had invaded his territory. He thought of the similarity of his position with the white man and the hawk. Both he and the hawk were forced to defend their territories against their enemies. First, each of them warned the trespasser to withdraw peacefully. If not, they would battle for possession of the same territory. The victor would be the stronger of the two, and the loser would be driven out or killed. Was this not the way it had been between his people and the white man or the Ojibwa? He watched the intruder fly off into the predawn light, wishing his enemy was as wise and relenting as that bird.

Quietly, he arose and walked a short distance away to relieve himself. He stretched and flexed his tight muscles. When the sun peeped over the mountains, he was still standing in the same place, thinking and planning.

He knew he had never wanted a woman as he wanted this small white girl who was his enemy. Was her total defeat really necessary? Yes, she had made it so. What if he had shown her more kindness sooner? How could he blame her for doubting him and wanting to escape? He was confused by his feelings for her more than ever.

He wondered if she had run in fear or in hate. He recalled their last night together and asked himself if she could have run because she was afraid to love him. He scoffed, how could she love me after what I have done to her and her people? It was all lies and deceptions on her part. She must have thought I would be more lenient and kind to her if she fooled me into thinking she loved me. Maybe she realized that last night she could not pretend to love and want me any longer. She had only been waiting until the day I trusted her enough to leave her unguarded. Maybe she has even guessed how I really feel about her and is trying to use those feelings against me. I cannot allow my desire for her to interfere with my honor or leadership. I do not have the power to grant you forgiveness, Lese. I wish I could see into your heart and know the truth which lives there.

His eyes must have deceived him yesterday when he thought he saw her face light up at the sight of him standing there on the hill. Maybe he had only seen what he had hoped to see. He could not understand why she did not let the snake bite her and end it all since she had been so desperate to flee him. She said she had prayed for him to come for her. How could he really know for sure how she felt and what she thought? How he longed to know what the real truth was . . .

When he returned, Alisha was awake and sitting up on the skin. She was drinking some water and splashing some on her face from a cupped hand. As she dried her face with the edge of the blanket, he stared at the bruises on her hands. When she lowered the blanket, he stared at the still visible bruises on her delicate cheekbones. He had given her those and many other reminders of his cruelty and power over her. Sadly, there was more to come.

She felt his eyes on her and looked up to meet his gaze, letting her gaze linger questioningly. His impassive look told her nothing, nor did his deadly, calm attitude.

He sat down and took the wasna and aguyapi from his pouch. When he had eaten his fill, he passed the pouch to her. After his treatment to her the day before, she carefully and suspiciously reached for the pouch. She knew she would have to wait until he was ready to reveal her fate to her. He passed her the mni skin. She ate and drank slowly. When she had finished, he repacked the pouch and skin and stood up to depart. He gathered the remainder of his possessions and called for her to come to him.

He retied her hands before they left. She was too confused and weary to resist his commands. Her only thoughts were to keep moving and follow him. They walked at a slow but steady pace, which was certainly easier for her. She did not stop to think or question that their pace was solely for her benefit. She wasn't even suspicious at his frequent, unnecessary stops all day. He would use various excuses of checking tracks, finding water to refill the mni skin, shifting his packs or just resting himself. But at each stop, she would immediately drop wearily to the ground to rest. He would conveniently leave the water skin within her reach and pretend not to notice her drinking from it so often.

By afternoon, they were back at the stream near his camp. When she caught sight of the water, she made a dash toward the stream. She was quickly jerked back by the leash on her wrists. "Water," she pleaded. He ignored her pleas. "Mni, yuzaza," she lapsed into his tongue, but he still ignored her pleas.

Although she had drunk sparingly from the water skin during the long, hot walk, the mni skin had been empty for the past hour and she was very thirsty. She was aware of the danger of drinking too much water when hot and excessively thirsty.

Gray Eagle knew how sweaty, hot and tired she was, but did not dare relent now. Nor did he trust himself to watch her bathe. He told himself he must remain cold to her until after her punishment was complete. He could not allow himself to show her any concern or mercy, especially before his people.

He pulled Alisha through a shallow spot in the stream and continued moving on. The short contact with the cool water felt deliriously wonderful to her tired, aching feet. She would have resisted his cruelty if she had had the strength to pull back on the leash. Mutely, she pressed on behind him.

White Arrow came to meet them as they approached the outer circle of camp. His keen eyes quickly scanned her for injuries, just as Gray Eagle's had done when he first saw her. Her eyes met his and lowered in shame. Not too bad yet, he thought. To his friend, he said, "I see you have found her alive and brought her back as you said. Do those bonds mean she resisted your bringing her back? Is she injured in some way?"

"She did not fight me this time. She is foolish, but not a fool, Wanhinkpe Ska. She has a few small injuries, but she is mostly weak and tired. I found her just in time to save her from the rattlesnake. I had to kill it to save her life." He held up the long row of rings for White Arrow to see.

Fearing the answer he might receive, he asked, "What will you do to her for this, Wanmdi Hota?"

Gray Eagle stared off into the far distance and replied, "You know the punishment for this act and her constant disobedience — the icapsinte . . ."

White Arrow's breath caught in his throat and

he hoped he had heard wrong. "The icapsinte! Surely I did not hear your words, my koda! She is no common slave, nor an Indian. She is the slave of Wanmdi Hota. You cannot do this! It would either kill her or scar her for life. Why do you wish such a punishment for her? You must find some other way to deal with this thing she has done."

"Is the slave of Wanmdi Hota any different than the slave of another warrior?" Gray Eagle asked. "A slave is a slave, Wanhinkpe Ska, and a bad one must be punished. I must do this. She has left me with no other choice this time. This is the punishment for her many deeds of rebellion. Can I treat her any differently than I would another? Do you think I can walk before the others in honor if I say I cannot punish this ska wayakayuha because I, Wanmdi Hota and son of a chief, wants and loves her as a man does a woman? I cannot yield to my enemy!" he retorted hotly.

"Yes, you are the chief's son and our leader while he is away. You have the power to withhold her punishment and give no reasons," White Arrow spoke sharply to him.

Gray Eagle's head jerked in White Arrow's direction and he glared at his best friend. He was alarmed at the tone in his voice and the angry expression on his face. "I would not have to give any reason. They would see and know why I do this. Can I say to them that we must hate the wasichu when I myself love one? Can I say to them that we must drive them from our lands and forests and then keep and protect one in my own teepee? A leader cannot speak one way and then live another. I must show my people I am strong and true to my teachings."

"You must find some way to do this for her and yourself. You are wise, my koda. Think upon this thing. Find some way to save and help her, and still hold on to your honor. You must!"

"She has disgraced me before my people," Gray Eagle insisted. "She has taken my trust in her and cast it aside in contempt. It is past time for her to show respect to me. As was her dishonor before my people, so will be her punishment. They will all see and know it is Wanmdi Hota who rules his teepee, not his ska kaskapi. I have spoken and it shall be."

"It shall be, my koda. But first, I must tell you this. For the second time, I feel the fingers of warning touching my spirit. I hear the voices speak to me once more. I have felt and heard this warning about her before. I felt it the night you took her to the teepee sa. I felt it when you refused to heed my warning about a guard for her when we left two moons ago. Now, I feel it again when you declare her punishment as the icapsinte. Heed me well, for I feel the chilling fingers brush my mind. I feel the wind from the wings of the black bird of death around me. I fear for her life, my koda. Must it be this way?"

Gray Eagle looked confused and bewildered by his words and asked, "I do not see your meaning, Wanhinkpe Ska. How can there be danger of death in my actions? I do not wish to kill her. I will control the apa myself. I do not seek great pain or death from her. I only seek the saving of my face. In time, she will forget and accept that this was as it had to be. Do not let your heart blind your reason, Wanhinkpe Ska. You know it must be."

White Arrow studied the words of Gray Eagle and knew they were true. There was no way out for either of them. If only he had heeded my warning, he thought, this would not be happening. I should have pressed harder when I felt those strange feelings haunting me. But that moon is gone and cannot be re-lived . . .

White Arrow gazed into the pale, tense face of Alisha and agreed, "Yes . . . it must be as you say, but it will bring much unhappiness and pain to both of you. I will not go against your words, my koda."

Alisha instinctively sensed that something was gravely wrong. White Arrow's empathy reached out to her like a lifeline and pulled at her. It appeared to her as if they were arguing about something which disturbed her friend greatly. The troubled looks he gave her and the tone of his voice warned her of some coming danger. It was clear Gray Eagle had the upper hand in the argument. She had seen White Arrow bow in submission to Gray Eagle's words, as she had done so often herself. However, White Arrow's submission looked reluctant.

Perhaps my fate is far worse than I imagined, she thought. Even Wanhinkpe Ska cannot accept it. What could possibly be so terrible that he could do to me to cause my friend to go against Wanmdi Hota in order to help me? She watched the two very closely as they argued. She noted Gray Eagle's victory and White Arrow's unwilling surrender.

Gray Eagle started to move forward again. She reached out and touched White Arrow's arm, gazing tenderly into his jet eyes. "I sense you plead mercy for me, my koda. I do not know how to make you understand how much that means to me. I wish I knew the words to thank you for all you have done and for your friendship. I know he would not listen to you. He will have his way. My destiny now lies in his hands. If it is death, then we cannot stop him or change his mind. Perhaps it is time for it to be over . . ."

She smiled up into his face and gently touched his cheek with her fingertips. "Good-bye koda. May we both find the peace and happiness we search for." She turned to follow Gray Eagle, leaving White Arrow standing there and staring after her.

Within a few feet, White Arrow caught up with them and walked along with his friend. He asked Gray Eagle what Alisha had just said to him. Looking straight forward, Gray Eagle repeated her words to White Arrow. The brave was touched and moved by her kindness and understanding.

White Arrow was concerned about the lack of vitality in Alisha's eyes and voice. Her wan face and the darkened patches beneath her eyes told him of her weakened condition and loss of spirit. He had said he would not plead with Gray Eagle again, but he knew he must. "I will ask you only once more, Wanmdi Hota, do not do this thing. She is weak and it is wrong. She has also felt the warnings of danger and death. I hear this in her words and voice. If she lives, she will turn from you forever."

Gray Eagle stared straight ahead in troubled, brooding silence before he answered. "As she has said, her destiny lies within my hands, and her life, too. This is a part of it. As with the great landslides, she has pushed the first rock down the hill and I cannot change its path. As it travels, it gathers more trouble with it and creates much havoc and often pain and death. For once, Wanhinkpe Ska, the great and daring warrior Wanmdi Hota is powerless."

White Arrow walked away and could not look at her again. It took many long, painful steps to reach the ceremonial lodge to get the apa for the icapsinte. When he had the apa in his hands, he trembled with the desire to cast it into the fire and destroy it. He lowered his head, but could not pray. How could he pray for the right thing to be done when it would cause such harm and hurt to the one he loved? And yet, he could not pray for something to happen to his friend to prevent the harm and hurt.

Alisha silently trailed behind Gray Eagle as he made his way between the rows of teepees in each circle. They encountered many curious, bewildered stares along their way. He led her to the center of camp to the very posts Ben and the others had died at. It seemed like ages ago now to Alisha. She thought, so my time has finally ended here as I always knew it must.

Time ceased to move. She felt suspended between minutes . . . waiting . . . for what or why or whom, she did not know. Surely not for rescue, for she could no longer hope for that.

She halted in mid-thought. She stiffened and what little color was left in her ashen face quickly drained. White Arrow was standing before them with a whip grasped tightly in his strong hands. Surely this was not the terrible punishment they had argued over.

With mounting alarm and disbelief, she realized it was. She had seen men whipped for crimes in the streets of London. Never had she witnessed a woman's flogging. She vividly recalled the damage and pain the lash inflicted on its victim. She knew men had died from flogging. Why and how could he do this to her?

His beating at her fortress flashed before her mind's eye. Does he seek revenge on me for his lashing, after all this time? she thought desperately. I had nothing to do with his whipping. Didn't he see I tried to stop it? I had nothing to do with any of his abuse or evil treatment. Why does he wish to do these terrible things to me?

There must be some mistake.

She turned panicked, emerald eyes to him and studied his handsome, rigid face and icy eyes. She was horrified at what she read there. Sarcastically, she asked, "Am I to be beaten to death or only properly punished for the terrible crime of fleeing from Hell itself?"

He did not acknowledge her question or the fact that she had even spoken. He bound her ankles to the posts with heavy rawhide thongs. "Somehow, I fear you aren't trying to only frighten me. I think you really intend to flog me. Or do you seek my life this time?" she asked fearfully. "I believed I had seen and felt the heights of your hatred and brutality, but I was so wrong. There is no limit to them, is there? Wanmdi Hota, the great and fierce Oglala warrior who thrives on the blood of his enemies," she threw the stinging accusation at him, his name spoken with contempt and her tone filled with sarcasm. He tried to ignore both her tone and words, but could not. He flinched inwardly at each.

It was as if she had been wearing blinders which had suddenly been ripped off. Her situation was revealed to her with crystal clarity. She had been dreaming and fooling herself all along. She had never really had any chance of a future here with him, nor any chance of happiness, let alone life. Her future was as grim and black as her past had been since the day she first met him. How could I have been so blind and stupid? she raged against herself. How could I have thought

for one minute that things would ever be any better or different between us?

She spat at him, "I shall pray to both our Gods
that today will finally end this tragic farce. My
death should be swift and final. I will welcome it.
It has been too long in coming. Why did I not see
long ago this was the only way to really be free
from you and this life you have chained me to?"

Reality caught her heart in a crushing vise. The
pain was almost too great for her to bear. She
lifted misty, green eyes skyward and prayed
softly, "I beg you to hear and answer this prayer.
Have mercy on me this day. Please let him kill me
and free me from this life of torment. Please
don't allow me to pass another day here in this
savage land as his captive. Take my life and spirit
out of his reach forever. Please, God, let me flee
him in death. Free me from his hold and curse
forever. I beg you to hear and grant me this
prayer. Have I not suffered enough for my sins?"

She lowered her head dejectedly to the post.
Her eyes fell on Gray Eagle as he was binding her
ankles to the post. Her gaze captured his and for
once, he was the one who could not look away.

"This day, Wanmdi Hota, you will regret above
all others . . ." A cold shiver ran over his body as
she spoke the very words he had used when he
discovered her escape. An omen — he feared to
ask of what. ". . . if you do this evil thing. God
forbid that I should live, but if I do, I will hate
you forever and never forgive you. Never! I will
die cursing the day I met you and your evil. You

chose to show no mercy or understanding. You chose to have a heart of stone. You are blinded by hate and vengeance. You chose to shut me out of your life and to reject me in every way. Now, you must choose to end it all with my death. I could have loved you with all my heart. I could have accepted you as a man, and perhaps made you forget I am white and an enemy."

Tears clouded her vision and emotions threatened to constrict her throat, but she continued with the words which had to be said. For once, she had to face her feelings. She could no longer deny them. Soon, it would be too late. Everything seemed to fall into place — all, that is, except Gray Eagle's role in her life and fate. How could she explain or understand his type of cruelty and hate?

"Your heart and mind is too full of evil to see what you give up. If only there was some reason for all of this, I could accept my fate and die in peace. I can find none. Is there ever a reason for hate and murder? That first day I saw you, Horace warned me I would live to regret my actions. He was right, but not for the reasons he thought. That first day I saw you, I lo . . ."

She ceased speaking to herself as she became aware of many voices and laughter behind her. She turned her head to see what was going on. Many of the Indians from his tribe were standing only a few yards back. She mistakenly thought they were talking, laughing and waiting for her punishment and death. They were there at the request and order of their leader to witness her punishment only.

Despair crossed her ashen face and her eyes riveted quickly back to him in disbelief and betrayal. She fought hard to control a fresh flood of tears which threatened to spill. She vowed, I will not cry! I will not cower before him or his people. She prayed once more, "God grant me the power to stay silent . . . no matter what he does to me. Do not let me cry out or plead for mercy. Take my voice away if I cry. Help me end this with honor. Please, do not let me cry . . ."

With a great and difficult effort, she swallowed several times to force the lump from her throat and chest. She clamped her teeth tightly together to prevent any pleas from escaping and to still her trembling lips and chin. She told herself over and over, do not cry . . . do not plead . . . ever . . .

White Arrow stepped before her line of vision. Their eyes met and locked and they spoke without words. She braved a last, sad smile to the only friend she had found in the Indian camp. For a brief moment, her grassy eyes had their old sparkle of life and innocence. Just as quickly as it had appeared, it vanished, to be replaced by her heart's pain.

His somber, ebony eyes scanned her features as if he memorized them for a last time. Perhaps he did. . . . He unwillingly handed the whip to Gray Eagle and looked at her once more. In his tongue, he whispered, "May the Great Spirit and your God protect you today, Pi-Zi Ista." He smiled into her eyes and gently stroked her ivory cheek with his hand, then walked away slowly.

Gray Eagle flinched at her parting words to White Arrow, "Would that I had met and loved you first, my koda . . ." She watched him depart, knowing he could not and would not watch this deed.

White Arrow was mumbling to himself as he walked away. His mind was in a maelstrom. Wanmdi Hota is a fool! He does not see it is not only the girl he will punish this day, but himself too for loving and wanting her. Would that she were mine . . .

Alisha closed her eyes, refusing to look at the people again. She did not want to see their stares and looks.

She heard the rich, deep voice of Gray Eagle speaking to his people. He was telling them the charges against her and what the punishment for her deeds would be. He announced five strokes of the apa. He came to her and with a swift jerk tore her garment down the back to her waist. He took his place behind and slightly to the side of her. He shook the coiled whip loose in his grasp. She stiffened in dread and fearful anticipation.

Gray Eagle flexed his fingers on the whip handle and tightened his grip as he stared at the snowy, smooth back before him. He hesitated a moment as she turned her head in his direction. She glared into his flinty eyes, letting him feel her anguish. That look would haunt him for a long time to come. Many nights, he would awaken seeing that last painful expression of betrayal, pain and shattered love.

She turned her face back to the post and rested her forehead on it. She clasped her fingers tightly together and closed her eyes. She clamped her lips shut. She tried to mentally prepare herself for what was shortly to come. She tensed all the muscles in her body and inhaled deeply several times. She prayed once more for the courage and strength to remain silent and die in dignity and honor. She determined she would not beg or scream, no matter what he did or how much it hurt.

The whip uncoiled and struck like a viper, biting into her soft, tender flesh and jarring her entire body. The searing pain swept through her body so forcefully she nearly fainted. It was far worse than she had ever imagined. No one could prepare himself for something like this. How many such lashes could one endure before death or insanity?

Another lash was delivered with such stunning force she lunged into the wooden post. She instantly saw bright stars before her eyes and her ears hummed. Her jaw was aching from her tight restraint on it. She stiffened her sagging body and gripped her fingers more tightly together, unaware the whip would bite deeper and harsher into taut flesh. Her respiration was coming in short, labored rasps.

Another snap of the whip and more excruciating agony. How could she possibly endure this much longer and keep silent? How could she not beg and plead for mercy? Would he continue this abuse until she yielded and screamed for the mercy he might not even grant? Perhaps he intended to beat her until she was dead or horribly disfigured. She prayed not. She preferred death!

Do not yield this time, Lese! she begged herself. Either he must stop because he wishes to or he must kill you. He will be solely responsible for his choice. Keep silent!

Her back throbbed and flamed like a sheet of fire. She was living a nightmare to which there was no awakening. Waves of nausea flooded her and she fought for control. Blood pounded in her ears. Still, the brutal flaying continued . . .

The muscles in her back twitched with pain. It was as if someone was cutting them out with a hot knife one by one. Another lash whistled through the air and landed with a jolt. She teetered between reality and unconsciousness. She had not even felt the minor pain in her lip where she had unknowingly bitten it. Blood trickled down her chin. She felt the warm, sticky blood. She tasted metallic blood. She saw fiery, red blood. Her vision began to blur red, then black, then red and black over and over. She clamped her teeth fiercely onto her hand to suppress a scream.

Silence! Silence! her mind commanded again and again to her mouth. Do not yield to him again!

She sagged against the post, losing count of the

lashes. Blood flowed down into her eyes and coursed down her ashen face. On the last lash, she had uncontrollably arched backwards with the impact of the whip, then forward, slamming her forehead into the post. A humming, ringing sound from far, far away filled her ears. She would never know it was partly the sound of people's voices joined in praise of her bravery and endurance, for to endure such pain and suffering in silence and bravery was greatly honored.

The agony was now unbearable, but no sound would come forth to help release the tension in her pain-racked body. It was as though she had willed herself mute.

She thought perhaps she had gone mad. She knew pain did that sometimes when it was so great and brutal. Just let me die, she prayed softly.

One last crack of the whip and she knew her body had been ripped apart by its force. Pain and fire shot through her. Her mind reeled in fuzziness. No more, merciful God, no more . . .

Her body was floating in a pot of boiling oil. There was bloody darkness and gloom all around her. Charon had come to ferry her soul across the river to Hades. What if Cerberus wouldn't let her pass? But of course he would, she was dead, wasn't she?

Delusions whispered in her ears. Reality had fled and in its place were phantoms. Each came with words and visions of hideous torments.

Then for one brief moment, she sensed total awareness of her surroundings. I am dying, she realized. At last, it's over. She lapsed into unconsciousness, void and black.

Gray Eagle had inwardly flinched at each blow he delivered. He cursed himself for not taking his friend's advice. He had tried to deliver the lashes lightly, but found the apa had a mind of its own and would not be cheated of its task. He gritted his teeth in remorse as he witnessed the soft ivory flesh torn and bleeding. He had watched the long, jagged gashes appear. Raw welts streaked across her slender back. He had announced five strokes and knew he could show no weakness by giving less.

He could feel the strike of the blow each time. Blood was flowing unchecked down her back and dripping into the dusty dirt. He could not understand how she had remained silent so long. He should have recalled how gruesome and painful a lashing was. His reasons for doing this to her seemed unimportant and unnecessary now, but it was too late for apologies.

He mentally punished himself for going through with this. I should have come up with a lesser punishment for her, he agonized. On the fourth lash, he had stiffened in anguish as she arched backwards in convulsive torment. He had almost dropped the whip and run to her side, but had caught himself. What would they think at his show of mercy for this white slave? He secretly wished their opinions and thoughts did not matter to him. Had it been possible, he would have exchanged places and taken the beating himself for her. He was torn between his love for her and his love and loyalty to his people. How could he explain his feelings to them when he did not even understand them himself? Why did the Great Spirit give his heart and love to an enemy when it was impossible for him to return her love or to have her openly?

On the last lash, she had finally sagged and gone completely limp. He had prayed to the Great Spirit for her to lose consciousness immediately to avoid the agony and shame she would be forced to endure. Never once had she cried out in pain or pleaded for mercy. How she must hate me to have such courage, he thought bitterly.

He heard praise all around him. He had even heard calls for mercy and words of sympathy for her. Was this what it had taken to win her a measure of acceptance and honor by his people? He scoffed, the debt is paid now. She had won great respect and face in their eyes, but would never know until the day he chose to reveal the entire truth to her — if he ever had the chance.

There were two people nearby who did not share in Alisha's new-found acceptance and favor: Kathy and Chela. They elated in her suffering and shame and wished her death.

Chela boldly stepped forward and spoke tersely, "She is not dead yet, Wanmdi Hota. A few more lashes of the apa will finish your work.

Even she deserves some mercy, doesn't she?" she queried sarcastically.

Gray Eagle was in no frame of mind or mood for her envy or sarcasm. He roughly shoved her aside and passed by. He turned and warned in an ominous tone, "If you continue to taunt me and my judgments, Chela, or continue this disrespect of me and my honor, I will beat you next and see if you can hold as silent as she!"

He sneered at her look of disbelief and rage, then went to Alisha. He glared angrily at the raw, bloody pulp of torn flesh. He cut her feet free, then went to her hands. Blood ran down her arms from injuries inflicted by the thongs. She had bitten into her hands to keep from screaming. Her wrists were burned and bleeding from straining against the rawhide thongs which bound her hands to the post.

He cut her hands free and leaned her head back against his shoulder. As he lifted her limp body gently, her head rolled backwards onto his arm. He winced as he saw the bloody, swollen lip and the laceration on her forehead. Both injuries ran blood freely down her face and into her damp hair. There were trails where tears had flowed unhalted and now mingled with her blood. He hurriedly walked to his teepee to tend her injuries.

He found White Arrow waiting for him with herbs and medicines. Quietly, he asked, "Does she still live, koda?"

Gray Eagle nodded, not trusting his voice to

speak. He took the water and cloth from White Arrow. While he held her in an upright position, Gray Eagle washed the tears, dirt and blood from her face and arms. Then, he laid her down on the buffalo mat. He placed the cloth under her forehead to staunch the flow of blood, which continued to flow unchecked.

White Arrow passed him the medicines from the pezuta teepee. Together they tended her injuries in silence and apprehension. Gray Eagle took his knife and cut the remainder of her dress off. He covered the lower half of her body with a blanket. White Arrow knew he had never seen such beauty and loveliness, which was now so marred by the angry red welts.

Gray Eagle carefully bathed her back, but still Alisha made no moves or sounds. Fearfully, he checked to see if she still breathed. Agony raced through his mind and tore at his heart. Yes, she was still living, but her respiration was very shallow and light. He recoiled in anguish as he touched the jagged welts. He had seen and given a great deal of punishments, but this was very different.

"I should not have done this thing, Wanhinkpe Ska," he admitted. "You were right, my koda. It was too harsh and deadly for Cinstinna. I could have easily killed or maimed her. I should have stayed her punishment until my anger cooled. It is too late, for the deed is done. The icapsinte was too much for one so helpless and weak. I heard her pray for silence and she did keep silent. She

415

is far braver than I had ever imagined, or her hatred for me is so great that it gave her the strength for silence. I heard her pray for death, but I shall not let her go." For the first time in his life, Gray Eagle felt guilt and remorse for a deed he had committed, even if it had seemed necessary and justified at the time.

"Maybe her God will grant her prayer, Wanmdi Hota. She is very weak and has suffered much at our hands. Too much . . . somehow, I feel this action will take her from you forever."

Gray Eagle flashed him a look of defiance and determination. "I will never let her go, not even to the bird of death! He must fly away with empty wings this time!"

He took the salve made from the mountain herbs and rubbed it on her flayed back. He reflected back on the time she had done this same thing for him. Unlike himself, she did not resist his aid or attack the one giving it. He forced a small amount of juice from the peyote between her lips and down her throat to lessen the pain. The juice was laced with horsemint to prevent shock from the loss of blood and the great pain. He placed some yellow dirt paste on the wound on her forehead and bandaged it tightly with a clean cloth. He then cleaned and treated the smaller injuries on her hands and wrists.

He gazed down into the pale face when he had finished all he could do for her and moaned in anguish. He sat beside her all night, occasionally dabbing more salve to her forehead and back as it was pushed away by the flow of blood. Frequently, he forced water down her throat and mopped her fevered brow. She never responded to his gentle ministrations. Only her light, steady breathing told him she still lived. Throughout the long night, he prayed and chanted the healing chant many times.

His deep timbered voice called out:

Wakantanka, Wanmdi Hota calls,
I seek your help with my prayer.
Return the life of the ska wincinyanna to me
Give her spirit the strength to fight and re-
    turn.
Call back her spirit leader and the bird of
    death.
Call not her feet to walk the Mahpiya
    Ocanku.
Protect her from harm and death.
Wakantanka, Wanmdi Hota calls,
I am a warrior and an Oglala.
I have known and faced death and danger
    many times.
Cinstinna is weak and afraid.
Hear me and answer.
Once more make her spirit and body strong
    and well.
Do not let her die upon the scaffold in the
    night.
Let her lie at my side instead in love and
    peace.
Wakantanka, Wanmdi Hota calls,

Give Cinstinna back to me for now and all
   days . . .

Gray Eagle knew he could not bear for Alisha
to die and be out of his life and reach forever. It
had taken him many winters to find the woman
he could love and desire with all his being. Now
he had nearly lost her with his own rejection.
Why was he throwing away the very thing he
wanted more than he had ever wanted anything?

Solemnly he vowed, I will never be forced into
hurting you again, Cinstinna. I will give you no
reasons to hate or resist me. I will give you the
time and patience to forgive and understand this
thing I have done to you this day and other days.
Perhaps in time, you will learn to forget and trust
me as it should have been from the beginning.

Even as Gray Eagle spoke these vows in his
heart, forces beyond his control were busy destroying them. Powers and emotions he could
not stop were strengthening against him and his
wishes. For a brief moment, he had allowed himself the same folly Alisha had in hoping things
could work out between them. He forgot for a
time that they were enemies — but his and her
people would never forget. Fate would not allow
him to keep the promises he had just made for a
very long time, if ever . . .

Close to sunrise, Gray Eagle finally dozed, but
could not rest for long. The haunting face of
Alisha appeared before him each time he closed
his eyes. He could not escape that last look she

had given him before the icapsinte, a face naked with humiliation and pain, eyes filled with hurt and anguish and stripped of pride and happiness. How would she ever be able to understand and forgive the things he had done to her? Perhaps, she never would . . .

He recalled the agony when his flesh was torn and bleeding in sacrifice to the Great Spirit at his Sun Dance. The only things that had made the sacrifice bearable were his beliefs in obedience to the Great Spirit and his own honor. He had proven his love and gratitude to the Great Spirit. He had shown his great strength and courage to his people. His scars were visible for all to see and know what he had endured. His bravery had been rewarded many times since that day. Was he not known as the bravest, most powerful warrior in the entire area? Were his honor and words not accepted and trusted by all, even those who hated him and his people?

But what reward did Alisha have to think upon and accept? What reason could she accept for her sacrifice and pain? He knew her forgiveness would be a long time coming, if ever. He softly said, "I would trade all my victories to have this morning back again and to have your love and forgiveness, Cinstinna. I wish I had the power to change what I have done this day. But man cannot recall the sun or moon when they have made their paths across the sky. He must right his deed on the new moon or sun, as I must do."

He stared down into the ashen face of his

woman, for that was truly what she was to him. She lay so near to death. For a moment, her face flashed before his mind's eye, alive with her first insight into love that night not long ago. He could visualize her sparkling smile, like the one she had given him the day he rescued her from the rattler. Sadly, he could hear her words, branded into his mind for all time: "Why, Wanmdi Hota? Why?" He had no answer.

Abruptly, a loud, excited voice called to him from outside his teepee flap. He realized it was Little Beaver calling to him to come and talk. He looked at Alisha and then rose to go and see what his friend wanted so early in the morning.

Alisha had not moved or stirred since he lay her down on his mats. At least, she was unaware of the pain and fever raging within her body. Gray Eagle flexed his muscles as he stepped outside in the grayish, pre-dawn light. He inhaled deeply several times as he brought his emotions back under his strict control. He thought it best if his friend believed he had been sleeping, instead of lying awake all night, praying for the life and healing of his woman. Once more, the cool, controlled facade of the warrior slipped easily and quickly back into place. His stoical mask revealed none of the inner turmoil of his heart, nor did his fathomless eyes reveal the pain and anguish he felt. To anyone looking, there stood a warrior with the traits of a man with an animalistic nature.

Little Beaver had walked a short way off from

Gray Eagle's teepee and paced anxiously back and forth as he waited for his leader and friend. He had observed the girl's effect on Gray Eagle many times. Little Beaver worried whether or not he should tell Gray Eagle that he understood his desire to keep the white girl. Hadn't she shown more bravery, intelligence and honor than many men did? Was his friend unaware of the fires of love and desire which lit her eyes when she looked upon him? Did he not see and know he was not truly her enemy, nor she, his? Why did he not demand for the others to accept his claim on her? Hadn't they both proven their courage before the Oglalas? But Little Beaver did not dare confide in Gray Eagle yet. This day there were other threats and problems requiring his full attention.

Gray Eagle came out of the teepee, and asked, "Capa Cistinna, what troubles you so early this day?"

Little Beaver began to relate his news rapidly and excitedly. He had ridden all night to bring his message from Chief Black Cloud of the Blackfoot tribe. He exclaimed, "The war council is meeting this coming moon in the camp of Chief Mahpiya Sapa. All chiefs, war leaders, band leaders and warriors are to gather to talk of war and to smoke the war canduhupa. They speak of a vote to war against the akicita-heyaketo at the wooden fort. They wish to purge our lands and forests of the wasichus and soldiers in our lands and those of our brothers. Mato Ki-in-yangki-yapi has called for us to join with all our brothers and even with our enemies to fight in eighteen moons. They ask Wanmdi Hota to lead them in this great battle."

Gray Eagle met his steady and proud gaze and answered, "We will meet our brothers to talk and vote. Will all the Otchenti Chakowia meet and prepare for war?"

"All tribes of the Seven Council Fires gather and wait for the Oglala and Wanmdi Hota. I saw warriors and leaders coming from the Brule, Hankpapa, Miniconjou, Sanc Arc, Two-Kettle and other tribes to the village of the Si-Ha Sapa. They spoke of others who were to come; the Cheyennes and Shosshone, our friends; and the Crow and Pawnee, our enemies. All will join in truce to drive the wasichus and bluecoats from our lands and back into their own lands to the East. There has been much talk to go on the warpath. Will Wanmdi Hota and the Oglala join with them and lead this battle?"

Gray Eagle deliberated on Little Beaver's words. "It will be a long and fierce battle to rid our lands of the wasichus and bluecoats. The bluecoats have the firesticks and great wall to protect them. We must conquer both for victory. Many will walk the mahpiya ocanku with the Great Spirit before our land is free of them all. The sacred burial grounds will have many new burial scaffolds before the fighting is over. May Wakantanka protect his children."

Gray Eagle thought aloud to Little Beaver. "It

is almost time for the winter buffalo hunt and the Sun Dance. We must end this matter soon and prepare for them. The time comes to leave for our winter camp in the sacred mountains. We cannot leave our lands for the wasichus to come and take while we are gone."

Gray Eagle paused, then decided, "Let it be as they say. I will go with my warriors and speak for the Oglala and war. We will make ready to ride to the village of the Si-Ha Sapa. Call the warriors and leaders together."

Little Beaver ran off with the message. But no sooner had Gray Eagle spoken, when his mind was in turmoil again. How could he leave Alisha so close to death and go to smoke the war pipe against her people? Yet, he knew he must and would. He was not a man, but a warrior and a leader. Even as his desire to remain with Alisha tugged at his heart, his excitement and eagerness to be with his warriors in this important battle flamed within him. Thoughts of pushing his enemies out of the red man's lands and hopes of victory glowed within him. With the help of the other tribes, total and final revenge against the wasichus was a bright reality. His heart soared with relief — and dread.

When this battle was over, all wasichus would be gone. But one would remain: Alisha. That is, Gray Eagle thought, if Wakantanka did not take her life while he was away. Surely, the Great Spirit would not send the Bird of Death for her while he was gone. Did the Great Spirit time this so that he would be away when He came for her? No! He would not take her now, not now, not when the cause of many of their problems would soon be destroyed. He would give the Great Spirit many wasichu lives in exchange for Alisha's. When all the wasichus were gone from their lands, his people would forget and forgive her for being white. When they no longer had to see and feel the wasichu greed and hatred, they would come to accept Alisha as his. In time, her presence in his life and teepee would be a normal, natural thing.

Gray Eagle knew he had no time to dream, and called to the old woman to come to his teepee. He ordered her to take care of and guard his kaskapi well during his absence. He cautioned, "I place her life and care in your hands, Matu. Do not fail me. The girl is mine. Let no one and nothing harm her. Care for her as you would your own cunwintku." He warned ominously, "I will hold you responsible for her life. Go. Bring your things here. Do not leave her side until I return. We go to the camp of the Si-Ha Sapa for war talk."

Matu left. She muttered under her breath all the way to her teepee and back. Once more, she would be responsible for a ska witkowin. This one should die just as the other one did so long ago. . . . Anger and resentment boiled within her bitter heart.

Whoops of excitement came to Gray Eagle's ears as his warriors prepared to depart. Tense expectation and joy filled the hearts of all the warriors, except one. His thoughts shifted from excitement to hesitation and from joy to sadness again and again.

He went over to the mat where Alisha lay, still unconscious. He studied her features for a time, then spoke softly, "Do not take your spirit from me, Cinstinna. I have loved you and wanted you as I have no other. Soon, this will be ended and we shall find the love and peace our hearts yearn for."

He stood up, gathered his weapons, and quickly left his teepee, unaware of the deadly trouble brewing nearby. He called to his warriors. "We ride, Oglalas." He mounted his steed and rode away, to face his destiny alone . . .

Matu stood outside his teepee watching him ride off with his band of warriors. Happiness filled her heart at the thoughts of revenge against the wasichu for whom she held a special hatred. No longer would there be any ska winyans to tempt the warriors, except this one here.

Angrily, she scoffed, he does not fool an old woman. He desires this winyan for his love, not as a slave. Once more, I am forced to protect the life of a white squaw for a chief. But no punishment could be as painful as the one for my last failure, not even death.

She could not deny Alisha's beauty and courage and it galled her to acknowledge them. She fumed hotly, it is not right for a warrior to give up his own winyans for a wasichu. These ska winyans come and take our best and bravest warriors. They cast their evil spells upon them and turn their eyes and hearts from their rightful mates. It should not be so! Must they take them to their hearts when they take them to their teepees?

Perhaps she could die just as the other one had. . . . Matu wondered if Wanmdi Hota would always mourn Alisha's death as Mahpiya Sapa did for the one called Jenny, Grass-Eyes. Do the spirits of lost loves linger near forever? Love? She would have to agree that Alisha did love Wanmdi Hota, just as Jenny had Mahpiya Sapa. But that did not change the truth of how things should be and remain.

She knew she could not risk killing Alisha. Wanmdi Hota would be sure to know. Oftentimes, the apple left a stain in the mouth and an odor on the breath after death. If she dared to kill Alisha for her own revenge or for Chela's sake, Gray Eagle's vengeance would know no limits.

Matu went to where Alisha lay and stared down at her. She asked herself, what does he see in a pale, skinny winyan like you? What magic do you have to make him desire you over his own kind? She lifted the blanket covering Alisha and asked, does he see the same things Mahpiya Sapa saw in his grass-eyed, flaming-haired, ska winyan? What made her life worth my sadness and banishment? How I long to return home to my people. I am old and wish to die among the

Si-Ha Sapa. I could not have changed what happened that day. Does he not see and know this yet, after all these winters? I have suffered long enough because of some such as you, ska witkowin.

But Matu's last words froze in her throat and her eyes widened in surprise at the sight before her. She sank to her knees for a better view. Her scowl was replaced by a smile as she shook her head. It cannot be, she murmured, excited by her discovery. But she knew instantly that her old eyes did not deceive her. "Thanks be to Napi!" she said aloud. She gently traced the scar on Alisha's left hip with her crooked finger. A mischievous, mysterious gleam flickered in her dull, ebony eyes as she fingered the little half moon.

It can be, it can be, she thought excitedly. I must tend to it now. Then, I will go to Mahpiya Sapa. Just as Jenny took me from my people, you will send me back in great honor and love . . .

Secretly, she left Wanmdi Hota's teepee to return to her own to fetch the needed items to bring her heart back to life once more. She returned to Gray Eagle's teepee carrying a small pouch clutched to her sagging bosom. Her task took only a short time for she had traced that same akito many times in the dirt.

Carefully, she rubbed salve onto Alisha's back and gently tucked the blanket securely around her. She called to Succoola. He had been left behind because of his age and weakness of body. She spoke with him quietly and secretly. She told him she must go immediately to the camp of Black Cloud with an urgent message. She told him to guard Alisha with his very life if necessary. She said no one was to enter Gray Eagle's teepee for any reason. No one was to tend her wounds or touch Alisha except him.

Succoola did not understand Matu's sudden concern for the life and safety of the ska winyan. She had not hidden her dislike or contempt for Gray Eagle's kaskapi. She told him she would explain it all when she returned. He had no reason to doubt her and agreed to do as she asked. He sat down crosslegged before Gray Eagle's teepee to watch over Alisha until Matu's return.

Matu had been gone only for a short time when the sound of the thunder of many horses' hooves and the noise of firesticks reached her ears. She halted quickly and listened. She knew the dreaded meaning of those sounds. Fear and anger gripped her heart. The bluecoats were attacking the Oglala village!

They had dared much to ride into the camp of Wanmdi Hota and Suntokca Ki-in-yangki-yapi. How did they know the warriors would be away? Surely they had, for they were not fools.

She prodded her horse to a fast pace. She must warn Wanmdi Hota of the raid on his camp. All other news must wait. If the girl were either killed or rescued, all her hopes and plans would be dashed.

"Napi protect you, Taopi Cikala," she prayed, using Gray Eagle's pet name for Alisha. She had heard him call her that many times, unaware that he was being overheard.

It would be to Matu's advantage that Black Cloud would not see the akito this day. She had not noticed in her excitement that Alisha's sensitive skin had turned very red from the irritation of the scratches. For all Matu had noticed was the akito showing a quarter moon with a star on either side of it. And Matu knew that was the symbol that would set her free . . .

Chapter Twelve

At the first sounds of gunfire and onrushing horses, the women and children fled to the safety of the forest. The few elderly warriors who were too slow to flee or too weak to resist were killed or wounded during the first minutes of the assault.

From their concealed position, the cavalry had observed the absence of warriors. The white truce flag was hastily replaced with the yellow and black standard of the cavalry. The commanding officer was elated at this excellent opportunity to teach the invincible Oglala and "that arrogant, fearless bastard" Gray Eagle a lesson they wouldn't quickly forget. In the process of showing their strength and boldness, they would liberate any white captives. The regiment's assignment was to seek out and trade any white prisoners being held by the Oglala, Si-ha Sapa and Cheyenne.

The troop of ruffians agreed with the ranking officer that it would be humiliating and degrading to ride into camp and beg to trade for the white captives these barbaric heathens had dared to take prisoner. Why trade or plead for what they could take by a show of force? They would find no resistance with the warriors away on a hunt. They would teach the fierce Oglala the cavalry was not to be taken lightly.

The white cavalry charged into the Oglala village like the scourge of the devil and his host of demons, shouting curses and firing at almost anything which moved. The thunder of the horses' hooves pounded like war drums, and the blast of many guns sounded like the call of death. They roped and pulled down many of the smaller teepees and set fire to others.

Some of the slower, feebler warriors were struck down with the butts of guns or skewered with sabers. The women who had not escaped to the forest were terrorized and taunted, but not ravished. Time did not permit this extra benefit. The witnesses would be left behind to tell the warriors of the daring and might of the akicita-heyake-to.

A sweeping search was made of the entire village. Kathy had been located and rescued from the teepee sa. When she was questioned concerning other white captives, she wickedly told them there were no other captives there. Her malicious tone and expression told them otherwise. When pressed for the entire truth, Kathy admitted there was one other white girl there.

She said acidly, "There ain't no need to free

her cause she stays with him willingly. When the Indians attacked our fortress, he saved her, brought her here with him, and treated her like a queen. He wouldn't let none of those other braves touch her. He didn't care to spare nobody's life except his harlot's. She's as much as a traitor and she's right in that teepee!"

Lieutenant Gordon and Captain Harrison ran to the teepee Kathy had pointed out. They lifted the flap, ducked and entered the teepee. After one glance at the shocking sight before them, they shook their heads with disbelief and horror.

Lieutenant Gordon walked over to the mat and knelt beside the delicate creature who appeared so small and vulnerable. It was evident to him that there was real beauty beneath the bruised and battered body of the girl before them.

"Damn those red bastards!" the lieutenant swore to his captain. "They'll have the devil to pay for this!"

He sent the captain to tell the men to prepare to mount up and move out promptly. They couldn't be sure how long the warriors had been away or how soon they would return. One thing Gordon was sure of — it would be stupid to confront the braves on their own home ground.

Gray Eagle had told Matu to hide all of Alisha's clothing. If she did recover while he was away, he wanted to be sure there was no chance of her escaping again. No matter how much she hated or feared him, she would never leave his teepee naked. Gordon looked around for something to dress her in. He cursed again when he found she wasn't even allowed to have garments of any kind. Seeing nothing he could use to cover the upper part of her slender body, he gallantly removed his uniform jacket and carefully put it on her. As he buttoned it securely, he took note of her slim, but ravishing, figure. She was neither child nor woman, but suspended momentarily between the two. He painfully realized he was much too aware of her loveliness and desirability as a woman. He wrapped a blanket around the lower half of her body and secured it about her tiny waist. He lifted her into his arms and carried her to his waiting mount. Captain Harrison held her while he mounted, then handed her up to him. He settled her in his strong embrace and cradled her protectively.

As the other men watched with growing interest and curiosity, Kathy harshly exclaimed, "I see you found the bitch. Too bad. She's not going to appreciate your help. She won't like being rescued and neither will her brave."

The lieutenant maneuvered his horse to stand before Kathy. He glared down at the bitter young woman, trying to detect the real meaning in her statement. He had loosened his grip on Alisha and her head had rolled away from his shoulder. A few gasps were audible as the closest men became aware of the mental state and physical condition of the beautiful girl in Gordon's arms. The cloth had slipped from around her forehead and the swollen, jagged cut stared them in the face. The slender ankles were raw and chafed from rawhide bindings. The arm which hung free displayed a bloody bandaged wrist and minor injuries on her small hand. The angelic features were also marred by a swollen lower lip.

Gordon retorted to Kathy, "Is this what you call a willing mistress? This girl's been brutally beaten into unconsciousness and inflicted with numerous other injuries. I saw from the lashing she took and the evidence of scars, she was far from being submissive and willing. From the looks of her abused body, I fail to understand how you think she's been treated like a queen. I think those were your exact words. Why would any man, even a savage, flog a woman to near death?"

Kathy spitefully replied, "He only whipped her yesterday. She tried to run away. He tracked her down and brought her back. The beating was for punishment. She's been living with him for months. She waits on him hand and foot. She does everything for him, Lieutenant, everything!"

Captain Harrison spoke up, "If she liked it here so much, then why'd she try to run away? 'Sides, how are you so sure she was crazy about him? Did you sleep in the same teepee with them?" His last question was a cutting joke and the soldiers nearby laughed at the jealous girl.

Lieutenant Gordon cut in before Kathy could

speak another word, "Prepare to ride to the fort, men! Or else your head will rest tonight on an Injun's belt!"

Gordon directed Harrison to take Kathy with them to Fort Pierre. The entire regiment fell into formation and headed swiftly out of the Oglala camp.

It was nearly midnight when they finally arrived at the fort. The guards hastily opened the gates at Lieutenant Gordon's command. He immediately went to the doctor's quarters with his precious survivor. He pounded loudly on the door with his boot. As Doctor Philsey opened the door, Gordon kicked it back and hurriedly went inside. Carrying the limp body of the girl, he headed straight for the examining table.

"What's going on, lieutenant?" asked the perplexed doctor.

Lieutenant Gordon shouted over his shoulder, "Doc, we found this white girl in a camp we raided this morning . . . appears she's been badly whipped . . . been unconscious since yesterday . . . signs of other injuries, too . . ."

Doc came forward to the table where Gordon placed Alisha and looked down at her. "My God!" he exclaimed. "She's no more than a girl! Damn these savages! Know who she is?"

Gordon carefully removed his jacket from the still girl. He shook his head and answered only the questions he could. "Her name's Alisha Williams. She's one of those settlers from that small fortress southwest of here. The one about two days' ride. You recall, the one that was raided about a month or so back. By the time we scouted the area, everyone was dead or captured. It was those Oglala, just like I thought. We brought back another girl, too; but she hasn't told us much. She said this one was the squaw of the chief's son. If you asked me, I'd say the other girl is just a mite too spiteful to be trusted. I think there's more between these two girls than she's told us."

Doc questioned, "Did you say Oglala camp?" Gordon nodded yes. "That would make the chief's son none other than Gray Eagle, wouldn't it, son?"

Gordon grinned like the Cheshire cat. "You're right there, Doc. Finally put one over on that son-of-a-bitch! Damn, how I'd like to see his face about now!"

"Don't you think that was a bit foolish, son? Gray Eagle isn't a man to be dallied with. His feathers will be mighty ruffled when he finds this treasure missing. You'll have to leave her here and I'll take care of her, if it isn't too late. From the looks of her condition, I'd say she doesn't have much of a chance to pull through. None, if infection sets in. Shame too, she's very young and pretty."

Mrs. Philsey came out to see what the fuss so late at night was all about. She noticed the girl lying on the table and went to her. She gasped. She moved backwards a few steps, slightly sickened by the sight of Alisha's raw back and ugly welts.

Doc had to force Gordon to leave to allow him to work on the injuries. He told Gordon he'd have to check her to see just how bad it was and see if he could fix her up. He maneuvered Gordon to the door and told him he would let him know her condition as soon as possible in the morning. He closed and bolted the door. He went back to join his wife at the girl's side.

Together they gently cleaned Alisha's back, which was a bloody pulp of torn, mangled flesh. They applied a salve and carefully bandaged it, then set to work on her other injuries. The worst scrapes, cuts and burns were painted with tincture of iodide. Her head wound was washed, balmed and dressed. This was about all they could do for her.

After talking it over with his wife, Doc decided it would be best if he kept her sedated for the next few days. He knew this would prevent him from knowing the full extent of her head injury, but the reality of her pain and the tortures she had recently undergone would be far worse for her at the present. Doc gave her a heavy dose of laudanum and put her in the spare room to the back of the their quarters.

The next few days passed slowly for the Philseys. They watched over Alisha as if she were their own daughter Elizabeth. Their hearts reached out to her when she would cry out for deliverance from her unseen enemy who haunted her even in her heavily drugged state. She had screamed out such terrible things. They would stare at each other in shock, wondering how she could have endured it all, if in fact her words were true. At those times, they would try to quiet and comfort her, but could not reach her. How could they doubt her words when her bodily injuries said she spoke the truth?

They daily bathed and dressed the wounds, keeping a close check for infection. Alisha's fever had finally broken and some of the angry redness in the welts began to subside slightly. The Philseys had forced soups and fluids down her throat numerous times during the day and night. They had been forced to change blood and sweat-soaked sheets twice a day. Things finally seemed to be coming under their control. Her cries would have pulled at even the hardest heartstrings.

By the sixth day, Doc knew he must allow the laudanum to wear off in order to check Alisha for any internal and brain injuries. He dreaded the thought of letting her regain consciousness, but knew it was necessary. In her delirium and pain, she had travelled back in time and relived many horrible events. Each tragedy claimed her energies, and Alisha would call out and whimper in her troubled sleep.

By mid-afternoon, the sedative began to wear off gradually. She began to stir restlessly and moan in discomfort. With each movement, her pain and awareness increased. Each action brought fresh waves of burning, stabbing pain to her back and head. Her mouth was so dry she could hardly swallow. Her head pounded and swam dizzily. She ached all over. Why was she so weak and groggy? She fought hard to regain consciousness, but couldn't quite bring herself above the dreamy level. Every so often she would hear soft whispering. Where was she and why was she in such terrible agony? Where were her parents and why didn't they stop this excruciating pain?

Alisha could hear someone screaming and crying. She realized it was she, but could not order her mouth to stop. Why didn't someone help her? Had she been in some accident? Couldn't they see how much she was suffering? It was so hot. Her back felt like a sheet of fire. Her limbs felt strangely dismembered. Her thoughts collided one with the other in a kaleidoscopic dream of varying colors and phantoms. Although her mind had travelled backward in time, it was swiftly hurling forward to the present with each passing minute. She would soon know the answers to her questions — only to wish for unconsciousness again.

A female voice startled her. She was stunned at the English she heard. "Don't cry, Sweetness. You're safe now. They can't ever hurt you again."

Alisha trod the twilight between consciousness and wakefulness. Her thoughts jumbled together and she moaned, "No . . . It can't be . . . It's not fair . . . Prayed to die . . . Suffered enough . . . Let it be over . . . Can bear no more . . . Others all dead . . . Why not me? . . . Can't wake up . . . Can't be kaskapi . . . No more cruelty and hatred . . . All blood and death . . . Torture . . ." She screamed out, "Please don't let him hurt me again. The pain . . . Hurts . . . My head . . . The fire . . . Untie me . . . Let me go . . . Please, water . . . Must escape . . . Papa, help me! . . . In the fire, burning, must save it . . . No-o-o . . . Beg you, mine . . . It's mine . . . Must help Kathy . . . Don't hurt her . . . Needs water, food . . . Hates us all . . . No place to run . . . Can't hide from his eyes and ears . . . All alone now . . . All dead . . . So hot . . . The pain . . ."

Her mental torment and agitation became so great, she bolted upright in the bed, face ashen with terror and eyes wide with fear. She screamed to her elusive antagonist, "No more, Gray Eagle. I beg you, no more . . ." The pleading softly faded as she lapsed back into unconsciousness, mumbling faintly, ". . . No more . . . Be good . . . No more, please . . ."

She lay there drenched in perspiration, mentally and physically exhausted. Mrs. Philsey stared down at her in shock and bewilderment. This girl's words and fears definitely did not match the accusations the Brown girl was spreading around the fort. Alisha certainly didn't sound like a willing squaw to her. All her pleas had been filled with hopes of escape from him and his brutality. It sounds to me like she was terrified of the bastard, Mrs. Philsey decided. Still, there were nagging doubts which pulled at her mind. Perhaps this girl was hallucinating part of the things she said. The head injury or the terror of her capture and ravishment could be responsible for the illusions in her mind.

One thing was sure — she had been the captive of Gray Eagle, for she had begged for mercy from him, only him . . . Mrs. Philsey begrudgingly wondered if this Gray Eagle were as handsome and virile as she had heard. The few women who had caught a glimpse of him during raids had spoken heatedly about his good looks, dashing boldness and brave manner. He had been likened to Adonis. Even the Brown girl couldn't hide her envy of Alisha's position. Mrs. Philsey suspiciously wondered if his cruelty had completely blocked out all that magnetism and sensuality. It definitely had not in the Brown girl. Still, Alisha had not spoken any words of love or desire. Confidently she vowed, I will know her thoughts and feelings for him and his kind very soon . . .

Powchutu had given a surprised start when Alisha had cried the name of Gray Eagle. He had been standing near the window of her room adjusting the bridle on his horse when she had cried out loud. He had listened to her rantings as he pretended to be busy with his gear. He had an overwhelming desire to hear and know more. He had overheard the gossip from the soldiers in the fort. They enviously discussed the beautiful white girl they had rescued from the camp of the Oglala, in fact, from the very teepee of Gray

Eagle himself! Powchutu was highly skeptical of the fact she was the private slave and captive of Wanmdi Hota. Gray Eagle capture and hold a white girl for his very own? Impossible! Why, he hasn't even taken an Indian winyan for his own! thought the Indian scout. Not that any one of them wouldn't give anything for that honor. Perhaps he is much like me. Perhaps he awaits that one special woman who will stir and awaken the heart. From the facts I have learned, the decision of choosing a winyan will soon be out of his hands.

But what is this white girl to him? She has called out to him in her sleep. Do the white soldiers speak the truth for once? Did that girl inside truly belong to the most feared and awed warrior in this entire area? All men, Indian and white, know the victories of Wanmdi Hota, and tremble to be called his enemy.

Powchutu recalled his past two years as a scout for the fort. He rarely believed anything these men said or did, but this time it might be true. In all his twenty-six years, they had shown him only contempt and hatred as they did all mixed-breeds, "hanke-wasichun" as the Indian would say. How he despised being called "that half-breed scout" by the white man and "hanke-wasichun" by the Indian. One day he would show them all! They will come to fear and respect the name of Powchutu as they did the name of Wanmdi Hota.

There was a great deal of deeply rooted bitterness, hatred and resentment in Powchutu against both peoples. His mixed lineage had caused him many problems and a good deal of suppressed anger and mental torment. His kind were rejected and hated by both sides. He had no real friends or family on either side of his blood line, and his life was empty and dismal. It was tormenting to be so all alone and alienated in a world of living, laughing, loving people.

Powchutu, cast out by both the red and white nations, swore his revenge against them both. Perhaps he would win his retaliation through the eventual confrontation between Gray Eagle and Lieutenant Gordon . . .

Later in the night, Alisha regained consciousness, screaming in the grips of pain and illusion. Doc and his wife finally calmed her down. She was trembling uncontrollably. Her cheeks were very flushed and huge tears escaped the luminous green eyes. She was thin and pale from the many days of undernourishment and illness. Her face revealed signs of the intense bodily pain and mental suffering she was undergoing.

She stared in disbelief and confusion at her unfamiliar surroundings and the two strangers who sat before her. She was hardly aware of what they were saying to her. She hastily blinked several times expecting the apparition to vanish. When it did not, she asked, "Where am I? How did I get here? Who are you?"

Before they could offer any explanation, her

terror-filled eyes scanned the room and she shrieked, "Where is he? Why did he bring me here?" Her tone changed to one of pleading, "Please don't let him hurt me again. Tell him I won't try to escape anymore. It's impossible . . . He'd only track me down again and . . ." She hesitated, then questioned, "What is he going to do with me now? Is the punishment over? Will he beat me again when I am well?"

Doc gently patted her hand and spoke comfortingly to her until she quieted down enough for him to go on with his explanation. He said, "You've been very ill. We weren't sure we could even help you. My wife and I have doctored you day and night for these past six days. Without proper care, I doubt you would have survived in that village. It's a good thing Lieutenant Jeffrey Gordon found you when he did and brought you here so promptly. Of course, the Indians are gonna be plenty mad when they learn of his raid on their camp, if they don't know already."

She gazed dumbfoundedly at him. His words hardly made any sense to Alisha. She stammered, "How did the cavalry know about us? Six days . . . Safe . . . Rescued . . . When I tried to escape, I was heading for Fort Pierre. Lieutenant Gordon? Will he come after me? Will he attack here?" She lowered her voice to a soft quiver, "You don't know what he's capable of. We're not safe even here. He destroyed our fortress and killed everyone. He'll come here and . . ."

She could not believe that it was over. How

could such a long, brutal ordeal suddenly halt? Could it really be possible and true? Free from torment and him?

Mrs. Philsey adamantly stated, "You're safe here, Sweetness. He can't harm you anymore. It's all over. He isn't strong enough to attack here. Why, our cavalry would cut him and his warriors to pieces if they tried to attack this fort! He's not that stupid." Alisha listened to the voice filled with positive assurance.

Doc caught Alisha as she fell backwards in a dead faint, "This news must be a great shock to her after all she's been through. Poor child, probably figured she'd never be free of those Indians again. When she realizes she's truly free and safe, she'll be all right. She's young and pretty. It'll take a little time, but she'll adjust and be fine." He laid her head on the pillow, adjusted her body and covered her up.

Mrs. Philsey replied caustically, "Little time! It'll take lots of time to get over what she's been through. I'll wager she never forgets it. There's no telling what those savages have done to her. I can't see why the cavalry doesn't ride in there and punish them all. They should stop this kind of thing from ever happening to innocent people. If it takes killing them all, then so be it. Go on and get it over with and stop all this brutality."

"Now, now, my dear. We can't just ride into their camps and slaughter them. Chances are things will settle down soon. You're just all riled up because she looks so much like our daughter."

"She's a white woman and they've dared to treat her like some animal! Mark my words, my husband, some day we will be forced to either wipe them all out or get off their lands. I would bet my life that those redskins would sooner die than give this area up. I'll wager that's the only way we can remain here or have others come later. Those Injuns will never be pushed aside or back. We'll be forced to get rid of them any way we can. You'll see . . ."

Doc was startled by the coldblooded gleam in his wife's eyes and the tone of her voice. He reasoned she was only more upset about this event than he had guessed. Evidently she was seeing Elizabeth instead of Alisha. He refused once more to see there was more to her meaning than he was ready to acknowledge. He dismissed the subject.

He sighed deeply and said, "Let's go to bed and get some rest. She's exhausted. She'll no doubt sleep through the night. I'll come in and check on her later. Forget about those Indians and their punishment. It doesn't concern us." They retired for the night.

The next few days were a confused time for Alisha, full of painful awakenings and slow-descending reality. It was true . . . she was safe at Fort Pierre. Her days were consumed with resting and eating. Gradually she began to regain her color and strength. The worst of the agony had receded. Now, it took only small doses of laudanum to ease the harshest of pain and relieve sleeplessness. The medication dulled the torment to a mild aching and eased the throbbing in her head. She became restless and agitated at having to sleep and lie on her sides and stomach all the time, but it was far too painful to lie on her back. When Doc placed the salve on her back she would cringe in distress. The headache gradually went away and the head wound healed leaving a dark bruise.

With more time, the weakness and soreness lessened. Longer periods of total awareness were brought on by the reduction in medication. Her mind was constantly bombarded with thoughts of her past. She fought hard to push all memories from her mind until she was stronger, but they refused to be suppressed for very long. She knew she must come to terms with all of it, or go insane. Alisha thought, which was more frightening — reality or insanity?

She had refused all visitors and saw no one but the Philseys. When Jeffery Gordon insisted on seeing her, she panicked. Doc had no choice but to forbid it for the time being because of her highly agitated mental state. Most of the time she remained calm and subdued. But other times, she would just sit and stare off into space with silent tears easing down her cheeks. Doc would shake his head sadly, knowing he couldn't offer any real comfort. He would convince himself it would all work itself out soon and she would be all right. She would come to learn her horror was over and life must go on.

He was deeply concerned about the look of terror in her eyes when she did not hear someone enter her room. On many nights the Philseys could hear her soft weeping, but had let her be. Doc said she had to work these fears and emotions out for herself.

As the days hastened by, Alisha tried to form a friendship with Mrs. Philsey. But the doctor's wife constantly pressed her for answers to questions Alisha did not want to recall. Alisha thought in exasperation, why was she so determined to have all the grisly, private details of her capture and life of captivity? When Mrs. Philsey pressed Alisha for information, Alisha would retreat into silence and gaze off into space as if there was no one else present. This action would greatly irritate and aggravate Mrs. Philsey. She was forced to cease her questioning for the time being. She would study the girl who was sitting before her, so distant, taciturn and fidgety. To be denied the information she wanted was eating at her like a great gnawing hunger.

Alisha's stubborn silence, as she called it, piqued her even more. Why did this girl refuse to tell her what had happened? What did she have to hide? Her captivity was no secret. Why did she refuse to discuss it with a sympathetic ear? Judging Alisha by her standards caused Mrs. Philsey's doubts as to what really did happen to Alisha in the Oglala camp. Memory of Kathy's accusations began to filter into Mrs. Philsey's mind.

She had coaxed Alisha with such arguments as, "It would help you to accept and deal with what happened to you if you would let us discuss it. Talk to me, Alisha. I can be very understanding. You can't keep all that tension, fear and hatred all corked up inside."

Alisha perceived Mrs. Philsey was only over-curious and a little too inquisitive. She couldn't possibly discuss the things which took place between her and Gray Eagle with this stranger. It was those intimate, personal things which tormented her. She wouldn't be able to conceal certain emotions and expressions if the discussion got out of hand. No one, no matter how considerate or sympathetic, would understand or accept how she felt and why. She must keep it all to herself, no matter how piqued or angry Mrs. Philsey became. She was grateful to her for all she had done for her, but this did not have to be repaid by baring her very heart and soul to the woman.

Alisha would try to talk politely and respectfully. When all else failed, she would plead with her, "Please, Mrs. Philsey. I just can't think or talk about what happened to me out there. I want to forget it ever did. It is too difficult and painful to recall it. I'm sorry, but I can't. I can't . . ."

Mrs. Philsey had done everything but demand she tell her everything. Reluctantly she would be forced to give in to Alisha's pleas. She was determined to have every gruesome, intimate detail of this girl's life in the Oglala village and those suspicious incidents back at their fortress. In time, she vowed. In time . . .

Alisha's back began to scab over and hasten the healing process. It mainly hurt when she made sudden moves or bends. The scabs were taut, and would sometimes break and bleed. Doc insisted she get up frequently to exercise. She would sit by the open window for fresh air and sunshine. Doc had taken a liking to this slip of a girl. His fondness for her deepened each day.

It became very easy to talk with her. She was very intelligent, and could converse on various topics. He became very much aware of her charm, wit and good breeding. She was fresh, alive, enchanting and lovely. But she was also vulnerable, artless and fragile. Such a combination in one so young, beautiful and abused. How had she managed to retain her air of innocence and dignity?

Much to Alisha's gratitude and relief, he never broached the subject of her slavery. He had a way of relaxing and comforting her with just his smile. For a few brief moments, she could be herself and forget reality.

The nights were the worst time for Alisha. She would see Gray Eagle's face when she closed her eyes and hear his voice call to her in her sleep. Even though I felt and saw his cruelty, she brooded, it seems so unreal now. I must forget him, and yet, I can't. How I long to go to him, to have him take me in his arms and tell me it was all a dreadful mistake, to have him love me!

She would admonish her thoughts and feelings. You live in a dream world, Lese, for you never really knew him at all. You love a man you have created in your mind. The Wanmdi Hota you love and desire is only an illusion — a beautiful, daring illusion. Why do you refuse to see and accept this truth? You must recognize the real Wanmdi Hota for who and what he truly is, not what and who you wish him to be.

After all he has been to me, what will my life be like without him? she wondered. How could I ever love another man as I have loved him? My heart betrays me for surely I should hate him with every fiber of my being. God help me, for I love him more than my own life.

How can I think of my future when my thoughts are living in my past? How do you tell the heart not to love, or the mind to forget, or the pain to cease? The longer I am here, the more I see his view of this brutal conflict. Still, it did not and will not change anything.

What now? her heart cried out. I can neither forget nor reclaim my past. It was distressing and alarming to realize the loss of Gray Eagle brought her more pain than the loss of anyone in her past life, or even than the beating he had inflicted upon her.

Why did he really beat me? she wondered. Had

she pushed him so far? I wonder if he regrets his action.

She couldn't forget the strange expression in his ebony eyes just before he began. Had it been one of guilt, compassion, hesitation or regret? She would never know. I would rather have died than lose him forever, she cried to herself. I must surely be mad, for I would accept him with his hatred rather than not have him at all. He is lost to me forever.

Their last night together forced its way into her thoughts. Would their life together have remained like that if she had not tried to escape? There was a strange closeness between them that night. For once, he had been only a man, not an Indian or a warrior. She had been only a woman, not his slave or his enemy. Had his budding acceptance and perhaps love been the cost of her freedom? Had she turned away just as he was reaching out to her? Had her escape and his beating cruelly torn his newfound feelings for her from his heart?

Alisha was abruptly aware of Lieutenant Gordon's voice. He was arguing with Mrs. Philsey again. She stiffened. What if he forces her to let him in? What will I do or say? I can't meet a stranger or anyone looking like this. I can't. I look a sight! My hair is dull and lifeless. I've no clothes to put on. My skin is pale and clammy. I'm thin, scarred and bruised. My appearance screams of captivity.

Alisha had been allowed only to sponge off.

Doc had said the welts must heal further before she could wet them. She had previously realized she did not have any clothes or possessions to enhance her looks, nor any money to purchase even a brush. Mrs. Philsey had given her two old, over-sized gowns, but that was almost the extent of her entire worldly possessions. What was she going to do? She couldn't expect these strangers to feed and clothe her indefinitely. She feared the day she would have to leave this room, but knew she certainly couldn't remain here forever. Mrs. Philsey's hospitality was already wearing thin. If only she had some way to repay or compensate them for their care, room and board. How could she even work or help without begging for money or clothes? She had never been this helpless in her entire life.

She listened . . . silence. He must have given up and gone away. The past must be laid to rest and you must begin a new life, Lese, she thought. But how and when?

The door opened and Mrs. Philsey strolled in. "The lieutenant was here to see you. He is getting more and more persistent and irritated. I believe he thinks I am the one who won't allow him in here to visit with you. I think you are being unfair and unkind, Alisha. After all, my dear, he is the one who risked his life and the lives of his men to locate and rescue you. I think you should see him and thank him properly. I'm not sure how much longer I can stall him with these dubious excuses of yours. Why won't you speak with him for just a few minutes? You do owe him that much."

"Why should he be concerned about someone he doesn't even know? I fail to see why he has any right to demand I receive his company if I do not wish it so. If he were a true gentleman, he would understand my hesitation. I am not ready to face the world, as you put it yesterday, Mrs. Philsey. Is a little more time too much to ask after all I've . . ." She turned away and did not finish her sentence. Why did the thought of meeting another man or speaking with him frighten her so much? Perhaps she was skeptical of his deep concern. His deep, mellow voice sparked an alarm in her mind. Why, she did not know.

"Jeffery is the officer who found you and brought you here to safety. Do you know how very dangerous it was for him to come into that camp to free you? 'That' gives him the right to know you are all right and recovering. He feels an obligation to your safety and welfare. He said as much himself. Besides, he's a very handsome young man. He could be just the one to take your mind off your troubles. Most girls around here, or anywhere for that matter, would give an arm to have him so solicitous about them. You should be glad he's concerned enough to call after . . . I mean, that he calls so frequently to inquire after you. If you continue to refuse to see him, he may lose interest and look elsewhere. I might add, Alisha, Jeffery is one of the richest, most charming and well-bred men out here. You would do well to think on your future and circumstances before you continue like this. You forget you are now alone and penniless. He would be a very good catch for you."

Alisha stared at the woman in such a way it caused Mrs. Philsey to feel very uncomfortable and defensive. Still, she continued, "I don't mean to sound so callous or unkind, but you must realize there aren't many solutions to your kind of problems, other than catching a man like Lieutenant Gordon. I promise you couldn't do any better. I suggest you had better think of the alternatives. The Brown girl isn't as fortunate as you to have your beauty and manner. It's obvious you're from a good background. The Brown girl is whoring for the fort. Is that what you want?" She boldly challenged Alisha to shock her into some action and decision.

Alisha's face flamed at her gaucherie, then paled at its implication. "I would never lower myself to . . ." she began, but was rudely interrupted by Mrs. Philsey.

"Sometimes, we have little to say about what we do or become. You, of all people, should know this!" Her speech was crisp and tart.

"I'm sorry if I have offended you in some way, Mrs. Philsey. Perhaps my seclusion does appear impolite and selfish to you and Lieutenant Gordon. I guess I haven't given any thought to my future yet. Your news about Kathy was such a shock to me. I only meant I could not become what she has. I would rather die first."

"Is your resistance and stubbornness what earned you that beating?" She was hoping to trick Alisha into some type of admission or revelation of some sort.

Alisha refused her baited question. "I was beaten for trying to escape, Mrs. Philsey, which I discovered was a terrible mistake on my part." But she did not explain what the "mistake" was.

There was a hushed, strained silence between them for a time. Alisha was the first one to break it. "I will see this Lieutenant Gordon if you think it best and if it will make you happy. But I must have a bath and shampoo first. Besides, I have nothing to wear. I certainly can't meet him filthy and draped in a bed sheet!"

Mrs. Philsey informed Alisha she would gladly furnish her with all three of her wants — a bath, a shampoo, and clothes. She told Alisha she had two dresses she had made for her daughter's birthday. She would happily give both of them to her if it would encourage her to return to the land of the living. She added she would borrow some undergarments and shoes from some of the other ladies at the fort. The number of females at the fort was small, so she would have to make do with the best they could lend. Mrs. Philsey knew they would donate a few items in order to speed up this mystery girl's public appearance. Many of them were anxious to meet her, or even to glimpse her.

Alisha thanked her for her help, but secretly speculated on her true motives. She couldn't quite put her finger on Mrs. Philsey's intentions. There was definitely more to it than compassion or kindness, but what?

Alisha softly said, "I am not up to a palaver at this time. I hope a few words and light banter with a very proper 'thank-you' will be sufficient for today. When I am bathed and dressed, you can send word to this Lieutenant Gordon that I will receive him."

Alisha was so close to Elizabeth's size, the dresses would fit as if they had been made for her instead. Mrs. Philsey decided it would be worth the donation of the two dresses for Jeffery's indebtedness. She herself would be sure to take all the credit for persuading Alisha to see him. She would soon be needing Jeffery in her corner. She would need a very special favor from this man, so any help she could give him with Alisha would be reciprocated in a most pleasing way. Within a few more months, she would no longer need to lick the boots of any man, no matter how rich or handsome.

Alisha sat calmly waiting for Mrs. Philsey to get things prepared. Mrs. Philsey eagerly sent word to Jeffery, informing him that Alisha would see him later that afternoon.

Alisha did not like having her personal life an open book for all the Fort Pierre people to read. Her face flamed at the remembrance of Lieutenant Gordon's having seen her nude when he rescued her. Doc had told her she had been dressed only in his jacket and a blanket. If he took the time to put his jacket on her, then why couldn't he have put one of her dresses on her? she thought with annoyance. At least that way she would have had something to put on now! To think of him touching and viewing her body while she was unconscious mortified her. How many of the other men had seen and helped him with her? She agonized over this realization.

Could this persistent interest be prompted by what the lieutenant viewed that day? Did he really care about her as a person? How could he? They didn't know each other. I do not trust him or his brotherly concern, she decided. For that matter, neither do I trust Mrs. Philsey's motives. They're anything but altruistic.

Alisha knew she had no real reason to doubt or mistrust either of them. Perhaps she had been too critical, too suspicious and too faithless. But neither of them has harmed me in any way, she chided herself. In fact, in different ways they have both helped me. It is not good to be so skeptical and untrusting of one's fellow beings.

Then why had Mrs. Philsey been so brutal with her news about Kathy? Why would she do such a thing? In the village Kathy had no choice, but here? The best thing for me is to get well and leave this savage land and its people for good. I must find some way back to England, for my heart is not up to my becoming an American — the cost is far too great to pay.

It would be dangerous to remain so close, and

yet so far away from Wanmdi Hota. I could not chance our meeting again under any circumstances. God help me and let it be over. I must forget him and all he did and was to me. It would be far easier if I did not have his scars on my heart and body to remind me of him.

Mrs. Philsey came in with the two dresses. One was a chambray of green and white. It was trimmed with a white collar and cuffs. The other dress was a beautiful paisley in blue, red, green and white designs. It was decorated with a white lace ruche and cuffs. Mrs. Philsey was also carrying undergarments and a pair of black, ankle-high, lace-up boots. She placed the things on Alisha's bed.

They talked about the clothes for a few minutes. She handed Alisha a volume of poetry left for her by Jeffery. As expected, Mrs. Philsey took all the credit for convincing Alisha to see him. She had coyly played up Alisha's shyness and embarrassment at her position in the Oglala camp.

Jeffery was satisfied with Mrs. Philsey's handling of the situation for a while. He knew she was blatantly lying when she told him Alisha had heard such raving compliments about him that she felt she had to wait until she was more presentable. Being of a roguish, conspiratorial nature himself, Jeffery knew there was far more to this woman's help than she let on. He would learn her reasons for her assistance with that bewitching, stubborn girl in the back room. He was positive she would be well worth his time and trouble.

Alisha looked at the book of poetry. It was an impersonal gift from a stranger to a stranger — or was it? It was a collection of sonnets by William Shakespeare. It included *The Sonnets, Venus and Adonis, The Passionate Pilgrim*, and *A Lover's Complaint*. The forepage was inscribed with a short, clear message: "For a speedy recovery and a long-anticipated meeting. Yours, Jeffery."

She studied the book and the inscription. Mrs. Philsey watched the radiant smile play across her lips. She likes poetry, especially love sonnets, she mused. Jeffery will be happy to know his gift pleased her so much. I shall be sure to tell him. I bet he's used that same tactic to woo the hearts of many an unsuspecting girl or lonely wife. Alisha can deal with his roving eye and rakish nature if and when she gets him.

But Alisha's smile was not because of the book, Jeffery's kindness or inscription or its kind. It was for the bittersweet memories of reading this same book with her father very long ago and far away in a flower-filled garden in Liverpool.

Still gazing down at the book, Alisha hesitantly asked, "What does he say about my being . . . a captive . . . about what . . . happened out there?"

"My dear Alisha, being a captive is no one's fault. He does not blame you for what you could not help or prevent. He has been here long enough to know what these savages are like. He will not hold any of this against you." She spoke gently to encourage Alisha, hoping she would not change her mind about seeing him. Not after all the trouble she had gone to. Let her discover for herself what Jeffery's opinion is of ex-slaves, especially an ex-slave of his worst enemy, Gray Eagle. She could not suppress a sardonic smile that Gray Eagle had put one more thing over on the aristocratic Jeffery Gordon — he had taken this girl he so greatly desired first. She grinned maliciously while thinking how it must gall Jeffery to know she had slept with that savage many, many times. What she couldn't understand was why Jeffery would lower himself to replace Gray Eagle.

Alisha should have felt the first hints of warning in the tone of Mrs. Philsey's voice or the gleam in her eyes. She would learn all too soon of this woman's hatred and contempt for the Indians and anyone who accepted them as people.

"But, Mrs. Philsey . . ."

"No buts, my dear. It's time to regain your youth and gaiety. Someone will bring you water for your bath and shampoo. Do not disappoint me and Jeffery. I will be back later to help you. The captain on duty is seeing to everything. Perk up! You're so young and lovely. Everything will be fine from now on."

Alisha sat down on the bed to wait for the tub and water to be sent in. She had to admit Mrs.

Philsey was right. It was time to bring the old Lese back to life, if she still lived somewhere deep inside.

Time . . . She could almost hear her father's deep voice as he quoted his favorite passage from the Good Book. ". . . To everything there is a season and a time to every purpose. A time to be born, a time to die; a time to kill; a time to heal; a time to destroy; a time to rebuild; a time to cry; a time to laugh; a time to grieve; a time to dance; a time to embrace; a time to refrain embracing; a time to get; a time to lose; a time to keep; a time to cast away; a time to be quiet; a time to speak up; a time for loving; a time for hating; a time for war; a time for peace . . ."

There was so much truth and good advice in those words. All of those things had been true about her at one time or another. She had found her time for love and hate, her time to cry; her time for getting and losing; and her time for war. Now was the time for her to find her rebuilding, healing, laughter, peace and casting away. All she lacked was the courage and strength to do it. It was the time for her new beginning . . . but why all alone?

She could not help but think on the words from her favorite passage. Today, they haunted her, for their meaning applied to her personally. She could understand the emotions and meanings of this passage since she had lived it herself.

"Entreat me not to leave thee . . . Where thou lodgest, I will lodge: Thy people shall be my people . . . If aught but death part thee and me . . ." She had always thought it such a beautiful, bittersweet love-story. It was far harder to accept hatred as the thing to part me from my love, she mused. It had not taken death to part us, my love. It was your vengeance and rejection. I shall go my way and you, yours. Why does my heart ache so for you?

The door behind Alisha silently opened. The tub and water were hauled in and set up. She did not take note of the task going on behind her, nor of the one who did it.

Powchutu finished his task. He observed the girl who sat so gracefully and proud on the bed, gazing out of the window in such deep thought. She had not seemed to know of his presence. She looked so small and vulnerable, like a fragile desert flower. He had hoped to see and learn more of this woman of Wanmdi Hota's. At least, more than her size and the color of her reddish-brown hair. He vowed, later, when I return . . .

Chapter Thirteen

The captain on duty should have realized the mistake he was making when he ordered Powchutu to go to Mrs. Philsey's. Every man at Fort Pierre was aware of her intense dislike of the Indians, including Powchutu. He was like a slap in the face to her, for he was an example of an Indian daring to touch a white. Mrs. Philsey would be overjoyed when her husband's tour of duty here would be over and they could return East, hopefully to that new post she was working so hard on.

She had spent enough time in this wilderness. She hungered for the day they could return to civilized living. She, like most of the others, had never tried to understand or accept the Indians. She considered them vile, filthy, low-born savages. Anyone who had anything to do with them also fell into that category.

Captain Tracy was thrilled with this golden opportunity to degrade Powchutu. When Powchutu was at the fort, he was under the orders of the captain on duty. The other two officers did not particularly care for Powchutu, but did not try to find ways to put him down in front of the others. But Captain Tracy was different. He looked for anything which was difficult or demeaning for Powchutu to do. He enjoyed nothing better than to stand over him while he performed this kind of service. Until Powchutu was ready to make his move, he tolerated Tracy's attitude.

In Tracy's attempts to belittle Powchutu, he loved to assign those jobs which were particularly female. He cackled to himself, thinking of the brawny, arrogant scout preparing a lady's bath. This is my best taunt yet, he crowed. Just wait until the other men heard about this one. What a stroke of luck! Thank heavens for finicky females!

Powchutu struggled hard to suppress his bitterness at these humiliating tasks. But today, he almost thanked Tracy for this assignment. His mounting curiosity to see this girl of Wanmdi Hota's outweighed his desire to refuse such a ridiculous order. He grinned mockingly and accepted the order, much to Tracy's chagrin.

If Mrs. Philsey had not been out back hanging out her wash, she would have prevented the hauntingly bittersweet friendship which would bloom and grow into a tangled vine which would soon entwine both Alisha and Powchutu in its strangling, binding grasp. She did not observe his coming or going, but neither did Alisha.

Alisha's rambling thoughts were interrupted

by Mrs. Philsey's voice and tap on her shoulder. "Ready, my dear. The water and tub are prepared. I checked and it isn't too hot for your back. I'll return later to rinse your hair for you. Just call out when you're ready." Mrs. Philsey closed the window and curtains for privacy, then departed.

Alisha slowly pulled the gown over her head and dropped it on the bed. She glowed with modesty as the door abruptly opened and Mrs. Philsey came back into the room, without even knocking! No stranger, except Wanmdi Hota, had ever seen her naked . . . that is, while she was aware of it! Mrs. Philsey placed soap, towel and cloth near the tub and departed again.

She lowered herself gradually into the oblong wooden tub. She relaxed as the warm, scented water surrounded her. Mrs. Philsey had thought of everything, right down to bath oil and fragrant jasmine soap. She scrubbed her hair and skin, feeling relaxed and clean for the first time since coming here. Mrs. Philsey had returned to rinse her hair with warm water from a small bucket. She immediately left after finishing, carrying the bucket and the soiled gown.

This bath and shampoo was perhaps the best she had ever taken in her entire life. She felt enlivened, refreshed and at ease, ready to face the world and Lieutenant Gordon, or so she believed.

She reluctantly rose from the water and dried herself. She dressed in the green and white chambray, a style of dress her mother would have called a morning dress. The paisley was a little too dressy for a first meeting, or even to wear at all in this part of the country. It was the kind of dress one would wear to dinner back East. Alisha almost regretted denying Elizabeth that beautiful dress, but she was positive she needed it far worse than Elizabeth did.

Alisha towelled her hair and brushed it until it was soft, shiny and silky. Without thinking, she braided it Indian style. Perturbed, she realized this dress buttoned down the back. She must wait for Mrs. Philsey to return to do her up. Either Elizabeth had servants to help her dress, or Mrs. Philsey did not want to place the buttons up the front of this dress. Feeling slightly weakened by this flurry of activity, she sat down on the edge of the bed to rest for a minute.

There came a soft, light tapping upon her door. Alisha had left the door slightly ajar to inform Mrs. Philsey she was finished. Thinking it was she, she called out for her to enter, "I am finished. Come in . . ." She was slightly amused at the woman's sudden politeness. Her back was to the door with her dress gaping open as she was putting the ill-fitting shoes on her small feet. How she wished she had her soft, comfortable moccasins.

She stood up and turned. A radiant smile touched her lips and eyes, making them sparkle with vitality. She began, "I feel so much better, Mrs. Philsey. This was just what I . . ." Her remaining words froze in her throat. She paled and stiffened in fear and disbelief. The smile had instantly faded, leaving her lips slightly parted. Her green eyes had darkened and widened with panic.

She stared into the handsome face of an Indian who was dressed like a white man, but who resembled Gray Eagle. Her eyes quickly registered his darkly tanned face; his collar-length ebony hair; his red cotton shirt; fawn-colored buckskin pants and vest; his knee-high, fringed moccasins; his height and size; the black hat with the wide brim and red braided band; and his strong, manly, arrogant features.

His tall, muscular body seemed to fill the room. It emanated power and pride. Her eyes were drawn to his by their most unusual, slaty color and the fierce emotions she could read there. It had taken only moments for all these details to reach her mind, but it seemed like hours before she was fully aware of her reaction to him and her bold, rude gaping. Was this man real or an apparition? He looked Indian, and yet, he did not.

Powchutu had alertly noted her reaction to him. He read the apprehension, disbelief, terror and confusion in her eyes, but he also read more. There had been a brief flickering of other emotions in her eyes. She stared at him more as if she were seeing a ghost, rather than an enemy.

He had not been prepared to see such an overwhelmingly beautiful, desirable woman. She was everything they had rumored her to be, but far more. He could easily understand both Gray Eagle's and Jeffery's interest in her. He was fascinated and astonished by her childlike innocence. She appeared so fragile and dainty, and yet, there was pride and dignity in her expression. Never had he met or seen a female to compare with this girl.

She spoke with her eyes, her vulnerability pulling at the strings of his embittered heart. She had not moved or screamed. She just stared at him as if she waited to see what he intended to do with her. He was surprised to see only shock and fear in her green eyes. There were no signs of hatred or contempt.

He moved slightly and spoke first, "I didn't mean to frighten you, Miss. I'm Powchutu. I scout for this fort. I'm here to remove the tub and water." Why was he bothering to explain, or to comfort her? He for damn sure couldn't explain the grin on his face or his crazy mood. He felt like he was the hot sun, beating down on a delicate white flower while it waited in fear of death or destruction from his power and heat.

When he spoke, her eyes riveted to his lips. Then without any warning, she began to slip to the floor in a faint. She was like a slender blade of grass succumbing to a heavy rainstorm. He was instantly at her side before she reached the floor. He tenderly lifted her and laid her on the bed, being very careful of her back. When he had first entered the room, he had seen the cruel marks of the lash upon her back through the gaped opening of her dress. He had inwardly flinched at the sight. Without knowing her, he was inflamed by her abuse. How could any man do something like that to such a girl, even a warrior like Wanmdi Hota?

He took a cloth and wet it in the tub. He came to sit beside her on the bed as he gently wiped her face with the cool, wet cloth. Her eyelids fluttered and slowly opened. He looked down into the most bewitching eyes he had ever seen. For a time, he was lost in their depths. She met his steady gaze in bewilderment as he repeated his former words, in case she had not really understood him.

Sensing no danger or evil in this man, her color quickly returned to her face and the fear disappeared from her eyes. He watched the transformation with pleasure. She relaxed when she realized who he was. Her eyes softened and she smiled up at him. Without being aware of it, she felt a strange warming and disarming attraction to this man. The idea she should fear and despise him never entered her mind. She was embarrassed at her reaction to him, for he had been sent here to help her.

When she answered him, her voice was as sweet and musical as the nightingale's. She smelled of wildflowers. Her skin was as soft as rabbit fur. An eternal flame of love and desire ignited in his heart at that moment.

There was no enmity in her eyes, only a light

he had never seen before — acceptance and friendship. He knew without a doubt, here was the girl he had waited for, hungered for and dreamed about. Here was a girl worth possessing, worth fighting the entire world to possess. She recognized him for what he was and it did not matter. She looked at him as a person, a man.

It only took a moment to recognize her value. Wanmdi Hota will suffer a great loss in you! he thought. Or will he? Would any man give up such a prize without a fight? He grinned as he thought about Jeffery's persistence and impatience about this girl. Now he understood why.

Alisha saw Powchutu return her friendly smile. "I am sorry, Powchutu. I guess you startled me. I was expecting Mrs. Philsey. You're the first person I've seen since I came here. You're an Indian, aren't you?" She had an urge to know who he truly was.

Automatically without thinking, he snapped, "I'm only half Indian! A hanke-wasichun . . . or half-breed as the white man says! At least, that's what I'm most frequently called." The intense bitterness, unsuppressed hostility and suffering in his eyes and voice tore at her heart. He had never revealed his very heart and soul to anyone before, until this girl . . .

Alisha could sympathize with his anger and pain. With all honesty and deep sincerity, she apologized to him, "I'm sorry, Powchutu. I didn't know. I wouldn't hurt or embarrass you intentionally. Sometimes we have no control over who or what we are. Do not be ashamed of your mixed blood. Be proud to carry some of both inside you. Each of them has something good to offer you."

He gazed at this girl in wonder. He thought, she speaks with intelligence, wisdom and understanding. How can one so young be so kind and knowledgeable? Her words are true, but she is the only one who realizes it. Why could the others not be as wise and kind?

Alisha did not know why she spoke so freely and openly to this total stranger, nor the reason she said what she did. The words and thoughts came to her mind and she knew them to be true. She noted how they touched and lightened his bitter heart. She thought, it must be terribly lonely and frightening to be so alone and misunderstood. I am happy I've helped him, if only in some small way. He seems so nice and pleasant. Why does anyone treat him so cruelly? A person cannot be held responsible for his parentage, nor can he change it.

Amazed, Powchutu thought, here is a white girl who calls me by my name and looks me in the eye. She apologizes for my suffering and humiliating by her people. She truly cares what I think and feel. How can this be? Yet, it is true, for I see it in those gentle, honest eyes and hear it in her voice. Now, I must comfort and help her.

"I know your fear of the Indian is great, but in time you will forget the pain they have inflicted on you. It was wrong for them to treat you this way. I am ashamed I carry their blood. If it were possible, I would punish them for this." He had a need to reassure her.

As he spoke to her, she lowered her eyes in pain and whispered, "Does anyone ever forget such hatred and cruelty, Powchutu? Never feel shame for the actions of others. We cannot control what others say and do. These people out here are confusing to me. We are much alike, you and I, for I cannot seem to fit in with either side."

There was a strong bond of understanding between them. Each was reaching out to the other. There existed a feeling of natural friendship, of finding a kindred spirit. It seemed the most natural thing in the world to sit together, to talk, to laugh and to share their happiness and pain. She felt she could discuss anything with him.

She raised imploring eyes to his and asked, "Why do they hate each other so much, Powchutu?" The soft way she spoke his name caused him to tremble as he listened to her words, both forgetting where they were and how she was dressed. "I mean the whites and the Indians? Except for their skin color and different customs, they're just alike. Why do they hate and kill each other?"

The door flew open and Mrs. Philsey marched in. She gaped at the intimate scene before her eyes in shock and horror. She became livid with rage.

Powchutu hastily rose from the bed and faced

her. He tried to explain what had happened to her. He wanted to protect Alisha from her anger, for she had no idea of how these people would view and treat her for befriending him. They would not allow them to be friends and she must be made to know this before she was hurt. He would rather give her up than see them do to her what they did to him every day of his life.

Mrs. Philsey's animosity filled the entire room. She shouted, "What the Hell are you doing in here? I don't allow Injuns in my quarters! How dare you come here! You . . . you savage! I'll have the stripes of the man who sent you in here. This is an outrage! An outrage, I tell you! If you're lying, I'll have you beaten and tossed in the stockade!"

Powchutu tried to calm her down, but she would hear nothing of his explanation. He gritted his teeth, trying to suppress his fury for Alisha's sake. He held back the words which threatened to spill forth. He forced himself to not stare at her with those darkened, angry eyes, which could bring fear with their very coldness of expression. He lowered his gaze to the floor to feign humility and respect, waiting for her tirade to cease.

It did not. "I'll kill you if you don't get out of here. This insult is unforgivable! The officer who sent you here will be sorry he ever laid eyes on you! Don't you ever come in here again, orders or no orders! Do you hear me? Get out! Get out!"

Alisha was taking in this entire exchange in shock and disbelief. Was this woman really saying what she was hearing? She could not believe the viciousness of her attack on Powchutu.

Finding her wits, Alisha spoke up, "Please, Mrs. Philsey. He was only helping me. I was startled and weakened. I nearly fainted. He only placed me on the bed and bathed my face with a cool cloth. He was very kind and helpful. He did nothing wrong."

She ignored Alisha's explanation. How dare she defend that scum? "He had the audacity to touch you! The heathen savage should never touch any white woman for any reason."

Alisha was flabbergasted by her attitude. "But I could have been injured if he had allowed me to fall! He said and did nothing improper. You can't mean those terrible things you said."

"It doesn't matter. The filthy savage put his hands on you and, worse, while you were unconscious. How do you know what he did or didn't do?"

"Mrs. Philsey!" she retorted. "Stop this immediately! You have no reason or right to accuse him or me of such things. I will not allow you to speak to him in this manner." Powchutu watched and listened to this defense of him. "He is not a savage. He's a scout for this fort. He lives and works here like all the other men."

Mrs. Philsey's anger skyrocketed. She screamed back, "How do you know that? You've been talking with him! I don't believe this! You

475

refused to meet the white officer who saved your life, but you'll sit here all cozy and friendly with one of the same savages who did this to you! Why you act like you prefer this . . . this scum to one of your own kind! I can't believe this after all you supposedly went through in their camp. You sit here, half naked, on your bed, unchaperoned, with a total stranger, laughing and talking like two old friends. How can you possibly befriend another one?" Her last sentence was spoken harshly between gritted teeth.

"Another one?" She was definitely insinuating something improper and wrong, even shameful. "What do you mean?"

She acidly answered Alisha's query. There was no doubt in her mind the Brown girl's accusations had just grounds. The proof of her love for Injuns was right in front of her. If she were innocent, she would fear and hate all of them. "That Brown girl has told us all about how you helped that Gray Eagle! I bet she told the truth when she claimed you helped him escape. She said you weren't a prisoner. She said you been living with him like some queen. Well, I say like some harlot! If it hadn't been for your help to him, all of your people would still be alive. I can see and hear for myself that you prefer them over your own kind. You chose his company over Jeffery's, didn't you?"

Alisha's mouth fell open in shock. Her eyes widened and she inhaled with a loud gasp. "You actually believe for one minute I could help him escape, to come back and kill my family and friends! You cannot possibly think I would do such a terrible thing! Kathy is mistaken. I was his prisoner! I did not live like some queen. I worked just the same as she did, as a slave, Mrs. Philsey, a slave! I was tortured and punished just like anyone else when I defied orders. As for choosing Powchutu's company over Jeffery's, we simply spoke! Perhaps you have forgotten why I was bathing and dressing — to meet this Jeffery of yours! And, as for being an Indian lover, if not hating or rejecting them because they are different from me qualifies me for that name and position, then all right — I guess I am an Indian lover! Your attack on both of us is unjust, cruel and untrue. You have no right to speak to either of us this way." Her green eyes flashed a challenge to the woman.

Mrs. Philsey's expression told Alisha her words had only brought on more coldness and contempt toward her and the scout. It was evident she believed Kathy's lies. "If you would befriend one, Alisha, then you would befriend others. You admitted just now you like and accept them. I have the right to say and think what I so choose in my home, and to the girl I nursed back from the door of death and waited on hand and foot for days. Can you deny you fed and doctored Gray Eagle when he was a captive in your fortress? Can you deny you touched and helped his vile, filthy body? Do you deny you held a gun on your own people, even threatened to shoot them, if they didn't stop beating and taunting him?"

Her tone, words and eyes challenged Alisha to deny the statements. Alisha knew it would be useless to try to explain humanity, compassion and understanding to this woman. There was nothing she could say or do which would change anything this woman thought.

At Alisha's silence, Mrs. Philsey demanded, "Can you deny any of it?"

Alisha defended herself, "Yes, I did help him that day; but I would have done the same for anyone who was being beaten without a just cause. I did feed and care for him because no one else would. For all they cared, he could have died! No one deserves such abuse and contempt, no one! They were whipping him like some wild animal. I think they would have flogged him to death without remorse. I tried to reason with them and they wouldn't listen, just like you're doing now. I had no other choice but to stop them with the only way open to me."

"Would you have shot one of them to protect him?"

Alisha did not have to say yes, for her eyes had. "Do you forget we're supposed to be the civilized Christians? I see none of you practicing this. I've seen white men behave more like savages than they do. As for Powchutu, he isn't like them and you know it. He is not to blame for his parentage, nor can he change it. How does his being of mixed blood harm you? How does it justify his abuse and hatred? I cannot accept these ideas of prejudice and hatred."

"They are wild animals!" Mrs. Philsey shot back. "Not only that, but cold-blooded, murdering savages! And you, my dear Alisha, are no better than they are. I can see it all now. That Brown girl was right about everything. Now I know why you wouldn't tell me what he did to you or about your life out there. You didn't dare! He wasn't holding you captive . . . you were staying with him because you wanted to! Is that why you've been so sad and lonely? Is Gray Eagle the reason you've refused to see Jellery? You're his woman, aren't you? And to think of all I've done for you! You, acting like the poor, innocent victim . . . like some fine lady!"

Alisha could not take any more of her hateful words. "It wasn't like that at all!"

Mrs. Philsey cut her off. "Understand and help an Injun lover, harlot? I have learned the truth about you, haven't I?"

Alisha knew there was no way she could reason with the vindictive woman. Would the others think the same way? Probably so, for this was the same type of hatred she had confronted with her own group at the fortress.

She turned her back to them and slowly sank down to the bed, her mind flooded with anguish and disbelief. Not here, too . . . Not all over again . . . The mere sight or mention of an Indian brought insanity to the minds of people like Mrs. Philsey. How could she deal with insanity in so many people? How could a woman who had cared for her for so many days turn on her so brutally just because she had been nice to a man who was only half-Indian? The look in the woman's eyes, the tone of her voice, and the words she used reminded Alisha of the same reaction from the settlers the day she first met Wanmdi Hota.

Powchutu had witnessed the entire exchange. He saw what the woman's words did to Alisha. Her stricken expression knifed his heart. For a moment he had been tempted to pull his knife from its sheath and cut the old bitch's tongue out. Perhaps he would one day . . . For now, the best thing for Alisha would be for him to quietly slip from the room. He did.

Finding no other insults she could hurl at the quiet girl, Mrs. Philsey whirled and left the room, slamming the door with a loud bang. She was seething in anger. She restlessly paced the floor of her room. The girl must surely be insane! Insane or not, she would have to leave her quarters immediately. She wouldn't allow an Injun lover in her home. Why, that would be the same as housing one of those savages, she thought in her fury. I took care of her like she was my own child and this is how she repays me! It's bad enough she's an Injun harlot, but she's taking my hold on Jeffery away. He'll no doubt blame me for not telling him this sooner. Damn her! I'll fix her good before I'm through with her. She'll be sorry she ever befriended that savage Gray Eagle!

Darkness gradually filled the room where Alisha sat immobile on the bed. For one so young, tender and blameless to be so hated and unwanted, was a tragic, crushing blow. How had everything gone so wrong? Her parents and uncle were dead. Every possession and penny she had ever had was gone. She was hurt and weak. She was hated and held in contempt by the strangers at Fort Pierre. There was not, and never could be, anything between her and the man she loved. She had nothing and no one. Her only hope for survival and a new future lay hundreds of miles of untamed wilderness and an ocean away. Hope . . . there wasn't any.

If only there was one person to help her, to tell her what to do, where to go. If only someone could care for her, protect her, love her. Was there no one to save her from this life of terrible suffering and emptiness?

Doc came in later. He slowly walked over to the bed and sat down beside Alisha. He studied the lonely, dejected expression on the lovely face. Mrs. Philsey had filled him in on all the details of this afternoon's events. He had never seen his wife so hostile. He asked Alisha to tell him in her words what took place here this afternoon. She related the tragic scene almost word for word.

He wondered how he could explain hatred, contempt, and prejudice to this girl who had not learned to feel any of them? The Doc tried to calm her. "Alisha, you don't seem to understand or recognize the bitter enmity there is between the white man and the Indian. I know how you feel and what you're thinking. This will be very hard for you, but you cannot, you must not, befriend any of them, not even one who befriends you. You cannot acknowledge any other Indian. You also cannot speak of your feelings openly. There is too much bitterness and hatred for these people to accept or tolerate your friendship with them. You cannot have any contact with the Indians. If you refuse to take this advice, you are in for a very rough and unhappy time."

Alisha lifted pathetic eyes to him and spoke despondently, "Doc, I've only been in this new land for about two years. I do not know of this hatred and bitterness between the people out here, nor do I understand why they wish to torture and murder each other. I have no part in this conflict. Why do you all insist I take sides? Why must I hate someone who has done me no wrong or injury simply because he is half Indian? It is not right to forcefully impress your beliefs on others. I have never seen such violence. I would never have come to this land if I had known or suspected I would be forced to endure the things I have. I am perhaps too naive or foolish, for I truly believe we could have peace and friendship if we tried, if we really tried. One thing you must believe, Doc, I did not help Gray Eagle escape, but I did try to prevent his brutal beating."

She walked to the window and gazed upward to the starry heavens. "My father taught me to respect a person for himself, not for his skin or his status. He always accepted a man for who and what he was, not what others said or thought about him. Perhaps you are right when you say I do not understand the gravity of this situation. I did not go to Gray Eagle willingly. We were and are enemies, but only because both he and you say we must be. The things he did to me . . ."

She did not continue. Later, she went on, "Your wife's hostility hurt me very deeply. If she reacts this way after knowing me for many days, what will Fort Pierre's people think? Why does your wife hate Powchutu so much, Doc? He had nothing to do with my captivity. In fact, he was very polite and kind to me this afternoon. If you all hate him as she does, then why is he allowed to live and work here at the fort?"

"To most people, Alis ha, he is Indian. Your father's teachings are fine for London or back East, but not for living out here. I am sorry to tell you this, but the others will also think and feel as Martha does. Before you leave this room, you must realize they will react the same, if not more violently, than she did this afternoon."

Doc talked on and on for a long time, trying to help her see the white man's point of view. He talked until there was no more he could say to her. A tear came to his eye as he painfully realized he would be unable to help her. She was a white rose growing in a garden of weeds. They would surround her and cut off her sunlight, for they would never allow such a precious flower to bloom among them. A rose will always be a rose, he reflected. She could never become a weed and for that she will suffer. How he wished he could pluck her and take her to safety far away.

"The best thing for me is to get well and leave here as soon as possible," Alisha decided. "You must help me, Doc! Please! I must find some way to get back East and catch a ship back to England. My father has many friends. I know I can find someone there to help me."

Doc shook his head and replied, "It will be a long time before you will be able to travel, or before anyone will be safe to leave. The Indians are making raids in all the surrounding areas. It won't be feasible for anyone to head anywhere for a long time. Get some sleep. Things will look brighter in the morning." It sounded right, but he only half believed his own words. Doc stood up and left, closing the door quietly behind him.

It was a long time before Alisha finally relaxed and went to sleep. For the time being, there was nothing she could do.

While leaning against the wall outside her window, Powchutu listened to everything which she and Doc had said. Hearing her even breathing now, he knew she had finally dropped off to sleep. He pondered all that had happened. It was easy to understand why the notorious Gray Eagle had captured this girl for his very own. Surely he will want her back, Powchutu thought. I am surprised he has not come for her already. He grinned as he mused, he has the power and courage to dare anything, even to attack this fort.

I await the day to see Lieutenant Gordon's face when he knocks on the door and demands his woman's return. I wonder if Wanmdi Hota knows who is responsible for the raid on his camp and the kidnapping of Alisha. He must wait for her to heal and regain her strength, or perhaps he does not know she is here. It would be good if the two of them would kill each other. If he comes for her, do I allow him to take her again? Could I lose her when I have just found her? She wishes to leave as I do. Perhaps we could depart together. But like Wanmdi Hota, once she is mine I will not give her up.

I must learn of the feelings in her heart for him. She did try to help and protect him, but why? I do not understand his harsh abuse of her. There are things I must know. There is more between them than warrior and captive. She will find many enemies here, as I have. I must watch over her and protect her. I will not allow anyone to harm her anymore, not even the great Wanmdi Hota!

An intense, overwhelming desire to protect her from everyone and everything surged within him. I will guard over you, my love, he swore. I will let no one . . . no one . . . harm you from this day on.

For four more long, grueling days, Alisha secluded herself in her room alone. A few times, she saw a sullen Mrs. Philsey when she brought her meals to her. But Alisha did manage to see

485

one person — Powchutu. He would sneak up to her window after dark and they would talk for hours.

She was getting stronger, better and more restless every day. Her back was mending rapidly and hurt less and less. The terrible pain had vanished, replaced by a dull soreness. The time had come for her to do something about her plight. She had given it a great deal of thought for the past few days. There was only one possible path for her to take.

She had decided to go to the post commander and solicit his help. He was the one with the authority to help her get away from Fort Pierre. Perhaps she could make some arrangement to borrow enough money from the cavalry to return to the East and on to England. Some friend there would give her the money to return it to the commander.

Her decision made, she went to find Mrs. Philsey to ask her for a bath. She related her plans to her. Nothing would suit that woman more than for me to not only leave her home, but the fort as well. She had surmised correctly. Mrs. Philsey beamed at her news and decisions.

She caustically said, "I'll send that Injun in with the tub and water since you don't seem to mind having him around you."

Alisha ignored the cutting remark and answered, "Thank you, Mrs. Philsey. I'm sorry I have been such a bother to you. I know you do not wish me to stay here any longer. I am truly sorry you harbor such hatred in your heart for me. I cannot help what I believe and think. I can be no different from what I am. I only wish you will someday come to understand my feelings and forgive any wrong you think I have done to you. I will try to be gone very soon."

When Powchutu came with the water, Alisha smiled and nodded to him, knowing Mrs. Philsey was eavesdropping outside her door. He grinned and nodded back to her. She closed the window and barred the door.

She eased down into the warm water. She bathed and shampooed. She carefully dressed, trying to look her best to go out for the first time since coming to Fort Pierre. She put on the green chambray. The color of the dress enhanced the jade green depths of her eyes. She looked as radiant and fresh as a newly opened flower in the morning. She brushed her auburn hair and let it hang loose and free down her back. It shone like the coat of a chestnut mare running in the sunlight.

Pleased with her appearance, she asked Mrs. Philsey for the directions to the commander's quarters. Mrs. Philsey harshly answered her, and silently envied Alisha's youth, beauty and freshness. She had no right to look so pure and proud . . . No right . . .

Alisha walked to the front door. She stood there for a few moments bracing herself to face the fort's people for the first time. She inhaled several deep breaths, opened the door, and stepped outside into the warm sunlight.

She remained motionless for a minute to allow her eyes to adjust to the bright sunlight and unfamiliar surroundings. As her eyes became accustomed to the glare, she looked all around her, taking note of the fort's construction and size. It was indeed very large and strong. Through the open gate, she could see it was a vast, enclosed area surrounded mostly by grassland and prairie. Here and there, she could see a few tall trees and many clumps of smaller trees and bushes. The fort seemed to rise like some giant, wooden boulder out of the semi-barren wasteland.

The fence which surrounded the fort was about ten feet tall. It had been constructed of small trees which had been trimmed to sharp points at the top, de-limbed, and lashed together by ropes and supporting poles. Wooden ramparts with lookout openings ran the lengths of the walls.

Her eyes travelled to the back wall. There she noted a row of two-story soldiers quarters, and from the appearance of the closeness of the doors and windows, the rooms were very small. Her eyes moved on to the two diagonally situated blockhouses. From the markings on the doors, those were the officers' quarters. There were two short rows of structures at either end of the fort. From the looks and smell of one of them, it was the cooking house and mess hall. The other structure, where she was now standing, was the doctor's quarters and infirmary.

In the front right corner, she viewed a small brig. It was a wooden, block-styled room with bars across the only window. There was a huge bar propped against the doorway to secure it when a prisoner was inside.

The fort was apparently very strong and protective. Now she could understand why Mrs. Philsey had spoken so confidently about their safety. It was a pity her own fortress had not been this sturdy. She recalled how she thought no fence or fortress was needed. How very naive and foolish she had been!

Her eyes were drawn to the center of the yard where a tall flagpole was standing. The two flags waved gently back and forth in the light breeze. She stared at one of the flags, the one whose colors were so dear and familiar to her heart.

She finished her intense scrutiny of the fort in the back left corner. There was where the stables were situated. She could see the racks for saddles and tack gear. She could tell where hay and feed were stored in the loft of the stables.

She leaned against the hitching post in front of her. The ground was dry and dusty. She watched it swirl in the gentle wind. As far as she could tell, there were not any trees or shrubs inside the fort. It was even too hot for flowers to grow in this barren earth. It was apparent there were other females at the fort by the flower boxes on many of the windows. But of course, Mrs. Philsey had told her this when she borrowed the things for her. Suddenly the question came to mind as to why none of them had tried to visit with her.

She saw men milling around, doing chores. She gazed up at the balcony-like platform which was used for a lookout tower and guard post. She noted the young man who was studying the horizon with his field glasses. How very far she had come from the streets of London!

A deeply masculine voice spoke up from behind her and pulled her from her observations. "Miss Williams?" She turned to stare up into the handsome, darkly tanned face of a young officer. He had the clearest crystal blue eyes she had ever seen. They were the color of aquamarine. Those eyes had a vitality all their own. She could see blond hair beneath the dark blue hat with yellow braid. He was the very picture of the elegant, dashing officer. His uniform was clean and neat. The dark blue color with the shiny brass buttons and yellow braid trim accented his good looks and charm.

His eyes engulfed her entire being with one quick sweep. She was even more beautiful than he had realized. In the brilliant sunlight, she could not see his look of animal lust. With a great effort, he glanced away.

He nodded politely and said, "Lieutenant Jeffery Gordon at your service, Ma'am." He gave a low, sweeping bow.

She returned the friendly smile with feminine modesty and thanked him for his kindness and help.

"You've been a naughty girl to refuse to receive

490

me. I've been very concerned about you." He spoke in a slightly mocking tone. His blue eyes glittered devilishly. He flashed her a broad grin which revealed even white teeth.

Mrs. Philsey had certainly described him and his charms correctly. He was a most beguiling, disarming man, but his expression sent warnings to her mind. She averted her eyes and paled slightly. His tone implied more than his words said. She wondered what Mrs. Philsey had told him about her and their argument. What was he thinking about her right now? She was unsure of how to respond to his light-hearted banter.

"I could not bring myself to face anyone until today. As a gentleman, I am sure you understand and accept my hesitation. I do wish to thank you for the volume of poetry. It is a favorite of mine. You have been most kind and thoughtful, Sir. I was just on my way to see the commanding officer."

He instantly sensed her timidity. He jested, "I was only teasing you. I knew you needed time to recover from your unfortunate experience. It was a most terrifying and brutal thing for a lady to endure. I am sorry I did not have the chance to prevent it."

He noted the far-away, tormented look which came into her eyes and the sad expression which crossed her features. Almost inaudibly she whispered, "I do not wish to discuss it or even remember it ever happened. I only want to get as far away from here as I can, and as soon as possible."

She turned to go but he caught her elbow. She tried to pull free but he would not release his hold — a hold which was gentle, but firm. She lifted her emerald eyes to his. "Please . . ."

"Don't go just yet," he pleaded. "I feel I have offended you in some way, perhaps even hurt you. I apologize for my breach of etiquette."

She relaxed the stiffness in her arm and gazed up into deep pools of blue. His tone bespoke sincerity. She nodded. He asked about her home and family, and learned she had neither. She did believe she could find friends back in London, but there was no way she could get from here to there. Lovely dreamer . . .

"A trip to England would be very expensive," he advised her. "Also you have to consider food, lodgings and necessities between here and there. Just how do you plan to pay for all of that? The colonies are a long way from here, England even further. It will be a dangerous trip for anyone. But for a beautiful young woman all alone, it will be impossible."

"You pose questions for which I have no answers, Lieutenant Gordon," Alisha replied. "As for the trip back East, I've made it before. I know the hardships involved. I do not know how, but I must find some way to leave here. I cannot remain in such a violent, uncivilized land with such bitter, cruel people. I not only refer to the Indians but the whites here as well. This is not where I belong." She assumed it was best to hint of her feelings now. If he did not already know what she thought, then let him begin to suspect now.

Unaware of the troubles with Mrs. Philsey and doubting Kathy's words, her statements went right past him. Mrs. Philsey had only told the lieutenant that Alisha had relapsed and must rest for a few more days.

"But," he said, "there is no one to take responsibility for you and your well-being?" He deeply emphasized "no one."

She sadly met his gaze and replied, "No. No one . . ." Then defiance sparkled in those grassy eyes and she added, "But I shall still find some way to leave this horrible place!" Suddenly angry for letting such personal feelings show to a total stranger, she yanked her arm free. She felt resentment at his prying and probing into her life and mind, and perturbed at herself for allowing it.

"I fully appreciate your help and concern, Lieutenant Gordon, but I can take care of myself and my problems! I do not have to excuse myself, nor my feelings to any of you people!" She whirled and rapidly walked away from him. She headed toward the commander's quarters, not daring to look back.

He grinned and stared after her until she was out of sight. Can you now? he challenged. We'll just wait and see about that. What a nice little diversion you'd make on some cold, lonely night! He laughed, and added, or hot, lonely night. Such a little spitfire; but I will tame her, soon — very soon.

He wondered how any woman could radiate such purity when she was not pure. Such childlike innocence and openness, he mused. Being guiltless does not make one innocent again. Damn, how beautiful and fiery she was. It's been too long since I've had a woman like that! My hooks are in you, Little Spitfire. I won't settle for anything less than your total surrender to me. You will provide a very nice *affaire d'amour* and I surely do need one about now.

Being accustomed to the finer things of life and coming from a refined upbringing, Jeffery assumed Alisha would fit nicely into his sparse existence at Fort Pierre. She was from the same class of society he was from. When he was ready to leave the fort or when he was finished with her, he would be grateful enough to furnish her with the passage back to England. When he knew her a little better and she was allowed time to realize her stranded, poverty-stricken state, then he would approach her with this suggestion and make all the arrangements. It would undoubtedly be to both their advantages. She would be well worth the trouble.

Jeffery Clayton Gordon was the eldest son of a rich, powerful, colonial family. His father had hoped this commission he had purchased for his son would instill some maturity in the youth. He had been educated in the finest schools back East and abroad. His father hoped he would sow his wild seeds and return ready to settle down to business, marriage and raising children.

Jeffery was thinking of the many holidays he had spent in England and on the continent. Perhaps he would return with Alisha when his tour of duty was over. They could share the long voyage, the holiday and some pleasure before he had to return to his father's plantation. He dreamed of how he could conquer the girl . . .

As Alisha hurried toward General Galt's office, her path was noted by another man. Powchutu had watched the meeting between Alisha and Jeffery. He studied Jeffery's expressions. He knew what the lieutenant was planning for this unsuspecting girl. He had overheard many accounts of Jeffery's prowess and charm with the females. Powchutu resolved, I must find some way to warn her about the lieutenant and his intentions, or she will surely be snared in his golden trap.

Alisha reached the door of General Galt's office and tapped lightly. A young private opened the door and stared dumbfoundedly at the girl. He flushed red as a beet when he realized he was gaping open-mouthed at her. He stepped aside and asked her to come in. She smiled sweetly and thanked him politely.

General Galt looked up at the lovely young lady standing before his massive oak desk. He blinked in confusion, arose and came around his desk to speak with her.

He smiled lazily and inquired, "What can I do for you, Miss . . . ?" He faltered, not recalling what they said her name was. This could only be the girl Doc was taking care of in his quarters.

"Miss Alisha Katrina Williams, Sir," she said courteously. "I have come to request your help in returning to the Colonies, hopefully to the coast where I can find a ship to return me to England. I have no other family here, but I do have friends in London who will repay your kindness promptly. I pray you can assist me in this matter."

General Galt had previously discussed the girl with Doc. He sighed heavily and shook his head. "I'm afraid that just isn't possible right now, Miss, and won't be for quite some time. At present, we're cut off from the other settlements and forts. I couldn't spare the men or funds to escort you anywhere." He watched the look of dismay cloud her face.

"Surely there is some way to leave here in the near future?"

"No, I'm afraid not. The Indians are kicking up quite a ruckus all around us. We're sitting on a loaded powder keg right here and it could blow up at any time. I only hope we can hold out until our new supplies and recruits arrive. We might all be in the same boat as you are if help doesn't come soon." He wanted to impress the danger of the fort's position upon her, in order to forestall all the begging and tears he was sure would soon be forthcoming from this lass.

But Alisha seized upon his information. "But couldn't I return with their escort when they arrive?"

He chewed on the cigar stub between his teeth

and nodded again. "I'm sorry, Lass. But all those who will be coming will be staying. That is, if any of them can make it through . . . You'll just have to remain here with us until this mess is cleared up one way or another. Things will settle down soon and we'll bring this crisis under our control."

She looked disheartened. "But when will that be, Sir? You must have some idea of how long it will take."

"Maybe a couple of months if we're lucky. Longer, if we're not . . ."

"Months?" She had perhaps expected him to say a few weeks, but months! "You mean I'm stranded here for that long? What will I do here? There must be some other way. At least, send me to another fort or settlement. I cannot remain with the Philseys indefinitely. If not, then find me some work to do to earn my board and keep."

"I'm sorry, Lass, but there isn't any work for a young lady here. I'm sure Doc and Martha won't mind your staying with them for a while longer. It isn't safe to try to send you anywhere else. Besides, you would only find the same problems there which you're finding here. Perhaps you can work in the infirmary with Doc."

He made it all sound so hopeless. He did not understand and did not care to. It angered her to see the man in power had no power to help her, and didn't give a care.

Alisha mumbled her thanks to the general and left. She leaned against the building for a short while, overcome with despair. Somehow, she didn't believe General Galt's excuses denying her help. The men seemed too at ease to be worried about an attack. The front gates were wide open. There were no extra guards on the rampart. If trouble was brewing, why weren't preparations being made to defend the fort? What Alisha didn't realize was that there was trouble of another sort in store for her at Fort Pierre . . .

A voice startled her from her melancholy state. "I see the General has given you sad news." She opened her eyes and looked up at Powchutu. He saw the tears which threatened to spill. She only nodded, afraid to speak lest she burst into tears.

"Come, I will walk you back to your quarters." He knew he was doing wrong. He knew he dared too much, but he could not stand there watching Alisha suffer all alone. He shouldn't even approach her, much less talk and walk with her. But he did, and Alisha accepted his company.

She was unaware of the aghast stares and malicious frowns cast their way as they walked along. She was only aware of her many problems and the friendship and comfort offered by this one man. She realized he was speaking to her. She turned to listen.

". . . not trust him, Alisha."

She questioned in confusion, "Who are you referring to, Powchutu? I did not hear who you were talking about. My mind was still in the general's office."

He stopped and faced her. He repeated his

warnings. "Lieutenant Gordon is known as a man who entraps women with his looks and charms. He will try to capture your heart. Do not trust him. He has made it known he is after you and will not rest until you are his."

The knowledge that the people at the fort were discussing her personal life was appalling. She recalled the looks the lieutenant had given her — the ones she had unconsciously dismissed which had made her feel so uneasy.

"Lieutenant Gordon is nothing to me, Powchutu. I will not allow him, or any man, to take advantage of me . . . ever again . . ."

"I only warn you to be careful of him, Alisha. You are still weak and hurt. I will give you protection from him and the others," he promised.

She smiled up at him and was about to thank him for his noble gesture. Abruptly, he was shoved backwards and fell into the dirt. A dark blue blur was at her side immediately. She whirled to face the flashing blue eyes and the furious mood of Jeffery. He glared at Powchutu with intense hatred and contempt. Alisha could see the livid rage beneath his tanned skin. His lips were curled into a snarl, revealing clenched teeth.

"How dare you speak to her, you filthy savage! If you so much as glance at her again, I'll skin you alive." His fists were balled into weapons, ready to kill. "You savvy, Injun?"

Alisha grabbed Jeffery's arm. "No! Stop this! He was not bothering me. We were only talking.

Your rude behavior is uncalled for, Lieutenant Gordon."

He glared at her in stunned surprise. "Stay out of this, Alisha! This is between that scout and me. It's none of your affair. I'll handle the red . . ."

"Lieutenant Gordon!" She screamed to silence his next few words. The familiar use of her given name and his presumptuous tone angered and alarmed her after what Powchutu had just told her. "Yes, this is my affair. It appears I started it by talking to him. I shall settle it. Both of you will . . ."

Powchutu had instantly leaped back to his feet like a cat. He took a defensive position — feet apart, shoulders hunched, fists clenched, eyes and ears alert, muscles taut and agile. He was ready to spring for an attack on Jeffery the moment he moved.

"You can't defend that savage!" Gordon fired at her.

"There aren't any sides in this argument! He did nothing improper. Also, Mr. Gordon, he is not a savage, no human being is! He is a soldier just like you. He has offered his friendship and I have accepted it, just as I accepted the friendship you offered minutes ago." She had hoped this last statement would cool his fiery temper.

Powchutu stepped forward. "I will fight my own battles, Alisha. He is right. This is between the two of us."

A small crowd was gathering around the three of them. As the heated words flew back and forth, some of the men began to shout encouragement to Jeffery and ridicule to Powchutu. The two men studied each other's eyes to watch for the first hint of attack. Neither of them would back down or apologize.

Alisha's head whirled with the feeling of *déjà vu*. She was suddenly back at her fortress, reliving that same nightmarish event which changed her entire life and brought her so much suffering. Mesmerized by the mob and its actions, she gazed around in fear of what they could entice Jeffery into doing. Her panicked eyes rested on the scout. The truth she had failed to acknowledge dawned on her: the icy eyes, the facial expression, the malevolent mood, his physical features and voice — he was the shadow, the counterpart of Gray Eagle! Alisha warned herself she must be very careful to remember he was Powchutu, her friend . . . Nothing more . . .

General Galt was somehow at her side, shouting orders and admonishing all the men. When he had the situation under control, he asked Jeffery and Powchutu to explain this outrageous behavior and conduct. The two men only glared at each other in silence. Alisha spoke up and gave the details of what had occurred. She related the entire incident without bias, much to Jeffery's and to Powchutu's vindication.

General Galt wisely decided he had better not take sides between these two men. He put an end to the matter, and said, "No damage has been done, Lieutenant. Miss Williams says Powchutu didn't insult her in any way. I order you men to forget this whole thing and get back to work. I might remind you, we have more urgent matters to take care of than hot tempers."

Over Jeffery's demands, the matter was dropped. The men muttered amongst themselves as they moved off to return to their duties. Only the lieutenant, Powchutu and Alisha remained in the yard. Powchutu knew it would be best for both himself and Alisha if he left things alone for the time being. He stalked off in silence.

Jeffery stared at his retreating back. He turned to face Alisha. "I fail to comprehend your tolerance and forgiving nature toward men like that. It was his kind who did to you those things you wish to forget. Why, Alisha, why?"

She met his gaze and answered, "Powchutu had nothing to do with my capture or treatment. A man cannot take the blame, nor the credit, for another man's words or deeds. It is I who fail to understand your behavior just now. He is a fellow soldier, not your enemy. If you despise and mistrust him so much, then why do you keep him here? I would think the position of scout would be deadly in the hands of one's foe."

He studied the emerald eyes and sweet face for a short time. He quipped, *"Chacun à son gout!"* He saw her confusion. Was it possible she truly did not understand why the scout must be ostracized? Perhaps she did not recall her French.

"You see, Powchutu is a *bête noire*. Even though

we need his services, we do not have to accept him or like him."

"Somehow, I do not see him as a necessary evil. Nor do I see any of you allowing free choice of friends and ideas. I think what you have here, Lieutenant Gordon, is an *état intolerable*." She had understood his words and fired back at him in perfect French, much to his pleasure. Her accent was impeccable.

Jeffery grinned mischievously at her choice of words. He made a mocking, sweeping bow and retorted, "*Touché, Alisha*."

His mocking gesture and tone were amusing. She smiled, knowing she had struck home. "I do not like to see anyone ill-used or abused. Suppose you were Powchutu . . . would you like to be viewed and treated as he is?"

How could he argue with such a lovely, tender-hearted, naive fool? He was using the wrong tactics on this girl and if he didn't alter them, he would be left out in the cold. He relented as far as she could tell. His voice was mellow and soft.

"I see your point, Little Heart. No, I would not care to trade places with him, or with anyone. Maybe I was a little hasty with my accusations. In the future, I will try to control these envious impulses to collar him. I just lost my head when I saw him with you. I assumed you were either too polite or frightened to tell him to leave you alone." He flashed her a boyish, innocent grin which she could not resist responding to. His charm was at its peak.

Seeing his change in behavior was winning him points, he pressed his advantage. "I'll have to instruct you about this land and its people. You'll understand then why I reacted in such a manner. Perhaps you will forget and forgive my rash behavior. *Trève?*"

Her guard was cast to the wind. She smiled and replied, "*Trève,* Jeffery . . ."

Score one, he mused. By the time I am finished with your education, you'll believe and trust anything I tell you. "I am afraid you have a great deal to learn about life out here. I am also afraid it will be difficult and painful for a girl like you, Alisha."

Anguish touched her teary eyes. She whispered, "That was the same thing my uncle told me just before he was killed. You are correct when you say this truth will be painful and difficult. Still, the fact remains — Powchutu did not personally have anything to do with my problems. I cannot blame him for what they did to me and my life."

He observed her very closely. He was more determined than ever to have this fresh, unspoiled girl. With a few changes in attitudes and emotions, she will be a treasure . . . a real treasure. These qualities must have cost her dearly in the Oglala camp. Even that bastard Gray Eagle knows a jewel when he sees one.

He clenched his teeth at the thought of that warrior brutally ravishing this fragile creature. Still, he could understand why even a savage would desire her. I will be the man to teach you

504

the gentle side of love, *ma petite*. You will gratefully come to me in time, he vowed confidently.

"Come, I'll see you back to your quarters." He took her elbow and escorted her to the Philseys' door. Once there, he asked to see her again the next day. She hesitated, but he would not allow her to say no. She was embarrassed and worried about her impecunious state.

She realized it would be unwise to antagonize her new ally, so she accepted. She would worry about her other problems later. She quickly entered the door, hoping to get to her room before Mrs. Philsey caught her. It was futile. From the expression on her face, Alisha could tell she knew about the scene outside. She quickly went to her room.

The days travelled by at snail's pace for Alisha. There was nothing to do. She read, rested, did her small laundry, did her grooming and sat. She was bored. She had come to a crossroad in her life and found all paths were blocked to her. Her fate lay in the hands of strangers.

Mrs. Philsey developed a pattern of sending her meals in by Doc, or leaving them at her door. She would not allow Alisha to socialize or eat with them. Even though Doc objected to this rule, he could not change his wife's mind, nor did he have the courage to go against her wishes.

Doc went to check on Alisha daily. They would banter lightly, for an invisible strain had developed between them. It was guilt on Doc's part and fear of pressing him too hard on Alisha's. Her injuries were mending nicely and would be completely healed in a few weeks. He told her one day the welts would soon vanish, leaving only small, lined, white scars to remind her it ever really happened. Alisha wondered if the scars on her heart and soul would also heal someday, or if there would always be scars to remind her of her visit to Hades.

She found herself looking forward to Jeffery's calling, if only to avoid her loneliness at the Philseys'. No one else visited Alisha. Certainly, the women did not. Powchutu avoided her, too, thinking it best to keep a low profile at the fort. He did not want to cause her any more trouble. So, as the days passed, Alisha found herself more and more in the young lieutenant's company.

Powchutu's warnings went unheeded. Alisha pushed his warnings to the back of her mind. She and Jeffery seemed to have so much in common, besides backgrounds and education. Her spirit hungered for the vitality he radiated. She needed to absorb some of the self-confidence which flowed from him to her. He represented a link to her past and hopefully to her future. In this rustic, crude wilderness, Jeffery was civilization and chivalry. He was all the things she missed and yearned to have once more.

Jeffery was cautious not to rush her, and kept her off her guard with his charm. Sir Lancelot himself would not have presented a more gallant knight than Jeffery did to Alisha during those long days. He reminded her of all she had lost, and refreshed the dreams of youth in her heart.

When he believed his hold was firm and secure, he became more demanding on her time and emotions. He began to ask more questions about her future plans and her recent past. She had come to delude herself as to what he was offering and preparing her for in the near future.

Struggling to retain this illusion, Alisha would attempt to restore their lighthearted banter. If this failed, she would withdraw into silence. She would refuse to continue the confusing, frightening discourse, forcing him to back off and attack from another front.

His subtle advances and personal remarks about the two of them became more frequent and more intimate. Most of his comments and actions were never quite clear in intent. She turned away and rebuffed his slightest touch.

Each time Jeffery tried to touch Alisha, Gray Eagle's face loomed before her like a dark specter. She would freeze and pull away. A light kiss on the forehead, or a brush across her lips did not bother her; in fact, she found it enjoyable and novel. But soon, Jeffery would try to kiss her more ardently and Alisha would only feel terror.

He determined to wear down her fear with persistent charm and romance. Even after what she had experienced with Gray Eagle, she was still naive and innocent. He would take her face between his hands and gaze down into her panicked eyes of green. But he never realized she panicked because of him.

He could feel her flinch when he touched her hair and nestled his face to her ear, or when he "accidentally" touched a forbidden place. He was very experienced in the art of seduction. This green, unsophisticated girl wouldn't stand a chance against his knowledge. With his persuasion, she would be in his bed in his arms before she knew what had taken place, he thought. Once there, she would have no desire to ever leave. His only problem was her terror of love and men, perhaps even of her own emotions. He had no doubts that he could not tear down that wall of fear around her heart and mind.

But the process of breaking down Alisha's defenses was not as easy as Jeffery schemed. For whenever Alisha was with him, thoughts and images of Gray Eagle haunted her mind. Her soul cried out in torment, why do I feel I betray Gray Eagle when Jeffery reaches out to me? She did not realize it was not Jeffery she was reaching out for. It was the love and security she thought he was offering to her.

Alisha dreamed she spoke to Gray Eagle: I hear your voice in the winds. I see your face in the night. I feel your touch in my slumber. Do you possess some power of voodoo? Can you bring me such suffering even though I am physically free of you? Did you cast some spell upon my heart which prevents me from loving another? Have you imprisoned my soul forever as you once did my body?

Jeffery is all the things I could ever want and need in a man. He is life and you are death. Why can I not respond to him? Is it love I fear, or Jeffery, or do I fear to allow him the same power you held over me? Jeffery is my one hope for a new life and freedom. He is the hope of regaining myself, my happiness and peace of mind.

Then Alisha would silently call out to the lieutenant: Help me! Jeffery. Help me to love you. Teach me to want you, to respond to you and your touch. In time, you can replace him in my heart as you have done in my life. You must! Free me from Wanmdi Hota!

"What troubles your thoughts, *ma petite?*" Jeffery broke into Alisha's reverie.

She paled even more, then flushed guiltily. Was she so transparent she had allowed her most intimate emotions and torment to show, and to him of all people? "No matter how hard I try to forget, Jeffery, sometimes my memories sneak in around the edges of my mind to torment me." She turned away from his keen eyes as tears began to roll down her cheeks. "Will it never go away or stop hurting, Jeffery? Will the terrible emptiness and humiliation always be there? I have no one . . ."

He reached out and pulled her into his arms to comfort her. She cried like a hurt, frightened child. She desperately clung to him for the strength and consolation he offered. He sensed how much she needed him and it gave him a feeling of power over her.

He embraced her tightly and possessively, whispering soft, soothing words into her ear. Her vulnerability and nearness overcame him and he began to cover her face and lips with hungry kisses. His hands moved up and down her back, caressing and fondling. His insistent tongue probed her mouth and one of his hands tenderly cupped her breast. He was so caught up in his hunger for her that he did not immediately realize she was trying to push him away. She pleaded fearfully with him to stop. This was the rash behavior such as Horace displayed that day, but there was no Ben here to help her this time. He was too powerful to fight and she could not seem to reach him with words. She struggled harder.

"Please, Jeffery, don't! You can't! I can't . . . stop! Please stop . . . Too soon . . . Not here, not now . . . Time, I need more time! Jeffery!" He was actually going to seduce her! He would take her in the grass like some harlot. He didn't want her; he wanted a woman, any woman. Her tears were from anger and bitterness and she fought like a cornered tiger.

He cooed in her ear, "I can make you forget what he did to you, Alisha. Don't pull away from me. Let me teach you the way of love and gentleness. I won't rush you or hurt you. Let me love you, Alisha. I want you . . . Need you . . . Here . . . Now . . ." He pleaded with her in a husky voice overcome with desire.

Jeffery gripped her wrists so tightly he was hurting her. His lips bruised hers. His breathing was rapid and hot against her face. His hands grew bolder with their caresses. He pressed his hardened manhood to her body and rubbed against her. He was at the point where she could not reason with him. His eyes held that same lustful, evil look the trapper's had held that day when he was about to rape her. Wild, sheer terror raced through her veins.

Shaking violently, she cried, "No! Jeffery. I said, stop it! Let me go!"

She slapped at him and clawed at his face. She beat on him with her small, ineffective fists. She frantically grabbed a handful of hair. She yanked and yanked with all her might.

He jerked his head back angrily and he glared down at her. His effort to seduce her was thwarted and the fires leaping in his body retaliated, "Soon, you'll come a-begging for what you now reject! You don't play with a man's emotions like that, then shy off like some frightened young virgin — which you're not!"

Alisha lowered her lashes in shame and guilt.

He brutally continued, "You can push a man only so far, Alisha, then he'll take by force what you freely offered, just like that savage did. Is that what you want, force to make it blameless for you?"

There had never been a time when he had not been in full command and control — until today, until Alisha . . .

The look on her face calmed his agitation. She looked like a hurt child. Never had he noticed such hurt and pain in a woman's eyes before. Tears flowed from her translucent eyes and slid down her rosy cheeks. She had lowered her head in submission. He chided himself sternly, this was the wrong time and way to reach her. Damn! Why had he lost control of the situation like that? Now, he would have to win her trust all over again. If only she weren't so innocent and beautiful. She was like a child in a woman's body.

He reached out his hand and lifted her chin. He spoke softly, in a tone filled with remorse and apology, "I'm sorry, Alisha. I guess I lost my head there for a time. It wasn't your fault. You've just got a way of getting to me. I apologize for my behavior. I want you like I've wanted no other woman.

"But my patience is short and my hunger for you so powerful. If you'll give me the time, I'll prove myself to you. Think about what I have to offer you and what you need. I need you, Alisha, and I think you need me. We're a lot alike and we have a lot to give to one another. For once, Alisha, don't be afraid to reach out and take what you want. I can promise you — it won't be like it was with those savages."

His tone was accomplishing everything he wished it would, for she was greatly tempted to throw herself into his arms and tell him she would belong to him forever.

Then Jeffery added, "I'm you're best hope here, Alisha. Just don't take too long with your decision . . ." He had hoped to help her see the light as quickly as possible. Perhaps if she feared he might lose interest or become discouraged, she might make some commitment to him sooner. But his words carried the tone of a threat, not a promise.

She mentally backed up. "I'm truly sorry if I misled you, Jeffery. I did not mean for you to think . . . I mean, I do find you most charming and attractive, but I'm not ready to commit myself to you or anyone just now. There are things I must work out in myself first. Please understand, it isn't you or what you did . . . It's just I . . . I can't bring myself to . . . You frightened me with the way you acted and the way you were looking at me. I have never known or met anyone like you and I'm unsure of what it is you want or expect from me. Whatever it is, I'm not ready or prepared to even know about it. Can we talk about it later? Maybe in time, I could . . . we could . . . All I ask is time, Jeffery, just a little more time."

He stepped back and smiled that beguiling smile of his, nodding acceptance of her terms. At least, for a while . . . He convinced her of his gallant intentions of waiting until she was ready to make the first move toward him.

Although Alisha tried to relax and suppress her fears about Jeffery, there was a hidden strain in her. She was on constant guard against another such incident between them and of allowing herself to trust him too much too soon.

She became agitated at his constant reminders of her vulnerable position. Jeffery would tell her how much he wanted her and allude to something special between them. Although he never proposed marriage, this or love was what she thought he wanted from her. His real intention never entered her pristine mind . . .

Chapter Fourteen

Alisha would not dare to think about what Fort Pierre would say about her nocturnal talks with Powchutu. They would no doubt be greatly shocked and enraged.

Several days after the confrontation between Powchutu and Jeffery, Alisha had been sitting by her open window in the dark to catch the cooler night breeze. When Powchutu passed nearby on his way to his room, she softly called out to him. He looked around to make sure no one saw him, then came over to her. She apologized for the scene she had caused, and he hastily explained it was not her fault. He assured her the men had only used her as an excuse to antagonize him. They would have found something else to use if she had not been there.

Thus began Alisha's friendship with the red man.

She would sit on the floor beside her window as he leaned against the outside wall. They would talk about the Fort Pierre people. They would often mimic some of them and snicker quietly, like two childish conspirators.

Most of the nights, their talks would center around this land, the settlers, their lives, and the Indians. Alisha did not realize that she thirsted for knowledge about the Indians in order to help her understand Gray Eagle and her interlude with him. There was so much to learn, and for some imperceptible reason, so little time to do so.

Powchutu also felt this urge to teach her all he knew, and to help her understand all these things, but especially all about the Oglala and the warrior Gray Eagle. He would talk with her for hours on end. Sometimes, she felt her head was brimming with facts; then other times, she felt she understood nothing of the things he told her.

He related the story of how the Sioux had received their name from the French, from a word "nadowes-sioux," which meant "enemies"; but the people called themselves "Dakotas," which meant "friends."

Powchutu told Alisha that the Sioux practiced what was called a Warrior Society. The braves earned their membership by bravery and generosity. A warrior had the right to go on hunts and raids as a member of the party and could be chosen as the leader for them. After his selection, the leader would then select the men to accompany him and the object of their hunt or raid. There were two times when all the hunters and warriors were joined in one band and this was for the spring and winter buffalo hunts or for tribal war.

Alisha recalled the many times she had seen Wanmdi Hota chosen as the leader. He was greatly loved and respected by his people. Wanmdi Hota's position was very important. She wondered how this council had voted on how she should be treated and punished, or if they had had any say in her relationship with their beloved warrior. Had he lacked the power to go against the council and change their demands, or had he willingly accepted their decisions about her?

She wondered what took place at those meetings he went to in the great teepee in the center of the village. Just how much did his laws and customs have to do with her troubles? Were his people angered by their great warrior taking and protecting one of their enemies, even one who had helped him? Perhaps that was the reason her life had been spared.

The truth hit her like a bright, blinding light: Her worst punishments followed public defiance of him. It appeared she was trying to force him to show favor to her or his people. Had she forced him into choosing between her abuse and his power? Had she pushed his back to a wall, leaving him no way out but to lash out at her? These doubts tore at her mind, for she would never know.

Alisha listened with great interest to Powchutu's stories about the calling of coup — the telling of his deeds of bravery, daring and generosity. The calling of coup was done at special ceremonies. The warrior's best friend usually did this before battle or before a contest. The people would cheer loudly for their favorite warrior or sing along when his coups were chanted.

Honor and respect were ingrained into the warriors from the time of birth. Powchutu said, "There is no greater shame to a warrior than the loss of face and his honor before his own people. This is even more vital to a great warrior or leader. He must never allow anything or anyone to darken his name or honor . . . no one . . ."

Alisha winced at this knowledge, for that was exactly what she had done many times. Perhaps her offer of help at her fortress had been an embarrassment to him. Had he thought it would damage his pride to allow her to help him? Had he believed she had been trying to taunt him, she a mere girl in control of a great warrior? Had she committed some grave error in etiquette by touching him?

One night, they discussed the white man's religion in comparison to the Indian's. The two religious concepts had many similarities, and yet, they were very different. He related the Sacred Circle of Life to her. She recalled its scenes from the ceremonial lodge. They honored mother earth Makakin and the sun Wi. They revered all of Wakantanka's creations.

They worshipped Wakantanka, ruler of the sky, water, land, animals and men. "All things are His creations and under His watchful eyes and protection. He sees, hears and knows all things."

Powchutu explained, "Wakantanka is to the Indian what God is to the white man. The Indian believes all things have spirits, good or evil. The Indian lives as one with the land and nature. We live, grow and learn together as Wakantanka planned."

They discussed the role and life of children in the Indian society. He told her of their training, love and protection by all adults. Each child was taught to know his proper place in the tribe. Respect was one of the main traits they were taught. Then came the preparation for girls to become wives and mothers, and for the boys to become hunters and warriors. The children were inured with honor, obedience, generosity and pride. They were instilled with the laws and customs of their tribe and those of nature. They were ingrained with these traits from the time of birth, and honored and practiced them until death.

Alisha plied Powchutu with many questions about the burial scaffolds she had seen and the red man's beliefs in death and the afterlife. Powchutu said, "They place the body of the fallen warrior on a high scaffold in sacrifice and to protect it from wild animals. The departed warrior's spirit is taken by the sun, wind and rain elements. They claim it and lead it to the Ghost Trail, the Mahpiya Ocanku. There, his spirit walks in peace and happiness until Wakantanka accepts his spirit unto himself forever. His people kill the warrior s horse and send it, along with his weapons and possessions, with him to aid him on his journey to his new life. White traders and trappers have been known to steal the weapons and possessions of dead warriors. This is a death punishment. No one must touch the sacred scaffold or the body of the fallen warrior."

They talked for many hours on the importance of dreams and visions in the lives of the Indian. "A dream is contact with the Great Spirit, Alisha, but a vision is a command or guidance from him. He gives the warrior instructions and warnings in these visions. The warrior must do as the vision commands, or face death and dishonor.

"Each young boy at the proper age goes out into the wilderness alone. He refuses drink, food and sleep until the Great Spirit comes to him in a special vision to give him this guidance for his life. At birth, a boy is given a child's name, but the Great Spirit gives the man his true name."

"Is this how Wanmdi Hota received his name?" Alisha eagerly inquired.

Powchutu nodded. "In his vision quest, he saw a gray eagle. He took this name and its meaning for guidance and strength. This is true of the others, like his koda Wanhinkpe Ska. His name White Arrow means straight and true. I have not sought my vision or a new name. I still carry my childhood name given me by my mother."

She humorously related the name White Arrow had given to her. He laughed as he agreed "Grass-Eyes" was a good and true name for her.

She hesitated a moment, afraid of his answer, then asked him what "Cinstinna" meant.

He asked who called her by this name. "Wanmdi Hota did so many times. What does it mean?"

"It means 'Little One.' Which beside him, you are surely that! I have heard he is a tall, powerful man."

"Yes. But to him, I am very small in many ways." She joked lightly as she secretly recalled the tone of his voice when he called her this. It had been soft, never mocking.

Powchutu did not want to discuss his rival and continued, "The young boys go through strict training and teaching before they are ready for their vision quest. It is a great ordeal for a young boy. Many have failed or died. To die is the will of Wakantanka, but to fail is a dishonor. After the boy receives his vision, he returns to his village and goes through a secret ceremony to be accepted into manhood and the first level of the Warrior Society. Each new level in the society is attained by age or coups. Only the very bravest of warriors gain this highest level. All leaders and chiefs come from this level."

He teased her with his next question. "Did you know Wanmdi Hota has earned the highest of all honors of any tribe? He is the most respected and famed warrior here. No man can stand up to his fame and honor."

Alisha gaped at him in astonishment. "Are you saying he is the most important and powerful warrior in this entire area?"

"Yes. In spite of your treatment, you were greatly envied by the others, and honored to be chosen by him." He observed the effect of those words on her.

She flushed at the way Powchutu was looking at her. She angrily retorted, "I do not call it an honor to be the slave of any man, not even a demi-god himself! Let any woman who envied my place take it! If they desire such a man as that, then they are most welcome to him."

His words had stung deeply. She does not lie or deceive well, Powchutu reasoned. I wonder if Wanmdi Hota knows she loves him. He must, for she does not have the eyes to fool him. He did not realize how lucky he was to have had her first.

On another occasion, Alisha asked what Jeffery had meant about the warriors meeting to smoke a war-pipe. Powchutu said, "Pipe smoking is done on many occasions, in prayer rituals, friendship parley, and meetings of the Society. A man's personal prayer pipe is thought to be sacred and is never to be touched by others. To steal the prayer pipe of an enemy is a very high coup. When members of different tribes meet, they smoke a pipe of friendship. When tribes join to declare war on another tribe, they smoke the same pipe to show oneness in will and spirit. The smoke from the prayer pipe is thought to be the breath of the Great Spirit. It is said to instill knowledge and courage in the warriors, and truce between those who share it."

Powchutu explained another custom to Alisha. "All events, battles and histories are recorded and remembered through chants and dances. One of the most important is the Buffalo Dance after the hunts. It depicts the fight with the big bulls, telling of the bravery and skill of the hunters. They act it out like what the white man calls a play. You were probably too scared to notice much about the Victory Dance, but I am sure you have witnessed one. This is done after great battles and raids. The warriors dance and chant their gratitude for their safety and success. It tells of their victory over their enemies.

"I suppose the most misunderstood dance is the War Dance. It is not to declare war but to call the warriors together and prepare them for the coming battle. The most important and meaningful ritual is the Sun Dance because of its meaning. It's held once a year at the end of the summer when the tribe is all together for the winter buffalo hunt. They feast and celebrate for four or five days and nights. This is a highly revered time for all the people." Suddenly, Powchutu stopped speaking.

Alisha looked out the window to see why he had abruptly stopped. Powchutu was gazing off into the darkness, as if his thoughts were miles away. He was vividly recalling the Sun Dance he had witnessed when he had been living with the Indians.

Alisha asked, "Powchutu, is something wrong?

Had you rather not speak of the Sun Dance to me?"

He looked over at her and smiled. "No, Alisha. I was just recalling the one I witnessed long ago. It was wonderful and inspiring, and yet gruesome and terrible. I do not believe I could go through what those warriors did, not even for such great honor and gratitude."

"Why is this ritual so different and important?"

"They prepare for it for many weeks. I will tell you the most important things. They take a buffalo skull and place it upon a pole cut from the sacred cottonwood tree. The warriors who have chosen to sacrifice their flesh and blood to the Great Spirit are made ready. It is done to show obedience and gratitude to Him. They are first taken to the Sweat Lodge for fasting and purifying. When the day for the Sun Dance comes, they are skewered to the pole in the center of camp. The ceremonial chief cuts two strips of skin and muscle in the warrior's chest. He secures the muscle to rawhide thongs and the thongs to the pole. The ceremony begins. The warriors dance, pray and chant around the pole. They blow on eagle-bone whistles to call on their spirit helpers to give them the strength and courage to endure this ordeal. They must endure the pain while trying to pull free from the pole. It is a disgrace to the warrior to cry out. Death is preferred. I have been told many warriors have died because of this ritual.

"When the warrior has managed to pull himself free, he is doctored and fed. This deed is added to his coups and all his coups are sung and chanted by the people in his honor. The torn strips of skin leave scars to prove this warrior has performed this great sacrifice.

"I believe I am a brave man, Alisha, but I do not think I could ever do this thing to myself."

Alisha had flinched and squirmed as he told her about the ritual. She nodded in agreement. "Nor could I, Powchutu. I cannot speak ill of these beliefs, but it seems such a horrible thing. I saw scars such as you just described on Wanmdi Hota's chest when I was doctoring him at our fortress. I had guessed they were from some other beating." Alisha thought, Wanmdi Hota, you are a man above all men. I am privileged to have known you . . .

One night Powchutu brought Alisha wildflowers he had found that day. The fragrant odor filled her room. He had recalled her telling him how much she loved the variety of flowers in this new land. She giggled with delight when he handed them to her, just like a child at Christmastime. She leaned forward and impulsively kissed him lightly upon his lips. As she inhaled the heady fragrance of the flowers, she missed the look which flickered in his eyes. Her touch had shocked him like a bolt of lightning. He felt tremors throughout his body and the stirring of desire in his loins. For a moment, he was overcome with the temptation to heave himself through her window and claim her for his very own.

He had been so distracted she had to repeat her question. She was asking him about the chief of the Oglala. Powchutu told her his name was Suntokca Ki-in-yangki-yapi, "Running Wolf" in her language.

"Why does it take so many words to say only two names?"

"For some things, there is no direct translation into your tongue. The Indians use many signs and symbols to communicate for which your tongue has no words of like meaning. The chief's name when translated means 'he who runs like the wolf.' The wolf is silent, daring, cunning and brave, and so is the chief. It is an excellent name for a leader of a pack of warriors. Evidently his son is much like he is.

"I have been told the chief was wounded in a fight with a sutler. It is said he has gone with the shaman to the Sacred Mountains for healing. The shaman had need of certain herbs and medicines which grow there. It is also believed the Thunderbirds live there and have the power to restore the health of the ones who go there to pray to them."

"Sutler?" asked Alisha confusedly.

"A sutler is a trader who works with the cavalry. I have learned Gray Eagle was tracking the sutler when your people took him prisoner. The sutler escaped and is now beyond his reach for revenge. It was said Gray Eagle swore vengeance on those who captured him and allowed the sutler to go free. We did not know of his plans to attack your fortress until it was too late. I am sure you know he is a man of his word. Your camp was destroyed and all your people were killed. Your people made one of the most deadly mistakes possible, Alisha — they beat and disgraced the son of a great chief. They dared to strike the body of their greatest warrior. This is never permitted. It is certain death to strike one such as Gray Eagle."

Alisha vividly recalled the night she had tried to slap him. He had nearly broken her hands. Why had he not killed her if it was an unforgivable sin? If anyone besides White Arrow had witnessed what I did, she thought, I would be dead now . . .

"This sutler and beating, they were the reasons for his intense hatred and violence to my people? He must have been furious to know the trader escaped while he had been captured. I suppose I understand his revenge toward my people, at least from his viewpoint. But surely he realized I had nothing to do with his capture and torture."

"I would guess that is why you are still alive now," explained Powchutu. "I venture you were the only one who resisted his treatment or tried to help him. He has repaid your help by sparing your life."

"But I was his prisoner. I was beaten and tormented!" Alisha protested.

"For rebellion and dishonor. He did not kill you as he did the others. Do you realize he is the son of Chief Running Wolf? He will be the next Oglala Chief."

Simon had been correct. Now I know his status and the reason for his power and respect. Son of a chief . . . the next chief . . . and I was his personal slave . . .

"Gray Eagle will lead his people until his father is healed and returned. He carries a great responsibility at this time. All eyes are on him. Even I am forced to respect him . . ."

"If he has so much power, then why did he treat so badly the very person who helped him? Doesn't he have the power to do as he wishes?"

"He is not a chief yet, Alisha, and even if he were, his honor and people would be more important than a slave who had helped him one time. He cannot change the laws and customs of his people for his own selfish desires. He must behave in the way expected of a leader. They see you as white, their enemy. It does not matter what you think or how you feel about them. It would take great patience, a great deal of time, and much understanding to ever hope to earn their respect and acceptance. I doubt if they have ever known any white woman like you, and so, they view and treat you as they would any other one. I am sure that in time they would have come to see you for yourself. From what you have told me of your life there, you kept reminding them, and Gray Eagle, you were white and a prisoner.

Gray Eagle has never cowered to any man or woman, and never will. He will always remain aloof and cool.

"Do you expect a man like him to open his heart and life to his enemy, even one who is brave and beautiful? If you do, you ask and dream for too much from a man like Gray Eagle. Why would he think he needed the love of his enemy to fulfill his happiness? He possesses everything he thinks he needs. Even if he desired you as a woman, he would not dare to love you. Or if by some slim chance he did love you, he would never tell you. He would never dishonor his name by allowing anyone to suspect such a thing."

Powchutu made everything sound so hopeless, and yet, his words were logical and true. Alisha asked herself if she had really believed she could win Gray Eagle's love and acceptance, if she had reached for that illusive pot of gold at the end of a rainbow. Yes was the answer to her questions.

Suddenly, Alisha thought of Chela. Alisha had to know who she was in the life of Wanmdi Hota. This uncertainty had plagued her mind in his village and at the fort. "Powchutu, do you know of the woman called Chela? Who is she to Wanmdi Hota?"

He studied her facial expression intently before he replied. "Chela is the Oglala shaman's daughter. She has been chosen to join with Gray Eagle."

"Join?"

"In your tongue, marry . . ."

She despised to hear him say aloud the words she had feared, but suspected. She had prayed she had wrongly surmised. "He is going to marry her? From his actions, I would doubt his love for her. He captured me and flaunted me before her as his harlot. How dare he! No wonder she hated me so much. I could see the desire in her eyes to have him, but I did not know they were promised. If he is to marry her, then why would he take me and keep me? Why would he treat her so vilely?"

There were intense emotions entwined in her words, more intense than even she realized. Powchutu recognized hurt and jealousy in her face. He knew for sure then, she cared too much, far too much for Gray Eagle. Should I let her think what she must, or do I tell her the whole truth? he wondered. Which will hurt most?

Powchutu chose to speak the truth. "Gray Eagle did not choose to join with Chela. It is the custom of their people that they join. If he has chosen no wife by his twenty-fifth winter, tribal custom declares he join with the shaman's daughter or another of the council's choosing. He has taken no wife, or woman before. That is until you . . . I would also guess she would hate you greatly. She would have been the only woman to have ever known the beloved warrior. It is only a few months before they are to be joined, but you have taken him first. Unlike most Indian women, Chela is known for her fiery temper and possessive nature. Most maidens would give anything to have been in your place. I, too, have heard of Gray Eagle's looks and virility."

She was almost tempted to tell him how much he favored the man he spoke of to her. Alisha wasn't sure if Powchutu's words made her feel better or worse. "But why would he do such a vile and cruel thing to either of us, Powchutu?"

There was an uncontrollable sharp edge to his tone. "It is obvious to anyone how very beautiful and special you are. Many men would trade anything to have you for their own. Gray Eagle is no different in this way. He saw and desired you, and had the power and courage to take what he wanted."

She blushed at the tone of Powchutu's voice. She dared not ask him to comment further. "If I were still his captive, what would have happened when he joined with Chela?"

"He would either sell you to another, or keep you for himself. Life would have changed very little for you. Chela would be his wife and you would be his . . . his witkowin. You two would share him."

Witkowin . . . She flinched at the thoughts of not only being a slave, but a harlot. "I am glad I did not have to endure such a humiliation. I will be no man's concubine!" Alisha's tender nature was repulsed at the thought of the warrior's going from her mat to Chela's and back again. Joined in a few months . . . Suddenly, she was grateful for Jeffery's rescue, and she resolved she

531

would never again dream of returning.

Alisha abruptly questioned, "Why do you always call him Gray Eagle instead of Wanmdi Hota?"

Powchutu shrugged as he looked away. He did not want to tell her he resented the caressing way she said the Oglala name which she did not do when she called him Gray Eagle. He spoke his name in English in hopes she would do the same.

Powchutu did not answer and bid her a hasty goodnight. This talk tonight had been painful and enlightening for both of them . . . but in very different ways.

Each of them lay awake for hours, recalling the things they had spoken of together. Each one was thinking of the one they loved, and of the wide breach between them. Somewhere along the way, each had felt a spark of love . . . but hers was for another. How could a man fight the ghost of one such as he?

The following day, when Alisha heard Powchutu's tapping at her window, she rushed over and peered outside. There he was as usual, leaning against the wall. She smiled to him and sat down.

He had some very startling news to tell her this night. First, he asked her if she had witnessed the torture and death of two white trappers recently. He described the two men for her. She recalled the event and its aftermath all too well. Powchutu told her they had killed and scalped three Oglala warriors, one of whom was a good friend of Gray Eagle's. She now knew how she had misjudged the situation . . . Wrong again . . .

"I did not know white men killed for scalps. I had heard tales and rumors, but for them to actually be true!" She recalled who one of the warriors was and how even she had grieved for his death.

Powchutu nodded yes. Alisha felt queasy at the thoughts of scalping a man, any man . . .

Powchutu said, "It is done many times. The scalps and jewelry are sold at trading posts for souvenirs, as the white man calls them."

His voice became quiet and low in warning, "You have spoken of your actions that day. You must always remember this warning, Alisha, never, never interfere with Gray Eagle's judgment, no matter if you understand it as wrong. This will bring shame to him and hurt to yourself. A man must pay for his crimes, and that is the way the Oglala punishes those who do wrong. The trappers had to pay for their deeds, just as your own people had to pay for theirs. Your attempted escape proved you had not learned respect and obedience to Gray Eagle."

Powchutu then explained Alisha's beating. "I feel I must tell you, Alisha, it was not Gray Eagle's idea. It was the law of the tribe. It is called 'icapsinte.' When a slave has earned the trust of her owner, she must never do anything to dishonor this faith. You had earned the trust of Gray Eagle or he would not have left you unguarded. When you tried to escape, you shamed the open show of trust he had placed in you. You proved his opinion of you was wrong. The punishment for such a deed is the icapsinte or slow death. But he only beat you rather than torture and kill you.

"I can only assume he did the beating himself to try and make it easier for you. It is the custom for the ceremonial chief to perform this punishment for the warrior. Perhaps it will ease your mind to know the whole truth."

"I did not know or understand these things," she murmured in an anguished tone. "If only I had known you before now, or if you had been in the village as my friend. Why did no one try to teach me what to do, Powchutu?"

He chided gently, "Teach your enemy, Alisha? Why should the Oglala tell a white woman what your people do and why? You should know why. Since you are white, they assume you to think and behave as other whites."

She summoned the courage to ask her most feared and tormented question. She had not even dared to speak the words before. "If only a small part of what you say is true, then why did he take me to the . . . to the teepee sa that night?"

The last few words were spoken so low he had to strain to catch them. When he did, he whirled to face the window. His jaw grew very taut and his slaty eyes blazed fury. Surely he had misunderstood her. Gray Eagle would not have dared to let others use his woman.

He demanded, "The teepee sa? Explain what treachery you speak of."

Painfully and hesitantly, she related the events of the night Gray Eagle took her there. It was a long time before Powchutu sorted out his own thoughts. When she had brought her tears and emotions under control, he gave the only explanation he could think logical.

"My only guess is he wanted to frighten you, perhaps teach you some lesson. Gray Eagle is very cunning, Alisha. He chose to use the one thing you would fear the most. If all the other punishments and threats had failed, he had to look for the one thing which would make you do anything he demanded. The lesson could have been to point out the protection he offered you, or to force you to realize you wanted no man but him.

"I do not believe White Arrow harmed you, for I do not think Gray Eagle would allow any man to take his woman. I am sure White Arrow was your true friend and would not have hurt you for any reason. Whatever the lesson, it must have succeeded, for you did say he never took you there again."

Powchutu concluded before he left Alisha's window, "It appears you and I have suffered at the hands of both peoples, my friend. To know you have had so many like sufferings is somehow comforting. I feel I am not the only person caught in the middle."

Jeffery came to call on Alisha the next afternoon. They walked to the big shade tree outside the fort. He had so far kept his word to her and made no more passionate advances toward her. All the knowledge Powchutu had given Alisha about Gray Eagle and the Oglala had dimmed her warming feelings for the dashing officer. She wanted his friendship and acceptance, but nothing more. How could she pretend he meant more to her than he did, or as much as he wanted to?

They chatted casually as they strolled along in the warm sunlight. The sky was a clear azure blue with fluffy white clouds. The countryside was beginning to change, preparing for the coming autumn. In the open, it looked as if the sky and land went on forever and ever in a sea of blue, green and gold.

Jeffery leaned against the tree with his broad shoulders and one foot. He teased, "You looked a million miles away just now. Where did that beautiful brain roam, Alisha?"

She replied easily, "To the south of France. I was thinking of how lovely and fresh it is there this time of year. We used to go there on a holiday every year about this time. We . . ." She faltered momentarily. ". . . My parents and I went a great many places together when we lived in Liverpool. But that seems So very long ago and so far away."

He took advantage of her wistful mood. "Perhaps you can return there some day soon.

Nothing is impossible if you want it badly enough. There are always things a smart person can do to get what they want or need in life." He leaned over and picked a large blade of grass. He began to chew on it as he continued nonchalantly, "You know you will shortly have to do something about your situation at the Philseys. Everyone is aware of the friction between you and Martha Philsey."

Alisha averted her eyes to the puffy clouds. She watched them for a time as they drifted along in the sea of blue. "I didn't realize our trouble was of such interest to everyone. You know I cannot leave her quarters at the present time. General Galt informed me there are no empty quarters available. Where would I go? If I have any other alternative, believe me, I will grab it. But for now, Mrs. Philsey and I have no choice but to tolerate each other."

He was staring past her toward the mountains. "She might evict you, you know. But, if she did, rest assured you could move into my quarters with me. A man gets awfully lonely out here away from family and friends. He needs a special woman to fill those lonely hours. There are other things he needs from a beautiful, vivacious woman too. I could use someone to take care of my quarters and spend those long, cold nights with. You and I are well-suited for each other, Alisha. You could move in with me and we could . . ."

There had been no mention, not even a hint,

about love or marriage. He was merely suggesting she move in with him as his mistress!

The reality of his suggestion stunned her. She cried out, "Jeffery! Surely you aren't suggesting what I think you are? Two single people of opposite sexes sharing the same quarters, surely you jest! We couldn't do that? What would everyone say about me then? I would only prove to them they are right about me. No!"

The lieutenant sought to convince her of his good intentions. "Sure you could. No one in that fort would dare to challenge my decisions. There is plenty of room for the two of us. I can easily take care of all your needs, financial and otherwise." Alisha needed no interpretation for the "otherwise."

"I am a man of wealth and reputation, here and back East. I can do as I wish and no one, no one, will dare to speak against me or mine. I need a beautiful, well-bred, refined woman like you with me. Who is there around here a man of my standing can socialize with? I'll provide you with anything you want or need. In return, you provide me with the companionship I need and want, day and night. I think this would be very pleasant for the both of us. After all, Alisha, you don't have too many solutions for your pressing problems. If you agree, then when my duty is over out here I'll either send you back to England, or take you there myself on a holiday. If you so wish, you can accompany me on the holiday, then return to England when I head back to the colonies. Either choice, your troubles would be over. There is no way you could have a better life here, or find a way to return to England."

She was gaping at him open-mouthed and wide-eyed. "You're not jesting! You're actually serious about this! I am supposed to trade my soul for a return trip to England? How dare you, Jeffery Gordon! How could you possibly suggest such a vile, filthy thing to me? I thought we were friends! I'm not some trollop you rescued from the gutters of London! Just because I was taken captive and forced to live with those Indians, doesn't give you the right to treat me like some harlot! Never!" She whirled to storm off.

Jeffery roughly seized Alisha's arm and yanked her back to him. "Just a damn minute, little spitfire. I think you're forgetting a few things." His face was a cold mask of rage. His grip was like a steel band. She thought for a moment he was going to strike her. His narrowed eyes were flashing blue fire at her.

"Just where the Hell do you think you'll go when Mrs. Philsey evicts you without a by-your-leave? You can bet she will, and pretty soon." Alisha noticed that he sounded as if he knew more than she did.

"You come begging for what you now reject. You'll be only too happy to share my room and board then. Just maybe I won't be so obliging when you're ready. You're not exactly the pure, innocent virgin anymore, so don't act like one! I would be gentle with you, Alisha, and that's more than you've been used to. Would you care to hear what those men in the fort think about you? Well I'll tell you. They think you're nothing more than a used Injun squaw."

Alisha drew herself up in righteous dignity. Struggling to control her rage, she said, "I am a lady."

He cruelly mocked her. "Lady! Lady . . ." He laughed sardonically. "I don't believe I see a lady around here, only a *trés belle ange tombée.*"

Alisha's self-control utterly deserted her and she screamed, "I am not a fallen angel, nor a fallen woman! What do I care what you or those vicious people in there think? You're cruel and heartless, Jeffery. I have never seen this side of you before. But I am glad I did before I made any decisions about how I truly felt about you. To think I actually believed I could fall in love with you! What a horrible joke!"

"Come on now, Alisha," he leered. "You're the only person here who doesn't realize what you face from now on. Stop living in that dream world! Wake up, my dear. Youth and innocence are lost to you forever. You're a woman — act like one!"

"You're vulgar and brash, Jeffery. All your charm, wit and gentility are specious. You have no honor! All this time, and all you wanted was a mistress. How dare you place me in the same class as Ka . . . I wouldn't want you for a friend, and never for a husband!"

He lunged like a tiger for the throat.

"Husband!" he scoffed. "Is that what you're looking for? Is that what all this flirtation has been about? You were trying to trick me into asking you to marry me?" He threw his head back and laughed long and hard. "My lovely vixen, you'll search forever for a man who would marry Gray Eagle's leftovers."

She blanched white at his words and stepped back slightly. Then Jeffery forcefully pulled her struggling body to him. He silenced her with a bruising kiss while gripping her in an iron embrace. She could hardly breathe! He backed her to the tree trunk and pinned her to it with his hard body. It took only minutes for her to realize she was no match for him. He planned to do exactly what he was whispering in her ear. No one would dare to come to her rescue against him. She was totally at his mercy, and he offered none. All gentleness and manners had been dismissed.

The dishonorable lieutenant thought, she'll change her mind after I've taken her a few times. When she learns what it's like to have a real man, she'll change her tune and dance to the one I play.

His hands roamed over her body and she was unable to stop him. She fought feverishly and wildly, but his strength was too much for her. With trembling fear, Alisha knew what he was going to do.

Wanmdi Hota, her mind screamed for help. I can't let him do this to me. She shoved at Jeffery but it was like pushing on a stone wall. She threw her body at his, trying to knock him off balance. The only thing she accomplished was to further inflame him.

His kisses became more and more demanding and his hands more insistent. She reasoned, feign response and perhaps he'll relax his grip. She relaxed into his arms, pressing her warm body to his, and offered her lips to his kiss. He moaned and deepened his kiss, instantly aware of her lack of resistance. He felt her submitting to him.

Loosening his taut grip on her, Jeffery leaned back to taunt Alisha with his victory over her weakness. She smiled up at him while managing to free one of her hands. She determined to wipe his smug sneer right off his proud face. She quickly drew back her hand and delivered a stinging slap.

For a moment, he was completely stunned into silence. She glared at him with hate and contempt, and shouted, *"Cochon! Chien!"*

He shook her violently by her shoulders and sneered, "You little vixen! You'll be sorry for that. The only reason the men have left you alone so far is because I ordered it. But I can just as easily and quickly dismiss that order! You'll come begging on hands and knees for my protection within two days."

"How dare you threaten me, Jeffery! I'll never come grovelling to you!"

He taunted unmercifully, "What's the matter, Alisha? Is a white man too good for you, or perhaps not good enough? You'd rather be bedded by that savage than by me, hadn't you?" He hesitated as he studied those lucid, innocent eyes. "Don't bother to deny it . . . I can see the truth in those big green eyes." He scoffed contemptuously, "Why, you don't even know what a good pleasuring is!"

Out of nowhere, Powchutu spun him around and shouted his name, "Lieutenant Gordon! You're out of line, Sir." The sir was said with a derogatory slur.

Jeffery looked like the scourge of the devil. He halted his retaliation as he eyed the scout's hand on the handle of his long hunting knife. He had witnessed Powchutu's skill with that blade many times. He furiously backed down.

Powchutu had slipped up silently and secretly. "General Galt sent me to find you. He wants to see you in his office immediately!" Jeffery was fuming at the scout's arrogant tone, and swore, one day I'll kill you, Powchutu . . .

"The commander believes there's trouble brewing west of here near the Blackfoot village. Would you like me to go tell him you can't come right now because you're far too busy assaulting Miss Williams?" He had alertly noticed the influence Jeffery had over the general at times, and mocked him.

"You get your ugly face out of my sight before I forget just how useful you are to us. I'm tired of you interfering in my affairs. You half-breed! One day, you're going to push me just a little too hard and too far . . ." he warned ominously.

Jeffery was seething in rage at the timing of the scout's interruption. A few more minutes and he would have forced Alisha's submission either by his power or threat. He would have proven to her she had no choice but to accept his offer. Damn the Indian and his infernal meddling! He released his grip on Alisha's wrist.

She leaned back against the tree, limp and quaking.

"We'll finish this later . . ." His statement was a threat. He stalked off in a black rage to return to the fort.

Powchutu gave her a few moments to compose herself. He could see how badly shaken she was. He had returned earlier after scouting the western valley area, and reported promptly to the commander on his findings. He had been about to ride out again when he had observed the scene taking place under the tree. He wasn't about to stand by and do nothing while he abused her that way. He had to first overcome his urge and desire to kill him on the very spot he stood. He quelled his emotions, for there would be no one to protect Alisha if he were killed for removing Jeffery from the scene. Powchutu dared to push and bluff Jeffery only so far. He must find some way to get Alisha away from here, to a place where no one knew her or what had happened to her. There was only one catch — he would have to wait until this new crisis was settled. When he had been scouting today, he had been unable to get close enough to the pow-wow to know what was going on, but it was something big and important. He hesitated to guess what a tribal meeting of that size meant. Right now, he had Alisha to think about.

"Lieutenant Gordon will be madder than a treed bobcat when he learns the commander didn't send for him," he scoffed, then laughed mischievously.

Alisha glanced at him in puzzlement, then burst out laughing. "He will be fit to be tied, Powchutu. You had better stay out of his sight and way for a few days. There's too much animosity between you two and this will only aggravate it."

"I could give you the same warning, Alisha. If my eyes and ears did not deceive me, you are in trouble not only with Jeffery, but with all of Fort Pierre."

She flushed in humiliation to know anyone, even her best friend, had overheard the words between them. "Did he speak the truth? Naturally, I've heard the little, vulgar remarks and hints behind my back and seen their leering looks. Do they all really say and think I am . . . unclean . . . like Kathy . . . a . . . whore?"

He observed the anguish in her eyes. They captured his and sought the truth. How could he lie to her? She watched him closely. He did not have to verbally answer her, for his expression of pain did.

"But why, Powchutu? Of all prisoners taken, women are the most helpless and vulnerable to strong men. How can we resist their attacks or cruelties? We cannot control our treatment. How can we be held responsible? They have no right to hate or resent us . . . no right!"

"I guess from their viewpoint, your sin is in remaining alive, Alisha. Perhaps it has to do with what our friend Ben told you — resist till death. They view life after Indian slavery a dishonor. If not physical death, then death of the spirit and heart. They expect and demand submission to anything they wish you to be or do. They resent, even misunderstand, your pride and self-respect after what you've been through.

"There is one thing I can tell you honestly, even if they consider you unclean: there isn't a man at that fort who would not give his right arm to have you for his own. From what I have seen and learned from my experiences, he speaks the truth, very brutally but honestly. Perhaps if it had not been Gray Eagle who took you, they might forgive and forget. He is the one man who strikes fear in the hearts of every one of them."

"But that was not my fault," Alisha protested. "I couldn't choose who took me captive. You don't feel this way about me, Powchutu. You are not like they are. I have learned from you that much of my suffering at the hands of Wanmdi Hota was from my own ignorance of him and his laws. Even if many of his ways are still strange and frightening, I understand why he did most of it. He hates me. They hate me. What shall I do, Powchutu?"

"I do not know, Alisha," Powchutu said, resigned. "I have tried to help you know why you suffered so much at his hands. I wished you to see and know these things so you could deal with them and forget. This thing with your own people, I cannot help you with. I am sure pride and honor was at the foot of many of your troubles in the Oglala camp, but here, they have no true reason to do this to you. I give you this warning, Alisha, knowing these things about him and his ways change nothing. If he re-captured you this very day, it would be the same as before. You would still be the enemy and slave, and he, the warrior. Also, he is still promised to Chela. Never forget this warning, no matter how you feel or believe. You will always be wasichun and he, Oglala. He could never treat you any other way . . ."

Alisha was crestfallen. She had no future with either the red or the white people. "Do not fret, Alisha," Powchutu soothed, "for I will find some way to get you away from here and these people. I will return you to the land across the great waters you have spoken of to me. You must be patient until this new trouble is over."

Alisha wondered what she would have done without Powchutu as her friend. He passed no judgments on her. He accepted her for herself. His promise of help and his kind words lifted the heavy burden off her shoulders which Jeffery and all of Fort Pierre had placed there.

Powchutu felt he must ease Alisha's mood

even more. "So much of this trouble is based on the misunderstanding between the white man and Indian. Both sides have suffered greatly since the white man came here. The white man kills to take the land, and the Indian fights back in the only way left open to them, in battle. You have been caught between the two warring sides. On the one side is the white man, jealous and angry because the Indian took you first. On the other hand is the Indian, desiring you but not accepting you because you are white. The pride and hatred on both sides prevents either one from having you."

"Why do you keep saying Gray Eagle wants me?" Alisha asked. "How could he and do the things he did to me? He only wanted to hurt and use me because I was white and helpless. If he cared for me at all, he would have freed me rather than treat me the way he did. I think my freedom was paid for with the blood of my people and the saving of his life!"

"Alisha," he chided her. "You have not been listening to me closely. He proved how much he wanted you by taking you as his captive and keeping you in his teepee. Gray Eagle does not take white slaves for himself, nor Indian slaves. He's never even taken a wife. He has shown his desire for you before his people and his promised mate. He feels he shows weakness before his warriors to take and keep one of the enemy for himself, especially when that lovely enemy refuses to be subdued and conquered. It is a frightening and disgusting thing for a man like him to feel he has shown weakness and a lack of wisdom. He makes up for this by showing his power over you and his lack of feelings for your pain and suffering. He tries to make a joke of your humiliation, to pretend this is why he keeps you. He uses harsh punishments to keep you in line and to prove you are only a slave to him, nothing more."

Powchutu wavered. Which was more important, for her not to know Gray Eagle's feelings for her and let her think she had only been taken as a whore; or tell her she must have been very special to him and let her see her true worth and value? To be taken with love and desire would be far less painful and shameful for her to accept than to have been taken for hate, spite and abuse as a whore. He would tell her the things she needed to hear, truth or not. Hopefully she would never see the warrior again and Powchutu's own words would not matter one way or the other, except to ease her shame.

"He must at all cost save face and dignity. Pride is most important to him, more important than his life or yours. You presented a very big problem to him. He finds it impossible to fight his mind with his heart. If I were you, Alisha, I would carefully study my feelings and place a guard over them. You have a tendency to reveal far too much with your eyes. When you speak his name or talk about him, your eyes soften and your voice is sweet and caressing. It would be a tragic mistake if the others guessed your true emotions . . ."

Alisha flashed him a look of guilt and panic. Was he saying it was evident to him because he knew her so well, or to everyone? She admitted, "I am so confused, Powchutu. How do you deal with emotions you cannot understand or explain? How can you control such feelings? By all that is sane, I should hate him for all he has done to me. Heaven help me, for I cannot. He has created feelings inside of me I never knew or felt before. It is like a fire I cannot control or extinguish. It burns at the very thought or sight of him. I must not . . . I cannot love him, for I can never have him. What shall I do?" she pleaded in anguish, ". . . for I shall never see him again, and yet, my heart cries out for him!"

Powchutu wished with all his heart she could feel and say those same things about Powchutu one day. Was there any hope she would turn to him if Gray Eagle was out of her life for good? Did he dare not warn her about the trouble brewing? "Do not be so positive you have seen the last of him. He is not a man to give up what he feels is his."

Alisha brightened. "Are you suggesting he might try to recapture me? But there is no way he could get to me here." Powchutu's words flashed vividly across her mind. She would never return as his concubine with Chela in the same teepee as his wife. "You said we could leave here and go to another place to live when this trouble is over, didn't you?"

The word "we" seared across Powchutu's brain, and he smiled. "Yes, I did, if you'll trust me enough to leave here alone with me."

She met his steady gaze and replied, "I would trust you with my very life, Powchutu. If I cannot trust the only friend I have, then I am doomed. You are all I have. I need you. When the time is right, we will go far away from this dreadful place and people. We will be a family, just you and I. We will always love and care for each other. Agreed?"

She was speaking of a brother-sister relationship. Deep inside he knew this, but allowed himself to hope that with time, it would be more, much more.

They were both silent and thoughtful for a time. Powchutu took her arm and they headed back for the fort. As they entered the gates and headed for the Philseys' quarters, they were quickly aware of the attention they were attracting. There was no way they could hide their meeting, so why try?

When the lieutenant strode into the general's office, Galt looked up. "I was just about to send for you, Jeffery," he said. "I don't like the trouble the Injuns are brewing. They are trying to wipe out every white settlement and fort in this entire area. Powchutu says the war councils are meeting in the camp of the Blackfoot with Black Cloud.

If they decide to attack here next, I'm not too sure we could hold them off for very long. If the war party is large, we won't be able to hold them off at all. If only those new men and supplies I requisitioned would get here soon! Hell, what good are guns without ball and powder? I hope to God those savages don't know how bad we're hurting."

Jeffery's eyes gleamed. He saw this as an excellent opportunity to be rid of Powchutu for a time, and with any luck, for good. "Sir, don't you think we should send someone for help? I'd say someone who knows this area and people the best."

The general rejected his idea, "No, Lieutenant Gordon. We've lost two men already. We had better hold onto the few men we have left. Those last few raids cost us too many men and supplies."

General Galt paced the floor nervously, muttering to himself. Jeffery tried again, "Why don't we send Powchutu out to scout around some more, see what he can learn? He might find out what they're up to or where they plan to attack next."

General Galt still refused his idea, "No, again. I'm afraid we'll need Powchutu here if they attack. He's the only one who could speak with them."

"Hell! General. Those savages wouldn't dare to attack here. They wouldn't stand a chance of a snowball in Hades in a fight against us! I wish Gray Eagle would try to raid here! I'll clip the great eagle's wings, and stuff my pillow with his feathers and scalp! I have a personal score to settle with him."

The general said, "I suggest we call in all the officers for a meeting. We had better plan some strategy if an attack comes. It will be imperative to make a strong showing in the beginning."

Jeffery rose, saluted lazily, and answered, "Yes, Sir. I'll see the men are here at 1800 hours." He left.

He halted just outside the general's door to watch a scene which had instantly caught his attention. Alisha was entering the gate on the arm of the scout. His arms stiffened, his fists clenched and unclenched, and his eyes burned with hatred and fury. Damn that vixen! he seethed. You've pulled your last insult at my expense, Mr. Scout! I'll fix you both! He caught the eyes of several nearby men. He nodded toward Alisha and Powchutu, and spitefully gave the signal they had seen many times before.

Several of the men were bewildered and surprised. He had expressly ordered all the men to leave that girl alone. The signal was unmistakably given once more. It was definite he wanted her included in on the raillery today. They surmised, she might be playing too hard to get, or being just a mite too friendly with that Injun. They figured he wanted to teach her a lesson or two. A few of them maliciously thought, she deserves it too, fraternizing with a red scum . . .

The men began to tag along behind Alisha and

Powchutu. They nudged and poked each other in the ribs, snickering and loudly whispering. The tempo and crudity steadily picked up as more men joined in. Alisha's face was flaming at the vulgarity and filthy gestures.

Powchutu tightened his grip on her elbow to let her know he stood by her. The group moved closer and closer to them as the ribaldry continued. They used words and signs she had never seen or heard before, but instinctively knew were obscene.

She walked on, head held high with pride and courage. Tears stung her eyes and she feared she would break down right in front of them. She silently prayed Powchutu would not be antagonized into defending her, for she had no doubts he was sorely tempted to do so. The grip on her arm and the look which had flickered in those slatey eyes betrayed his inner turmoil. His muscles were tight and tense. She longed to tell him it was all right, and give him a smile to prove it, but she dared not look at him again. If he read the expression on her face, he would instantly assail the closest man. She also had no desire for any of them to see the full impact of their cruelty upon her.

She was totally correct in her assessment of Powchutu's emotions. But he was wise enough to know it would be foolish and futile to take on so many men at the same time, at least in front of Alisha. If he were injured defending her honor, she would be hurt even more. His death would be even more destructive. She would be helpless and alone without him. He felt lightheaded knowing she relied so very much on him.

Powchutu swore to himself to find the time and place to singly take on every one of the men involved in this humiliation. This thought gave him the strength to close his ears to their words and his eyes to their gestures. He concentrated on getting her to her quarters as quickly as possible, but with her pride intact.

Without warning, a loud, spiteful voice ripped across the air, "Slut! Red whore! Where you hurrying to? Prefer Injuns to soldiers?"

Alisha's heart sank. It was Kathy.

Kathy launched into a vicious attack. "I saw the way you carried on with that Injun in his camp. Now here you are trying to act like Miss Goody-Two-Shoes. Well you ain't fooling nobody. They all know what you are and what you done."

Kathy had been viewing the whole scene from the captain's window. She had waited a long time to publicly humiliate Alisha and now had the chance — and everyone's approval. Kathy raced out of the captain's room.

Alisha was so stunned she stopped in her tracks. In just a moment, Kathy stepped in front of her and blocked her path.

Alisha stared at Kathy in astonishment. She could not believe a woman would say such things, or even think them. Her malevolence and crudity shocked Alisha. She said, "Kathy! You can't possibly mean such awful things! How can you stand there and spit out such vicious fabrications? You were there also and you know how we were both treated. Why would you say such terrible things?"

"Ha!" she wildly exclaimed. "Sure I saw how we were 'both' treated. I was forced to live and work like a dog, while you paraded around like some ivory goddess. You, a slave? That's a joke! You were nothing more than his harlot. You had the gall to live and sleep with the very man who murdered all our people. Why, you care more about him than your own kind. I saw you two, walking and talking like two lovers. You trailed around behind him like some lost puppy."

Kathy warmed to her diatribe. The soldiers jostled and surrounded the two women and the scout. Kathy shrieked to a rapt audience, "I even saw you bathing with him and you didn't even mind a bit! You looked at him with that sweet, innocent look, and smiled that sickening smile, and fondled him at every chance like he was your knight in shining armour. Why, you couldn't keep your hands and eyes off of him! Don't try to tell me you didn't like him! I got eyes in my head, ears too! I ain't dumb neither! You're just a cheap slut!"

Alisha had paled at her obscene attack. Her face was almost colorless, except for the two bright patches on her cheeks. She whispered, "You're wrong, Kathy. How could you hate me so much? You know you're lying, but they don't.

Why are you doing this to me? How can you stoop so low?"

"I see your little game. You're trying to convince these men you were innocently and badly used. Poor thing!" she sneered. "It won't work. I've already told them everything about you and him. They know about how you tried to help him back at our fortress, feeding and doctoring him. If you asked me, I bet you're the one who released him during the night so he could escape."

Alisha shouted back at her, "You're a liar! I did not help him escape. I had about as much to say about his taking me, as you had to say about who took you."

Alisha glanced around her at the expressions on the men's faces. She studied the distorted hatred on Kathy's face. She looked into the vengeful, bitter face of Jeffery. His face fairly shouted, "I told you so," and "beg me to stop it." She was only an outcast, unwanted, hated and mistrusted.

Their faces swam before her vision and she wavered slightly. Powchutu feared she was about to faint. He pulled her away from the crowd and hastily led her the remaining distance to the Philseys'. He could hear the tirade of curses and insults coming from the group left behind. Kathy was beaming with pleasure for finally getting a chance to knife Alisha in the back.

Alisha immediately went to her room and closed the door. She ran to the bed and threw herself upon it. She dissolved into heartbreaking sobs. Why had they been so mean? she cried in anguish. What have I ever done to any of them, or to Kathy? They seemed to be enjoying what they were doing to me. Their hatred and brutality is far worse than yours, Wanmdi Hota. At least, you believed you had reasons to hate and abuse me. They do not. Oh God, will it never end? How much more can I bear? What shall I do? I would rather be back at the village than live through another scene like that one.

Hatred and cruelty from the enemy does not hurt like hatred from one's own people. Had they already forgotten her condition when she was brought here? Besides, she had not asked to be rescued. And if they knew she would be treated like this, why did they bother to do so? If they believed she was truly Gray Eagle's woman, how did they account for her torture and abuse? This contradiction made absolutely no sense. How could she ever go out of the room and face any of them again?

Her heart beat sad and heavy in her chest. She remained in her room, all alone, for the next day. She refused to see Doc. She did not eat. She did not light the lantern that night. She just lay on her bed in the dark, staring up at the ceiling. She did not move when the light tapping came on her window that night. Time could not lessen the pain in her heart, for nothing could ever remove the sting of humiliation she had suffered. Except for Powchutu, she was all alone, orphaned, penniless and friendless.

There was no escape from her torment and agony.

Powchutu had hastily left the fort. He rode his horse swift and hard to release the pent-up fury in his body. He had seen Alisha safely to her room, then mounted up and rode off. He knew he might kill somebody if he didn't get away from the fort for time to cool his rage.

When he had returned after dark, he was hurt she could not even reach out to him in her pain. When she did not come to answer his signal, he realized she would need time to recover from the pain she had undergone. He swore, I cannot wait for the trouble to be over here. I must take her and leave here immediately. In a few days, we will be gone . . .

He gazed at her darkened window, wishing he could share this good news with her. He would see her tomorrow and tell her then.

At that same time, Jeffery was properly thanking Kathy for her help that afternoon. She had really knocked the wind out of Alisha. Only a few more days and he knew Alisha and not Kathy would be lying beneath him. After she's mine, Jeffery thought, I'll kill Kathy if she ever comes near me and mine ever again. Within three more days, that damned scout will be dead, and Alisha will be my slave for a change . . .

Chapter Fifteen

Matu had ridden hard and fast toward the camp of Black Cloud to tell Gray Eagle of the raid on his camp. All her plans would be in vain if the girl died in the raid or was rescued.

Gray Eagle, his warriors and those from many of the other tribes and villages swiftly rode back to the Oglala camp. They arrived to find many dead and wounded scattered about the village. Others were hiding in the nearby forest. The camp had been ransacked and many teepees turned over and burned. Fortunately, most of the teepees and supplies were still intact. They had attacked quickly, without warning, and left the same way. He dismounted and hurriedly went to his own teepee. He was furious when he saw Alisha's mat empty and the deep boot prints all around the mat.

Old Succoola ran in, panting. "They took her, Wanmdi Hota. I could not stop them. There were too many of them and they carried the maza-wakan. I was to guard her while Matu came to the camp of Black Cloud, but I have failed. She was still sleeping and never awoke when they took her. I watched from the edge of the forest. It was the one with the yellow hair, as before. He placed her on his horse and rode away. I am shamed, great leader of the Oglala." The old man lowered his head dejectedly.

Gray Eagle looked at the old man and spoke softly, as he would to his own father, "You were brave to remain so close and watch. The one with the yellow hair should take only the white girl, not the life of an old warrior, my koda. You did well. It does not show wisdom to remain in the face of death. You could not have saved her. The one with the yellow hair has dared the vengeance of Wanmdi Hota for the last time. He and all his kind will die before the snows touch our lands once more. I have spoken and so it shall be."

Gray Eagle's rage knew no bounds when he was alone in his own teepee. He clenched his hands into hard fists and ranted to himself, how dare they raid my camp and take what is mine! I will kill every one of them in our lands and forests. Their blood will soak our soil. We will do as Mahpiya Sapa says, we will band together and ride against them in twenty-eight suns. We will destroy them all.

Gray Eagle inwardly hoped Alisha would be cared for until he could reclaim her, for surely he would. She was as much his as his own body. It would be a very long moon before all the tribes would gather and be ready to slay the bluecoats.

As he paced around his teepee, he wondered what she would think when she awoke to find herself freed from his hold. She will no doubt be happy to be free of me. But not for long, Cinstinna! You are mine, and no man will take you from me, ever! You will once again share my teepee.

Each of the tribes returned to its own camp to prepare for war against the wasichu cavalry. Many arrows, lances, war clubs, knives and tomahawks had to be made, sharpened and repaired. Shields and lances were decorated with feathers and scalp hairs. War paints were mixed and readied for use on the promised day of justice. Hunting parties killed and stored game for the women, children and elderly warriors to be used during their absence. There was chanting, singing, and praying for the Great Spirit's help and guidance. The Owacitipi Hunska, asking for help and protection, was chanted and danced many times in the following days. All things necessary were being done and made ready for the largest raid ever attempted, and hopefully, the last.

For Gray Eagle, the nights were the hardest time for him in the twenty-eight day period. The busy days flew swift upon their course of time; but the nights were lonely, crawling by slowly. They moved like caterpillars on the bark of the cottonwood tree. His arms ached to hold his Lese, to be sure she was all right, to show her he loved her and wanted her close. His body hungered for her touch, her smell, her love, her kiss.

Wanhinkpe Ska had been right, the beating had taken her from him and his care. If she had not been unconscious, she could have been hidden by Succolu in the forest. She will surely hate me for the beating and for not letting her know why it was necessary, Gray Eagle mourned. Will she also hate me for recapturing her and bringing her back if I explain these things to her? Even not, I must have her back! Our lives and hearts have touched; now I cannot live without her. What life and happiness could I find with another?

As the days passed on and on, White Arrow would find him pacing anxiously back and forth, which was unusual for this man of great and long patience. He would stop and stare in the direction of the fort and mentally besiege it by himself.

White Arrow commented once, "So, you miss Pi-Zi Ista. I would not have guessed you cared this much by your actions, my koda."

Gray Eagle scowled at him and retorted, "I only miss her warmth in my mats and her duties as my slave. I am angry because they have dared to defile my camp and take what is mine."

White Arrow laughed, seeing through his facade. He proclaimed innocently, "They only took back what you had stolen from them. If you do not care for her, then why does she haunt your heart these many nights?"

Gray Eagle exclaimed, "She is mine! I shall

have her back. She is no longer one of them, Wanhinkpe Ska. But you speak wise and true, my koda, for even now I see her face before me . . ."

White Arrow spoke the words he had refused to think upon until now, "Suppose she is dead . . . or she could be wounded or killed in the attack on the fort? Also, one of the other warriors might find and capture her first." They both flinched at these thoughts.

"I can allow none of those things, my koda. I will tell them she is mine and will kill the first man who dares to take her with a challenge. They know and respect the honor and courage of Wanmdi Hota. They will not refuse."

His words sounded more confident and daring than he felt deep within his heart. If it came to a challenge, he would die defending her, or kill her before he would allow another to take her.

Gray Eagle's eyes narrowed in concentration. He knew he must find a way to get her out of the fort before the battle. He tumbled different plans over in his keen mind. Then a plan struck him by surprise. He could pull a white man's trick — speak with a double tongue and bluff them.

He excitedly related his idea to White Arrow. "When the akicita-heyake-to sees such a large band of warriors outside the wooden fort, all I have to do is convince them we will not attack if they give me the girl they took from my village. They will not dare to refuse. We know they are very low on supplies and men, for we have not allowed them to pass our scouts for a long time. We have also prevented their hunting parties from taking game. They cannot have enough food or mazawakans to ward off a heavy attack for very long. They will be in great fear of this raid.

"I will be very careful not to allow them to see her importance to me, or they may try to hold her as hostage. I also cannot allow the other warriors to see this is more than a show of power and humiliation. All must see only hatred and vengeance in my words for the raid upon my camp. I will tell them her life is demanded in payment for the damages to my camp and people. I will say I demand apology and sacrifice from them for what they did to me. I will say the cause of the raid must be returned to me for punishment."

White Arrow listened to his words and was impressed by his koda's intelligence and boldness. "It will work! I am sure of it. Who could dare to stand before the mighty Wanmdi Hota and not tremble with fear? They will be happy to give up her life rather than their own. But what if she begs for their protection? Will they not listen to one such as she and refuse to give her up to us without a fight?" He laughed as he answered his own question, "No, for the white-eyes are frightened and helpless. Besides, Pi-Zi Ista is brave and she would not allow others to die for her safety." He agreed with his friend.

Gray Eagle gazed in the fort's direction again, but this time with a smug smile upon his lips and deviltry glimmering in his inky black eyes.

Soon, I shall feel the softness of your body next to mine and taste the sweetness of your mouth, he thought. I will see the sparkle in your eyes and hear the music of your voice. This time, you will be far too frightened to fight or defy me. You will submit and I will not have to be harsh or cold to you. Yes, Cinstinna, this time will be different . . .

The entire day before the raid, the chiefs and leaders went into one sweat lodge, and the warriors went into another. This was a teepee with very little ventilation and was covered with thick, heavy buffalo hides. They built a large, hot fire in the center of the teepee and placed many rocks in it. As the rocks heated, the teepee became very hot, causing the men to sweat profusely. This ritual was done to release all impurities, evil spirits and fear from their bodies. This was always done before all battles and contests to renew and cleanse them in body and mind.

After they left the sweat lodge, they went to the ceremonial lodge to the Warrior Society meeting. The pezuta yutas were passed around and eaten to instill endurance and courage for the next day. They chanted and prayed to the Great Spirit as the euphoric hallucination began. Gray Eagle prayed silently:

Wakantanka, hear us;
We call to you for help and guidance.
The white bird you gave to me has been
    taken away.

The white bird you gave to me must be re-
turned.
She holds my heart and spirit with hers,
Return her to my teepee,
Return her to my heart and life.
Wakantanka, hear me;
Send me your sign . . .

Gray Eagle weaved to and fro as he spoke of the vision he saw. Under the influence of the peyote, the others believed they heard and saw the same vision he was experiencing. Mass hallu cination was taking place under those circumstances of close contact and empathy of mind and body.

He spoke of the great eagle soaring free and wild in the heavens when it spied a small white bird lying injured on the ground far below him. He gave a shrill cry and swooped down. He gently gathered the little bird into his sharp talons. As he flew homeward, many other birds tried to steal her from him. Being of superior strength and courage, he protected the little bird from further harm. He cared for her and protected her until she was almost healed.

One day while he was out hunting food for them, a large flock of bluejays came and stole her away from his nest. She vainly tried to resist them and flee, but she was still too weak. She called out for him to come and help her, to free her. When he returned home, he found her gone and saw the blue feathers all around his nest.

He soared high into the heavens to search for her. He untiringly flew all around the skies and lands day and night for a sight of her. At last, when he was about to lose hope, the great Thunderbird appeared to him and told him where to seek her. He quickly flew there and engaged in a fierce battle with the bluejays. He killed all his enemies and freed his little bird. She flew home with him, protected under his great wing, to live forever in his domain and under his care.

Gray Eagle talked on and on under the influence of the peyote. All of the others could mentally see and hear the battle and the other events he described in vivid detail. The hallucination began to slowly fade and relaxation came to each of them. Later, they related the vision from the Great Spirit to all the other warriors in the council meeting. They believed the mutually shared vision to be powerful magic and of great importance.

The Oglala understood what the vision signified — what Matu had known the moment she saw the strange half-moon scar on Alisha. The tribe concluded, "The white girl has been given to you by the Great Spirit for your bravery and generosity. She has shown courage and friendship to our people. We did not understand the Great Spirit meant for her to live here. That is why you were sent to their fortress many moons ago. He wished you to find her and save her, and now you must do this once more. She has been taken by our enemy, but we have been told to help you bring her back here. The Great Spirit has a purpose for wishing her life spared. We will do as he has commanded when he allowed us to share his vision guidance to you. We will be your spirit helpers. We will free the girl before the battle and restore her to you. You will place her under your wing and guard her well until the Great Spirit chooses to reveal her purpose to you. We shall kill the invaders of our lands and forests. We will tell the other chiefs and warriors of this message when Wi rises in the heavens. She will be spared and returned. We listen and obey you, Great Spirit, knower of all things." The council had decided and voted to return Alisha's destiny to the hands of Gray Eagle.

Gray Eagle and White Arrow were so excited about the vision of her rescue and return, neither of them could sleep. By the time of the new sun, she would once more be among the Oglala.

The pre-dawn light found the warriors prepared in their linked-bone breastplates and dressed for war. They took their weapons and mounted their finest, fastest war ponies. Their breastplates were an important item of their dress, for they were believed to protect the warrior's heart from the magic of the mazawakan. Their hair was adorned with varying colors of feathers, which by the number and position of the feathers indicated that brave's coups.

They were prepared to ride away as the Tokenpi-i-ceyapi Itancan's voice sang loud and clear.

He could still be heard as they rode away as he repeated the war chant for the fifth time:

Wakantanka, hear us,
We call to you for help;
Give us your sign,
Give us your guidance;
Show us your great love and protection.
Wakantanka, hear us,
Our Mother Earth cries;
Our forests and their creatures cry,
Our slain warriors and brothers cry,
Our winyans and papoose cry,
The waters and Wi cry,
All cry for the leaving of the wasichus from
    our lands.
Wakantanka, hear us,
We will take the wasichus mazawakans;
We will take the wasichus woyetu;
We will take the wasichus sunka;
We will take the wasichus spirits and lives.
Wakantanka, hear us,
We will be revenged;
We will free the forests and the creatures,
We will free the plains, and our brothers the
    buffalo,
We will free the children of Wakantanka and
    Makakin;
Wakantanka, hear us and help us . . .

The cry as they left was thunderous: "Yekiya wo! Ku-wa, Oglala, kodas, ihakan ya!"

They rode like the wind until they neared the fort, then halted. In the early morning of the twenty-eighth day since the raid upon the camp of the Oglala, dawn was approaching with breathtaking majesty, as if she sent her own, special blessing to the Indian.

Gray Eagle sat proud and erect upon his appaloosa before the entrancing sunrise. Its tawny hues sent rays like shimmers from heaven to outline him against the cobalt skyline. He appeared awesome and forbidding, sitting there like a god of war ready to swoop down and conquer the entire world.

It was time.

Gray Eagle urged his horse forward and forcefully hurled the lance he carried into the dirt. It struck with a great force and stood quivering at the vigorous impact. The two feathers at its end began to gently waver in the light wind.

Gray Eagle sat waiting for the fort to respond to his signal to talk. He sat proudly and boldly before Fort Pierre and the warriors. There was no indication of fear in him.

Tension and panic ran rampant throughout the fort. The sight of the enormous band of Indians outside their walls was alarming. Terror broke loose at the vision of the awesome event about to take place. The soldiers scurried about like mice, getting their weapons and preparing to defend their lives and the fort. The few civilians present hurried inside their quarters to hide in dread. Everyone anticipated death; or worse, torture.

The lookout watched the Indians closely for any movement. He stared at the tall, arrogant warrior sitting before the others. He wondered if that was the infamous Gray Eagle of the Oglalas. Who else would be so daring and fearless?

General Galt called up to the lookout, "How many would you say are out there? Can you tell the tribes involved?"

"About two thousand, maybe more, Sir," came the reply. "I'd guess there are five or six different tribes out there. They appear to be waiting for something. Could be for others to join them or . . ." That was when it happened. He called down, "There it is, Sir! They want to talk. That warrior out front has thrown the talking lance into the ground and is waiting for an answer. My God!" he shouted excitedly. "The feather is yellow! It's him, Sir. It's Gray Eagle himself!"

Jeffery quickly spoke up, "Best we send Powchutu out to see what he wants."

"After that raid you pulled on his camp, lieutenant, it should be obvious what he wants! It'll take some doing to talk ourselves out of this predicament." Still, the general heeded the lieutenant's suggestion. He ordered, "Powchutu, it looks like they want to talk. I'm sending you out there to see what they're up to." His apprehension was apparent to the scout and Jeffery.

"Yes Sir," he replied and nodded. He walked to the gates and waited for the guards to swing the huge wooden doors open. He walked outside. He listened as the gates were pushed shut and re-locked. He gazed out at the sight before him and fearlessly walked up to the warrior who sat in the place of the tiospaya itancan. He knew he had nothing to fear at the talk. The Indian was a man of his word and would not attack under the talking lance. Later, maybe . . . but not now.

He halted before the warrior and spoke, "I am Powchutu, scout and speaker for the cavalry. The general wishes to know what you want. Why have so many braves and chiefs come dressed and painted for war?"

The noble warrior answered in a deep, steady voice, "I am Wanmdi Hota of the Oglala, son of Chief Suntokca Ki-in-yangki-yapi." He had alertly noticed the effect of his name on the scout. The scout's face had registered recognition; then had it been hatred and anger?

Powchutu thought and felt exactly that, and more. I guessed who he is from his bearing and courage, he thought. He is indeed all I have heard — a man to melt the heart of a woman, but bring terror to the heart of a man.

Gray Eagle continued, "I have come to demand an apology for the raid on my village and payment for the ruin your bluecoats did there. You will give me the ska wincinyanna as this payment. I demand insult and shame from you through her, for the disgrace and suffering you brought to me and my people! If you value your lives and this fort, you will bring her to me, now!

"If you refuse, we will attack the fort and destroy it and all inside. If she survives the raid, she would still become my kaskapi. A battle would cost many lives from both sides. But you must be made to suffer as my people did because of the contempt of the one with the yellow hair. I will teach your people torment and dishonor through the girl. They will see and know the foolishness of such actions. They will be made to know humiliation by giving the girl to me willingly to save their own lives." He spoke with confidence and boldness as he observed the scout's expressions.

Powchutu fired at him, "She is innocent of the raid on your camp! Demand the lives of the men who did this thing, not hers! You have caused her enough pain and dishonor. Why should we give her back to you for more, or worse? Why do you not ask for the life of the other white girl?" Powchutu suddenly wished he had told Gray Eagle that Alisha had died from the beating. But he had not thought quickly enough.

Gray Eagle answered calmly, "The life and sacrifice of a witkowin means nothing to either of us, but the life and sacrifice of the pi-zi ista girl would bring much dishonor and anguish from all of you. The men responsible for the raid would be tortured and killed quickly and the deed soon forgotten; but living with the knowledge of what they had been forced to sacrifice for this evil deed would go on in their hearts and minds for a very long time. It is far easier to die with honor than to live with shame."

Powchutu realized how very cunning the warrior was. Just like the angry wolf, he went for the jugular vein of his prey. Powchutu's muscles stiffened uncontrollably. His voice was tinged with both sadness and fury as he accused, "So, you have really come for Alisha, just as I believed you would one day. But I will not allow them to send her back to you and your cruelty." Powchutu's expression belied his words.

Gray Eagle appeared to ignore his statement. He spoke with an icy, deadly calm in his tone, "She will be brought here to me before the sun is straight above my head, or we will attack at that hour. If we are forced to attack, no life will be spared."

Powchutu challenged, "What if she will not come?"

Gray Eagle's eyes narrowed and darkened and his jawline tightened. His expression warned Powchutu he had overstepped his bounds in meddling in a warrior's demands. He glared at Powchutu and demanded, "If she will not come willingly, then you will force her to come."

Powchutu tried for another opening, "What if the cavalry holds her as a hostage or refuses your demands?"

Gray Eagle handed him a rawhide leash and thongs. He vowed, "In the time given, you will talk, vote and decide on life or death. If you choose life, lead her here to me, bound and secured with these. If you choose death, then prepare for all inside the fort to perish, including the girl, if need be." He sounded cold and daring.

Powchutu struggled to suppress his anger and

bitterness. He could not resist one last plea for the girl he loved. He asked through gritted teeth, "Has she not suffered enough at your hands? Why do you hate her so? Is it right to make her pay and suffer for the evil deeds of others? She has done no harm to you or your people. She is as gentle as the morning light and as pure as the snows in the sacred mountains.

"I see why she hates and fears you. But I tell you this, Wanmdi Hota, if you harm her again, I will hunt you down and kill you with my bare hands!" Gray Eagle could not miss the look of anguish which touched his eyes as Powchutu continued. "You have judged the ista skas well and true. I am sure they will return her to you to save themselves. But I tell you this, it will be by force!"

Gray Eagle stared as he walked away, wondering at his strange words and pleas. How could a hanke-wasichun know her so well and in such a short time? Had she dared to befriend an Indian? Would she not fear and hate all of us? he thought. Once more I have underestimated her gentleness and strength. Will I ever fully know this woman I love and want?

Perhaps this scout secretly wishes and desires her for his own. Their friendship is too close I fear. I will know more of this man and Alisha. I do not trust the look of love which filled his eyes when he spoke of her, nor the look of hatred and revenge at my coming for her.

The white men and the scout are convinced I

hate Alisha and only want her back for vengeance. This is good for now, but you must soon know the truth, Cinstinna. I fear they would kill you if they guessed the real truth. The scout's love for you is very strong if he would risk a challenge to me to save you. He dares much in his speech and manner.

Bird of my heart, fly to me quickly and safely . . . It has been too lonely and long without you. Great Spirit help me if they reject my bluff and we are forced to attack . . .

Powchutu walked back toward the fort with a heavy heart. He knew what the outcome of this day was going to cost him. Why hadn't he taken her away from here before now? The fort will easily give her up, he thought, but will she go willingly? What choice will they give her? Damn them all! he fumed angrily.

Could he possibly let Gray Eagle have her back without a fight? There was no way he could stop him from taking her, or the others from sending her to him. He hides his feelings well, for I am not sure if he desires her, or if he might love her. Will he truly attack and kill us all, including Alisha, if we do not turn her over to him? Gray Eagle does not make idle threats. There is no doubt he would attack, but kill Alisha? Powchutu could not venture the answer to this haunting query.

I will find a way to save her from all of them, Powchutu vowed. I will take her far away from this place and all of those who would harm her.

She will one day be mine. I will give her back the happiness and love they have denied her for so long.

A wishful thought suddenly touched him. What if this was only a bluff? What if he wished to protect her from disgrace and harm?

The wooden gates opened to let him re-enter. He quickly walked over to the general's office, ignoring the many questions from those around. He tapped lightly on the door and was let inside. He went to stand before the general's desk. He disregarded all the other officers and Jeffery as he gave his report.

He repeated the words of Gray Eagle and placed the leash and ties down on the desk. The general listened, white-faced. The others glanced from one to the other in surprise and confusion. Powchutu's face was void of all emotion as he related the terms of withdrawal and truce. He said nothing of his own pleas concerning Alisha. He tried to make the demands sound cold and brutal for Alisha's sake and honor.

The general exclaimed incredulously, "He what? Surely you misunderstood, or is this some kind of joke? Why would he want the girl back so badly? His pride and honor, you say?" He glanced around as he thought on the perplexing demands. His face brightened with an idea. "Maybe this Brown girl's right. Maybe she is his squaw and he wants her back. Well, well, well, this puts a different light on things. I'd say she's managed to fool us all, hasn't she? The little tramp! Trying to get us all killed, is she? How the hell did he convince the others to help him get his white squaw back?"

Captain Tracy spoke up, "From what I hear, Sir, those Injuns would cut off their right hand for that Gray Eagle. Half of 'em love and respect him, and the other half fear and honor him. You're damn right they would help him do anything! No matter why he wants her back, he'll get her one way or another. You know what shape we're in. We don't dare call his bluff."

The general paced the floor nervously as he weighed the possibilities. He could either return the girl and take the chance Gray Eagle spoke the truth and would leave, or he could keep the girl as hostage. What if she was being innocently, but vilely, used as a taunt to them? No matter, either choice was dangerous and deadly. Without a doubt, Gray Eagle could take the fort apart and kill them all.

Powchutu's heart flamed in anger at their cowardice. He spoke acidly, "She is not, and was not, his squaw. Not for the reasons you think. She was his slave and prisoner. He only uses her to taunt the white man. He hopes to punish you by forcing you to witness his taking her, and to shame you by forcing you to give her to him willingly. He cares nothing for her as a man would for a woman. I have seen this hatred of the white man in his eyes. If you return her to him, it will go worse for her than before. He will be more brutal to her this time out of anger and spite for the raid on his camp. He holds her responsible for the raid, for it was done to rescue her. It is wrong to treat her as you have, but far worse to return her to him!"

The general retorted, "Don't moralize to me, half-breed!" But Galt knew he had been forced into a corner. He said, "Powchutu, you fetch the girl. Let's hear what she has to say about all of this."

Powchutu went directly to the Philseys' quarters and rapped loudly on the door. Mrs. Philsey answered it and glared contemptuously at him. He told her what his orders were before she could open her mouth. She backed away from the door and let him pass her to head for Alisha's room.

He knew he must talk quickly if he was going to have time to tell Alisha everything before he took her to the general's office. He wanted her to know the truth from him. He knocked on her door and called her name. Mrs. Philsey informed him she had not shown herself since that incident the day before. His malevolent look silenced the spiteful woman.

Alisha slowly opened her door and stepped aside for him to enter. What possible difference could it make now for him to visit her? Things couldn't be any worse than they were now. Why should she deny entrance to the only friend she had? She realized that something was afoot, for this was the first time he ever visited her during the daytime.

Powchutu guessed from her appearance that she had no idea what was taking place outside. Her red swollen eyes told him she had been weeping.

Anger flooded him. He knew he must relate the dreaded news as hastily as possible. Bluntly and simply, he stated, "He is here, Alisha. He has come for you, just as I warned he might."

She looked at him blankly. The last person to come to mind at this time was Gray Eagle. She queried, "Who has come, Powchutu? What are you talking about?"

His tone became soft and gentle. "Wanmdi Hota! He waits outside the fort walls for you to be brought to him as a prisoner. He has come with a large band of warriors. He demands you be returned to him as an apology for the raid on his camp. He demands your life as a peace-offering, or he will attack us."

He watched her face blanch and her green eyes widen in disbelief. Her lips parted to speak, but she could utter no words.

She had dreamed he might come back for her one day, but not like this. He had not come to rescue her, as she had so often prayed. He had come to shame her, maybe even kill her. It wasn't supposed to be like this . . . She began to tremble.

Powchutu went on, "The general wishes to see you and talk with you about this." He lifted her chin to force her to look into his eyes. He placed his hands on her shoulders to steady their quivering. "They will ask you questions about your life with him. You must get ahold of your wits and emotions. Fear does strange things to a man's judgment," he warned.

She desperately asked, "What did he say when you spoke with him, Powchutu? After all this time, why does he want me back now? Does he intend to execute me right before them for revenge? Surely they would not send me back to him?"

He knew it was cold and brutal, but she had to know what she faced. He reluctantly repeated, word for word, his talk with Gray Eagle and the general. She was totally stunned by both their words. She wavered slightly and caught Powchutu's arms to steady herself.

She hesitantly asked, "He says he'll kill everyone here, including me, if I am not returned to him, willing or not? Is this also a matter of his honor and pride, Powchutu? I think not! This is but a matter of hatred and spite. I was wrong . . ."

Powchutu tried to calm some of her greatest fears and doubts. He spoke of how he would act if he were Gray Eagle. "I believe he wants you back for himself. He uses this trick to save face with the Indian. Also the need for your honor and safety makes this trickery necessary. If it would punish him, the cavalry would turn you over to him dead."

He allowed his words to sink in before he continued. "I do not know how he convinced the other warriors to go along with this deceit. They must think it is a proper humiliation to the whites for them to be forced to apologize and sacrifice you to their worst enemy. He is awed and loved enough they might permit it anyway, even if they were aware of his true motives. I just do not know."

He could not tell if she understood any of his reasoning. He added, "For his and your pride and honor, he must treat you coldly and cruelly before all of them. You must not be harmed."

"Pride and honor! Face and shame!" she cried. "I have none of those left! Between my people here and his there, they have taken everything from me but my life. What does my life or freedom matter to any of them? It is only a trick! It does not take a whole band of warriors to reclaim war booty! I would not trust him this time."

She walked over to the window and peeped out at the frantic people moving about outside. In a subdued tone she murmured, "He will surely kill me this time. I have been too much trouble to him. He holds me to blame for things I have no control over. How could I have so foolishly forgotten what he did to me before I was rescued . . . rescued!"

She laughed and cried at the same time. "He knows no mercy or kindness. I could have died that day for all he cared."

All the suppressed doubts, fears and hurts resurfaced to fill and frighten her anew. She had unwisely allowed herself to forget for a time; to forgive, when forgiveness was not honored; and worst of all, she had foolishly allowed her heart to fall more deeply and strongly in love with him. Her illusive lover was not the man who sat outside the fort waiting for her to be brought to him in disgrace and sacrifice. She had been en-snared in the trap of blind trust and love, and the hope of his love in return someday. Her shat-tered illusions cut into her heart like a white-hot knife.

"Alisha, you have forgotten. He did not kill you. He must not have wished your death, for he was caring for you." As much as he hated de-fending his rival, Powchutu hoped his argument would ease her pain, but it did not.

"Only so he could have the pleasure of hurting me again, Powchutu. Such a powerful warrior wouldn't let a little thing like death steal his best slave," she spoke bitterly. She began to cry and he pulled her into his embrace to comfort her.

She looked up into his eyes and pleaded, "Please don't let him take me back, Powchutu. You are the only one who can help me. You are my only hope."

Powchutu crushed her to his chest and held her tightly and possessively. He answered, "I would give anything to save or help you, my love. If I tried to stop them, they would be happy to kill me and send you to him anyway. You would only feel guilt at my useless death. I cannot fight them, Alisha. There are too many on both sides. But I promise you, I will find some way to help you. I will get you away from him and here. Somehow . . ."

She leaned back and gazed up into his face, knowing he spoke the truth. "I am sorry. This is one time no one can help me, not even you. We can do nothing to stop or alter their decisions. I will live for you to come and fulfill this promise." She smiled bravely into his sad eyes and kissed him lightly on his lips.

He tenderly cupped her face between his hands and gazed lovingly into her emerald eyes. He spoke to her without words, but she misread his meaning. She had not realized he spoke of love, the love of a man for a woman, not the love of friends. He leaned over and kissed her full on the mouth. She did not pull away or refuse his kiss. It was a kiss of sharing love and promise, comfort and hope. It was soft and gentle in the giving and taking. He hugged her fiercely once more as he whispered into her ear, "Remember, I will come for you, little heart. Do all he says and he will not harm you."

She thought on his words, "all he says," and trembled.

The general would be sending someone to look for them. Alisha seemed to have regained her courage. He stated, "Alisha, come. The general will have to decide what is to be done. Let the final word be his. It will be best for you if he orders your return." The solution now out of her hands; she went with Powchutu.

Gossip had spread the news around the fort.

The word was out that Gray Eagle had come for his captive and would attack if she were not promptly returned to him. As she and Powchutu walked toward the general's office, the people glared at them in open hostility. Their cool, hard stares caused her to falter. This was the first time they had seen her since the episode the day before. Here was the girl who had chosen a half-breed scout over a dashing white lieutenant!

Some of the men hurled insults and threats at her. Soon, others from the crowd joined the derision. "Go back to your Injun lover, slut!" "We don't want no Injun squaws here!" "We ain't gonna die for no white whore!" "Harlot! Bloody red harlot!"

She somehow found the strength to get to the general's office. She felt she was walking into her own grave. Powchutu blazed in fury at the people's words.

Alisha forced a brave smile to him. She softly said, "It doesn't matter anymore, Powchutu. They only prove this is necessary. I couldn't stay here now. They're scared children, and I'm the only one around they can vent their fear and anger on. They don't dare do it to Gray Eagle so they choose the next best person — me, because he wants me. It doesn't matter why. Maybe they're right. Maybe I will be better off back with him, dead or alive." Her last rays of hope had dimmed for she knew the outcome of the meeting before she went inside the general's office.

The door opened and they quietly slipped inside. General Galt tried to avoid the eyes of the girl standing before his desk. He got up and moved about nervously. He tried to decide how to begin this sour, unpleasant task.

"I suppose Powchutu has filled you in on our crisis here?"

She nodded yes, but did not speak. He looked into the ashen face with the somber green eyes which were filled with anguish. Damn! He realized she was going to make it hard for him. He tried to ignore the shame of what he was about to do.

He asked her bluntly, "What do you think we should do, Miss Williams? You've lived with him. Will he do as he says? Could he want you back so badly?" His words carried double meanings, and she caught both.

She swallowed hard and spoke softly, "Why do you ask me, Sir? You're in command here. The final decision is yours. I have only seen and known one side of him — the brutal, vindictive warrior. He never made promises to me, only threats. If he knew of your abuse of me, he probably would ask you to keep me. All of our lives would be more miserable that way, and that is what he hopes to accomplish with this demand. He has his revenge on us all now, regardless of your decision. You know the truth, Sir, but refuse to look it in the face."

General Galt spit the tip of his cigar into the bowl on his desk and turned to face her. "I have hopes this Gray Eagle won't be as cruel to you this time. Maybe Powchutu can plead with him to go easy on you. He can tell him you had nothing to do with the raid on his camp. One thing I'm sure of, those people out there won't stand for my giving you sanction here at the fort at the cost of their lives. I have no doubts he will carry out his threat if you remain here. I'm afraid I have no choice but to turn you over to him."

There, it was said and done! He waited for any of his officers to plead her case, but none did. The reality and finality of it hit Alisha instantly. She bravely accepted the inevitable. The men sat stunned.

Alisha challenged, "Are you all sitting there and waiting for me to offer myself as a martyr for you and this fort? You should know I would never willingly agree to return to him and his brutality. I have seen and felt his hatred for the white man. I carry the scars to prove it. If you order me to go, then I will not refuse. But never will I volunteer! I place my safety and life in your 'capable' hands, Sir."

General Galt nervously cleared his throat and voiced his decision. "I think it best for all concerned that you be sent back to him. The safety of this fort and its people depends upon it. There is no other choice possible."

"Then you are ordering me to go?" He nodded yes. "The safety and best you speak of does not include mine?" she mockingly queried. His black, angry scowl answered for him.

"No, I guess I am not that important," Alisha

spat at him. "You certainly can't allow such a dangerous, despicable person to live among decent, honest folk, now can you, Sir?"

Powchutu was leaning against the door, silently cheering her on. He wore a smug, pleased grin on his face. General Galt reddened in guilt and fury. "If I had more men and supplies, Miss Williams, I would gladly offer you sanctuary here with us, and to hell with what anyone thought or said!"

Alisha turned to Jeffery with a sweet, innocent smile and asked, "Does this decision also include your approval, Jeffery?"

Jeffery boldly locked gazes with her and replied, "Go with your brave, Alisha. That is where you belong now."

Alisha walked to the lieutenant and spoke softly. She had no need to shame him publicly. Her refusal of him had already accomplished that. She said, "One thing I know for certain, Jeffery. You are less than half the man he is, in every possible way."

She turned to Powchutu and stated, "Since I have no personal belongings, I'm ready to go."

As she reached the door, she turned and spoke to them for the last time, "Tell yourselves each night for the rest of your lives that you are sorry that this could not have been prevented. But you all know it is a lie. I would have been better off if you had never rescued me, for then I would never have known the evil and hate which lives here in the hearts of all of you. I hope you always remember you held my life and fate in your hands for a brief moment before you cast it upon a pagan altar in sacrifice for your own. May my death be upon your heads, and my blood upon your hands! There is only one real man in this entire fort, and he stands here at my side!"

She walked out, leaving the men shamefully avoiding each other's glances. She and Powchutu made their way through the sullen crowd to the gate. The crowd had instantly known the outcome of the meeting in the general's office. A hushed, embarrassed quiet settled in the fort as Alisha walked to her fate with head held high.

But Alisha felt strangely detached from the whole scene. Her thoughts were on what awaited her outside the gates. She and Powchutu halted by the heavy gates to allow the guards to open them just enough for them to pass through. Her eyes touched Kathy's who stood smiling triumphantly. She gazed at the pathetic girl and said, "I hope this vengeance tastes sweet, Kathy. You surely worked for it. You might have won the victory here, but what have you really gained? All you have left is your hatred and bitterness. And now, you will have no Alisha to vent them upon. Be certain that you wash my blood from your hands tonight. And remember: while you sleep with every bit of scum in this fort, I will be sleeping with only one man — the brave and handsome Gray Eagle."

For once, Kathy was completely speechless. She could not believe that the gentle Alisha had struck back. But Alisha's walk to her own death made her brave — and brutally honest.

The gates closed behind Alisha and Powchutu. She listened as the huge bar fell heavily back into place. Eternally and brutally she was being shut out of their lives; and they, from hers. The inhabitants of the fort did not realize that their destinies had just been sealed with the closing of the gate. She was free; the fort was helpless. The warriors quickly realized that things were going just as the Great Spirit had shown them in their vision.

Alisha and Powchutu walked a short distance from the fort, just out of earshot of its traitorous inhabitants. He tugged at her elbow to halt her steps. She lifted inquiring eyes to his pain-filled ones. His heart was aching at her obvious anguish and raging at his inability to help her. They both sensed that this moment could be their last time even to talk.

She stood beside him in the bright morning light, wishing that time could be suspended, and with it, the torment and shame that it had brought into her life. She lifted her face up to the sun and inhaled deeply several times, trying to calm her racing heart and to bring some small measure of comprehension into her confused brain. The need to show courage and dignity was past.

Powchutu could read the desperation and hopelessness in her misty eyes. He cursed both the Indians and the white man for what they were doing to her, for never had there been one so beautiful and so blameless as she. The abject voice which spoke to him sliced his heart more quickly and expertly than his own hunting knife could have done.

"How is such injustice and hatred possible? Why can't Gray Eagle leave me alone if he refuses to have a meaningful truce with me? Why must he continue to torment me this way? He has even turned my own people against me. It isn't fair, Powchutu. I have done nothing to deserve all of this. Why must it be this way?"

He lowered his head, ashamed for his own guiltless part in her sufferings. "How can I explain what I do not understand myself? The Great Spirit will surely punish all of them for this dishonorable deed," he declared heatedly.

Alisha felt as if her tender heart was being pierced by countless tiny arrows. "My whole life has gone topsy-turvy in only a few short months, months which seem more like years. I feel as if each side has a cruel grip upon my life and is tearing it down the middle. I have no strength or means to stop them. I have seen such evil in this land, in these people. I hate the ugliness which surrounds me here. I hate what they have done to me. Worst of all, I hate these feelings of hatred and revenge which they have instilled within my heart," she murmured sadly, just above a slight whisper.

He studied the face of the English girl that he had come to love more than life itself. He wondered at the drastic changes that she had brought into his life and his heart. He, a half-breed scout, was in love with a white girl whose heart and life were imprisoned by the fiercest warrior of all time. Far worse, she had unwisely allowed herself to fall in love with her dreaded enemy. He could not imagine how Gray Eagle could bring himself to hurt such a fragile woman.

Powchutu recognized what his friendship had cost Alisha. He recognized emotions within her that she herself was unaware of possessing. He recognized that there was far more to this strange demand of Gray Eagle's than met the eye. He gazed longingly into her tearful eyes and spoke from his heart, "I will pray to both our gods that he will not harm you this time. He is no fool, Alisha; he knows that you cannot be blamed for the raid upon his camp," he stated to reassure her.

She sadly shook her head, auburn curls swaying gently around her slender shoulders. "But he can and will blame me. To him, I am white; I am his enemy. My innocence or guilt will not matter to him. They never have before." Yet, even as she spoke these words, she had the strangest feeling that they were not wholly true.

The sun had slowly climbed higher and higher, until it was almost directly over head. The midday air was arid and motionless. As she stood halfway between the long rows of painted warriors and the spiked fence of the fort, she could almost feel the surfaced hostilities. The moment of her fate had arrived; yet, she felt almost as much excitement as she did fear.

Both the warriors and the soldiers watched the tender and baffling scene taking place between the stunning white girl and the half-breed scout. Everyone was wondering what was being said between them. They wondered what was causing their delay. They pondered why the scout was not bringing the girl promptly to Gray Eagle. They had waited for a long time.

The people inside the fort became very apprehensive and angry as more time passed and Alisha did not make a move to go directly to the waiting warrior. The thought crossed many minds that she and the scout were intentionally trying to antagonize him, perhaps hoping for revenge upon all of them. Fearfully they asked themselves, why not? Hadn't they forced her to return to that savage warrior? Had any of them cared that she had come from his camp only a few weeks ago, come with a mass of welts from the flogging that he had given her? They feared that she only wanted to force a fight between them, a way to punish both sides. They could not help but fear that she would not help the people who had refused to befriend her.

It was much the same with the numerous colorful warriors. They were greatly perplexed by her actions. If eyes and senses could be trusted, she and the scout were good friends. The inexplicable thing was that she could like or trust any Indian, even a half-blooded one, after what

Wanmdi Hota had done to her and to her people. She was indeed a mystery. Some decided that Gray Eagle's torture had sent her mind to dwell in another land, that mystical land of nothingness. . . .

At the same time, Gray Eagle was alertly studying the expressions which came and went on both Alisha's and the scout's faces. He did not like the look of tenderness and love which she sent to the scout; those belonged to him alone. He inwardly flinched each time that she gazed up into Powchutu's face with that warm look that he had known so well. From what he could see, she appeared to be pleading with him. It could not be for help, for what could one man do against so many? Gray Eagle was very tense.

Finally, she looked out toward the warriors. She let her gaze slowly travel the lines of painted warriors and colorfully arrayed chiefs. They seemed to spread out endlessly and threateningly upon the vast blue horizon.

Gray Eagle once more held her fate within his powerful hands. She suddenly realized that she felt more betrayed by her own emotions than by him or by her own people. He would make certain that there was never another escape or rescue for her. She knew that he would not have to worry, for she would never try either. She would submit herself to his control, for only in that way could she ever find any measure of peace. Hopefully her love and desire for him would make such a decision easier to keep in the future.

She smiled at her friend, knowing that she would always love and remember him. He had done so much for her. It was doubtful that she would ever be given the opportunity to repay his kindness and help. In her heart she knew that she would lay down her very life for him if ever necessary. Noting the awesome sight before her, she thought of the people inside the fort. Each one had his own selfish reason for her being here now, facing only God knew what fate. Their hatred, jealousy, and fear were once again placing her at Gray Eagle's mercy.

She reflected aloud, "Even during his worst hatred and cruelty, Powchutu, Gray Eagle never hurt me or abused me as my own people have done. The pain and shame that I felt in his camp would not compare with what I have known here at the fort. Then they call themselves the civilized ones. They are far more savage than he ever was, or ever could be. No matter what he has done to me, or will do to me in the future, I will find the courage to do as he commands. I do not belong with the white man any longer. I can only hope to find some place with him and with his people. If my future is with him, then I must make the best of it."

She trembled with fear. She dreaded the thought that Gray Eagle might not permit a truce between them. Yet, she could vividly recall the time when he had been pleased with her submission; she could just as easily recall how she had forced him to shame and to hurt her many times. She realized that she must bend her will to his; she must put her pride in the right place. She knew so many things that she had not known when she first met him, things which could help her to understand him, his people, and herself.

Poised between the two peoples, in the moment that sealed her fate, the first moment she met Gray Eagle flashed before her. He had drawn her to him with his powerful magnetism. In an inexplicable way, she had become emotionally captivated by him that very first day. He had taken the punishment of her people with great dignity and courage. His hard, muscular physique had appeared indestructible. She would always remember that first impression of him. Even now, those memories brought a hunger for him to her.

Her eyes scanned the horizon once more, resting on Gray Eagle. He sat like a conqueror upon his majestic gray and white horse. He was indeed the height of power and masculinity. She could not help but notice his noble bearing and fierce pride. He was such an important man. A look of uncontrollable pride and pleasure crossed her face very briefly. It did not go unnoticed by him, even at that distance.

She realized anew that he had a way of making everyone and everything around him dim with his very presence. Their eyes met and fused. His seemed to bore into her very soul, reading all its secrets. A tingling warm sensation spread over her entire body. He had expected to read fear and hatred in her eyes. Instead, he read something very different, something which made his heart sing with joy.

So many thoughts raced through both their minds. He had never said that he loved her, but perhaps, Alisha thought, he had shown her many times. Had they both not enjoyed their close relationship? Had there not been countless times of happiness and relaxation between them? For certain, life with him seemed the only place for her.

She studied his handsome, stoic features for a time. How she wished she knew what went on inside his head and heart! He was the passion that ruled her body; he was her life and her future. He had made her a woman, his chosen woman. If she were not special to him, then why had he captured her and held her prisoner in his teepee, his first woman, and a white woman at that? Dare she imagine that he truly wanted her? He was a man of great pride and important rank. Surely total capitulation would have some good effect upon his view of her and his treatment in the future.

If her future was with him, then she would make the very best of it. After all, she did love him. There was no need to worry about what her own people might say or think about her. They could not hate or scorn her any more than they already did. There was no one to consider now except Gray Eagle and herself. There was no turning back now. She must go to him completely and willingly. Regardless of how he received her, her place was with him, just as her heart was now. It would be his decision as to what their relationship would be.

Her green eyes softened and warmed as they roamed over his face and body. Her respiration quickened in response. Yes, she would try to win his heart and his trust. A light smile unconsciously played upon her soft pink lips as she made her final decision.

Gray Eagle's obsidian eyes locked with her forest green ones, seeming to inflame her from a distance. The tension and sadness quickly left his taut, powerful body. His prayers and dreams would surely be answered this very day. He could read it in her smouldering gaze and in her trusting smile.

Her love for him was clearly evident. This time, they would find the path to love and to acceptance. This time, she would know and understand the secrets of his heart as well as those of her own. Like the pre-dawn, life passed too swiftly to live it in sadness and in sacrifice. She had been given to him by the Great Spirit to make his suns beautiful and meaningful. The Great Spirit would find some way for her to be accepted by his people. With her at his side, he could wait for that day. In time, it would not matter to anyone that she was white. She was not, and never had been, his enemy. He had already determined not to punish her any more for the deeds of her people.

His gaze never left hers as he thought, from this day forward, there will be only a man and a woman in our teepee, only Lese and Wanmdi Hota. His heart drummed heavily in his broad chest as she headed toward him and toward their new future together . . .